PENGU

Ralph

'Deliciously enjoyable . . . although there have been many books trying to decipher the new rules of engagement, Jewell's is one of the most refreshing: addictively readable without being irritating or glib' *Times*

'A party worth gatecrashing! Lisa Jewell pulls off a rare trick which even the likes of Helen Fielding and Nick Hornby couldn't quite manage. She has written a book about relationships which appeals to men and women . . . It's a spicy lamb kofta in a sea of bland chicken masala' *Daily Mirror*

'A joy . . . a fun, summer read' *Guardian*

'A lovely, modern, urban tale of interconnecting relationships, desires and disasters. Quite the nicest in this vein for some time' *Bookseller*

'A breath of fresh air' Tom Paulin, *Late Review*

'Addictive . . . Jilly Cooper for the combat-trouser generation' *Metro*

www.lisa-jewell.co.uk

Ralph's Party

LISA JEWELL

PENGUIN BOOKS

PENGUIN BOOKS

UK | USA | Canada | Ireland | Australia
India | New Zealand | South Africa

Penguin Books is part of the Penguin Random House group of companies
whose addresses can be found at global.penguinrandomhouse.com.

First published in Penguin Books 1999
Reissued in this edition 2024
056

'Jessie's Girl', words and music by Rick Springfield, copyright © 1981 Vogue Music,
Polygram Music Publishing, 47 British Grove, London W4.
Used by permission of Music Sales Ltd. All rights reserved.
International Copyright Secured.

Set in 12.5/14.75pt Garamond MT Std
Typeset by Jouve (UK), Milton Keynes
Printed and bound in Great Britain by Clays Ltd, Elcograf S.p.A.

The authorized representative in the EEA is Penguin Random House Ireland,
Morrison Chambers, 32 Nassau Street, Dublin D02 YH68

A CIP catalogue record for this book is available from the British Library

ISBN: 978-1-405-97219-2

www.greenpenguin.co.uk

MIX
Paper | Supporting
responsible forestry
FSC® C018179

Penguin Random House is committed to a
sustainable future for our business, our readers
and our planet. This book is made from Forest
Stewardship Council® certified paper.

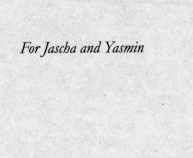

For Jascha and Yasmin

An Introduction by Lisa Jewell

In October 1996 I was a twenty-eight-year-old out-of-work secretary sitting in my boyfriend's flat in Kilburn in front of a big fat plastic computer monitor typing some words into a big clunky plug-in keyboard. I was lucky to have access to a home computer at that point and without access to a home computer, it's unlikely I'd have taken up my friend Yasmin's challenge, made drunkenly on holiday the week before, to write the first three chapters of the novel I'd just drunkenly told her I wanted to write.

I'd been made redundant from my job as the PA to the marketing director of a shirt-making company the week before my friend's challenge and had given myself a month to write the three chapters, but then I would need to get a job. After leaving a five-year starter marriage, I was living at the time with my sister and her boyfriend and I had rent to pay and a busy social life to support.

But little did I know that as I started writing tentatively about a boy called Ralph who lives in Battersea with his friend Smith and is about to meet a girl called Jem, that I was in fact writing my first novel. Three chapters, that was the agreement, and then back to business as usual. But my friend Yasmin read the three chapters I passed her under the table of an Indian restaurant one Friday night and emailed me to say: this is brilliant. You have to send it out to some agents!

It seemed little effort at the time; I titled the (as yet unwritten) book 'Third Person', wrote a covering letter, and a synopsis (even though I had no idea what the book was actually going to be about), took it all to the copy shop and asked for ten sets which I shoved in ten envelopes and sent off to ten agents selected at random from a copy of the Writers & Artists' Yearbook (bought via a brand new online book retailer called 'Amazon'.)

Over the next few weeks, the rejection letters trickled in. One was very encouraging and praised my voice and made some suggestions to improve the work. I took them on board because I was so tickled to have a real-life literary agent talk about my work as if it was something serious and real. But still, it all felt like a thing I'd done that was now over, and I took on some temping jobs and went back to the path I thought my life was on.

Little did I know what vast life changes were just around the corner for me.

In January 1997, two months after I'd received my 9th rejection letter, the 10th agent wrote to me. She told me that she'd enjoyed my work, but that it was 'going to need a lot of work' and that she didn't like my font. She also included a photocopy of some guidelines for layout and punctuations, as apparently my commas and apostrophes were all over the place. But she said she wanted to see the rest of it.

But there was no 'rest of it'. That was all there was. My instinct at that moment was to tuck her letter away in a drawer to show to my grandchildren. 'Look,' I could say, 'I nearly had a literary agent once, but I was too busy going out drinking with my friends to finish writing the book.'

Luckily my boyfriend had different ideas.

'Do you know how few people get a letter like that from a literary agent?' he said. 'You have to finish the book!'

He told me I could move into his flat and use his computer, that he'd cover all my drinking expenses and I could stop paying rent and work part-time.

And so that's exactly what happened, I moved in with my boyfriend and I got a job working two and a half days a week for a recruitment consultancy in the west end. The other two and a half days I sat at my boyfriend's huge computer and wrote a book.

I thought it was going to be edgy, possibly thrillery, certainly dark. Certainly that was what the synopsis I'd sent out to all the agents had suggested. But the book that came out of me during 1997 was none of those things. Inspired by the cultural zeitgeist of the late 90s, I channelled Nick Hornby, I channelled the TV show *This Life*, I channelled Britpop and Radiohead, I channelled the nights I spent with my boyfriend and his mates in Firkin pubs and eating late night Peking duck in Chinatown, the other nights in friends' flatshares getting stoned and watching stupid late night TV shows, I channelled the feeling of being in love in your twenties in the coolest city in the world during the coolest time to be in that city. I used the setting of one of the many London neighbourhoods I'd lived in during my young adulthood, Clapham Junction, and replicated the house I'd lived in there, and then I thought about who else might have lived in that house in the flats above and below, I thought about the views of the backs of London houses from the trains I sat in to get to my office jobs. A boss at one of my temping jobs told me about a young lover of his who'd messed him about and I put her in the book. My landlord when I was sharing bunks with another girl in Holland Park had taught Ceroc and I put that in there. My boyfriend and I on one of our very first dates had bought fresh bird's eye chillis from Chinatown to make a Thai curry and ended up having a raw chilli-eating competition (it was a draw) which I also put in there. And yes, I did once strike up a conversation with a Mancunian butcher in Chinatown.

On New Year's Eve, 1997, I typed The End and early in 1998 I handed my complete manuscript to the agent who'd wanted to see it (and yes, I'd changed the font) and I thought at that time, I really did, that it was terrible and that at the very most she might be able to sell it to a small publisher for a few hundred pounds and that a few people might read it and think it was quite quirky and cool.

But that is not what happened. What happened is that the agent called me into her office and told me she was going to put the book into a bidding war with five of the top publishers. She also told me it was good that the book was set all over one season as it 'made the film rights easier to sell.'

I still sometimes walk past the bus stop in Chalk Farm where I stood after this seismic meeting with the literary agent and I remember, vividly, standing there, twenty-nine-years-old, in a fake fur coat from Dorothy Perkins, my cheeks burning hot, wondering what on earth had just happened to me. I'd gone into the agent's office a secretarial temp who'd written a book for a bet, and I'd come out as a writer. It felt unreal and unlikely. Had it even happened I wondered? Was the agent maybe a little mad?

But the agent was not a little mad. She told me to rewrite the last third of the book, which I dutifully did, and now it ended with a party, which had not been there in the first draft. 'Let's call it Ralph's Party,' she said. So we called it *Ralph's Party* and she sent it out to some of the biggest publishers in the UK and got me a big fat two-book deal from Penguin, no less.

It was published with a bang on May 6th 1999 when I was thirty years old. It was reviewed on the *Late Review*, a highbrow late-night review show on BBC2; it was reviewed in all the broadsheets; I was interviewed on the radio and the TV. It hit the bestsellers at no. 3 and it sold 250k copies in its first year. The whole thing was all a ridiculous fairytale and my feet barely touched the ground for a year or two afterwards.

But the real magic has happened since. Somehow I managed to live beyond the hype of that insane debut publication experience and built a career that is still going strong, if not even stronger. I now write the sort of dark psychological books that I thought I'd write back then, in the 90s, and wonderfully, many of the people who read *Ralph's Party* back then when they were young and finding their way in the city, or even younger still and stealing books off their parents' nightstands, have stayed with me and are reading me now, twenty-five years later, having grown up alongside me. They even bring their daughters to my book events!

But now it's time for Ralph and Jen and Smith and Cheri and Siobhan and Carl to find their way into new hands of new readers and see how they stand up in this very different world. So many things have changed – nobody in this book has a mobile phone, nobody uses a computer – but so many other things have changed not a jot. People still live in cities and look for love and get drunk and cry and obsess over things they cannot have and find ways to turn things round. They get on buses and share flats and have terrible jobs and get stoned and kiss people they don't want to kiss. They still live their lives to a soundtrack of music that moves them, they dance and dream and eat raw chillis and stick their heads in the fridge (except now they'd film it and put it on TikTok!).

So I hope you enjoy this old book that so many people loved so much back in the 90s and that it resonates still, even in the high-tech, high-stress 2020s.

All my love

Lisa Jewell
6th February 2024

... IT IS ALWAYS LIKE THAT AT PARTIES, WE
NEVER SEE THE PEOPLE, WE NEVER SAY THE
THINGS WE SHOULD LIKE TO SAY, BUT IT IS
THE SAME EVERYWHERE IN THIS LIFE ...

— *A la recherche du temps perdu,* Proust

Prologue

Smith put the phone down and glanced around the living room. A few people had already been round that night, and the flat was still relatively tidy after an earlier blitzing.

He picked up empty mugs and glasses and carried them through to the kitchen. It was strange and vaguely unsettling to think that these objects still carried the lip marks, the fingerprints, the traces of saliva and microscopic organisms left there by the strangers who had been into his home that evening, strangers he had shown his bathroom, who had seen his grubby dressing-gown hanging behind his bedroom door, strangers who had sat on his sofa in unfamiliar clothes with unfamiliar mannerisms and names and lives, strangers who had been given the opportunity to peer into other strangers' private lives.

Ralph and he had reached decisions quickly and cruelly. It would be obvious in a moment that someone was unsuitable, but they all got the tour: 'And this is the kitchen – you'll be pleased to hear we've got a dishwasher *and* a washer-dryer!'; the talk: 'Smith's up with the lark during the week but we both like a lie-in at the weekends'; the interview: 'What do you do for a living?'; and the conclusion: 'Well, there's still a few more people to see the flat – give us your phone number and we'll let you know.'

Always the full fifteen minutes, so that the unwanted stranger would leave feeling like he'd been in the running, like he'd been given serious consideration.

Jason had sounded hopeful on the phone but turned out to be looking for a ready-made social life. 'I just want to live somewhere that's got a bit of life – d'you know what I mean?' he'd said, his eyes wide and overkeen.

'Erm, maybe you could explain?' Ralph had asked, thinking of the nights that he and Smith spent hopping mindlessly through forty-seven cable channels without talking and going to bed, stoned, at midnight.

Jason sat forward on the sofa and cupped his kneecaps with his hands. 'Like, for example, where I live at the moment, all that happens is I get home from work every night and nobody wants to do anything. It pisses me off, d'you know what I mean?'

Ralph and Smith had nodded sympathetically and felt old.

Monica had been a born-again Christian – would it bother them if she spoke in tongues occasionally? – and Ruth appeared to be on the run from an abusive marriage. Her hands shook throughout the meeting, her dark eyes unable to rest on one object or hold a gaze. She explained that she and her husband were having a 'trial separation'. Ralph and Smith decided that a permanent separation from Ruth's sad but unpalatable situation would be best for them.

Rachel had the sort of skin condition that made them want to hoover the flat the minute she'd left, and John smelt of Pedigree Chum. They'd just about given up hope.

'Who was that on the phone?' Ralph switched on the television and spread-eagled himself on to the sofa, the remote control poised for action in his hand.

'Someone about the flat,' Smith replied from the kitchen, 'a girl – she's on her way over now. She sounded nice.' He kicked the door of the dishwasher closed. 'Her name's Jem.'

Jem took the first turning off Battersea Rise, which brought her into Almanac Road, a small sweep of three-storey Edwardian houses, long and thin with basements – unusual for this part of South London.

As she walked down the road, peering nosily into uncurtained basement flats, she began to feel strangely like she had been here before. There was something familiar about the proportions, the width of the pavement, the colour of the bricks and the spacing between the weedy saplings that lined the road.

Jem stopped outside number thirty-one, and the feeling of familiarity increased further. She suddenly felt safe, like a child coming home after a tiring day out, to a warm house and Saturday-afternoon television.

Jem glanced down into the basement flat and saw a young man, his back to the window, talking to someone out of view. It was then that she knew she had been here before. Maybe not this exact place, but somewhere very similar. In her dreams, since she was a teenager – a basement flat in a tall house in a terrace; a view through the window, at night, the room lit up; a man on a sofa smoking a cigarette, whose face she couldn't see. Her destiny. Was this him?

Jem rang the doorbell.

I

The girl standing in the doorway was tiny, about five foot two, black curly hair held on top of her head with pins and clips in some complicated but very feminine style that looked as if it should have sported ivy wreaths. She was post-coitally pretty, with cherry-red cheeks and a bitter-sweet mouth, the bottom lip drawn back very slightly under the top, and her eyes were bright and mustardy, framed by mascaraed lashes and faint but lively eyebrows. She should have been wearing wood-nymph muslins and lacy leather sandals but instead had on an equally beguiling soft flannel suit with fur at the collar and cuffs and a short skirt that would have looked obvious on a taller woman. The tip of her nose was winsomely pink.

Smith let Jem walk in front of him down the hall, watching her as she turned her head this way and that, examining the pictures on the walls, peering through half-open doors and patting table-tops as she went. She was definitely cute. She turned to Smith.

'This is lovely, really, really lovely.' She smiled widely and suddenly turned to face the wall, grabbing the top of the radiator with both hands and letting out a sigh of relief. 'Sorry,' she laughed, 'my hands are freezing, like blocks of ice – feel.' She made her small white hands into fists and placed one on each of Smith's cheeks. 'It's so cold out there!' Smith started and felt suddenly shy.

'Shall we go to the kitchen? I'd love a cup of tea.'

'It's just through the living room,' offered Smith, attempting to overtake her.

'Oh, yes. I know where the kitchen is. I saw it through the window. Outside.' She laughed again. 'Sorry, I'm really nosy. And I've seen so many horrible flats tonight I don't think I could have faced coming in here if it hadn't looked nice.'

They walked into the kitchen.

'My flatmate's around somewhere,' said Smith, filling the kettle. 'He's probably in his room. He's called Ralph. I'll take you to meet him when the tea's done.'

Jem was examining a rack of herbs and spices. The plastic lids of the jars were covered in a layer of greasy dust; all of them were full. 'Do you and Ralph ever cook?' she asked.

Smith laughed. 'Erm, I think this speaks for itself.' He opened the door of the fridge to reveal shelves laden with colourful packets proclaiming 'Thai-style Green Curry', 'Creole Chicken with Cajun Rice', 'Chicken Tikka Masala', and floppy see-through bags containing fresh pasta sauces and soups.

'Oh, God – typical boys! That's such an expensive way to eat!' exclaimed Jem. 'Cooking's brilliant, you know – I'll teach you. And Ralph, if you like.' She used the name Ralph comfortably, as if she knew him. 'I'm very good. I think. Well, so I've been told. I can cook a Thai curry. These ready-made things are dreadful for you – it's all the salt they put in them to make them taste of something.' She closed the fridge and wandered back into the living room.

'Do you want to ask me some questions?' she called, picking up a paperback from a shelf and examining the back cover.

'Milk and sugar?' Smith called back.

'Have you got any honey?'

Smith futilely opened and closed a few cupboards. 'No,' he shouted. 'Got some golden syrup, though.'

'This is a gorgeous room, you know. No offence or anything, but it doesn't look like two boys live here.'

'Thank you.' Smith was embarrassed, and slightly shocked at being referred to as a boy in his thirtieth year.

Jem quickly took note of the objects strewn around the top of the dark wooden coffee table inlaid with ornate brass work. She approved of a good messy coffee table – they held so many interesting clues to the day-to-day content and clutter of people's lives. Smith and Ralph's coffee table held a selection of remote controls, a satellite TV guide, an ashtray full of stubs, two packets of red Marlboro, a business card, a box of matches and a home-delivery pizza menu. Somewhere underneath it all she could make out a proper coffee-table art book, a set of car keys and, barely visible but unmistakable, a small piece of green cardboard torn from a packet of Rizlas. Jem smiled quietly at her discovery.

'Let's go and say hello to Ralph,' Smith was lingering in the doorway, his face cocooned in wreaths of steam from his tea, 'and then I'll show you around.'

Ralph barely noticed Jem the first time he saw her. He was arguing with his girlfriend Claudia, sitting at his desk, the phone cradled under his chin as he carelessly pulled elastic bands into tight ligatures around his wrists in an apparently subconscious attempt to cut off his blood supply and end the painful predictability of it all.

As Smith entered he grimaced and took the phone from under his chin, holding it a foot or two from his ear so that Smith could hear the tinny drone of the unhappy woman. He hit the speakerphone button:

'I just feel like I'm the one doing all the work here, Ralph, d'you know what I'm talking about? No, of course you don't. Who am I kidding? You can't see anything beyond the remote control – as long as you've got a piece of technical equipment in your hand that will prevent you from doing something else, something that might, just might involve you getting up off your arse and doing something . . .'

'Ralph,' whispered Smith, 'this is Jem.'

Jem twinkled at Ralph from the doorway.

Ralph saw a small, smiley girl, tendrils of hair framing her face.

'Are you listening to me, Ralph, or have you put me on that fucking speakerphone?'

Ralph smiled apologetically at Jem and mouthed a 'Nice to meet you' as he hit the speakerphone button again and began murmuring inaudibly into the phone.

Smith and Jem left the room, closing the door quietly behind them.

'Claudia can be very . . . demanding. They could go on like that for hours. Poor bastard.' Smith smiled smugly and took a slurp of tea.

'You don't have a girlfriend, then, Smith?'

'Very perceptive,' he replied ungraciously. 'No, I don't.'

Not for the first time since Jem's arrival, he found himself feeling uncomfortable. He wanted to be friendly and welcoming, to create a good impression, but try as he might, he just couldn't, and was coming across instead as frosty and impolite. He put his hand out to grasp the antique door-handle in front of him and pushed the door open.

'This would be your room.' He reached to the left for the light switch. 'It's quite small, as you can see, but it's got everything.'

The room was tiny and L-shaped. The walls were clad in caramel-coloured wood-panelling, and the room was lit centrally by a ceiling lamp housed in a brass and glass star-shaped shade. A single bed stood at the far end, covered with a vivacious Indian throw and several large cushions with tassels and fringes. A 1920s wardrobe with mirrored front panels stood in front of it, and at the other end of the room was a single sash window hung with densely patterned heavy curtains and a small chest of black-lacquerwork drawers.

Jem turned and grasped hold of Smith's hands. 'I absolutely love it. I love it. I knew I would. Please can I live here? Please!' Her face was glowing and childlike, her hands felt small and warmed by her mug of tea.

'Let me show you the rest of the flat first and then we can have a chat.' Smith could still feel where Jem's hands had covered his. 'I need to talk to Ralph as well – lots of other people have been to see the room. I'll need to consult him.' He could feel himself blushing and turned his back on Jem.

'OK,' she said lightly. She wasn't worried. She already knew that the room was hers.

2

Siobhan knew she should feel happy. I mean – ALR, All London Radio. That was something else, it really was.

When Karl had first told her, earlier on that evening, she had felt ecstatic – all his dreams come true. He was on the phone to his Irish mother and Russian father in Sligo now, telling them the news. She looked at him over the top of her book; his soft, handsome face was alive with an energy she hadn't seen for years as he explained to his no doubt bursting-at-the-seams-with-pride mother that her one and only son, her precious, sweet Karl, had just been handed a peaktime slot on London's biggest radio station.

She couldn't quite imagine it: 'Good evening, London, and welcome to the Karl Kasparov Show.' Her Karl, not some faceless, naff DJ, but her Karl, having thousands of listeners, his own jingles, doing interviews. His name would be there in the radio listings: '3.30–6.30 p.m. – Karl Kasparov.' *Drive Time,* that's what they called it, Karl's slot. Karl was going to have a *Drive Time* radio show.

Siobhan imagined a classic 'Hot in the City' scenario, a traffic jam on a steaming summer's day, bumper-to-bumper gridlocked traffic and the sound of Karl's voice purring from car radios, 'It's hot out there – so keep cool by staying tuned to *Drive Time* ALR' before seguing into 'Up on the Roof'.

A barely perceptible whimper jolted Siobhan from her train of thought. It was a quarter to eleven – they'd forgotten about Rosanne in all the excitement. She was now sitting stoically by the living-room door, aware that tonight was not a normal night and trying, without irritating, to convey the message that she still had a bladder and it was getting late.

'Oh, baby, did we forget about you?' The sympathetic tone of Siobhan's voice elicited a tentative wag from Rosanne's tail, which increased with velocity and force as Siobhan headed towards the hook in the hall that bore her lead.

'Karl, I'm taking Rosanne out for a pee. Come on, baby! Come on, we're going out!'

Siobhan struggled into her winter coat, so much tighter around her upper arms and chest than it had been last year, and Rosanne panted delightedly at the door waiting for her mistress to join her.

Siobhan was glad to be out in the cold night air. The central heating, the excitement and the champagne had fuzzed up her mind. It was a beautiful October night and the tall, elderly houses of Almanac Road looked elegant beneath a jet-black sky brightly illuminated by a huge full moon.

Rosanne seemed to sense the fullness of the moon above, uncertainly sniffing the air around her, her black coat looking extra glossy beneath the bright white light. They walked to the end of the road, Siobhan thinking hard about her feelings. She'd got so used to she and Karl bumbling along in their unimpressive lifestyle. It had never mattered to her before that she hadn't really worked since losing her job as a technician at a fashion college in Surrey – she'd made ends meet with the odd wedding-dress commission and handmade cushions for an interior-design shop on Wandsworth Bridge Road. And Karl's weekend deejaying at local pubs and functions, plus what he earned at the Sol y Sombra teaching Ceroc had been plenty to meet their paltry mortgage repayments and modest-lifestyle expenses.

Karl and Siobhan—a strictly small-time couple. That's how Siobhan had always seen them, and she knew plenty of people who were jealous of their way of life, and their relationship. She couldn't have wanted for any more really – they had a lovely flat which they'd been lucky enough to buy for next to nothing before Battersea had up and come, a beautiful dog, friends they'd known since university, a relationship full of laughter and ease that was, their friends informed them, the strongest they knew, an example to everyone else, a yardstick. Neither of them was going to suffer from executive burn-out. The idea that all this might change, would change, filled Siobhan with dread.

Suddenly it would matter that she was getting fat, Karl would notice that her life was going nowhere. He would get back from his *Drive Time* slot, hyped and driven, full of fame and crappy Top Ten pop songs and find Siobhan's bulk sprawled all over the sofa, glued to *Coronation Street,* her belly swollen from the enormous meal she'd eaten while he was out because she didn't like to eat in front of Karl any more, and what would he think?

Would he still drive the little black 1966 Embassy he'd shipped back from India the year after university? Would he still wear his old American Classics chinos with the split on the knee and the scuffed old Bass Weejun loafers he'd had since before she even knew him? Would he still put on his funny Tibetan socks with the leather soles when he got in and make them both a cup of tea and watch documentaries on the sofa with Rosanne on his lap?

Would he still love her?

It was cold now – winter had stopped knocking tentatively at the door, had forced its way in and made itself at home. Siobhan looked up in time to see a wispy violet cloud pass over the moon and then disappear back into the blackness.

'Come on, baby, let's go back.'

They moved briskly up Almanac Road towards the light and warmth of number thirty-one. As Siobhan felt in her coat pocket for her front-door keys she heard voices and looked down to see a pretty dark-haired girl leaving the basement flat below theirs. There'd been visitors in and out of that flat all night. She wondered what was going on.

She unclipped Rosanne's lead in the hall and the dog dashed into the living room and straight on to Karl's lap. Karl hugged her and let her lick his face and Siobhan watched the scene from the hall while she tugged at her too-tight coat sleeves. She smiled deeply and warmly to herself and allowed the scene to etch itself firmly on the slate of her mind, allowed the joy of her current life to overcome her, because, she knew for sure, it was all about to change.

3

Ralph and Smith had been best friends for fifteen years. They had been enemies for four years before that, since day one at grammar school, Smith offended by Ralph's creative aura and vaguely effeminate manner and Ralph threatened by Smith's easily gained popularity and effortless academic success. They kept different circles of friends and, on the rare occasion that their paths crossed, they sniffed and snarled at each other like unfriendly dogs passing in the park, their friends keeping them at bay like impatient owners tugging on leads.

It took a girl to bring them together. She was a foreign-exchange student from Baltimore called Shirelle and she was staying with Smith and his family for two months. She arrived in London in May wearing flared jeans with turnups and a hairy turquoise woollen jumper with a cowl neck. Her hair was long and plain, like her face.

She spotted Ralph getting off the bus on her first morning at Croydon Grammar. His trousers were tighter than school rules allowed, his dark-blue blazer was held together at the back with a safety-pin and his hair was dirtily tousled, sticking up in meringue-like peaks sculpted with soap. He had a smudge of something black and sooty under each eye. Smith thought he looked like a right tosser. Shirelle fell in love.

Over the course of that term Shirelle became Skunk.

She shaved her hair and dyed it black with a peroxide streak running through the middle. She spent her allowance in Carnaby Street on fishnets and studded belts and leather skirts. She smoked and drank snakebites and followed Ralph around like a lovesick Rottweiler. She asked him over to the Smith residence with the invitation 'Fuck me,' an offer that, although it scared him half witless, Ralph as a hormonal young man of sixteen felt he could not refuse.

Smith as a hormonal young man of sixteen was both fascinated and repulsed by these sessions and the fact that they were happening, audibly, under his own suburban roof. Any previously held notion of Ralph's dubious sexuality was well and truly rubbished by the noises that emanated from the Smiths' spare room. As time went by, his curiosity got the better of him and one afternoon, feigning interest in the phone book in the hall, he watched Ralph saunter down the stairs, tucking his T-shirt into his combat trousers in an awe-inspiringly macho way, smelling of something unfamiliar and exciting.

'So, what's going down, then, Ralphie-boy?' Smith enquired, in what he hoped sounded like a casually off-hand, sneeringly condescending manner. 'How's it going with the skunk-woman?'

Ralph glanced ceilingwards. 'Fancy a walk?' he'd said, shoving his hands deep into his pockets.

And that was that. Shirelle went home at the end of term, despite her threats to stay and bear Ralph's children, bring them up in the squat they would share with the Sex Pistols and Siouxsie Sioux, take heroin and die of an overdose, and Ralph and Smith became friends.

Theirs had developed into a friendship based around the ability to comfortably spend hours in each other's company without the need to speak or move. Now, as it had been at school, they each maintained different circles of friends and took part in different activities outside the flat, but their time together there was a precious opportunity mutually to make no effort whatsoever, a form of behaviour that they found unacceptable to themselves and their friends in any other circumstance.

Obviously they weren't always silent. Sometimes they would discuss which channel to watch, occasionally they even bickered about it and conducted small tussles over the remote control when one felt the other lacked the judgement required for captaincy of such an important tool. And sometimes they would talk about women.

Women were a pain in the arse, they were balls and chains, never pleased, always aggrieved. Smith and Ralph thought of themselves as nice blokes. They weren't bastards, they didn't have affairs or lie to women, or stand them up, or hit them, or expect them to perform menial tasks. They didn't ignore their women when they were with their mates or go out with the lads and refuse to see them; they didn't stick pictures of Melinda Messenger over their beds. They were *nice blokes*. Phoned when they said they'd phone, gave their girlfriends lifts, paid for things, didn't demand sex, even handed out the odd compliment. Ralph and Smith tried to treat women as equals, they really did, but women just kept proving to them that they weren't worthy of it – they were a strange, alien breed with a list of unreasonable expectations as long as the M1 and a feast of paranoias and insecurities that Smith and Ralph were expected to deal with, daily. And then of course there were the women who weren't like that. They were the ones you fell in love with almost immediately, told all your mates about, made fantastical plans for the future with and then felt surprised when three weeks later they dumped you in a pool of your own foolishness and went off with someone who *would* have affairs, lie to them, stand them up, hit them and expect them to perform menial tasks.

Ralph, blessed with an insatiable libido, couldn't do without the sex and still threw himself regularly into the fray, emerging every now and then broken and crippled, hobbling and limping, his over-enthusiastic genitalia still pointing proudly like a bayonet towards the next battle. But Smith had given up fighting this frightening nineties version of the battle of the sexes years ago and retired, bruised but intact, to his corner.

Smith was saving himself anyway, so he said. Saving himself for a woman about whom he knew nearly nothing, a woman with whom he'd never progressed beyond the occasional awkward exchange of smiles, waves and nods, a woman who, in his opinion, encapsulated in one blissful arrangement of cells, organs, pigment and genes, the absolute epitome of female loveliness. For five years he'd imagined a day when their paths would cross. He'd bestow upon her a charming smile of teeth and self-confidence, engage her briefly in witty conversation, extend an invitation to dinner at the wonderful restaurant that had just opened up in St James, smile again at her acceptance, drape his overcoat over his shoulder and walk away with a well-paced swagger.

Instead, he'd spent five years grimacing gruesomely at

her like a socially and intellectually inept toad, sometimes raising a limp, sweaty hand to wave at her if he chanced upon her from a distance and occasionally adding yet more to his plight by tripping over obstacles, dropping fragile objects, missing steps and failing to find his door keys whenever he was within her sights. He was in love with a vision of blonde, honeyed gorgeousness, a tall, slender, toned slip of perfection that no other girl he'd encountered before or since had come close to matching in any way. He was in love with a girl called Cheri, a girl who lived two floors above in the flat at the top of the house, a girl who shared his address. Until he made her his, no other girl would do.

Smith's love for Cheri remained undiminished by her haughty arrogance, her sneering indifference to his attempts at friendliness. It remained unsullied by the frequency of middle-aged men visiting her flat, their Porsches and BMWs double-parked on Almanac Road, by the thought of wives left at home while their husbands wooed his beloved with gifts of jewellery and perfume and dinner at all the best restaurants in London. Smith failed to see beyond her beauty; all he knew was her cool exterior, the layers of self-protective skin she wore to hide the nothingness inside.

While Smith waited on a fantasy that he was emotionally incapable of engineering into reality, Ralph filled his life with a succession of vacuous blondes with accommodating beds, and the two of them killed time . . . until what? Until they were too old to do anything about it? Until all the opportunities in life had gone, like unclaimed raffle prizes, to other people?

Smith knew that they needed a change. Things had

been the same for too long. They were grinding each other down. He'd put an ad in *Loot,* one in the *Standard* and a card in the newsagent's window. And along had come Jem.

As far as Ralph was concerned, things hadn't changed too much in the week since Jem had moved in. She was out most nights, and when she was around she was barely noticeable. There were a few strange things in the bathroom, like cotton-wool balls and jumbo boxes of Tampax, and the fridge had suddenly become home to fresh vegetables, chicken breasts and skimmed milk. But apart from surface changes, it was still, to all intents and purposes, the same flat.

Except it felt different. The dynamics had changed. Ralph no longer felt comfortable walking around in nothing but his boxers; he became self-conscious about his toilet habits, which had always been protracted and unpleasant-smelling but which Smith had learned to live with a long time ago. And, more unexpectedly, Ralph was curious, very curious. Here was a stranger, in his home, a stranger about whom he knew no more than a first name, a strange woman at that, with all the exotic and delightful paraphernalia that surrounded women – knickers, bras, make-up, heels, roll-on deodorants in pink bottles, hair-brushes entangled with long, clean-smelling hairs, Pearl Drops, lacy things, silky things, fluffy things. He'd spent many hours extracting varying degrees of enjoyment from the women in his life, but he'd never, in all his thirty-odd years, lived with one before.

And now there was one in his flat. His curiosity was

aflame and, really, he had only peeped into Jem's bedroom. He hadn't searched through her things or opened drawers or anything, just walked around a bit and looked at stuff. He was sure there wasn't anything wrong with that. If there'd been anything she hadn't wanted anyone to see she'd have put it away somewhere, out of sight. And besides, she'd left the door open. Ralph didn't like to think of himself as a snoop and was feeling slightly guilty now about his little investigation, especially in the light of what he'd seen.

Ralph had intended to spend this week at the studio. He hadn't been for over three months now. He'd made that brochure-design job for the travel company last more than a fortnight when he could have finished it in a week and had spent the last ten days or so cocooned in his room working his way through all thirty-three levels of some computer game or other. He'd reached the end this morning and, after the rapturous programme of congratulations and flattery from the computer had died down, he'd sat back in his chair and realized with some sadness that he now, officially, had nothing to do.

He'd persuaded himself that at eleven-forty it was way too late to make it to the studio but that he would definitely go tomorrow. He'd thought about the possibility of calling Claudia at work and decided against it – he always called her at the wrong time: 'Not now, Ralph, I'm in the middle of something'; 'Not now, Ralph – I'm on my way out'; 'Not now, Ralph – I've only just got in.' He imagined Claudia, in one of her silly shiny suits, busily walking in and out of the office all day, endlessly, like a film on a loop. It made him smile to himself.

The usual cloud of boredom descended upon him, and he decided to go for a short walk. As he strolled down Northcote Road, past market stalls of jewel-coloured autumn flowers and cheap plastic toys and joss sticks and African beads he began to think about Jem. He really hadn't wanted another flatmate – he liked his lifestyle with Smith, an easy life, watching telly, getting stoned – but it was Smith's flat and so he'd gone along with it, and anyway, Jem seemed quite nice and he trusted Smith's judgement.

The first week had been a bit awkward. Smith and he weren't very good at making an effort with strangers, and he'd felt guilty ordering that home-delivery Indian without asking Jem if she wanted any and then embarrassed when he'd heard her slipping into the bathroom moments after he'd made that festering rodent-corpse smell in there. She'd offered to cook for them tonight, and although he appreciated the gesture he found himself rather selfishly resenting this disruption of his normal routine. Monday night was his staying-in night and he liked it to be as socially undemanding as possible; when Smith was out he quite often switched on the answer-phone and ruthlessly screened his calls. But it was nice of Jem to offer and he would try to rise to the occasion.

To give his walk a purpose he went into his local overpriced 'corner shop', one of those ubiquitous upmarket chains which sell bags of imported tortilla chips for extortionate amounts of money but never stock anything you really want to eat, which sell only one kind of washing powder but at least twenty-two brands of Mexican chilli sauce. Ralph didn't know why he frequented these places – they were so obviously designed to line the pockets of some youthful laughing-all-the-way-to-the-bank ex-City-boy types ('Ere, Paul, let's buy some retail space and flog the yuppies a load of wine and tortilla chips for three times the recommended retail price') and they annoyed him intensely. He bought himself a packet of Marlboro, although he had two packs at the flat, and walked back to Almanac Road.

Lunchtime television consisted of a selection of cookery programmes and Australian soaps, and Ralph found himself mindlessly absorbed in some frenetic shopping-channel programme, watching a suntanned guy with a tape measure around his neck feverishly extolling the myriad virtues of a horrible acrylic tunic with beading around the neck: 'Not just one, not two, but three, *three* different types of beading. You've got the bugle beading here, the button beading around the appliqué and, look – this *beautiful* tear-drop beading on both sides!'

Ralph wondered what planet these presenters came from and what drugs the channel fed them to make them sound so sincerely and genuinely excited about the naff and uninspiring products they were being asked to pay homage to.

He switched off the television and felt silence engulf the room. He felt empty and useless. He had nothing to do. He picked up a mug of lukewarm tea he'd made earlier and a packet of Tuc biscuits and walked aimlessly into the hall. It was then that he found himself, almost subconsciously, pushing open the door to Jem's little room.

It was strange to see the spare room full of someone's things. He'd only ever seen it empty before. It already had an unfamiliar smell. Jem's belongings lay semi-unpacked

22

in boxes around the edges of the room – empty boxes had been flattened and folded and left near the door. The bed was unmade and there was a blue cotton dressing-gown draped across it with a white Chinese dragon embroidered on the back.

Ralph stepped further into the room to examine a pile of CDs balanced on the table next to Jem's bed. He was impressed with her taste in music, like his, still stuck somewhere in 1979: the Jam, Madness, the Cure, Generation X, the Ramones – he might ask if he could borrow them. Next to the CDs was a framed photograph of Jem in a thick winter coat, her nose reddened by the cold, crouching to hug a handsome golden retriever. Ralph looked closely at the photograph, realizing that he couldn't really remember what Jem looked like – he hadn't paid her much attention – and that she was extremely pretty. Not particularly his type, though. He always went for blondes, blondes with long legs and designer clothes and attitude problems, blondes with names like Georgia, Natasha and, of course, Claudia, blondes who worked in PR or for art galleries or fashion houses, blondes who wished he was wealthier, trendier, tidier, smarter, earlier, later, cooler – someone else.

In contrast, Jem was tiny and quirkily pretty. She had good taste in music and she kept a picture of her dog by her bed. She was also nice and polite and gave the impression that she'd be a pleasure to be with. Not Ralph's type at all.

He bit into a biscuit and a large chunk fell to the floor. As he stooped to pick it up he noticed a pile of books under the table, worn and battered looking, with various years inscribed down their spines in gold blocking, or handwritten in pen and marker. They were diaries – and, by the look of them, not impersonal desk diaries but proper, from-the-heart, highly personal girls' diaries. They stretched from 1986 to 1995. He wondered what had happened to 1996, the current diary, and then he saw it just peeping out from under Jem's dressing-gown.

It was open but obscured by the gown; he could see the date – it was last Thursday's – and snatches of handwriting, small and curly like Jem herself: '. . . beautiful flat . . . might be shy – I'm sure they're not . . . this be my destiny – I'm so excited . . . Smith could be him but seems a bit . . . Ralph . . .' Ralph stopped abruptly. What the hell did he think he was doing, snooping around in this poor girl's room looking at her fucking diary, of all things? This really was very, very sad indeed. He almost left at that point, but his interest had been stimulated to boiling-point.

His heart was racing as he pulled the dressing-gown out of the way and his jaw dropped as he read the entry in full. It seemed Jem thought she was here because of some dream or other, she was following her destiny, she was excited because she thought that either Smith or himself would be the man of her dreams – literally. Ralph was inclined to think that Jem was some sort of fruitcake, but as he read on he found himself warming to her dream, her destiny. Not only was he in the running, he had the advantage. Look, she'd written it: 'Smith seems a bit uptight, and he's not really my type to be honest. Ralph seems more likely – very lean and sexy and sort of dangerous looking' – Ralph's stomach tingled pleasantly as he absorbed the compliment – 'he seems like he'd be more fun to be with. The problem is, he's got a girlfriend.'

This was all true, thought Ralph – apart from the bit about Claudia being a problem. He *was* more fun to be with than Smith these days. That hadn't always been the way, but over the last few years, since his obsession with Cheri had taken over his life, Smith had lost some of his old sparkle and self-confidence.

There was no entry after that. Ralph put down the book and took a deep breath, resisting the urge to turn back the page, to read more. He placed the diary on the bed at the same angle he'd found it, painstakingly re-arranging the blue gown over it and hoping she hadn't left a hair draped across it, to trap sad, snooping diary-readers.

He sat on her crumpled bed now, so unlike Claudia's, which took ten minutes to make, with new bedsheets every day and complicated throw and cushion arrangements that had to be just so, otherwise she'd complain. One of Jem's bras was folded into the sheets. It was black and plain and old looking. He picked it up and examined the label – little Jem was not so little: 34D. Where the hell had she been hiding those? Claudia had breasts that complemented her willowy stick-insect frame, small and pointy and incapable of forming a cleavage even when pushed firmly together from both sides. Ralph realized that he missed breasts, he missed that projection of soft voluminous womanliness that moved when it was touched and was always warm and welcoming. Other bits of women's bodies sometimes felt like they might bite or strangle or constrict, but never the breasts – they were friendly and relaxed.

Ralph was disturbed to find himself running the strap

of Jem's bra across his top lip and smelling the thin strip of worn black elastic. He removed it quickly and placed it on his lap, turning his hand into a fist, which he inserted into the cup. It fitted easily, leaving plenty of room for a second fist. My God, he thought, Jem is what Claudia would describe as a 'clever dresser'. Whenever Ralph disagreed with Claudia's assessment of another woman as fat she would explain that he had been fooled by clever dressing – underneath that strategically placed scarf or sweater the woman was actually a little overweight, he just couldn't see it because he was a man and oblivious to the tricks that women played. Maybe she was right, he thought now, admiring the capacity of Jem's bra. He certainly hadn't noticed those before.

He placed the bra back into its crevice in the bed-sheets. He was beginning to feel a bit seedy and uncomfortable with himself and was relieved to note that he didn't have an erection.

Ralph was tempted to stay in Jem's room; he was enjoying its snugness and femininity. He wanted to see what she kept in the drawers, take the top off her deodorant and smell the ball, read all her diaries and find out what she was doing on specific days years ago, he wanted to climb into her bedclothes, under her duvet and between her sheets, his head on her aquamarine-cased pillows, to smell her and feel the echo of her warmth.

Instead, he stood up slowly and ruffled the duvet back into shape, checked there were no traces of his visit, left the door ajar as he'd found it and stepped back into the hall. Tonight could be quite interesting.

As he sat back down at his desk, trying to think of

something constructive to do which didn't involve leaving the flat, using the phone or expending too much energy, his thoughts kept returning to the tantalizing snippets he'd read in Jem's diary, and he felt an overwhelming wave of intrigue and curiosity. What was all this about dreams and destiny? What else had she written about them? And more to the point, what else had she written about *him*? He couldn't quite explain it, but for some reason Ralph suddenly had the feeling that life was about to become very complicated.

4

It seemed to Siobhan that her body was just one big hair-sprouting machine. She'd expected to wrinkle as she aged, she'd expected her hair to lose its pigment, her skin to lose its tautness, but she hadn't been expecting the slow but insistent arrival of so much bloody body hair.

Starting from the bottom up, she had developed little lawns of mousy hair on the fleshy bits on her big toes. Then of course there were the legs, but she'd always had hair there – that was socially acceptable. Even supermodels had hairy legs, and there were aisles full of products in Boots that you could buy without shame or embarrassment.

It was what happened at the top of her legs that bothered Siobhan the most, the dense jungle of coarse hair that seemed more and more intent as the years went by to find its way out of her underwear and join the party taking place on her thighs and creep up her stomach in a thin arrow pointing to her belly button. The line looked particularly unpleasant in the winter, standing out starkly against the now-spongey white expanse of her stomach.

But it didn't stop there. She had noticed lately, among the pale soft down that slept between her breasts, a few renegade hairs growing longer, darker and thicker than the rest. Why? And nipple hair, spidery legs forcing their way through the otherwise unblemished surface of her breasts to spoil the aesthetics and make her feel ugly. Hair on her upper lip, too, that made her self-conscious when people stood too close to her, and even the odd whisker growing quietly but determinedly from cheeks and chin.

The soul-destroying, time-consuming rituals to rid herself of so much unwanted hair were almost daily now. Bleach for her moustache, a razor for her legs and under her arms, rancid-smelling cream for her pubic hair, and tweezers for her toes, nipples, chin and eyebrows. Did men have even the vaguest idea how much work went into women keeping themselves smooth and childlike, into removing anything from their bodies that might even begin to be described as masculine? Would men themselves be prepared to do it if fashion and society had decreed that they, too, should be alabaster-smooth?

And how come in other countries it was acceptable? How come a million Italian women could walk shamelessly and proudly along beaches every year, a veritable bearskin of black hair cascading from their bikinis and lush pelts of foliage dangling from their armpits? How come in France they had a special and affectionate word to describe the female moustache, yet an English woman would be embarrassed to walk down the street with more than a quarter-millimetre of stubble on her legs?

How high would it be, if she were to pile up the last ten years' worth of hateful hair? It was all so thankless. Like housework. From the very second it was done it was getting worse again, closer to needing to be done again. Hair was so insidiously persistent and never ending – it just grew and grew and grew, relentlessly. It never went on holiday or had a day off and it didn't care how fond you were of a particular part of your anatomy, it just decided to grow there anyway, like weeds on a smooth stone wall.

Siobhan had once tried to cultivate an interest in gardening, thinking herself the type, but it had quickly become clear to her that it was just like housework and unwanted hair – frustrating and for ever. Hair, weeds and dust – Siobhan hated them.

She was doing something that she seemed to spend more and more of her time doing lately – hating her body. Not only was she getting hairier by the day but she was also getting fatter, and it was now no longer a case of having put on a few pounds and her clothes being a bit tight – she had reached a size that meant people who didn't know her might refer to her as the 'fat woman'. Most of her clothes now hung redundant in her wardrobe, while she lived in the same pair of leggings and a small selection of shapeless tunic tops and jumpers. If she bought anything new it would mean having to go to shops she'd never been to before and buying clothes in sizes that screamed to the world 'I am fat.'

Karl never said anything about it – and it remained unspoken. He still touched her and stroked her and hugged her, still held her hand in public and told her he loved her. He'd never really been a compliment man anyway. Siobhan wondered what he really thought. She certainly didn't undress in front of him now or walk around the flat naked, and their habit of taking baths together had petered out unnoticed and, again, unremarked upon. She could always ask him straight out like other women would, 'Karl, do you think I've got fat?', but she knew that he wouldn't lie like other men would, he was the most honest man she'd ever known, and he would say, 'Yes, Shuv, you have,' and then where would the conversation go? What would happen next? It might emerge that he found her repulsive, that he hated her for letting herself go, for not loving him enough any more to care what she looked like.

The truth was that Karl didn't find her repulsive. He actually quite liked the shape of Siobhan's body now. She'd always been a bit out of proportion, with skinny legs, a too-wide back and a flat bottom, and now she was more balanced, her breasts looking less incongruous, her bottom more rounded and feminine. She felt nice, especially in the dark, firm and ripe and plump, her arms solid and corpulent, her thighs smooth and soft. It was almost as if the extra layers of fat had given her body a new lease of life, put the bounce back into her thirty-six-year-old skin – she felt like a chubby young schoolgirl, and Karl had never slept with a chubby young schoolgirl, even when he was a chubby young schoolboy.

Siobhan still had the most beautiful hair he'd ever seen, thick swags of summer corn down to her waist, always shiny and clean and smelling of good things. So much of the early romance and attraction in their relationship had revolved around her magnificent hair. He would see it everywhere he went around campus, either swinging freely to her waist, catching the light even on a cloudy day, or tantalizingly folded and pinned up like lustrous puckered gold. That hair tormented his soul for six months. His heart would miss a beat and then pump uncontrollably whenever he saw it; it was like a deafening siren signifying the faint possibility that he might have to walk past

Siobhan and display his blush, his desire, his embarrassment. He fantasized about removing those tortoiseshell
combs and clips, seeing her hair spread thickly like freshly
churned butter over his pillowcase, or spilling over the
back of the passenger seat of his 2CV. He wanted to wash
it for her, comb and look after it for her, almost like it was
a pet, an animate part of her – something living and breathing that encapsulated everything he wanted in a woman
and everything that was wonderful about Siobhan.

Siobhan had been unaware of any of this. As far as she
was concerned, Karl was the good-looking Student Union
guy, the one with the Russian name and the Irish accent,
the one she saw pinning posters up on noticeboards, the
one who seemed to know everyone on campus, the one
with the 2CV and the rockabilly quiff, and the one who
had been quite conspicuously going out with Angel, a
bleached-blonde, gamine-cropped, baby-faced wet dream
of a girl from the first year, since for ever. Siobhan found
him charming and attractive, loved his Irish accent, his
sunny disposition, his well-formed bottom but, as far as
she was concerned, there was a certain level of inevitabil-
ity when a couple were as attractive and popular as Angel
and Karl, and it was hard to imagine them enjoying anything less than a flawless, companionable and highly
sexually charged relationship. She imagined the two of
them sometimes, legs entwined on sun-drenched pure-
white sheets, biting and digging their fingernails into each
other, or laughing together in a pub with friends, their
chemistry overwhelming and infectious. She smiled at
him from time to time, and he smiled back, but that was
as far as she imagined it would ever go.

Siobhan's hopes and her heart were hydraulically lifted one day by a conversation with a friend who was on the Student Union with Karl.

'She's a little cow,' he said, unprompted, of Angel.

Zing! Hope Alert!

'Really? I always presumed she'd be nice, you know, going out with Karl and everything. They seem like a perfect couple.'

'The man has the patience of a saint. I don't know how he puts up with her, I really don't. They row nonstop, and she gives him such a hard time. Karl's a great bloke, he could do much better than her, and between you and me, I don't think it's going to last much longer anyway. I reckon she's seeing someone else – but I didn't tell you that.' He tapped the side of his nose and winked at her.

Siobhan didn't need to hear anything else. The passing smiles turned into passing chats, which evolved into long, animated lunches in the park when Angel was in lectures. And, when Karl told her one night after they'd officially been going out together for six weeks that their mutual friend had been so sick of Angel and so tired of hearing Karl going on and on about Siobhan that he'd taken it upon himself to set the wheels of romance in forward motion, it had filled Siobhan with such a deep glow of warmth that she hadn't needed to wear her coat home.

Her hair had lived up to his expectations, and even up until a few months ago when they stopped sharing baths, he had shampooed it for her occasionally, gently and meticulously, marvelling at its quality and length and the fact that it was in his hands and he was allowed to touch it whenever he wanted.

Some men were breast men, some were leg men and some were bottom men. Karl was a hair man. It was hair that turned his head and made mincemeat of his senses.

Cheri had lovely hair too – not impressive, imposing hair like Siobhan's, but it was silky and long and a pretty shade of vanilla. He'd noticed her hair before he'd noticed her, last summer; it shone with streaks of sunshine-bleached blonde. It hadn't been too long before he'd also noticed her long brown legs dangling from tiny summer dresses and short cotton skirts, her elegant shoulders, tanned and angular, and her finely featured face with those wonderful cheekbones and perfect teeth.

He admired Cheri's hair now, in an aesthetic, casual sort of way, over the top of his *Evening Standard,* as he sat behind a large window in a Covent Garden dance studio and watched her in a crop top and Lycra knickers high-kicking her way through the last five minutes of her Acid Jazz class.

While Siobhan sat naked on the side of the bath rue-fully grabbing handfuls of wretched, hateful flesh, three miles across town Karl stood up, folded his paper, greeted Cheri with a kiss and a stroke of her firm, neat buttocks and took her out for lunch to her favourite Modern European restaurant.

5

It was just starting to get dark as Jem walked from her office in Leicester Square to Gerrard Street to buy ingredients for the moving-in meal she had promised to cook for Smith and Ralph. She'd been living with them for just over a week now and she still knew absolutely nothing about them. She'd been out a lot and spent the rest of the time in her room, giving them their space, but now it was time to make friends.

On the day she'd moved in they had chivalrously although unenthusiastically helped her transport her boxed and bagged belongings from her dirty, French-mustard-coloured Austin Allegro to her room, the three of them processing quietly and industriously up and down the concrete steps like some sort of modern day chain-gang. They had then left her to her own devices for the remainder of the evening while she unpacked in the now somewhat cramped confines of her tiny room, popping their heads around the door every now and then, proffering tea and coffee and asking her politely how it was going.

Funny, this modern day thing of sharing homes with strangers, Jem had thought. Strangers had always lived together, of course – domestic staff and their employers, lodgers and their landlords – but not like today. Today people were expected to share an equal footing in their homes with strangers; there was no hierarchy. You watched the same television in the same living room, you used the same toilet and bath, shared the fridge, cooked on the same cooker and had some sort of obligation to treat this new person in your home as a friend, not an employee, not a lodger. Jem had moved around a lot from flatshare to flatshare and always found the first few nights strange and lonely. She had felt Smith and Ralph's awkwardness as they tried to go about their normal business but she knew that they didn't feel as relaxed as they would usually as they watched the Australian Grand Prix or Topless Darts. Even though she wasn't in the room with them, the fact that there was a third person in their home had thrown the dynamics of their nightly routines slightly out of kilter.

She thought about them now as she crossed over Lisle Street and remembered with a thrill that one of these two awkward but seemingly likeable men might be her destiny. It sounded daft, she was well aware of that, but fate had always made itself very plain to Jem and she had learned to trust in it unquestioningly. The only cloudy issue that fate had left her to deal with this time (and it was a very cloudy issue indeed) was which of the two men it was. Since it wasn't about to hit her between the eyes, she'd spent the last week looking for signs.

She couldn't go on looks, although they were both good-looking men, in very different ways. Smith had the public-school, floppy-haired, well-structured sort of look that she would have swooned over when she was eighteen. He was tall and nicely but unathletically built, with soft brown eyes, handfuls of thick minky hair and a fine nose with the most perfect nostrils. But he was a bit 'grown up' for her tastes, a bit too mannered, a bit restrained, too much the gentleman. She got the impression he'd be taken aback if she ordered a pint in the pub and that his idea of romance would involve long-stemmed roses and surprise trips to the theatre – yuck. She liked her men quite rough and ready, men who didn't treat women like 'ladies'.

Jem sorted through a box of shiny red and green chillies, long, thin and beautifully misshapen, feeling for firmness, while she contemplated her destiny. She placed the chosen ones into a clear plastic bag torn with some effort from one of those useless bag-dispensing contraptions and moved her pale hands to a box of baby aubergines, small and apply-green with waxy skin.

Jem found this sort of shopping therapeutic. A packet of M&S picked, peeled, topped and tailed, polished and prepacked vegetables just couldn't compare. How much nicer to wade with your hands through boxes of colourful and excitingly exotic produce, fresh from Thailand, China, India that morning, the scent of distant sunshine still clinging to their skins.

Ralph was probably more what she would have called 'her type'. He had the lean, slightly undernourished look that she liked, emphasized by his shorn hair and too-large clothes. His face was sharp but the angles were well-defined and his round blue eyes were set inscrutably deep into his face, giving him a streetwise but somehow sweet look. And he had one of those wonderful lazy, lop-sided smiles that started on one side of his face before the other side caught up. Sexy. He had the traces of a South London accent, which she loved, and he would *defi*nitely not expect her to drink dry white wine when they went to the pub or be impressed by expensive meals for two in trendy restaurants.

She reached the butcher's counter.

'Hello, Jem!' The butcher smiled widely as she approached. He was wrapping a large slab of pork belly for the elderly Chinese customer in front of her. 'What'll it be today?' he asked in a soft Mancunian accent. She'd always wanted to ask him how he'd ended up being the only English person working in a Chinatown supermarket.

'Hello, Pete.'

She surveyed the trays of ducks' feet and pigs' ears, the yards of shiny lilac intestines, the hunks of glistening white fat and rows of pink trotters.

'I'll have a pound of chicken breast, please, with the skins off.'

'What are you cooking tonight, then?' he asked. He always wanted to know what she was cooking.

'Oh, just a Thai Green Curry.'

'Making your own paste, are you?'

'Of course,' she smiled. 'Don't I always?'

'Thin slices?'

'Yes, please.'

'Who's the lucky dinner-guest tonight then?' he asked, deftly slicing through the pink meat with a lethal-looking knife.

'New flatmates – I'm trying to make a good impression.'

Jem took the chicken and put it in her basket. Who knows where the chickens from which these breasts had been wrenched came from? There was no handy label explaining their origin, no soft white-paper duvet for the breasts to rest on as they travelled from supermarket shelf to the purchaser's fridge. They were anonymous, and Jem felt that bit more adventurous for choosing them from among the gory remnants which other supermarkets would never put on view.

The shop was crowded, full of Chinese locals buying food for supper, of souschefs from Chinatown restaurants picking up an extra sack of rice or two for the evening rush, of tourists just looking, and amateurs. Amateurs were people who liked the atmosphere but didn't know what to buy, and their baskets invariably held a couple of packets of twenty-five-pence instant noodles, a jar of oyster sauce and a can of something preposterous like Squid in Malaysian Curry Sauce that Jem knew would end up in the bin because it stood to reason that squid in a can would be disgusting. Jem always felt a rather nasty sense of superiority as her basket went through the check-out in front of an amateur, feeling proud of her bunches of fragrant fresh coriander, packets of glossy green lime leaves, cans of creamy coconut milk, spindly sprays of lemongrass and hairy bunches of rose-pink shallots.

She looped her carrier bags over her wrists and headed for Shaftesbury Avenue. The sky was darkening to a deep plummy shade of black and the streets of Soho were assuming the night-time air of temptation and provocation that always excited her. She glimpsed the animated faces of couples over pints in pub windows, absorbed and stimulated even on a Monday night by the conversation and facial expressions of their obviously new-found love, and she felt lonely for a moment, until she remembered where she was going and the romantic potential that lay ahead.

Smith couldn't tell whether Jem was a wine girl or a beer girl so he picked up both. Maybe she didn't drink at all – he grabbed a bottle of Perrier. He was in the vintner's around the corner from his office in Liverpool Street. 'Vintner's.' The City was just as pretentious as the West End in some ways, with its fake antiquity and overblown traditions. What was wrong with calling it an off-licence, for Christ's sake?

He took his purchases to the recently distressed mahogany counter and a traditional shopkeeper wearing a deep-green cotton apron and steel-framed glasses zapped them through the till with an olde-worlde barcode gun. Smith realized he was in a bad mood. He almost threw his card at the unfortunate vintner and bristled with unnecessary impatience as he rolled the bottles in tissue paper and put them into a bag. The copper bell on a spring which rang as he closed the door behind him irritated him.

He walked across Finsbury Circus noticing how cold it was and thinking how it had seemed like only days ago that he had sat here basking in his shirtsleeves watching old farts playing bowls in his lunch hour. He was always much happier in the summer.

He wished that Jem wasn't cooking tonight. He really wasn't in the mood to be pleasant and interested and conversational, he just wanted to sit in front of the television and have a big fat spliff and a lager and not talk to anyone. He was aware that this was exactly why he had decided that a flatmate would be a good idea in the first place, but just not tonight, that's all. Tomorrow night would be fine. The presentation would be finished by then, James would be off his back and he would probably have bought a bottle of champagne and a bunch of flowers to celebrate, and Jem would have been impressed by how friendly he was, how amusing and how sincere in his appreciation of the great effort she had made to cook them this meal. Just not tonight.

Smith arranged his briefcase and bag in one hand to grab the escalator rail with his other as he descended into Liverpool Street station. He took large confident strides and fumed as someone in front of him, a tourist who obviously had absolutely no understanding of escalator etiquette on the Underground, came to a halt.

'Excuse me, please,' he muttered huffily. The tourist turned and shuffled into the space to the right good-naturedly, apologizing with a smile. Smith felt guilty for a second, thinking of the times he had been a tourist himself.

He sweated on the Circle line, feeling irritated by every other person in the carriage with him – they were too smelly, too noisy, too close, too tall, too fat, holding too much newspaper or just offensively unattractive. Smith had fantasies about embedding pickaxes into their skulls.

He wondered what he and Ralph and Jem were going to talk about that evening over supper. As he thought about it, it occurred to him how little he knew about Jem. He'd avoided talking to her whenever possible and didn't even know how old she was, where abouts in London she worked, whether or not she had a boyfriend – for some reason he found himself hoping that she didn't – all he knew was that she had a name nearly as silly as his, she liked honey in her tea, she drove a horrible Austin Allegro and she was really quite attractive. Not a Cheri, of course, not a magnificent specimen of well-toned, shiny, angelic goldenness like Cheri. But she was approachably pretty, small and sexy and sort of fluffy, like a proper girl. She had a sweet, unthreatening voice and she never wore trousers – Smith respected that in a woman. But for some reason, he had no idea why, she made him feel uncomfortable.

The doors of the Tube train opened at Sloane Square and Smith tumbled out of the carriage gratefully, glad to breathe in the fresh, crisp night air. When he'd first bought the flat in Battersea, eight years ago, Smith had got a real kick out of alighting at Sloane Square. After all, the plebs waiting for friends and dates outside the station weren't to know that he didn't live in sw3, as he breezed past them swinging his briefcase confidently down the King's Road. He couldn't give a toss now what anyone thought. He was way past that sort of immature posing and knew that nobody waiting outside the station even noticed him, let alone gave a shit about where he lived.

The flower stand outside the station caught his attention – it looked brave and colourful against the now almost leafless, grey October backdrop of Sloane Square and he decided that he would buy some flowers for Jem after all. She was paying for dinner and he didn't suppose she had much money. He selected three fat posies of peonies, bright and unpretentious – he didn't want it to look like a come-on.

The act of buying the flowers seemed to trigger a calm-ing chemical in his brain and he felt his mood improve as he boarded the bus, flashed his pass at the driver and took his usual seat at the back.

As the bus passed over Battersea Bridge and filled with the glow of the pomegranate sunset filtering through the birthday-cake lights of Albert Bridge, Smith felt a small rush of euphoria. He allowed himself a little smile, and began to look forward to the novelty of a home-cooked meal and a conversation with a pretty girl.

6

As usual, Siobhan had eaten by the time Karl got home after his Ceroc class. Siobhan had gone with him when he first started teaching. She would don one of her old fifties dresses bought from Kensington Market and fill it out with frothy petticoats, slide on some ruby-red lipstick and black eyeliner, put her hair up in a pony-tail, and the two of them would get into the black Embassy and drive down to the Sol y Sombra feeling like Natalie Wood and James Dean. But when they got Rosanne she felt guilty about leaving her on her own five nights a week and had gradually stopped going. And these days she wouldn't be able to fit into any of her old dresses anyway.

Now she would watch Karl as he slicked Black and White gel through his black curls and slid into his peg trousers and genuine Hawaiian shirt, looking, apart from a little less hair along his hair-line, exactly as he'd looked fifteen years ago. He was a brilliant dancer and an even better teacher; some of his ex-pupils had gone on to teach their own classes. He was always much in demand at weddings and parties because he made women look and feel as if they could dance.

'Has someone else moved in downstairs?' he asked, unlacing his worn but shiny brogues. 'There was a girl in the kitchen just now when I walked past, cooking.'

'Was she small and dark?'

'Yes.'

'I've seen her coming in and out all week. She must be a new flatmate or something.'

Karl wandered into the kitchen and put his arms around Siobhan's substantial waist and his chin on her shoulder. She reached back to ruffle his hair and realized, too late, that it was Ceroc night.

'Eugh, I've got Black and White all over my hands. Yuck!' She made a dash for the tap. Karl slapped her bottom gently.

As he left the room, the smile disappeared from his face. He sat down on the sofa and put his head in his hands. He could hear Siobhan next door, singing softly as she washed her hands. Her voice was gentle and melodic. She sounded like a little girl, an innocent little girl. He wanted to cry. He wished he was on his own so that he could sob and sob until his heart broke. He had been robbed, robbed of his baby. It had been taken away from him without his permission, without his knowledge.

Just one floor away, in the flat upstairs, his baby had been growing and breathing and sleeping in Cheri's womb, a mass of cells the size of a fingernail, with eyes and feet and thumbs, carrying in it the strands of his DNA, of his black curly hair and his bad temper in the mornings and his funny big toes, and she'd killed it without even thinking to mention it to him.

The fact that she'd ended their affair today, casually, over pan-fried scallops with lime juice and fresh coriander, meant nothing. *Cheri* meant nothing to him, except hair and sex and a dancing partner. But she'd killed his baby and she really didn't seem to care. He'd looked at her cold and untroubled face – she'd seemed more concerned with the texture of her scallops than the murder she'd committed – and he'd hated her, really, really hated her.

'One in three pregnancies ends in miscarriage, you know, it's not such a big deal. It could have just died anyway and you'd never have known, neither of us would ever have known,' she'd explained wearily, as if she had to explain away an abortion to some distraught, cheated-out-of-fatherhood ex-lover every lunchtime. 'And what would you have said to Siobhan anyway? "Oh, darling, you know that girl who lives upstairs, that one you don't like, well, I've been fucking her and guess what? Marvellous news, she's pregnant." Yes, I'm sure dear, fat, barren Shuv would have been *very* pleased for you.' She'd arched her perfect eyebrows impatiently and turned to inform a passing waiter that her scallops were too tough, and would he mind bringing her a linguine with chilli and clams?

Karl had no idea what he would have said to Siobhan had circumstances been otherwise; practicalities were not prevalent in his helter-skelter thought processes – all he could think about was the fact that his chance had gone. His baby had been in a womb. Suppose he and Siobhan had been so desperate for a child that they'd gone to a surrogate mother – it would still have been his sperm, another woman's egg, another woman's womb – what was the difference? He had about as much feeling for Cheri as a plastic syringe would have.

As he sat listening to Siobhan preparing his dinner in the next room, remembering the pain on her face when she'd been told at the age of twenty-one that she was infertile, that she'd never be able to have a baby, he vowed

46

he'd have his revenge. He wasn't sure how he'd do it, but when the opportunity arose, he would make Cheri feel bad, as bad as he felt now.

Smith hadn't known whether to laugh or cry all day. He'd had two hours' sleep, eight cans of lager and two tequilas the night before and now it was Tuesday and he only had another couple of hours to complete the presentation that his financial P R company was putting together for one of the largest banks in the country. The office was in a state of complete panic and James was being more painful than Smith could have ever thought possible. He was usually an unruffled, dignified sort of a chap, who prided himself on his elegance, but when the heat was on, the loose brush of silvery hair that usually covered his balding skull stood upright, his silk tie refused to sit in a neat vertical line and small wet patches appeared under the arms of his Jermyn Street shirt.

His face was florid now, and he was shouting at Diana to 'Open some fucking windows in here! It smells like a Bedouin fucking-tent.' Diana, who hated working and was waiting for her pink-faced jellybaby of a boyfriend to propose and allow her to live the life of leisure she felt she deserved, had reached breaking-point half an hour ago and was about to cry.

Smith moved back to his desk and looked at his screen. He'd written one line of the proposal so far, 'Quirk & Quirk is one of the City's longest established PR houses with a reputation for . . . ', and it sat on the screen now, reminding him vindictively of his hungover state, mocking him for being so irresponsible, daring him, challenging him to write another line without thinking about last night.

Smith felt his bowels begin to move. He picked up a copy of *PR Week,* and checking that James wasn't watching his every move, as he tended to do when he was in a panic, he walked towards the toilets.

Sitting in the shiny white cubicle staring blankly at the magazine on his lap, his reflections on the previous evening persisted. What a night, what a completely unexpected night. And what a mess. He put his face into his hands and smoothed back his thick hair with his palms, enjoying the feeling of the skin on his face stretching taut.

What was he supposed to do now? It was all going to be so horribly embarrassing. Smith just wasn't used to women coming on to him. In the days before Cheri, before he'd given up on women, it had always been up to him, he'd always made the running. Jem had really taken him by surprise last night, and he'd been too drunk to think about what he was doing. He felt guilty now, almost like he'd been unfaithful to Cheri. He'd saved himself for five years, five whole years, and now he'd blown it – just like that. It was all very flattering, the first time in years his ego had received a massage. And it had been enjoyable, *extremely* enjoyable. But he really shouldn't let it go any further. He hoped to God that Jem regretted it as much as he did. Maybe she would prefer to forget about it too. And if not? He'd have to tell her, tonight, tell her it was all a dreadful mistake. Then what? Shit. The atmosphere would be terrible. She'd move out and he'd have to find another flatmate. What was he supposed to say to her? What the hell were they going to do? And why the fuck hadn't he thought about this at the time?

He stared dismally at his reflection in the mirror above the sink. He looked appalling. He felt appalling. He had to write that proposal. He felt like storming into James's office, slamming his fists on the desk and saying, 'I'm sorry, James, but I have a life, and I don't give a shit about Quirk & Quirk's long-established reputation. Write it yourself, you manic old bastard – I'm going home.' But he wouldn't, of course. He took a deep breath and walked back into the claustrophobic mayhem of the office. James was frantically pressing buttons on the fax machine.

'Diana, Diana, what the hell is the matter with this stupid machine?' he was muttering, his upright hair making him look like some kind of ageing budgerigar.

'Have you pressed Send, Mr Quirk?' she asked with weary impatience.

'Of course, I pressed Send. Look, can someone else please do this, I really don't have the time.'

Diana made a face at James's retreating back and headed towards the fax machine. She noticed that Smith was back.

'Someone called for you while you were out, a girl. There's a message on your desk.' She raised her eyebrows.

Smith peeled the yellow note from his computer screen. *'Gem called – thanks for last night and fancy going for a drink tonight? Please call back.'* His heart lurched in his chest, and he felt a hot flush rise up from his neck.

Oh, shit. Now what?

7

'Morning, Stella.' Jem was exhausted and hungover and could feel the bags beneath her eyes pulling at her eyelids.

'Morning, Jem, you look well today. Is that a new lipstick you're wearing? It suits you.'

'Thanks, Stella.'

Ridiculous. Jem knew she looked like shit. Jem and Stella had been working together at the theatrical agency for over three years now, and every single morning without fail Stella would furnish Jem with a compliment and every single morning it would be one that she had never heard before. Taking account of holidays, Jem had calculated that five compliments a week equalled two hundred and forty compliments a year and a grand total of seven hundred and twenty compliments in all, all of them different.

'How did it go last night?' Stella enquired, in her usual ingratiating manner. She was hovering over Jem's desk with that desperate look on her face, like she'd been waiting since six o'clock that morning for Jem to get into work so she could ask her just that question.

Stella was thirty-three years old, six foot two, and still a virgin. She had hair the colour of yellowing newspaper, the remains of a perm at the ends, which never seemed to grow or change. She wore the same pale-blue eyeliner every day, which only succeeded in making her round eyes look even more damp and watery than they were. As far as Jem could tell she had no life whatsoever, and chewed gratefully on whatever scraps of Jem's not particularly exciting life she chose to throw her. 'How did your sister's eye test go?' she'd ask concernedly. 'How's your friend Lily getting on with her new boyfriend?' (She'd never met Lily.) 'What colour wallpaper did your mother choose in the end?' (She didn't know Jem's mother.) 'Oh, the duck-egg . . . lovely.'

Jem wished she could say she was fond of Stella, that she had a soft spot for her, that she'd miss her if she wasn't around, but it wasn't true. She was a huge galumphing giant of a pain in the arse, and on a morning like this morning, with a thumping dehydrated headache and a lot on her mind, she found it took all the patience and civility she could muster to form even the curtest of replies.

'Oh, fine, fine. It went fine, thank you.' Jem smiled tightly and tried to look busy.

'Good,' trilled Stella, thrilled that Jem had had a Monday night good enough to be described as fine. 'Still enjoying the new flat?'

'Oh, yes, lovely – super. Very much, thank you.' Jem was running out of fake enthusiasm.

Stella's phone rang at that moment and Jem breathed a sigh of relief. She felt a small blush of coy embarrassment and excitement spread across her face and towards her chest as snapshot images of last night's events flashed unbidden through her mind. Smith had bought her peonies – he'd actually bought her peonies, her favourite flowers in the whole world. The minute he walked in and shyly handed them to her muttering, 'Just to say thanks for the meal,' she'd known without the slightest doubt that it was *him*. She'd stood in the kitchen and looked at the two men last night, and it was blindingly obvious in an instant. On one side was Smith looking handsomely care-worn in a nice grey suit and a pale lilac shirt and tie, and on the other was Ralph wearing a foul baggy grey jumper that he appeared to wear every day and a most unbecoming pair of vaguely obscene-looking longjohns.

'D'you need any help?' Smith had asked, as Ralph wandered back into the living room and back on to the sofa to watch *EastEnders*. Smith – two; Ralph – nil.

Finally they sat down to eat. The entire flat was infused with the aroma of coconut, garlic and coriander and the almost heavenly scent of Thai fragrant rice. Ralph and Smith were in raptures.

'This is the most delicious thing I have ever eaten in my whole life!' declared Ralph.

'Better than anything I've had in a restaurant,' agreed Smith.

It had taken a few of cans of lager to lubricate the evening, after the seam of compliments on the quality of the food had run dry, and Jem had found herself doing most of the work to start with, asking the two men about themselves.

Smith worked in the City, she discovered, for a PR company dealing largely with financial institutions. He'd worked as a City dealer before that but had been in danger of burning himself out so had taken a fairly substantial cut in salary to change career. But, reading between the lines, he was still earning somewhere in the region of four times Jem's modest salary. He'd lived in Almanac Road for eight years – he'd saved vast amounts of money working in the City during the boom and living with his parents in Croydon after he left university and paid cash for the flat when Battersea was still relatively good value. Ralph had moved in shortly afterwards.

To her surprise she'd learned that Ralph was an artist. She had a clichéd idea of what an artist looked like and it wasn't Ralph. She'd been wondering what he did for a living and had noticed that he never seemed to leave the house. He hadn't painted for a few months, he'd been doing sporadic freelance graphic design on his Apple Mac, but it seemed that his income was chicken-feed, just enough to cover living expenses, beer, cigarettes and drugs and the odd cab home. He seemed uncomfortable talking about his lack of direction and stalled career. He'd been the star of his year at the Royal College of Art, and his degree show had been met with much over-excitement from critics and buyers. He showed Jem a small book of press cuttings from the time, moody black-and-white photographs of 'the artist' accompanying glowing articles full of phrases like 'formidable talent', 'genius', 'exciting new star of his generation'. He'd had a few successful exhibitions, sold some paintings for what had felt at the time like extraordinary amounts of money and then everything had gone quiet. New 'exciting stars of their generation' had displaced him and for the last few years he'd been relegated to exhibiting his work in City wine bars and hotel foyers.

'I'd love to see some of your work,' Jem had said. 'Have you got any of it here?'

'Yeah, Ralph, I'd love to see some of your work too,'

said Smith, turning to Jem. 'I've lived with this bloke for eight years and I've never seen anything he's done at the studio. Not a Polaroid, nothing. Show her your degree-show book, Ralphie.'

Ralph grunted but loped off to find it.

He'd returned with a large hardback book which fell open easily to a double-page spread headed 'Ralph McLeary' and a picture entitled 'Dangerous Sands Shifting 1985.' Jem didn't understand or care much for modern art but the picture made an instantaneous impact, and she turned the page with interest, to 'Noxious Gases and Ultraviolet 1985' and a smaller picture entitled 'Violent Electrical Storms 1985'.

The paintings were abstract but rich in colour and although seemingly flat and one-dimensional, Jem felt surges of energy bursting from them.

'Ralph, these are great, really . . .' She searched for a word that wouldn't sound ignorant, '. . . dramatic, energetic, scary almost. And I don't usually like modern stuff. These are brilliant!'

'Thanks.' Ralph had looked pleased despite himself and closed the book. 'Anyway, you've had to ask enough questions tonight. Tell us about yourself.'

Jem always hated talking about herself, but she told them in as few words as possible about Smallhead Management, the theatrical agency where she'd worked for three years, how she'd recently been promoted from secretary to Junior Talent Manager and was learning the ropes from Jarvis Smallhead (they'd laughed at his name), the outrageously camp agency boss who had high hopes for her. She recounted the almost never-ending series of mini-dramas and crises she had to deal with every day involving a bizarre collection of aged luvvies and prima donnas. She told them about the painful Stella and her obsession with Jem's life, about her eccentric mother and her long-suffering father and her idyllic childhood growing up in a cottage in Devon. She explained that her name was short for Jemima and that before she moved into Almanac Road she'd been living with her sister Lulu in a vast, partially furnished flat off Queenstown Road. Lulu was moving her boyfriend in, and his three children from a previous marriage, and although she'd been welcome to stay, Jem had decided to move on.

They'd carried on chatting as Smith and Jem cleared the table (Smith – three; Ralph – nil), and the more Jem watched Smith the more she felt sure. He was definitely the quieter of the two, the more restrained. He sat straighter at the table, his table manners were more precise, his laugh more controlled than Ralph's, and there was something vulnerable about him that appealed to her, a certain sadness, a loneliness. Ralph was good fun and probably more similar to Jem in a lot of ways, but although Smith seemed more uptight, she felt a closeness to him.

Once she'd decided she knew it wouldn't take much to set the ball rolling, to lead Smith gently by the hand into a relationship. She just hadn't expected the ball to start rolling quite so soon, or quite so fast.

Ralph had got up from the table at about eleven, kissed Jem unsteadily on the hand, thanked her profusely for the meal, proclaimed it a milestone in his gastronomic life and gone to bed, leaving Jem and Smith alone.

Jem hadn't wasted any time. 'Do you believe in fate?'

she'd asked, rolling a spliff on the pine surface of the kitchen table.

'What do you mean?'

'You know, everything happening for a reason, events and moments being preordained. Like me being here tonight. If I'd seen a double room I liked last week I wouldn't have come to see your room. I would be sitting in someone else's kitchen now, talking to someone completely different, and I wouldn't even know you and your lovely flat existed.' She paused briefly. 'Except, that's not quite true.' She stopped to search for a Tube ticket in her handbag to use for a roach. She wondered how much she could say to Smith.

Smith wondered what on earth she was going on about and wished he could focus on her a bit more clearly.

'This is going to sound weird – do you promise you won't think I'm a nutcase?' she asked, tearing off a small piece of cardboard.

Smith reached for a bottle of tequila. 'Promise,' he said.

'Well, ever since I was a teenager, I've had a recurring dream.'

'Ye-es,' Smith slid the shot glass in front of her. God, she really was cute.

'Just a really nice image of a tall house on a curved road with a basement and little trees outside. I'm walking down the road and I look into one of the flats and there's a man sitting on the sofa with his back to the window. He's smoking and talking to someone I can't see and he's smiling and happy and relaxed and I really, really want to go in. The flat looks warm and welcoming and I just have this very strong feeling I'm supposed to be living there – it doesn't feel right that I don't, that I have to walk past and never get to know the man inside, never be part of his life. And that's it, that's the dream. And then, that night I came to see the flat, I just knew it was the same flat – I felt it. It was so familiar, so safe, just the way it felt in the dream. And I looked down, just like in the dream, and I saw a man sitting on the sofa and talking to someone out of view.' She paused. 'Do you think I'm mad? Are you going to kick me out?' Jem laughed nervously.

Smith fought the smile that was twitching at the corners of his mouth. He didn't know where this weird conversation was going, but for some reason, he felt compelled to keep it going. He arranged his features into an expression of serious consideration. 'No, I don't think you're mad at all. I think that's really rather amazing.'

'But that's not all. I hope you don't think this is really heavy or anything . . . Oh, I don't know whether to say this or not . . .'

Smith looked at her intently and rested his head on his hands. 'Please – go on. This is fascinating – I promise you.'

'Well, it's not just the flat. It's the man. I know in my dream that I'm supposed to be with the man on the sofa – he's my destiny. Do you realize what I'm saying?'

Smith had no idea what she was saying, but she was getting cuter and more attainable by the minute. All of a sudden he could imagine taking her face in his hands and kissing her sweet little red mouth, and then he thought about Cheri, imagined her upstairs now, while they spoke, elegantly tucked up between her ivory silk sheets (he'd never actually seen them, of course, but they had to be, didn't they?), her lithe, supple body encased in a tiny slip of satin and lace, her perfect head ever so slightly denting her pillow while she slept. He imagined her lace-clad chest rising gently up and down as she breathed, pictured her turning in her sleep, stretching and writhing slightly, the slippery sheet sliding off her body for a second and revealing one long, brown perfectly formed leg. She would sigh as she turned, a long, deep, sensual sigh, and then drift back into sleep . . .

'You do think I'm mad, don't you? Shit. I knew it. I knew I shouldn't have said anything.' Jem was staring at the floor and wringing her hands.

'What? No! No. God, I'm sorry – I was just thinking, that's all.' Smith smiled modestly and sincerely at her. He still wanted to kiss her, and all of a sudden it didn't seem like too much of a challenge. He lifted his shot glass and nodded towards hers.

'Cheers, then,' he said, watching her as they downed the repulsive liquid and grimaced.

'Yeek,' scowled Jem.

'Bleugh,' shuddered Smith.

They fell silent for a moment, looking into their glasses and glancing at each other every now and then, both waiting for something to happen.

'Smith,' said Jem eventually, 'I hope you don't think I'm being unbelievably forward, but – I've just had this overwhelming compulsion to hug you. What do you think?' She grinned nervously and put out her arms.

It had been a monumental hug, a coming-home hug. Jem had almost felt the energy flowing between them as she pushed her head into his chest and breathed him in deeply, his smell enveloping her in the same feeling of rightness and safety and destiny as her dream, but better, because this was real.

Smith had gripped her tightly, unexpectedly enjoying the sensation of shared physicality; it had been so long, so bloody long since he'd had any kind of decent human contact. He'd forgotten what it felt like to put your arms around another human being, without embarrassment, and share their warmth and their body. He'd always thought this moment would've happened to him and Cheri, but this was good, this was nice. Jem was nice.

They had stood like that for what felt like hours, their arms around each other, Jem's head in Smith's chest, Smith's chin on her head, breathing deeply, sighing, allowing unspoken feelings to flow through them, a silent communication between two people looking for entirely different things and finding them in exactly the same place.

8

Ralph could not believe it. He really could not believe it. It was beyond the pale, it defied belief, it was rude and . . . and . . . and . . . unbelievable. He could not believe it. The girl had only been here two minutes and already Smith was . . . was . . . fucking her. He was fucking her. He was fucking well fucking her. Unbelievable!

He could not understand how it had happened. One minute they'd all been sitting together having a nice chat and a laugh and breaking the ice very nicely, thank you, and they were all friends, all equals and then Ralph had taken himself off to bed and then – then what? What the hell had old Smithie said or done to that girl to get her into the sack so fucking quickly? Maybe she was some kind of nymphomaniac who moved from flat to flat shagging her flatmates – saved getting cabs home, he supposed. Jesus.

Ralph had lain in bed all morning with an achingly full bladder, waiting for the other two to leave the flat so that he wouldn't have to bump into either one of them on his way to the bathroom. Smith was gone by eight o'clock and then Jem had got up and left at nine. He was standing over the bowl now, watching the colourless jet of piss escaping gratefully into the water below, and breathing a pleasurable sigh of relief.

Jem just didn't seem the type. A nice girl, a decent girl.

He'd found her completely charming over dinner the previous night and had been thinking how refreshing it was to meet a girl who was intelligent and funny and pretty, and drank lager from the can, and loved curry as much as he did, and who was a good talker as well as a good listener. He'd been delighted and flattered by her reaction when he'd shown her some of his paintings. He'd been overwhelmed by her culinary ability and her highly impressive capacity for searingly hot food. He'd been entranced by her stories about her family and the strange characters she worked with at the theatrical agency. He'd found her Italianate hand gestures and scrunchy facial expressions beguiling and endearing. She wasn't like any of the girls he normally met. She was special.

So what was a lovely girl like Jem doing, leaping willy-nilly into bed with a prat like Smith? Ralph was intrigued. He was confused. And he was also a little jealous.

He headed for the kitchen and a pint glass of tap water, gulping greedily. It was a filthy day, just visible outside the kitchen window; the sky was uniform paper-flat white, and a fine drizzle was slowly moistening the bricks and concrete of South London, turning the crunchy leaves strewn messily around the streets into mulch. The combination of bad weather and bad hangover was rapidly making the journey through London to his draught-ridden, rat-infested studio in Cable Street seem unlikely.

Maybe all that stuff in her diary was rubbish and she'd wanted Smith from the first moment she saw him. Maybe something had happened between them that night when she'd come to see the flat and Ralph had been in his

61

room. Maybe the air had been thick with the scent of unbridled lust since Jem had moved in and Ralph just hadn't noticed, like some sad insensitive bastard. Maybe (Ralph hated to think it) maybe the dinner was only really intended for Smith, and they'd both been waiting all night for him to go to bed, giving each other looks across the table every time he'd opened his mouth to say something else, thinking 'Fuck off, Ralph, Fuck off, Ralph.' Ralph felt stupid.

For five years he'd had to listen to Smith droning on and on about that God-awful woman upstairs, that snotty, stuck-up bitch with the attitude problem from hell, who didn't have even the slightest awareness of Smith's existence. And now, the first time an eligible woman set foot in their flat and showed a little interest, he'd bedded her. Just like that. That really was the epitome of laziness.

The post landed on the doormat and Ralph padded down the hall. A cheque from the travel company – £540. Just enough to clear some of his overdraft so that he could start building it up again. Ralph could not remember the last time his account had been in credit. He put the cheque on the hall table – he'd make a trip to the bank later in the day. He noticed that the door to Jem's room was ajar again. He remembered the tantalizing passage he'd read in her diary yesterday and, his resolve and sense of honour weakened yet more by curiosity, he pushed open the door and scanned the room for the book. Maybe there would be a clue in there, something to explain the extraordinary goings-on of last night.

The room was still in disarray. Jem's bed had been slept in, so she'd obviously managed to find her way out of

Smith's bed at some point, the curtains were drawn and the weak light outside struggled through the thick fabric, casting a pink glow over the room. Ralph reached for the light switch and the little glass star lit up. The diary sat with its predecessors under the table by the bed.

Ralph was caught off guard by his reflection in the wardrobe mirror – so, this is what he looked like, snooping in someone else's bedroom. He was wearing a pair of old grey longjohns and a baggy grey V-neck jumper, displaying a spray of dark chest hair and a silver chain he'd bought in Bangkok. His hair was short but dishevelled, receding into two gentle dips of baldness, which seemed to retreat at exactly the same rate of acceleration as the hairs on his chest, back and shoulders advanced. His blue eyes were looking a little dull this morning, as they always did when he'd been drinking. But, on the whole, not at all bad for a totally unfit, twenty-Marlboro-a-day, very nearly thirty-one-year-old man.

Ralph wasn't a vain man, just one who appreciated how lucky he was not to have to worry about being unattractive – life was difficult enough without being ugly as well. His image looked after itself; he didn't need to cultivate it. He never put on weight, and the muscles he'd developed during a summer spent labouring on a building site when he was twenty-two had somehow lasted him almost a decade. Losing his hair suited him, and hair care was just a matter of going to the same barber's he'd been frequenting since art school and asking for a number two. And girls always seemed to buy him clothes. Especially these PR fashion types who got discounts all over the place and half-price designer samples. The jumper he was wearing had been bought for him by Oriel, a beautiful but tedious girl with an obsession with handbags and a small dog called Valentino. He'd seen the same jumper in a shop a few weeks after they split up and had been shocked to see it sporting a price tag of £225. That hadn't stopped him wearing it at least five times a week without washing it; it was now peppered with small burns caused by hot rocks falling from spliffs, and smelt at close range like an ashtray full of curry which had been stuffed up someone's armpit for an hour during a heatwave.

Ralph turned away from the mirror. He wasn't used to studying himself – it wasn't unpleasant, just vaguely unsettling. He pushed open the dark wooden doors of the wardrobe.

The floor was lined with shoes, lots and lots of shoes, little tiny shoes. Some were flat and some had heels, but they all looked as if they had been worn; unlike the impulse buys that constituted the extravagant shoe collections of other girls, these were old friends.

Her clothes formed an eclectic kaleidoscope of rich browns and reds and greens, and floral prints on chiffon, velvet, suede and silk. They emitted a sweet odour, perfumed with subtle undertones of pubs, cooking oil, wood smoke and spicy food; an aromatic diary of her social life. Ralph pulled out a particularly pretty dress, ankle-length diaphanous georgette printed with small red roses, with thin straps and a stream of impossibly small buttons down the back. He could picture Jem in it, her black curls studded with flowers, her abundant bosom pushing upwards, running barefoot through the grounds of some imaginary grand house, a pink-cheeked Renaissance babe.

No no no no no *no* NO! Ralph stopped himself abruptly. He hadn't come in here to sniff Jem's clothes and form elaborate Mills and Boon-style fantasies about her. He hadn't come in here to get a crush on her. Jem was not, was most definitely not, *not*, NOT, Ralph's type. No. Blonde, tall, whippet-chested, cool, arrogant, wine-drinking, label-wearing, *Elle*-reading, ball-attending – that was Ralph's type.

Time to get down to business; time to find out what was going on here. Yesterday he'd been in the running, had been, in fact, ahead of the game; yesterday he'd been 'lean' and 'sexy' and 'more fun to be with'. Yesterday he had been the object of Jem's strange and mysterious dreams. Yesterday he'd been Jem's 'type'. One day later and he was a spare part.

All of a sudden he could see the future mapped out before him, and it wasn't pretty. Jem and Smith were going to become inseparable; he would have to spend hours listening to them having sex, sitting on his own in the armchair while they snuggled together on the sofa. They would decide to get married, and Smith would approach Ralph nervously after the engagement party to broach the subject of him moving out. He'd end up in a cardboard box (no one else would be as understanding about Ralph's sporadic rent-payment style), and he'd have one Tennents Super too many and be set on fire by hooligans while he lay unconscious in a doorway.

Why the hell had she gone for Smith? What had he, Ralph, done to put her off? Maybe it was all those smelly shits he'd done; she always seemed to walk into the toilet moments after he'd exited. Or it could be because he hadn't fussed around her, offering to help when she was cooking, like Smith had. She must have got a fair idea last night of how much money Smith earned – that was always attractive in a man. And Smith had bought her flowers as well, the smarmy bastard – that had to be it. Girls liked flowers. God, if only he'd thought of that. Why Smith? Why not him? Why not him when she'd fancied him more to start with? What was wrong with him? Smith already had a flat and a great job and loads of money, he didn't need a girlfriend, too. And besides, he was in love with someone else. Ralph felt suddenly nauseous with rancid jealousy, rising to the surface of his soul like lumps of wet toilet paper in a blocked toilet bowl.

His pulse racing, his resolve and sense of honour now absent, Ralph sat down on Jem's bed and pulled the diary from the top of the pile. He began to read from the beginning, from January 1996, when Jem had been somewhere else, non-existent, someone he was yet to meet. If Smith was going to go out with her and sleep with her, then *he* was going to get to know her.

Lunchtime came and went, and elsewhere people with jobs went out, shopped in Boots, ate sandwiches, bought the *Evening Standard,* walked around town in suits and shoes and coats. Ralph read.

By mid afternoon the people with jobs were on the phone, in meetings, making cups of coffee, flirting at the photocopier, immersed in the safety of office life. Ralph read on.

As the light died at five o'clock and the people with jobs rushed to meet deadlines, tidy their desks, switch off their computers and frank the mail, Ralph still read.

At six o'clock, or thereabouts, he closed the book, put it back under the table, ruffled the duvet, turned out the light and left the room. He sat at his desk, tapped a Marlboro out of its packet, lit it, smoked it and waited for Jem and Smith to get home.

9

'What's she doing here?' Siobhan asked, in a tone which she hoped sounded casual and light-hearted and didn't betray what she felt inside – insecure, jealous, nervous. She was just so bloody pretty and sort of fit looking, glowing with health and vitality; all the stuff that had waved goodbye to Siobhan years before. And she had such lovely hair.

It was Karl's leaving party at the Sol y Sombra, just a few drinks with his students, some of whom he'd been teaching for five years, to wish him luck in his glittering new career.

'She's one of my students, didn't I tell you?' Karl was drinking from a bottle of lager.

Definitely not. 'I don't think so. You might have, I don't remember.'

Cheri didn't really strike Siobhan as the Ceroc type, she seemed more aerobic, more of a sweating-at-the-gym sort of girl.

'She's very, very good actually. She was my partner for a while, after you stopped coming.'

'Oh, really.' A filthy flash of unaccustomed jealousy pierced her stomach. Brightly, brightly, keep smiling, Siobhan; don't let him know you're jealous.

'You really don't like her, do you?' Karl asked unexpectedly.

'Well, I mean, I don't know her. She just doesn't seem like a particularly nice girl, that's all. Not really my type. She doesn't pass the Pub Test.' Karl knew about Siobhan's Pub Test; it was her way of ascertaining whether or not a girl was her type. She imagined being in a pub with the girl in question. If she could envisage sharing a couple of pints, a bag of crisps and some easy chat with her, she passed; if not, she was happily consigned to the not-my-sort-of girl pile.

'Yeah, I don't like her either.'

Brilliant! 'Oh really, I thought you thought she was all right.'

'No, you were right, Shuv. She's a selfish cow. I didn't even invite her tonight, one of the other girls did.'

'So what don't you like about her?' Siobhan's curiosity was aflame. She wasn't used to Karl forming such forthright opinions about people, doing vindictive things like deliberately not inviting people to parties, calling people 'selfish cows'.

'I don't know. I just agree with you, that's all. There's something about her I don't like. I can't put my finger on it.' In fact, Karl was furious. He'd told the little bitch not to come tonight and she'd promised she wouldn't.

'Why would I want to come to some sad little drinks with all those sad little Ceroc people? Don't worry. Bring your fat girlfriend – she'll be safe, I promise you.'

And now here she was, dressed up to the nines in some skin-tight black cotton dress with a low-cut back, drinking lager from a glass and flirting with poor Joe Thomas, the permanently sweaty looking bank clerk with the Buddy Holly glasses and too much Brylcream, who looked as if he was about to die of entirely unconcealed excitement.

Karl couldn't remember who'd started this whole mess any more. Obviously he'd noticed Cheri – any man would notice Cheri. But then, life was full of women to be noticed; if you started doomed affairs with all of them you'd never get anywhere. Picking up women wasn't Karl's style. It must have been Cheri.

He'd bumped into her one day at the front door, struggling for her key. He'd just got back from a dance class, so he had on all his fifties gear, and she'd asked him if he'd been to a fancy-dress party. When he'd explained about Ceroc, she told him that she was a dancer, that she'd trained as a ballerina until she was twenty, that she loved rock 'n' roll, her father had taught her to jive as a child. So Karl had invited her along to the Sol y Sombra, and she'd come. In retrospect, knowing what sort of a girl she was, she'd probably been flirting like mad with him then, sending out frantic sexual signals that he – honestly – had been completely oblivious to.

It wasn't until the first time he danced with her that he felt anything beyond a purely aesthetic appreciation of her. She was quite simply the best dancing partner he'd ever had. Her classical training added beauty and grace to the most basic Ceroc moves and she felt like a hollow doll, light and effortless, feathery and feminine. Ceroc was a man-led dance, and she followed his moves almost telepathically, injecting just the right amount of energy and enthusiasm into her dancing, smiling all the time.

Karl had been blown away. So blown away, in fact, that he hadn't mentioned it to Siobhan when he got home that night – not because of guilt, but because he knew he would blush vivid red and Siobhan would ask him why, and then he'd blush even more vivid red, and it just wasn't worth sowing seeds of doubt in her mind over nothing. So he hadn't said anything. He hadn't hidden it either, but Siobhan was obviously never looking out of the window when he and Cheri got back from class together, and since there was no chance of Siobhan and Cheri forming any sort of neighbourly friendship, she had never known.

Which of course made it easier for Karl neatly to compartmentalize his life when the dancing partnership turned into something a little more carnal. Karl had been shocked rigid when Cheri had first kissed him. It was definitely a scenario that had been swirling pleasantly through his mind for a few weeks, but then, life is full of enjoyable imaginary scenarios, and it would be impossible to enact all of them.

'Let me buy you a beer,' she'd said one night. And then, when the beer was gone and it was time for them to go, 'I really fancy another drink. Let me buy you a tequila.' And then, when those were gone, 'Let's have another, go on.' She'd had to persuade him, jolly him along, but he'd agreed in the end. After a third tequila they were laughing and relaxed, and Cheri had swivelled around towards him on her barstool, smooth brown legs conspicuously crossed, eyelids lowered, her body closing the gap between them and, before any embarrassment had a chance to creep in, she'd locked her eyes on his and kissed him. Gently at first, hoping that she wouldn't have to do all the work, that he'd respond to the sensual brush of her lips and kiss her back. She'd looked at him again. 'I love dancers,' she'd said, her eyes moving from his lips back to his eyes and to his lips again. She'd grazed his lips, a little harder this time. 'I especially love Irish dancers,' she'd drawled, 'with soft lips.' He'd kissed her then, and Cheri felt a rush of triumph.

Their kisses had become longer and harder, and his tongue probed deeply into her mouth. He'd brought his chest up close to hers, gripped her back and emitted a small, slightly animal grunt. 'Let's go to the office,' he'd groaned, searching his pockets for the key, and they'd stumbled into the small, stifling room, pungent with the smell of stale cigarette smoke and warm plastic at the end of a long, hot summer's day.

Cheri had let her dress drop to the floor, a practised procedure, and smiled at the look on Karl's face as he saw her for the first time, unwrapped, pert, smooth and naked. He'd been awkward, fumbling with his clothes, clearing a space, never taking his eyes from her body. 'God you're beautiful,' he'd said, rolling a condom on to his erect penis. It was all over in five minutes, hard, fast and uncomfortable. Karl was sweating profusely, his trousers still around his ankles, his quiff drooping and falling into his eyes. 'Oh, Jeez,' he kept saying as he came, 'Oh, Jeez.' And then he'd pulled up his trousers. 'Shit, it's hot in here,' he'd said, and handed her her dress from where it lay on the floor. 'I'm going to wash my hands.'

That should have been it really. They should have left it there. But, it seemed, as far as Cheri was concerned, it wasn't over. It wasn't over because, although she'd seduced him and aroused him and led him astray, he wasn't grateful. And she wanted him to be grateful.

But he wasn't. He never asked for more than Cheri offered him and took even that with an affronting lack of graciousness. She'd almost had to drag him up to her flat one weekend when he'd told her that Siobhan was away. She'd cleaned the flat from top to bottom, cooked a romantic meal, and Frank Sinatra, his favourite, wafted alluringly from room to room. There were clean sheets, new underwear, flowers. But it hadn't made any difference. It was longer and more comfortable and less sweaty, but it was still entirely perfunctory, and Karl had wolfed down his dinner afterwards and gone back to his flat to watch telly on his own.

For his part, Karl wasn't sure why it had dragged on for so long. In a strange way which he couldn't quite explain, he was scared of Cheri. Her emptiness and coldness frightened him, and he couldn't help feeling that if he tried to extricate himself, he might pay dearly for it – Rosanne in a pot of boiling water sort of thing. She'd been so determined to have him, so determined to make him want her that he hadn't dared go against her wishes. And if he was honest with himself, there'd been something strangely aphrodisiac about that intensity, about his fear – pathetically, it had turned him on.

He had truly believed that he would never, ever, in a month of forevers be unfaithful to Siobhan; it was more than unthinkable, it was ridiculous. And he certainly would never have thought it possible that he'd end up having a torrid affair with a bimbo – which is all Cheri was, a blonde bimbo with legs up to here and lovely tits, who could dance like an angel.

He knew he was nothing special to Cheri, but then he didn't suppose that anyone would be anything special to Cheri. It was, had been, purely and simply, fucking as an extension of dancing, a natural conclusion in a way to a traditionally sexual art form. They danced so well together that it stood to reason they would fuck well together.

It had been much easier than Karl could have imagined, lying to Siobhan, facing her fresh from the Sol y Sombra, coital sweat still drying on the back of his neck, the tang of rubber still perceptible in his boxer shorts. Funny how he didn't blush now, now that he actually had something to feel guilty about. He'd spent his entire life blushing at inopportune moments, his face reddening for no reason whatsoever, and now, he could walk into his flat, face his faithful and trusting girlfriend of fifteen years, his dick smeared with the vaginal secretions of the blonde bimbo from upstairs, and remain perfectly alabaster white. Ironic.

It hadn't occurred to him that girls like Cheri got pregnant. She was just so utterly soulless, so cold, so vacant and devoid of emotion, so different to how he expected a real woman to be that he hadn't thought for a moment that she even possessed a womb. Cheri was a dancer, a looker, not a mother. The thought of a baby suckling at those perfect rose-coloured nipples was ludicrous, the idea of Cheri pushing a pram, of Cheri changing a nappy, was laughable.

Siobhan was what Karl imagined a mother to be like. Siobhan was real, she was alive, she had a heart so big she could have mothered the entire country and still had room for the rest of the world. Karl had never been loved by anyone the way he'd been loved by Siobhan, such clean, easy, honest love, not the possessive, clingy, insecure love so many people mistook for the real thing. She had never tried to change him, to alter him in any way. She loved him just the way he was, and Karl didn't think you could ask for much more than that. Except, for some reason, passionate sex with unsuitable, unpleasant women.

Karl was feeling incredibly uncomfortable now, with Cheri and Siobhan in the same room. And Cheri had a look about her, like she was here for a reason, had a hidden agenda. She turned away from Joe Thomas for a moment and caught Karl's eye – she smiled widely at him and, to Joe's obvious disappointment, started to make her way over towards Karl and Siobhan.

'Hi!' she beamed, 'Hi! It's Siobhan, isn't it? I haven't seen you around for ages. Haven't you been getting out much lately?' she held out her tanned hand for Siobhan to shake. Karl felt sick as the two women's flesh touched. 'I'm going to miss your boyfriend so much.'

'Oh, really?' Siobhan replied amiably.

'Yes, Tuesday nights will never be the same again,' she said, looking at Karl.

Karl found himself almost glued to the spot, his bottle of lager frozen halfway between his mouth and the table, watching the scene unfold before his eyes.

'You must be so proud. When do you go on the air, Karl?'

He collected himself, conscious of a small stream of sweat wriggling down his temples. 'Erm, Monday week, isn't it, Shuv?' he said, handing the conversation back to the women.

'Yes, that's right. He's at the station all next week, though, to learn the ropes, you know, learning how to put those jingle cartridges in the jingle machine, all that technical stuff,' Siobhan replied with a little laugh.

'Well, Karl, good luck and everything. I'd have to have stopped coming to the lessons anyway soon. Look' – she held out her left hand, palm down – 'I'm getting married.'

'Oh, what a beautiful ring.' Siobhan held Cheri's finger-tips gently in hers while she examined it, turning it to catch the light.

'Yes, it belonged to my fiancé's mother. She was one of the most beautiful women you've ever seen.'

'Your fiancé – is that the tall guy with the blond hair?' Siobhan asked.

'Oh, no, that's Martin. Oh, God, I wouldn't marry him. No, it's Giles. I've known him since I was nineteen. He's very wealthy, very important in the City. He's got a house in Wiltshire and one in Australia and a flat in Docklands.'

'Where will you live? Are you going to move out of Almanac Road?'

'No, I think I'll keep it as a *pied-à-terre*.' She sounded uncomfortable using the expression. 'You've got to have a bit of space, haven't you?' She tossed her hair over her shoulder and laughed. 'Anyway, you two, I hope you don't mind but I'm leaving now. I've got a big day tomorrow looking at dresses, and I've got to find a venue for the reception.'

Karl and Siobhan both murmured their lack of disappointment.

'Karl, my coat's in the office. Would you mind opening it up for me?' Cheri placed her hand on his bare arm and he jumped slightly, the first time he'd moved since Cheri had approached them.

'Erm, why don't I just give you the key?' he said, fumbling in his pockets.

'Oh, you know how awkward that lock is – I can never get the hang of it. Do you mind?' She was wearing a sickly smile, one of her eyebrows raised slightly higher than the other.

Karl gripped Siobhan's hand. 'I won't be a second. Will you be all right?'

'Yeah, sure,' she replied weakly, wondering why she was feeling so uncomfortable about Cheri and Karl going to the office together.

He returned a few minutes later, looking red faced and flustered. 'Do you mind if we go?'

Siobhan was secretly relieved. 'No, of course not. What's the matter?'

'Nothing. I've just had enough, that's all,' he said distractedly, surreptitiously trying to wipe away the now solid stream of sweat rolling down the sides of his face.

He was so angry he could hardly breathe. That little bitch, casually moving from man to man, taking things as she went, holidays in Antigua, engagement rings, flats, babies, honesty, decency. What was she going to do to this poor Giles character?

Everyone seemed to let her get away with it, just carried on giving her things and giving her things and never expecting anything in return. Well, he was different. He expected things. He wasn't going to let her walk away just like that, into some cosy life with a rich man who'd give her anything she wanted for the rest of her life. Especially when she'd come here tonight to show him she was in control, to flaunt herself at him, to prove to him that she could fuck him, finish with him, abort his baby and still get a decent man to marry her.

That was why he'd done that to her in the office just now, forced his hand down the front of her dress, squeezed those perfect breasts hard with his sweaty fingers until she'd yelped with pain and then kissed her hard, ignoring the clash of his teeth against hers, sucking hard on her tongue and grabbing her crotch with the other hand, kneading the hot flesh inside her knickers while she struggled against him. He'd thrown her coat at her then and held the door open. He wasn't scared of her any more.

'Go home, you slut,' he'd said. 'If you ever come anywhere near Siobhan again . . .' He was shaking, and the anger inside him filled out the whole of his six-foot frame.

She was a whore, a slut – it didn't matter whose engagement ring she was wearing – and he wanted her to feel it, wanted her to leave the Sol y Sombra cheap and dirty, not the righteous, virtuous wife-to-be she'd convinced herself she was tonight. She'd looked frightened when she left, clutching her coat, her lipstick smudged around her mouth, her dress dishevelled. He'd ruined it for her, her little wedding fantasy. Good.

'Shuv,' he said later on when they'd got home and he'd regained his composure, 'let's have a baby.' He hadn't planned to say it, it just came out. But the moment he said it he realized it was right. It was what he wanted, more than anything.

'Oh, Karl, you know . . .' Siobhan began sadly.

'Yes, yes, I know. It's going to be difficult, it's going to be hard. Especially for you. But let's try. Properly. We'll be able to afford it now – you know, different treatments and stuff. Shuv, please. I really want us to have a baby.'

He was on his knees now, holding Siobhan's hand. 'Please . . .' He laid his head on her lap.

Siobhan was still feeling unsettled by the incident in the club, and this was the last thing she'd expected. She thought they'd written it off years ago, after the doctor had told her that the infection in her ovaries had made her infertile. That's why they'd got Rosanne. She hadn't thought the subject would arise again; it had been philosophically dealt with and it was closed.

'But what if it doesn't work, you know? It could take years and years, and I'm thirty-six now. Maybe I'm too old – they don't like dealing with older mothers, more risks, it would take up all our time. I've seen the documentaries – it might tear us apart, and you and I are more important to me than a baby. I couldn't bear it, all the disappointments and the waiting . . .'

'Please, Shuv, please.'

Siobhan looked down at the mop of black glossy curls on her lap, the solid neck and the curve of his wide shoulders, the bright design of his Hawaiian shirt. His legs were bent up under him, his whole being prostrate and vulnerable. God, she loved him. All she wanted in the whole world was for Karl to be happy. That was all she'd ever wanted, from the day she'd met him.

'OK – we'll see.'

Karl grasped her tightly and buried his head further into her warm flesh. 'Thank you, thank you, thank you,' she heard him breathe. 'Thank you.'

She stroked his hair, ignoring the slick gel, and felt quietly scared.

10

Ralph should have gone out, he realized that now. He shouldn't have sat in on his own all night. Claudia had invited him out to some press party for the launch of a new perfume her agency was handling. It would have been a nightmare, but there would have been free food and booze and lots of PR babes to admire and he could have just got totally pissed and spent the night at Claudia's and let the two of them have the flat to themselves. But instead he'd decided to be selfish and interfering and hang around to see what happened next with the red-hot lovers. He'd been expecting to hear the key in the lock all night and was positioned ready for the entrance of either one of them, feet up on the coffee table, spliff on the go, lager in one hand, remote control in the other.

At about nine o'clock he'd got bored of maintaining this pose even though it was a fairly natural one, and had decided that a reading-the-paper-in-the-kitchen pose would be more suitable. By ten o'clock he'd read the obituaries and the gardening column, had tried and failed to get even one word on the cryptic crossword and had thoroughly depressed himself by reading the executive job pages. Was he ever, ever, going to be in a position to earn £120,000 p.a. *plus* car *plus* healthcare *plus* bonus? No, he wasn't, and the thought made him miserable.

By half-past ten he had concluded resentfully that

Smith and Jem must be together somewhere and he'd made toast and experimented with a lying-on-the-sofa-making-a-phone-call-and-eating-toast pose but couldn't think of anyone he wanted to speak to.

By the time Jem and Smith finally got home he was back in his original sofa, spliff, beer and telly pose. They were glowing horribly and the noise of their playful chatter in the hall had preceded them upsettingly.

They stood in the doorway, all teeth and smiles and breathless hilarity.

'All right, mate. Had a heavy night?' Smith enquired sarcastically. Sarcasm was not something Ralph was in the mood for.

'Yeah, well, I was going to go to one of Claudia's poncey press things but I couldn't face it. I didn't fancy another heavy night after last night, so I thought I'd have a quiet one. Where've you two been, then?' He was trying to be pleasant. He really didn't want to know where they'd been, he didn't give a shit where they'd been.

'Just for a drink with a couple of Jem's friends and out for a meal.' Smith placed his hand on Jem's shoulder as he spoke; Ralph felt dejected.

'You missed a great programme on Discovery,' he countered, 'about killer sharks. They cut this one shark open on the beach and found the partially consumed remains of four men inside it, including their oxygen tanks.'

'Aw, fuck, what a way to go,' Smith said. Ralph could tell that he was feigning interest; he was looking at Jem and playing with her hair.

'Does anyone need to use the bathroom? I'm going to

get ready for bed,' she said, taking Smith's hand from her hair and holding it at her side. Ralph watched her gently.

I know about you, he wanted to say. I've been inside your head all day long and I know everything. I know every thought you've had for the last ten months, every place you've been, every meal you've eaten, I know more than Smith. I know you haven't had a single date all year, that you've been starved of sex but resisted the temptation to go to bed with your friend Paul.

I know you eat curry at least twice a week.

I know that you're not as confident as you make out and that you hate yourself sometimes. I know you worry what people think of you, that you're sensitive, that you can be paranoid sometimes, that when you're being chirpy you think you're getting on people's nerves.

I know that you haven't spoken to your mother for two years and how unhappy that makes you.

I know you get terrible PMT. I know your periods are as regular as clockwork (thirty-one-day cycle, first thing in the morning) and that you worry obsessively about your bowel movements and that's why you eat two pounds of All-Bran every morning.

I know you had chronic piles in June.

I know you think you're two-faced because you think dreadful things about people you're nice to in the flesh.

I know you chose Smith because he bought you your favourite flowers. I know about your dream and I can see why you thought that Smith was the one. I should have made more of an effort, I should have put some decent clothes on and offered to help, I shouldn't have been so offhand and I shouldn't have gone to bed. And I know you're wrong, Jem – it's not Smith, that was just a coinci-dence: buying flowers is a cheerful thing to do. It was me sitting on the sofa when you looked through the window and it's me you should be with.

But how could he say it, when it would mean admitting that he was a sneak of the lowest sort, the kind of person who reads other people's diaries? He looked at Jem now and realized that she was a different person to the stranger he heard leave the house that morning. He'd been inside her head all day, inside her thoughts. He knew more about her than Smith did, Smith who'd spent the evening with her and met her friends and had sex with her last night. He knew her secrets and insecurities. He desperately wanted to be close to her.

'Na, na, go ahead. I'm going to be up for a while,' he replied.

'You go first,' Smith said, pulling Jem back towards him with both arms around her waist.

'OK. Night night, Ralph, see you tomorrow.'

'Don't I get a kiss?' he said, getting up from the sofa. He suddenly wanted to touch her, too.

'Why not?' Jem smiled. 'Night night, Ralph,' she said again and gave him a peck on the cheek.

'Sleep tight, Jemima.'

'So, what do you think, then?' Smith whispered excit-edly, as the door closed behind her.

'About what?' muttered Ralph. He really didn't want to discuss Smith's revolting good luck with him.

'Jem, of course. What do you think of Jem? Of me and Jem? Oh, come on – you must have worked out what's going on.'

'Oh, right, very nice. Yes, very nice.' Then, seeing from the look on Smith's face that something further was required, 'Lovely hair, very pretty, very nice. I'm very pleased for you, Smithie, really I am.'

Glancing at Smith, he could sense that this line of new-girlfriend flattery still wasn't sufficient.

'I'm not talking about what she looks like, I'm not asking you to fancy the girl, I just want to know what you think of her – of us.'

'Look, what the fuck do you want me to say? The girl's only been here five minutes. She's very nice – I like her. I just hope you know what you're doing, you know, after the last few girls. You've got a bit of a track record for rushing things . . . remember Greta? You asked her to marry you after two weeks and then couldn't understand it when she ran a million miles in the opposite direction. And then that fuck-awful Dawn girl, the one you told you loved on the first night you met her and then she turned up the next day with all her stuff, expecting to move in. And *I* had to get rid of her for you. And that Polish girl you took home to meet your parents after less than a week, who made off with their Camcorder and your dad's laptop to support her boyfriend's crack addiction. And . . .'

'OK, OK,' Smith conceded, 'I know what you're saying, but this is different. Jem's different. I feel different. That's what's so great. I'm not going to fall in love with her, it's all under control! I was going to tell her tonight, tell her that I didn't want to take this any further, tell her about Cheri and everything. And then I thought, why? Why the hell shouldn't I have a bit of fun for a change, a bit of sex? I forgot how much I enjoyed it and I think I deserve it, don't you? Jem's a really lovely girl, I really like her. But for once, I've got the upper hand, I'm in control. I'm older and wiser and I won't make the same mistakes again. It's just a bit of fun. Really,' he stressed, noticing the look of scepticism on Ralph's face.

'So you haven't told her about Cheri – about your deeply unhealthy five-year obsession with an unattainable woman.'

'Of course I haven't! You've got to be kidding, haven't you? I'm not going to mess it up before it's even started. She thinks I'm great, she thinks I'm the man of her dreams – really! She told me last night. She thinks – now get this – she thinks that this flat has appeared in her dreams and that I'm her destiny. Isn't that hysterical! Anyway, Cheri's a different thing entirely. Cheri's a dream-woman. I've waited long enough. It's time to get on with my life. And maybe if she sees me getting on with my life, you know, without her, with a pretty girlfriend who worships the ground I walk on, she'll see me in a different light, come round a bit. It might make me more attractive to her.' Smith's face brightened at the thought.

'But you will tell Jem – at some point – won't you? I think she has a right to know what sort of a prat you really are.'

'Yeah, yeah, and I suppose you've told Claudia all about your colourful past, have you?' said Smith, knowing full well that Ralph hadn't.

'Yeah, but that's different, I don't love Claudia. She doesn't need to know.'

'Whoa! Who said anything about love?' Smith laughed, 'I think you're rushing things a bit here! That's what's so fantastic – I actually think, for the first time in my life, that I've met a woman who's more into me than I'm into her. D'you have any idea how great that feels? And she lives here, which means I don't have to worry about all that phone-call and date hell – I've got her on tap. This, Ralph my old mate, is what I would call a result!'

Ralph swallowed the bile-like sensation of distaste that rose in his gut as he listened to Smith. He pulled a cigarette from the packet in front of him and tried to bring the conversation to a halt. 'Well, can you keep it down tonight, please? I've got to get up early tomorrow morning and I don't want to have to put up with you two caterwauling all night.'

'Why not? I've had to put up with Claudia the Queen of Grief for the last six months. And I can assure you that Jem is as quiet as a kitten compared to that bloody banshee. You know, Ralphie, there are decent women out there. You don't have to go out with a nightmare like Claudia.'

'Look, I don't want to piss on your only-just-ignited fireworks here, but all girls seem great when you first start going out with them. Claudia seemed great: "Hey, I don't want commitment, I don't want to be tied down, I just want to have fun, I just want you to have fun, of course I don't mind if you go out with your ex-girlfriend tonight, of course I don't mind if you cancel dinner, I'm a grown-up woman, I'm cool." And now look at her. Just watch it, Smith – women, they're all the same, and don't you forget it.'

They heard the light in the bathroom being switched off, and the door being shut. Smith got to his feet and stretched.

'Yeah, yeah. Just you wait. Once you get to know Jem, you'll know what I mean – she's just not like that. You'll love her too.'

'Nah, Smithie – not my type,' Ralph said, forcing a grin. 'And anyway, I thought we weren't allowed to talk about love.'

As the door shut behind him, and Ralph found himself as he had been all night – alone – he felt a great sense of loss. Things were never going to be the same again. For years life had unfolded nicely, predictably, easily. Now everything was in jeopardy – his home life, his relationship with Smith, his finances, his security, his routines and habits. And, he realized suddenly, more than anything, his heart.

1 1

'Look, I like the music, I'm not saying that I don't like it. I think it's great music, classic stuff. But I'm fifty-three, I'm a balding fifty-three-year-old executive with three kids, a house in the country, a Land Rover and acid indigestion, I'm supposed to like it. Hmm, hmm . . . d'you see what I'm getting at?'

Jeff, programming director at ALR and Karl's new boss, looked at him across his huge status-symbol desk with his hands held palms up and his face wearing an expression that said 'There's a queue of people outside my door waiting to talk to me about budgets and scheduling and I'd really rather just bawl you out and get you out of my office, but because you're a new boy I'm going to have to be pleasant about this.'

'Hmm, hmm . . . d'you see what I'm saying, Karl? Hmm, hmm.'

Karl wished he'd stop doing that 'hmm, hmm' thing.

'Kids just don't want to listen to Al Green or Jerry Lee Lewis – I do, oh yeah, yeah, I do – but they don't. D'you understand? Hmm, hmm . . .'

Karl was beginning to feel like the only guest at a party who hadn't been told that it wasn't fancy dress. He'd been brought in to ALR to play a wide range of music, from Top Ten to Tom Jones. That was what had appealed to Jeff when he'd been a guest at a wedding Karl was

88

Deejaying at and that was why he'd got the job, over the heads of all those other DJs struggling for years in hospital radio and small-time local radio stations in Nuneaton and Truro. He was knowledgeable, not just poppy and happy and chirpy. They'd wanted someone their listeners could respect, someone with impeccable taste in music. They'd wanted him to build some sort of reputation – if it's on the Karl Kasparov show then it must be good.

Drive Time was captive-audience time, listeners trapped in cars. People did other things during the breakfast show, they brushed their teeth, they fed the kids, they made love. Daytime radio was for working to, background noise; as long as the DJ churned out a lot of pop and fun nobody was going to turn the dial.

Drive Time was different, a time for unwinding at the end of a hard day, a time to be selective and demanding and to turn that dial if the DJ was getting on your nerves or the music was repetitive.

Karl, with his deep, lilting Irish accent, his unabrasive sense of humour and his intelligent taste in music was exactly what they were looking for.

And now, after less than two months, they were telling him that they were wrong, that they were losing listeners. The critics loved him, but his audience was 'turning the dial' in its thousands.

'Phone-ins, celebrities, characters, comedy, chat, that's what you need, Karl, and more Top Ten, hmm, hmm.' He picked up his phone and dialled. 'Rick, you got a second, mate? I'm here with Karl, you know, discussing the show, hmm, hmm. We need your expertise here mate, some

Rick-style advice. Could you come and see us? Yeah, yeah now, that's right, great, OK great . . .'

'Rick – you know Rick, don't you – he's the producer, you know, on Jules's show? Yeah, right, anyway, he's got some great ideas, he's a great bloke full of energy, and funny? – God, he's funny – I want you to spend some time with Rick, you know, talk talk talk. I'm talking about your free time here, Karl, I'm talking about . . .'

He stopped and began to search in the top drawer of his vast cyclamen melamine-topped desk with one hand outstretched as if ready to pull Karl back by the lapels were he to attempt to escape. His other hand surfaced with a large bunch of keys. He looked at Karl triumphantly.

'I'm talking about Glencoe. I've got a place up there, an old Presbyterian chapel, converted, miles away from any-where, it's ab-so-*lute*-ly be-*yew*-tiful, right on the banks of the loch. At this time of year the sun sets right over it – it's stunning, Karl, really, really stunning – makes you feel kind of small and pointless, that sort of landscape. Puts everything into perspective . . .' He fell into a thoughtful silence and then suddenly slammed his hands down hard on the desk. Karl jumped slightly in his seat. 'And I want *you*,' he pointed at Karl, 'and my mate Rick to get your-selves up there this weekend, with your partners of course, and really have a mess-around, you know, hmm, hmm, get pissed, get off your faces if you want, you know, really unwind and relax, get to know each other and start throw-ing some ideas about – anything that makes you laugh, anything that makes your girls laugh. You got kids, Karl?'

Karl shook his head numbly.

'Good. Anyway, I'll get Sue to give you directions and

stuff and money for booze and anything else you want . . . yeah, that's a good idea . . . yeah, take some drugs with you, I want you to come back with some really zany ideas, something for the kids, hmm, hmm. And take some watchables up – you know, Jack Dee, Lee Evans – I'll get Sue to sort that out for you. Don't worry about it, I'll get Sue to sort everything . . . ah, Rick.' Jeff stood up. 'Rick, my favourite producer. Karl, mate, this is Rick de Largy.'

Karl turned around in his chair.

'Good to meet you – I love your show.' The man standing in the doorway smiled and held out his hand. He was ridiculously good looking, not in a flash way but quietly and horribly handsome. Karl could suddenly imagine how women felt in the presence of greater beauty. With all this talk of 'zany' and 'kids' and 'chat' Karl had imagined that this Rick character would be naff and toothy and unpleasantly sweatered, with too much hair and a fake tan. Even his name had sounded tasteless and gaudy. But the man standing in front of him was elegantly dressed in a white cotton shirt, well-cut jeans and what looked like handmade shoes, his gentle-featured face framed by understated wire-framed glasses and his hair a soft champagne blond, short at the back and sides and thick and effortlessly unkempt on the top. He looked about the same age as Karl but much healthier. His skin actually glowed – Karl had thought that only women's skin glowed.

'You two,' said Jeff leaning forward into his desk, 'are going to be great, great friends – just you wait.' He beamed like a proud father. 'Now, what about a bit of lunch then, boys, hmm, hmm?' He laughed and shook both men's hands. 'Let's go and talk about how Rick here is going to make you the funniest man on *Drive Time*.'

Funny? *Funny?* Karl felt his heart drop. He'd never felt less funny in his life. His home life was falling apart. Things just hadn't been the same since that night at the Sol y Sombra and afterwards, when Karl had begged Siobhan to have a baby. The atmosphere of warmth and love in their little flat had died and Karl didn't know why. It should have grown from that night – Cheri was out of his life, he and Siobhan were making plans for the future, he was just about to embark on a fantastic new career, everything should seem new and fresh.

He'd lain in bed on the night of his leaving party and watched Siobhan sitting on the edge of the bed swiftly removing garments, pulling her top over her head, her hair spilling over her smooth white back, and he'd felt a strong rush of love and arousal, not just a need to ejaculate but a need to probe every area of her body, to explore her like he used to when they were younger. He stroked her hair and wound it around his hand into a thick coil that gleamed in the muted lamplight and brushed it against his face – it felt like satin and the lustrous silkiness aroused him further. He placed his arm around her waist, feeling it melt into the pliant rolls of flesh, and reached his hand upwards until it found her breast. He'd groaned then and buried his face into her back and breathed in the scent of her skin deeply, gently massaging her breast, feeling her nipple suddenly bloom under his fingertips, a small warm bullet of flesh.

For years their sexual routine had been fun and frolicsome, rollicking romps, good clean fun. Tonight he wanted more. Every bone and muscle in his body had quivered with desire as he gently pulled Siobhan around and lay on top of her. He pulled her hair from around her shoulders and arranged it carefully into an abundant fan over the pillow – she looked like a Titian archangel. He kissed her hair, her forehead, her plump white cheeks, her eyelids, her ear lobes, her neck – oh God, he wanted to feel every part of her with his lips, his tongue, his fingers. He groaned again and slid his face between her breasts, the tip of his nose feeling the moist pool of sweat that lay between them, damp and hot and pungent. He licked at it, enjoying the taste of the sweat on his tongue while his hands pushed her breasts gently together – 'oh God oh God' – he could come now, he really could. His erection was bursting, ripe and angry and pressed hard into Siobhan's groin – he rubbed it up and down against the coarse hair, the abrasion spreading feelings of desire from the shaft of his penis to the tips of his fingers. He felt Siobhan wriggling slightly under him and stroked her face, wanting the love he was feeling for her to spill from his fingertips into her head, so that she'd know without him breaking the spellbinding silence that was fuelling his desire.

'Karl . . . Karl . . . please, please.' Siobhan's voice had sounded like a distant echo, her hands gently pressed down on his shoulders. His tongue continued to forage, his hands grasped her flesh harder and harder . . .

'Karl, stop it, please . . . I . . . I . . . don't want to.' Karl took Siobhan's nipple into his mouth and sucked hard on it, running his tongue around the hard warm flesh . . .

'Karl, STOP IT, STOP IT, STOP IT! Get off me!' She pushed hard down on to his shoulders and tried to roll him away.

'WHAT?' screamed Karl. 'What the fuck is wrong?' He was on his side of the bed now, his hair wild and on end. He turned to look at Siobhan, who had pulled the duvet up over her body and still lay in the same position. She was crying, silently, huge effortless tears flowing down the sides of her face and on to the pillowcase, a completely blank expression on her reddening face.

'I don't want to, Karl, I just don't want to . . .'

'You don't want to what? What don't you want to do, Siobhan? Tell me, for fuck's sake.'

'I . . . I . . . I don't know.' She wiped away the teeming tears with the back of her hand to make room for the endless flow.

'You don't want me to make love to you – is that it? You don't want me to love you, to love your body – what, Siobhan? What?' Karl demanded.

Siobhan sniffed but the tears kept coming. 'I don't know Karl. I don't know . . . I'm so sorry, I just can't. I'm sorry . . .'

'Well if it's all the same with you, I'm going to have a wank,' he snapped, striding through the bedroom towards the bathroom and slamming the door behind him.

Siobhan had watched his angry naked body, still in good shape, defined back muscles, firm round buttocks, his scrotum just visible as the light from the hallway silhouetted him briefly. It was a body she was so familiar with, had loved for so many years, enjoyed for so many years, and as she watched it walk out of the room, away from her, she cried and cried and cried.

She didn't know what the matter was, or how good her

intuition was. But it was something to do with the party at the Sol y Sombra, something to do with that girl, the blonde from upstairs, the one who was getting married. She made Siobhan feel ugly, she made her feel insecure, and for some reason she made Siobhan feel sad and scared, as if something until now immutable had changed for ever.

She wanted to tell Karl, but she couldn't. How could she explain that she'd rejected him because she thought he wished he was doing those things to Cheri? That she'd lain there while he caressed her and licked her and loved her, and all she could think was that he was fantasizing about that girl, fantasizing that Siobhan's fat unkempt flesh was Cheri's taut brown flesh, that her densely haired, pungent genitals were Cheri's neat soft mound, that the woman underneath him was young and firm and beautiful?

She'd seen the way he looked at Cheri, how he'd blushed, the way he used to blush on campus all those years ago. And what had happened in the office, why had he looked so flustered when he got back? There was no doubt in Siobhan's mind that Karl fancied Cheri, that he wanted her. It all tied in with the glamour of his new job. How could a top DJ possibly be satisfied with a fat, lazy, hairy woman? He wanted more now, even the way they had sex wasn't good enough for him now – he wanted steamy Hollywood sex, passion and heavy breathing and grasping flesh, not the usual routine of fun and laughter.

He was probably thinking about Cheri now as he sat on the toilet and vented his frustration, probably enjoying it more than he would writhing around on top of Siobhan's vast, wobbling body pretending she was someone else.

He obviously didn't see her as a woman any more. It all made sense. That was why he suddenly wanted her to have a baby after all these years, so she would become a mother, a vessel, not his lover. Young fresh girls were for fucking; fat ugly women were for staying at home and having babies and getting even fatter. Their breasts were for suckling, for hard greedy babies' mouths to drain of their suppleness and femininity and leave dry and pendulous and ugly, hanging like strips of biltong. And while she nursed his child he would be fucking one of those awe-struck girls who congregated outside the ALR building, wanting a piece of DJ.

The door opened quietly and Karl tiptoed in. 'Shuv, I've brought you someone.'

A weight fell on to the bed and a wet tongue stroked Siobhan's cheek. The aroma of dog wafted in the air. Siobhan hugged Rosanne to her and cried until the tears stopped coming. Karl put a hand on her shoulder.

'Shuv, I'm sorry, I didn't mean to storm out like that. I didn't mean to shout. I was just so . . . so . . . I just wanted to make love to you so badly tonight.' He stroked her hair. 'Please, Shuv, talk to me, tell me what's on your mind.'

Siobhan just shook her head sadly, put the dog at the foot of the bed and turned on her side away from Karl.

'I love you,' he whispered in her ear, 'I need you.'

He turned over then, the other way, and a heavy wall of silence divided the room, a dense knot of unresolved unhappiness and uncommunicated thoughts hung in the air.

They hadn't made love since. They hadn't really talked either. They'd gone about their lives in an apparently normal fashion. Siobhan had given him a hero's welcome when he returned after the transmission of his first show, and he'd given her flowers. They'd been out to buy a new sofa together and bid an emotional farewell to the old one when they left it at the tip. But things just weren't the same, there was a distance between them that would have taken a million yards of rope to bridge, an intolerable distance that they were both too afraid to cross, because below was infinite darkness, impossible depth.

The baby had been forgotten about; it hadn't been mentioned since that night.

Things were not good and now they were getting worse.

No, Karl had never felt less funny in his life.

12

Jem had always found that men seemed to fall in love very quickly. The full-blown declaration of love usually came within the first week, sometimes sooner. When she was younger she'd been so shocked by these revelations that she would clumsily repeat this much-abused statement in reply, not knowing how else to bring the embarrassing moment to a close. And then, of course, after it had been said once it had to be repeated like a mantra every time it was offered to her like a desperate gift from the love-afflicted soul. She soon learned when the 'I Love You' moment was imminent and discovered that when it was countered by a firm but affectionate 'Don't be silly, of course you don't', it rendered the afflicted one even more desperately in love and devoted.

Which is why, even though she'd been going out with Smith for nearly two months now, she wasn't in the least worried that he still hadn't said it, that he still hadn't told her he loved her. He didn't have to. Jem knew he loved her, without a word leaving his lips. As far as she was concerned it was yet another sign that Smith was the One. It was all so easy, so effortless. Smith was so undemanding, he didn't put any pressure on her.

Jem found it refreshing that he didn't plague her with romantic gestures and overblown declarations and gifts and pukey tokens and acts of love. He didn't go on about how beautiful she was, or how she was the most amazing woman he'd ever met, or how she was *so* sexy and *so* wonderful and *so* special. She'd had enough of all that to last her a lifetime and she knew that such devotion usually came with a price tag attached – the jealousy and possessiveness of an insecure man.

Jem was aware that other women might find her attitude hard to understand. She realized that many women spent the majority of their lives dreaming of a man who would finally notice the dazzling flecks of amber in their eyes, the fine golden hair on the back of their necks, the porcelain smoothness of their skin, a man who would stroke, caress and soothe, utter words of adoration and talk endlessly of the years to come and the joys of commitment, a man who would place them carefully and reverently upon a diamond-encrusted pedestal, throw rose petals at their feet and hand-feed them morsels of their favourite food, all the while unable to unglue their eyes from them for fear of missing just one second of their incomparable beauty.

Not Jem. All that stuff turned her stomach and made her want to vomit.

She'd loved it the first time it had happened, of course she had, especially coming as it had at the tail-end of a hideously awkward adolescence just as she'd finally convinced herself that she was to remain unloved and unpenetrated for ever.

His name was Nick and he was a comfortable-looking bloke with a strong jaw and the sweetest smile imaginable. He'd just come through an equally awkward adolescence and at the ripe old age of nineteen was just about to resign himself to a lifetime of virginity when Jem came along.

It was a classic summer romance, full of picnics and trips to the cinema, drunken nights in beer gardens and hours of fumbling in the front seat of his mother's car, where Jem had found herself, after years of trying to keep other boys' hands out of her knickers, frankly, quite desperate to get hers into his.

They finally dispensed with their long-standing virginities that summer, the day after Jem's eighteenth birthday and, in comparison to stories Jem had heard subsequently from her female friends, it was a truly magical event that had lived up to both their expectations. They were madly, madly in love with each other.

So everything was perfect and Jem was happy.

Until one night, a few weeks later. She'd been well into her third pint and enjoying a raucous conversation with a raucous friend at a raucous girls' night out – when in walked Nick. He'd ambled self-consciously into the bar, scanning the room for his precious Jem, his face opening up like a blossoming flower when he spotted her, his pace quickening as he approached, his arms outstretched to pull her into a desperate embrace.

'I was missing you,' he said, 'my mates were boring me. I just wanted to be with you,' and he'd gripped her to him, burying his face in her hair and Jem had *tried* to smile, *tried* to reciprocate the depth of feeling, the strength of passion, but failed miserably, feeling instead completely suffocated, trapped and compromised. Nick felt like someone different after that night. They were no longer equals. The scales had been tipped. And try as she might, Jem just couldn't revive the warm, solid, easy love she'd felt for him before.

At the end of that summer, she went to university in London and he went to university in Newcastle, and although things were OK at first, their weekend meetings gradually became more and more stressful. Nick would spend hours interrogating Jem about her newfound male friends in London, about her every movement and action, and quiz her about every boy she'd kissed before they met. Then he started to cry with alarming frequency, huge, wailing, snotty, unstoppable tears. 'I only went to Newcastle to prove to myself that I could live without you – and I can't! I can't live without you, Jem!' When he'd started talking about transferring to a London university, Jem decided it was time. Enough was enough.

It was one of the hardest things she'd ever done and he reacted badly when she phoned him, blowing his grant on a flight from Newcastle to London because the train would have taken too long, and searching London's student community, house to house, for her. He'd finally found her, trying to hide from him in Lincoln's Inn Fields. They spent three traumatic hours going over and over the details of their relationship, Nick begging and pleading for another chance, until the sun started to sink and the vagrants began to set up their makeshift homes, and Nick finally gave up and went home.

Jason hadn't believed Jem loved him, either and demanded her attention, her love and her reassurance constantly, for ten months, disappearing into huge black sulks for days on end when he felt that she had wronged him in some way. Danny had insisted that she stop seeing her friends – he couldn't understand why she should possibly need friends, now that they'd found each other. Clem wanted to marry her after six weeks and then fell into a deep depression when she said no, claiming that he no longer wanted to see her because 'it just hurt too fucking much.'

And then, finally, there was Freddie, a fantastically charismatic, hysterically funny and deeply sexy saxophonist, who Jem had been all set to fall miserably in love with. He was totally removed from all the 'nice' boys she'd loved before and she was more than ready to experience the other side of the coin, to hand him her heart on a plate. But he beat her to it. Within weeks he'd had his long tousled locks cut short, swapped his jeans and waistcoat for a pair of chinos and a check shirt and was talking seriously about selling his sax and getting a job in sales so that they could get a mortgage and maybe think about starting a family.

Jem had been amazed. Wasn't that the way girls were supposed to behave? Wasn't it women who wanted commitment, security, babies, and men who just wanted to get drunk with their mates, have fun and play the field for as long as possible? Not in her experience. As far as Jem could tell, men were the ones with a strong need for commitment and security. How else could you explain the fact that at least nine times out of ten it was the man who proposed marriage? They can't *all* have been arm-wrestled into it.

Another thing Jem had learned about men was that they were threatened by a woman who *didn't* crave commitment and security, who wasn't straining at the leash to walk up the aisle, who didn't stop and drool at the windows of every jewellery shop she passed or turn to melted butter at the sight of every passing pink-cheeked cherub in a pushchair. As much as men might moan and whinge about these traditionally female traits, at least they knew what they were dealing with – 'the nag', 'the ball and chain', 'her indoors'. It had all been tried and tested by their father and their father's father and his father before them; women like that were a known quantity. It gave joyous meaning to nights at the pub or out with the lads – you deserved it after all you'd had to put up with from the demanding old harridan all week. It was part of life's rich tapestry and eventually, a couple of years down the line, the man would pretend to be strong-armed up the aisle, just to keep the tradition going, even though it was really what he wanted, too.

But these days – well. These days all the rules were broken and for some reason a lads night out isn't quite so enjoyable when you're worrying about what your free-spirited girlfriend is up to with her mates, and it takes the edge off rolling home pissed at one in the morning when she rolls in at two in the morning, completely slaughtered and having had a much better night than you. Where's the fun in being a bloke if you can't dangle the carrot of commitment in front of your girlfriend for years on end? And if she doesn't want commitment, the ring, the babies, then what the hell does she want? So Jem had found that most men, when confronted with a girl who just wanted to have fun, became confused and for some reason took over the role of the traditional woman, going to extraordinary lengths to try to tie their girlfriend down, break her spirit and control her.

But not Smith. Smith was perfect. He was happy for

Jem to do her own thing, in her own way. He was generous and kind and easygoing and so affectionate. Jem had never known such an affectionate man. He never left her alone, was always dropping kisses on the top of her head, squeezing her hands, stroking her neck and grasping her to him in rib-crunching bear-hugs. Jem knew why. He'd confided to her on their first date that he'd been celibate for five years. Five years! He hadn't had any physical contact with a woman for five years. It was another sign. It had to be more than a coincidence, his celibacy. He must have been waiting for her, waiting for Jem. And she was more than happy for him to make up for lost time with her.

He smelt nice, he looked nice, he dressed beautifully and he felt gorgeous. He didn't hassle her with his emotions and insecurities, he gave her space, he gave her time. She really liked all his friends. He really liked all her friends. And the fact that he was rich enough to pay for meals out and cabs home without Jem feeling guilty was just the cherry on top of it all.

OK, so it wasn't love's young dream. OK, so they'd bypassed all the usual courting rituals – the long, animated talks over late-night drinks, the endless hours spent in bed inspecting each other's moles and scars and belly buttons, the hour-long phonecalls you never wanted to end and pizzas in the park on freezing winter afternoons. And maybe they didn't really have all that much in common – she'd been right about the dry white wine and the fancy restaurants. But they were so easy in each other's company. Even now, at this early stage in their relationship, they were able to sit comfortably in silence, in public. It didn't matter when they ran out of things to say. There was no embarrassment. And Smith wasn't the most adventurous and spontaneous of people. But that didn't matter to Jem. She'd had her share of romance, and she didn't want any more.

She really didn't mind that Smith had forgotten both their one-month anniversary and their two-month anniversary. She found it refreshing. And she didn't mind that he never paid her compliments or noticed when she changed her hair or wore a new dress. She certainly didn't mind his lack of discomfort about her nights *à deux* with her close friend Paul or his complete lack of jealousy about her ex-boyfriends and old loves. She was happy that he spent so much time at work and didn't put any part of his life on hold to make room for her. She didn't want any of that. She didn't want the attention, the demands, the neediness. She'd been under the magnifying glass, the spotlight of insecure love for long enough. And now, she just wanted Smith.

13

Ralph had given up reading Jem's diary over the last two months. Well, the current diary, anyway. It was just full of Smith this, Smith that and Smith the bloody other. It was like Ralph had ceased to exist the moment Jem had slept with Smith. He had been hoping for some doubts to creep into her entries, some reference to the fact that Smith wasn't quite right for her, wasn't good enough, that she'd made her decision too soon. But it hadn't come. She was utterly blind to it, she was 'in love' with Smith and her diary was a constant, gurgling, gushing, vomit-inducing account of how perfect he was and how wonderful they were and how great the sex was.

But Ralph hadn't given up the long periods of time spent just sitting in her room. He liked it in there. It smelt good and he felt safe and warm with all Jem's feminine artefacts, it was second-best to her actually being there herself. He felt close to her when he was in her room.

He was sitting on her bed now, thumbing through her old *A–Z*, taking note of all the little roads that had been circled and wondering what they'd been circled for. Parties? Job interviews? Flatshares?

It was two o'clock in the afternoon. Claudia was away. All his mates were staying in with their girlfriends. A Friday night in. Ralph had felt unloved and depressed so he'd headed straight for Jem's room.

He put the *A–Z* back in her top drawer and his eye fell again upon the pile of old diaries under her table. He'd managed to resist the temptation of looking at them so far – it made him feel more disciplined, less unethical, marginally better about himself and his underhand behaviour. He looked at them and looked away again. No – he mustn't. He looked again. Fuck it, he thought, and reached for the bottom diary, an old accounting book covered in UCL stickers and smiley faces. Written on the cover was '1986'. He pulled back the front cover, the old, brittle paper crackling slightly as he turned over the first page. He started reading.

Six hours later, he stopped. A whole day had gone by and Ralph had learned an awful lot more about Jem. He'd learned about her adolescence, how much she'd hated her frizzy hair and her anaemic complexion and the fact that she was so short; how while other girls were losing their virginity and getting pregnant and coming into school with florid lovebites adorning their necks, Jem was busy crossing streets to avoid having to walk past anyone remotely resembling a teenage boy. She'd been painfully shy and painfully unconfident, crying into her pillow every night because she was so ugly and no man would ever want her. She'd been fifteen before she'd had her first kiss and then it had been so unpleasant and shared with such an ugly specimen of male youth that she'd rubbed at her mouth with the back of her hand for a good ten minutes after it was over, shuddering at the memory.

She'd then gone out, briefly, with a succession of ugly youths, desperately trying to cling on to her honour and her virginity, before Justin Jones had asked her out. Justin

Jones had, apparently, been the school heart-throb, a dark-haired dish with the pick of the school's girls at his feet.

'Why me?' she'd asked, referring obliquely to the contrast between herself and the more overtly attractive female students who would queue up daily just to stand in Justin's wake. 'I dunno,' he'd said, half-smiling, 'it's not the way you look, it's just something about you. I just really fancy you.' Justin Jones had unwittingly instilled in Jem with that one, long-ago, offhand comment a confidence that any amount of fawning compliments from lovesick suitors could not have achieved. He had paid her *personality* a compliment. He'd flattered her *spirit,* and Jem knew she didn't have to be anyone else but herself. She was an attractive person and anyone who couldn't see that was not worth knowing.

Since then, it seemed, Jem had had a whole string of relationships with nice blokes who'd made complete pains of themselves, smothering her with love and making unreasonable demands of her. Until Smith.

At last Ralph was beginning to understand what Jem saw in Smith, why she was so in love with him. Smith didn't call on her emotionally, he didn't restrict her or control her.

How ironic that she should have fallen in love with him because he didn't give a shit about her. How ironic that she thought he was so different from the other boys when, in reality, he was exactly the same, and the only reason he wasn't showering her with gifts and adoration and proposals of marriage was because he was in love with another woman. How ironic . . .

Ralph took a beer out of the fridge and flopped on to the sofa, searching through the rubble on the coffee table for the remote control. He'd just missed *The Simpsons* and now *Real TV* was on Sky, a series of totally unamusing real-life videos of people nearly drowning under white-water rafts and being rescued from burning buildings.

Smith was out tonight, at a press do. It was possible that he and Jem might be alone tonight. Maybe, instead of shuffling around trying to find reasons not to talk to her like he usually did, he should use it as an opportunity to get her to open up. Find out even more about her. He already knew more about her than he'd known about even his longest-standing girlfriends. He knew all her insecurities, her romantic history and her needs and desires. Now he wanted to get to know her better than anyone had ever known her before.

He heard female voices outside and shifted round on the sofa to peep through the open curtains. It was Jem, laden down with shopping as ever – he'd never met a girl who spent so much time in supermarkets – and she was talking to that blonde tart from upstairs. He strained his ears trying to catch what they were saying, but it was muffled. He smiled at the irony of Smith's girlfriend so easily and quickly engaging herself in a situation which Smith himself had been dreaming of, ineffectually, for the last five years. He stood up to check his reflection in the mirror, ruffled his shorn hair and sat down again.

Eventually he heard the front door open, and seconds later Jem burst into the room – Jem always burst into rooms, such was the force of her enthusiasm – all parcelled up in a big black coat and a deep-purple furry stole.

'I've just had a really nice chat with that girl from upstairs. She's very friendly, isn't she?'

Ralph had always found Cheri to be absolutely the opposite, but maybe Jem was a better judge of character than he was.

'She's a dancer, you know. She trained to be a ballerina until she grew too tall. It explains why she's so elegant, she holds herself very well.'

Ralph just thought she was a stuck-up bitch with too much attitude even for him.

'What are you doing tonight, Ralph?'

He shrugged and scratched his head, 'Um, fuck all actually. Pretty sad for a Friday night.'

'Excellent. Look, I've been blown out by my friends so I thought I'd just cook a curry, drink a load of lager, have a bit to smoke and then go to bed early. D'you fancy joining me? Well, apart from the going to bed early bit, of course.' She giggled adorably.

Ralph couldn't think of anything else he'd rather do tonight, he tried to hide his excitement: 'That sounds absolutely perfect – I'd love to. I can't promise to be much help in the kitchen, but I'll skin up.'

'Done.'

It was all Ralph could do to stop himself punching the air as Jem left the room.

'Right, I've decided,' Jem was back, barefoot in thick black stockings and a short dark-green jersey dress with capped sleeves and a flirty skirt, 'Have you ever seen that programme *Can't Cook Won't Cook*?'

Ralph looked blank.

'Oh, come on, you must have, you're at home all day. It's for people like you' – she pointed at him – 'people who write off cooking without even trying it. This chef guy gets two pathetic people to cook a dish by watching what he does – well, anyway, it's crap but that's not the point. I think every bachelor should know how to cook at least one dish, and since you like curry so much I thought I'd teach you. Come on, get up.' She held out her hand for him and he smiled and followed her into the kitchen, enjoying the feeling of her tiny little hand on his.

'I thought we said that I'd skin up and you'd cook.'

'Yes, well, I've changed my mind. OK, as you know, there are many, many different kinds of curry. Tonight I'm making a chicken jal frezi – actually, you can make a spliff while I'm doing the talk bit – yes, tonight I'm making a chicken jal frezi, it's very, very easy. You can pretty much do it to your own taste – I like mine quite green and stinking hot! So, I've got the chicken breasts, we can chop those later, and a really big bunch of coriander, lots of these monster-hot little green chillies – the big ones are crap, don't bother with them. Keeping up so far?'

'Oh, yes, so far so simple.' Ralph was sitting at the table crumbling grass into a translucent paper balanced on an upside-down box of Shreddies. He was entranced: why had none of his girlfriends ever taught him to cook before?

'You can get ready-made pastes but it's better to make your own – you can put what you want in really. OK, I'm going to put in loads of this coriander, some fresh fenugreek leaves and some ground fenugreek – smell that' – she held the plastic packet under Ralph's nose – 'that's what your armpits smell of the day after a curry . . .'

Soon enough Ralph was chopping up pieces of chicken and slicing onions and mincing garlic. He must have eaten a million curries in his life but he'd never heard of half the things that went into one. Ghee? Cumin? Curry leaves? He was amazed to find that he was thoroughly enjoying himself, even suggesting additions and asking for more jobs to do, and he was feeling wonderfully relaxed with Jem, for the first time since he'd found out about her and Smith. They were chatting and laughing together like old friends, singing along to the Pogues and dancing around the kitchen.

They laid the table together, and Ralph was ecstatic to be served with a plate of curry and rice that he'd helped to cook. And even more ecstatic when he tasted it – it was delicious.

'Ralph,' Jem began as they ate, 'can I ask you a question?'

Oh, Lord, one of life's most worrying openers.

'How do you feel about me and Smith – be honest?'

Oh, gawd. What was he supposed to say? '*I* want you *I* want you *I* want you, that's how I feel about you and Smith.' That would have been honest. Smith doesn't know you like I know you; you don't know Smith like I know Smith; it's all wrong and I'm as jealous as hell.

'I'm very happy for you both,' he said. How about that for honesty.

'So you don't feel excluded or, or left out or anything? It's just that you and Smith have lived alone together for so long, maybe you feel I'm crowding you, pushing you out?'

'Ooh, no, not at all, it's nice having you around.' Well, that was true at least.

'You would tell me if it was a problem, wouldn't you? I'd hate you to feel uncomfortable in your own home.'

'I promise you, it's not a problem, it's been so long since

Smith was even interested in a woman, it's a relief in a way.' Pinocchio, eat your heart out. 'I'm glad to see him happy. I've never seen him this happy before, you're very good for him.' But you'd be even better for me.

'Oh, good, that's a weight off my mind. So why aren't you seeing Claudia tonight?'

Claudia, Claudia? That was a conversational quantum leap. Ralph had to think hard to remember exactly who Claudia was, let alone why he wasn't seeing her.

'Oh, yes, yeah, she's gone to Paris for the weekend, something to do with work – fashion shows or something.'

'Ooh, very glamorous. I've not met Claudia yet, what's she like?'

'What, honestly?'

'Yes, we're being honest, aren't we?' She tore off a piece of kitchen roll and blew her nose, which was running from the heat of the curry.

'Well, she's very attractive, very tall and slim. And she can be quite sweet sometimes. But mainly she's a real pain. Everything I do is wrong. If I phone her it's inconvenient, if I don't I'm a bastard. If I invite her out with my mates she complains that she doesn't like them, if I go out without her she complains that I'm leaving her out. She tells me I'm scruffy and should make more of an effort, and then when I buy something new she says, "Oh, you can afford to buy new clothes but you can't afford to take me out for dinner." I can't do anything right.'

'Do you love her?'

'No.'

'Do you like her?'

'Sometimes.'

'So why are you going out with her?'

'For the sex, I suppose.'

'Well, that's honest, I guess. Wouldn't you like to be with someone you were in love with?'

Ralph reached for the kitchen roll – the heat was getting to him too. 'I have to admit, just lately I've wanted something more. I've been too scared for a long time, you know – the emotional investment, the insecurity, the vulnerability.'

'You've been hurt in the past?'

'Well, not hurt as such, just too involved, drained almost – it took over my life and I haven't wanted to risk getting entangled like that again. But now, I don't know, I think I might be ready for something real – the love thang.' He laughed nervously. He couldn't believe he was talking like this, he hadn't talked to anyone about real feelings for so long.

'Just haven't met the right girl yet?'

Oh, Jem, if only you knew.

'Yeah, something like that.' Time to redirect the conversation: 'So, you and Smith – is it a love thang?'

Jem smiled. 'Oh, yes, definitely. Very, very much so. Smith is everything I ever wanted, he really is. He's perfect.'

No, Jem, he's not. He's a prat and he doesn't deserve you.

'Yeah, he's a great bloke.' Ralph wanted to say something bad about Smith, put him down, but that was really small-minded and mean. He wanted to tell Jem about Smith's disastrous romantic history, that would take the shine off her rose-tinted glasses. He wanted to tell her that Smith thought her ideas about dreams and destiny were

114

ludicrous but a good way to get into her knickers. He wanted to tell her that Smith would drop her like a hot potato if Cheri was so much as to glance in his direction. There was so much he wanted to say but he couldn't possibly say any of it. Jem saved him from his thoughts.

'How come you don't paint any more?'

Well, they really were getting to the nitty-gritty tonight.

'Phew – that's a big question. I wouldn't say that I don't paint any more, more that I don't paint at the moment. I've tried, but the inspiration just isn't there. Maybe I've got too complacent. I was very unhappy when I was younger, very introspective – it was easy to paint then.'

'You've cut yourself off, haven't you? Cut yourself off from feeling things. I bet if you were to meet someone and fall in love it would all come back, all those emotions would be unlocked and you'd be straight down to the studio. It wouldn't feel like a chore, like an effort. Yes, that's Dr Jem's remedy. Get yourself a decent woman and fall in love.'

Irony was just so painful sometimes.

Ralph's eyes were starting to stream now, the chilli heat was on slow-release and his mouth was burning, his lips were swollen, his nose was running and his mind was in overdrive, full of things he wanted to say but couldn't.

'Not finding this too hot, are you, Ralph? All that talk about how you've never had a curry that defeated you?' Jem teased.

'Absolutely not.' Another lie, but there was no way he was going to admit that to this girl! 'Just how I like it. You look like you're suffering yourself, Miss I'm-So-Hard.'

'Humph – no way! This is mild compared to my usual curries, I was being kind for your sake.'

'Oh, I see, you think you're a bit of a chilli queen, do you?'

'I don't think it, I *know* it. I've never met anyone who can eat food as hot as I can.'

'Well, I think you've just met your match.' Ralph was well and truly fired up with competitive enthusiasm now. He leapt up from the table and took a handful of raw chillies from the bag on the counter.

'OK, one chilli each, whole, no nibbling. Let's separate the men from the mice.'

'No problem. Go on, let me have it.'

Oh, the pain, the sweet searing pain as the astringent oils from the chillies slowly released themselves over their tongues, first a crack as the shiny green skin broke under teeth, then a hint of flavour followed by an exhilarating burst of fire ineffectually doused by a sudden flow of saliva.

'You can't swallow it, you've got to chew the whole thing and display it on your tongue,' said Ralph.

Fingers of fire licked at the back of their throats, their brains sending frantic signals to all areas of the body. Jem and Ralph chewed feverishly, rapidly inhaling and exhaling through puckered lips like antenatal mothers and waving their hands in front of their mouths in a futile attempt to calm the flames.

'Oh, fuck – fuck fuck fuck – it's burning a hole through my tongue!'

'It's burning a hole into the back of my throat!'

Heart racing, sweat flowing, Ralph beat his fists off the tabletop, his eyes bulging slightly out of his head and tears rolling down his cheeks.

'OK, OK, time to show, time to show – I've got to swallow this thing before it kills me,' Jem shouted, her cheeks pinker than ever. 'Tongue out, please.'

Ralph and Jem stuck out their tongues, displaying small beds of green mush, and swallowed.

'Water, water!!!' yelled Ralph.

'No, water makes it worse. Lager!'

They gulped greedily but the liquid made no difference.

'Oh, God, I think I'm going to die! Rice, eat some plain rice!'

They both made a dash to the cooker and picked up handfuls of rice with their fingers, stuffing it into their mouths.

'Ice! Is there any ice in the freezer?!' cried Jem.

Ralph pulled open the door to the freezer and frantically searched through its contents. 'Got some, got some!' He turned the ice tray upside-down and bashed it hard against the work surface, ice cubes flying out in all directions, on to the floor and into the sink. They each picked one up and stuffed them into their mouths, sucking hard to extract every last drop of icy coolness.

'Oh, Jesus,' cried Ralph, 'Jesus Christ!' The flames were finally beginning to subside but his whole body was still in a state of sublime shock, endorphins flowing through him like some sort of wonderful drug.

'My God!' Jem was sliding the ice cube around her swollen lips. 'That was unbelievable! That was like sex!'

Their heads were spinning and their pulses racing. Both of them were laughing uncontrollably at nothing.

'That was *better* than sex,' replied Ralph.

Slowly they sat down again at the table.

'So, who won?' asked Jem.

'I think we can call that a draw!'

'Oh, no, I don't think so. Someone's got to win. Best of three!'

By the time Smith got home the flat was filled with an air of barely contained hysteria. He followed the sound of insane laughter into the kitchen and found Ralph and Jem with their heads in the freezer.

'What the hell are you two doing?' he asked, putting his briefcase down on the table amid the sea of empty lager cans, dirty plates and melting ice cubes.

They spun around guiltily, mouths full of ice, cheeks aflame, eyes streaming.

'Chilli Challenge,' replied Ralph through his ice cube, desperately fanning his mouth, 'five each – raw ones – it's a draw.'

'What! You're both fucking mad,' said Smith, shaking his head slowly. He caught Jem's eye. 'Look at you, you look like a lunatic. You look deranged!'

Ralph didn't think Jem looked deranged, he thought she looked absolutely stunning. Her hair was down now, long black curls framing her brilliant red face, glowing with heat and exhilaration as she hugged Smith. She was hugging Smith. It hurt Ralph to see how quickly she was drawn away from the special cocoon of madness they had woven for themselves tonight and into the arms of Smith, like she was a child he'd been baby-sitting all night whose beloved parent had returned. It had been him and Jem, close and totally together, and then Smith had walked in and crushed the atmosphere like a beetle under the weight of his stupid fucking briefcase. There'd been one brief beautiful moment when Smith had walked into the kitchen and he'd felt like Smith was the odd one out, the spare part, and Jem was his.

But now the night was over, painfully over. Jem was clearing away the debris on the kitchen table, Smith was unknotting his tie and talking about his night with a load of Swiss bankers. It was over.

Ralph was anchored to the spot by the weight of his sadness. 'Um, I reckon I'll push off to bed then,' he murmured quietly. 'Thanks for a lovely evening, Jem. Thanks for the Chilli Challenge and the curry and everything – it's been brilliant.'

He leaned down to kiss her on the cheek, just as she turned her face towards him, and caught her fully on the lips. The unexpected sensation sent shock waves through his system, a current of excitement from his lips, down via his heart to a loop-the-loop through his stomach, and ended in a hot glow of pleasure in his groin. It was more powerful than the chillies!

' 'Night, then.' His body was suddenly contorted by the conflicting desires to stay and ravish Jem and to leave the room as fast as his legs could carry him. He stumbled into the bathroom and sat down hard on the covered toilet. He was shaking.

He loved her. He was totally and utterly, stupidly and wonderfully in love with her. Shit.

14

'Och aye, this is the life, is it noo?'

'Och, and so it is, Siobhan, it's a bonny wee country and that's to be sure.'

Rosanne sat in the back seat of the Embassy, her snout stuck through the small aperture in the window, her eyes slanted closed against the bitter December wind that was blowing through her long black ears.

'Considering you're the Gaelic one, you do a crap Scottish accent, Mr Kasparov.'

'Well,' retorted Karl, 'have you ever heard Sean Connery trying to do an Irish accent? Bloody dreadful!'

Siobhan and Karl had left urban Scotland behind them now, and the landscape was slowly building up momentum, growing from tentative undulations in the south to the full-blown tidal-wave formations they were driving through now, along unending, empty roads, a wonder of nature, a spectacle of breathtaking beauty around every corner. For the last forty-five minutes, since they'd hit the Highlands, their conversation had consisted of nothing else but 'ooh's and 'aah's as the sharp Scottish light picked out shimmering threads of silvery water cascading down sheer black hills, or a tiny enchanted island artistically placed in the middle of a loch. The voluptuous landscape that loomed all around them was soft and womanly, carpeted in what looked from a distance like bright-green velvet, and the late-afternoon sky touched the land below with gentle wreaths of pale-blue mist.

Neither of them had been to Scotland before, and they felt like over-excited children now, dying to see what lay around the next corner yet wanting to linger every time they encountered a view which they knew would stay in their dreams.

'I hate to say it, but this knocks spots off Ireland. I've never seen anything like it,' said Karl.

Siobhan was studying the atlas on her lap. 'One more loch and we're there,' she said, brushing her windswept hair out of her face.

'That's a shame, I could keep driving for ever.' This was definitely the easiest they'd been with each other for weeks. They'd obviously needed this, a break from London, some distance from their problems. Karl wished it was just going to be the two of them for the weekend, but he liked this Rick de Largy character. He was a nice bloke, maybe it wouldn't be so bad.

It was four o'clock now and the low northern sun was already starting to set.

'Should be just in time to see the sunset over the loch. Jeff said it's breathtaking.' Karl couldn't wipe the smile off his face. He took his left hand from the steering wheel and placed it around Siobhan's shoulders, giving her a little squeeze. 'Are you nervous?' he asked.

'No, well, not really. A tiny bit maybe.'

'Yeah, me too. It's going to be fine though, you'll see. And if you don't want to join in you can just say you're not feeling well and sit and watch the view.'

Siobhan forced a laugh. Karl registered its false sound

with pain. He couldn't remember the last time he'd heard a genuine, raucous Siobhan belly-laugh. He loved that laugh; it was a laugh which resonated throughout restaurants, which made people on buses turn and look, which would have got her kicked out of public libraries. Now it was paper-thin, so brittle it sounded as if it could turn to tears, just like that.

They drove on for a while, deep in singular thought, while the sky hung above them like a kaleidoscopic mosquito net, changing colour every second.

'Glencoe two miles: we're nearly there. Are you ready to party, girl, hmm hmm? Ready to take some class A narcotics and just be wild and crazy, hmm hmm!!'

They were looking out for a tiny turning off the main road. The trees were painted white apparently; that was the only way of identifying it.

'There – there!' Siobhan pointed to the left.

They pulled off and followed a short dirt-track to a fork. A peeling green wooden sign to the right said 'St Colombas.'

'That's the place.'

The little black car bumped up the track for a while in darkness, but within a couple of minutes Siobhan and Karl were transported to Fairyland; the sides of the tiny lane were lined with bright pink and red Chinese lanterns, hooked on to the branches of diminutive cherry trees, prettily delineating the meandering route through the dark towards the chapel.

'My God, this is beautiful,' whispered Siobhan.

More was waiting for them at the head of the lane: the last dramatic red moments of the sunset reflected in the loch, the clapboard chapel lit up with fairy lights, a set of winding wooden steps from the graveyard down to the banks of the loch hung with more Chinese lanterns, shining the same warm crimson as the sinking sun, a picturesque wooden boat tied to an ancient wooden jetty bobbing blissfully in the still, icy water. An owl called from one of the towering chestnut trees around the chapel clearing, and windchimes hanging from the windowframes tinkled gently in a small gust of refreshingly clean air.

'I want to be buried here,' said Karl, his jaw hanging.

Even Rosanne was extra quiet, seemingly as enchanted as her masters by the unbelievable beauty of the place.

'I thought it was going to be really flash but it's not, it's just beautiful. I reckon Jeff must have been a real old hippie when he did this place up.'

They slowly unbuckled their seat-belts and collected their bags from the boot. There was already another car in front of the chapel.

'OK. Ready, Shuv?' Karl held his hand out for Siobhan.

'As I'll ever be.'

Karl rang the large copper bell hanging outside the vast wooden doors. Within seconds the door was answered.

'Karl, mate, good to see you. What a place!' Rick was barefoot, in jeans and a big jumper, and holding a glass of wine.

'Yeah, isn't it! I've never seen anything like it.' The two men shook hands.

'Rick, this is Siobhan, my girlfriend.'

'Lovely to meet you, Siobhan – Karl never stops talking about you.'

Siobhan attempted to smile, but she could barely breathe. This man was absolutely gorgeous! He was beautiful. She almost felt weak at the knees. Why did men never tell you things like that; they never said 'Oh, by the way, so and so's really good looking.' She wished Karl had warned her.

'Pleased to meet you, too.' Siobhan had suddenly remembered how to behave in a social situation. She smiled her most gorgeous smile and shook his hand firmly and confidently. She was *not* going to be a fat aunt in front of this angelic man, in this magical place. 'Isn't this the most beautiful place you've ever seen?' She was thin, thin and beautiful and desirable. She shook her hair round so that it framed her face.

'Stunning. I can't believe old Jeff would be capable of doing something so nicely. I thought it was going to be all shagpile and satellite dishes and log-effect gas fires. Anyway, come in the two of you – it's freezing out there. We've put the central heating on and Tamsin's just lighting a fire.'

They followed him into the chapel – the damp stone hallway was full of wellingtons and waterproofs and piles of wood – and then through the main hall and into the body of the building. They both gasped. The room was at least thirty foot high, raftered, galleried and cavernous. It was floored with antique boards and old rugs and lit up by an eclectic mix of dozens of Art Deco lamps and Victorian chandeliers. There were three enormous cream sofas at the far end, dressed in Chinese tapestries and an old oak banqueting table at the near end, covered in candelabras and vases of flowers.

'Wow!'

The girl kneeling in front of the monstrously large

sandstone fireplace around which the sofas huddled got to her feet and rubbed at the knees of her jeans.

She was small, petite even, with soft, sandy-coloured curly hair tied back in a pony-tail and a light smattering of freckles over her nose and forehead. She wasn't wearing any make-up, and she was, Siobhan was pleased to notice, ordinary – pretty, but ordinary.

'Siobhan, Karl – this is Tamsin.' Karl and Tamsin looked at each other quizzically as their hands touched and a strange atmosphere suddenly descended upon the group.

'Shit – Tamsin – what a coincidence!' Karl was saying.

'Oh – yeah – hi.' Tamsin was looking slightly uncomfortable, stepping from foot to foot.

Siobhan looked at Karl in confusion. Rick looked at Tamsin in confusion.

'You two know each other?' asked Rick.

'Erm, Tamsin used to be a student of mine – Ceroc – last summer . . .'

'Aaaah,' said Siobhan.

'Oh, right,' smiled Rick. 'Cool! What an amazing coincidence. I didn't know you'd been a dance teacher.'

'Well . . . you know . . . mortgage to pay.'

'Yeah, yeah.'

The atmosphere was inexplicably and negatively charged and, instinctively, Rick changed the subject. 'Well,' he said, clapping his hands together in an attempt to quell the unsettled mood, 'let's show you your room.'

Karl and Siobhan exchanged glances and followed Rick up the stairs and on to the gallery.

'What's going on, Karl?' whispered Siobhan, as they unpacked in their over-the-top Rococo bedroom, walled with swathes of dusty satin Jacquard and batches of browning Victorian and Edwardian photographs in chipped wooden frames.

'That's that girl,' whispered Karl. 'Remember? That one I told you about. The nympho, steam-train chick – it's her. The one who had that *ménage à trois* with those two French guys.'

'What?' Siobhan put her hands to her mouth to muffle her delighted shriek. 'God, no wonder she looked so awkward. D'you think she was going out with Rick then?'

'God knows. Probably,' said Karl, painstakingly arranging his trousers over a large wooden hanger. 'They live together.'

Siobhan suddenly felt that everything was going to be all right. The house was beautiful, Rick was gorgeous, and his girlfriend was ordinary – an ordinary girl with an extraordinary secret that she bet Rick didn't know about: it was Tamsin's place to feel uncomfortable this weekend, not hers. She smiled as her hopes for the weekend elevated towards the woodworm-ridden rafters like big pink helium balloons. She was going to enjoy herself. This was going to be fun.

She flopped backwards on to the huge four-poster, her hair flying out around her head. 'Isn't this brilliant! I feel like a princess, the one in the Princess and the Pea!' She began to bounce around on the vast bed. She was suddenly feeling unbelievably overexcited.

'Careful, Shuv, that's a really old bed. You might break it.'

Siobhan stopped bouncing and looked at Karl with disbelief. 'Oh, charming! You wouldn't say that if I was some slender young size-eight thing.'

'I'd say it if you were Will o' the Wisp, Shuv. Don't be so sensitive, for God's sake. It's probably an antique, and it wasn't made for bouncing up and down on, that's all I'm saying.' Karl zipped up his holdall and shoved it into the back of the towering tallboy.

A few of Siobhan's pink helium balloons had burst, leaving her feeling resentful and annoyed. 'He's very good looking isn't he, Rick? You didn't tell me he was so handsome.' Siobhan felt the insecure need to wind Karl up, get a reaction.

'Yeah, he is, isn't he? Especially for a radio producer!'

Typical – no reaction whatsoever. Siobhan had never tried to make Karl jealous before. She'd never felt the need to test his love, to push him to see how far he could go, how much he could take. But after the way things had been between them for the last two months, since that night at the Sol y Sombra, Siobhan didn't trust him any more.

Well, sod it. She certainly wasn't going to let Karl's attitude stop her from having fun for the first time in, oh, as long as she could remember. She was going to flirt with Rick, she was going to get roaring drunk, take any drugs that were offered to her and she was going to shine, even if it was only for a day and a half.

She decided to get changed, she suddenly felt uncomfortable in her old leggings and Aran cardigan. And she was going to put on make-up and do her hair. Just because Karl hated her fat, it didn't mean that other men would.

She pulled her neglected make-up bag from her case and sat at the dressing-table under the huge stained-glass window. Two small pink glass lamps illuminated the area, casting a soft flattering glow. As Siobhan delicately puffed at her face with a big soft brush and carefully applied a thin line of black liquid-liner to her eyelids she felt prettier than she'd felt in months. This was a magical house: it wasn't 1996 any more, it could be any time, past or future, but it was a time when your dress size was irrelevant, a time when you could be beautiful just because of where you were, because of the particular light of a pretty pink lamp. Fairy lights; magic lamps.

Karl watched her from the bed. 'I guess we should try not to bring up the subject again,' he said.

'What?' murmured Siobhan, disturbed from her reverie.

'Tamsin. We shouldn't say anything else about Tamsin and the dance class.'

'Oh, no, you're right. I don't want to talk about London and everything anyway, I just want to get lost under the spell of this place.' She was twisting her mane into an intricate knot of golden strands and stabbing it aggressively from behind with pins from a cardboard holder.

'Do you want a hand, Shuv?' asked Karl eagerly. Siobhan always asked him to put pins in her hair in the old days, when she used to wear it up regularly. He'd loved doing it, it was such a feminine act, and he'd thought himself privileged to be allowed to play such a vital role in Siobhan's grooming.

'No, I'm all right, thanks, nearly finished. You can go down if you like, I'm going to get changed now.'

'I don't mind waiting for you.'

'No, really, you go down. It'll spare you the unpleasantness of watching me get undressed.' Siobhan hadn't meant to say that, it had just come spilling out; an unbridled, feral thought had just escaped from her mouth. It was something she'd thought a million times over the last few weeks, few months in reality, and had never, ever intended to say, and now it was out, free, independent of her. She waited the split second for a reaction with her breath held.

'Shuv, what the fuck are you going on about?' Karl was incredulous. 'You think I don't like seeing you naked – Jeez, you're so wrong – I love you naked.'

Oh, nice try, Karl, thought Siobhan, you expect me to believe that? 'Karl, go downstairs. We'll talk about this another time.'

'No! I'm staying here and we're going to talk about this now. Is this what everything's been about, all this, all this . . . sadness, this sadness between us?'

'Karl, go downstairs. Go downstairs now or I'll scream. I do not want to talk about this. I do not want to listen to your bullshit. Get out!'

Bald-faced lies. Bullshit. Bullshit, Karl Kasparov. If you liked me this size, why would you be getting sweaty and flustered by that girl from upstairs, why would you think I'd break the bed, why would you want me to get pregnant? Liar.

Karl slowly left the room, and Rosanne followed him, unsettled by the unfamiliar atmosphere, and scared by the anger on Siobhan's usually placid face.

Siobhan felt no regret; she'd show *him* tonight. She'd be the old Siobhan, happy, poised, funny and attractive, except it wouldn't be for Karl's benefit – he wasn't worthy of such a performance – this would be for Rick.

She slipped on her black tunic, the one she'd made for herself, with the indiscreet split down the front that revealed a good few inches of cleavage – this was the first time she'd had the nerve to wear it – and matching trousers, and slid her feet into strappy sandals.

She opened the door out on to the gallery and looked down into the room below. Karl and Rick and Tamsin were all sitting on the sofas, drinking wine and talking quietly and politely. As the door closed behind her the trio turned around and looked upwards. Siobhan saw Rick gulp.

'Siobhan' – Rick stood up – 'just in time. I was just about to break open the champagne.'

Siobhan moved as elegantly as she could down the stairs, her heels making a feminine click against the wood as she walked. She felt like a contestant in a beauty pageant.

'I feel a bit underdressed now,' said Tamsin lightheartedly, gesturing at her jeans and fleecy top. 'You look fantastic.'

Rick handed Siobhan a champagne flute. 'Here's to a wild and wacky weekend!'

'Here's to Jeff!'

'Here's to Scotland!'

The four almost-strangers clinked their glasses together. Siobhan met Rick's glass with a smile that emanated almost entirely from beneath her eyelashes.

'And here's to new friends,' she beamed.

15

The first bottle of champagne lasted half an hour, the second twenty minutes, and the third was gone almost before it was opened. Siobhan was feeling flushed and was waving goodbye to the last vestiges of her inhibitions. She, Karl and Rick were talking animatedly and frankly about work, and Tamsin was in the kitchen heating through a fortune's worth of party food from M & S. Siobhan would usually have volunteered immediately to help in the kitchen, and it had crossed her mind, but she didn't want to, not this time. She wanted to stay out here with the men and elegantly cross and uncross her legs and join in the conversation. She was preoccupied with her posture, keeping her back straight and her chest out and her stomach in, occasionally smoothing her hair back with her hand or fiddling with her rings, watching Rick's body language and responses, gauging his interest in her and then turning to Karl, wondering if he'd noticed yet.

Tamsin appeared, laden with plates of chicken wings and pizza squares and trout goujons. She put them down on the table unnecessarily hard, hoping to attract attention to herself and her efforts, but none of them even looked around from their conversation.

'If anyone's interested,' she began, then decided to take the unattractive sarcasm from her voice, 'there's some food here – it'll soak up the champagne.'

'Excellent,' someone murmured, but still no one moved, still they sat there and laughed and joked and revolved around Siobhan like balls on a weather-vane.

Rick poured the dregs of the champagne into Siobhan's glass.

'Oh,' said Tamsin, clutching her empty glass, 'was that the last of the champagne?'

'Sorry, darling,' said Rick, 'it was only a drop. There's some wine in the kitchen, do you want me to get you some?'

'No, it's all right,' said Tamsin, unashamedly playing the martyr. 'I'll get it. The food's getting cold, by the way,' she added as nicely as she could.

'Oh, go ahead – I won't be eating anything,' said Siobhan. No way. There was only one thing more unattractive than a fat woman and that was a fat woman eating. Things were going really well with Rick, she was feeling wonderfully in control, she'd forgotten just how easy it was to turn a man to mush. She didn't want to blow it now by stuffing her face with chicken and pizza.

'Are you sure you wouldn't like me to bring you back a little something?' asked Rick, getting to his feet.

'Oh, no, really, we had a big lunch on the way down. Maybe I'll have something later.'

As Tamsin and Rick made their way over to the table, Karl approached Siobhan shyly.

'Are you all right?' he asked tenderly, leaning into her shoulder to whisper in her ear, brushing her neck with the tip of his nose.

'Never better,' she replied stiffly, trying to ignore the bolt of sadness and bitter-sweet love that coursed through her at his touch and the feeling that she wanted to comfort Karl, to reassure him.

'You look a lot happier,' he whispered.

'Well, I'm having a great time. Rick's fantastic.'

'Yes, he's great, isn't he? I told you you'd like him.'

Siobhan gritted her teeth in irritation. 'I'm going to get some more wine,' she said, getting to her feet, suddenly aware that she was drunk, as she felt her legs wobble slightly underneath her. She quickly gauged the distance from her seat to the kitchen door and the number of obstacles she would encounter on the way. The last thing she'd want to do now was trip over something or start weaving across the room like a dodgy shopping-trolley.

Unfortunately, she was already too drunk to start trying to regulate her drinking. But then, so was everyone else. The little bag of white powder made an entrance at about eleven o'clock and Siobhan was the first to accept the rolled-up fiver and square mirror from Rick. She turned away slightly in case she messed it up and dabbed lightly at her nose, dislodging a couple of small crumbs before passing the mirror on to Karl.

'I guess this is when we're supposed to start being wild and wacky,' she said.

'Ah, well remembered,' said Rick. 'I brought a tape recorder.' He walked to the hallway and returned with a tiny, state-of-the-art machine. 'It occurred to me that we'd come up with all these brilliantly witty ideas and we'd be so pissed that none of us would remember them. This thing's brilliant, it tapes for six hours and the sound quality is breathtaking.' He placed it on the mantelpiece. 'Are we feeling funny yet?'

A general cheer went up and he switched on the machine.

Jeff was right about Rick. He was very funny and his humour infected the other three. They sat for three hours and talked complete nonsense, inventing quiz games and characters and role-playing, Siobhan and Tamsin pretending to be listeners phoning in. It was actually working. Jeff obviously knew what he was doing – there was no way they'd have managed to come up with so many good ideas sitting in a boardroom in the ALR building. The coke had given them all the confidence to contribute ideas they might have felt foolish about in other circumstances, and the alcohol had also lowered their inhibitions and freed up their imaginations.

Siobhan was having the best time ever. Rick thought she was marvellous, and her confidence was sky-high: she knew she was being funny, funnier than Tamsin, and she was thrilled to find that she hadn't lost the ability to flirt, to twist men around her little finger. Rick was hers, and she sat close to him on the sofa, her arm draped carelessly behind his back, not touching, but possessing him none the less. She'd forgotten how good it felt to be the centre of attention.

Finally the hilarity began to die down. It was early morning, the coke was wearing off and the conversation began to pall. Siobhan got up and stretched.

'Do you think we've got enough stuff?' she asked Rick.

'We've got enough stuff to last us the next five years,' he replied happily.

'Well, I need some fresh air,' she said.

'That's an excellent idea,' Rick said, standing up quickly. 'Let me get my coat – I'll come with you. Are you coming?' He turned to Karl and Tamsin, as an afterthought.

Siobhan went up to her room to fetch her sheepskin jacket. She checked her reflection quickly in the mirror and tidied up her hair, smoothed her eyebrows and applied a little more lipstick. Adrenalin was coursing through her. What was going to happen? Would Rick try it on? How would she react? She thought of Karl and then quickly put him to the back of her mind. She'd go with the flow, see what happened – the worst thing that could happen was a kiss; it was too cold outside for anything else.

The night air hit them like a cold shower as they closed the chapel door. A wind had picked up now, a gentle low wind that whipped around their legs like a cold, ghostly cat. They wandered in silence towards the banks of the loch and sat down on the wooden steps leading to the jetty, listening to the windchimes and hugging their clothes to them to keep warm.

'Blissful, isn't it?' murmured Rick.

'Heavenly,' agreed Siobhan, her elbows on her knees, her face in her hands, watching the loch rippling in the pink glow of the Chinese lanterns.

'You could fall in love here.'

Siobhan bristled slightly. 'Yes,' she said, 'I suppose you could.'

They fell silent again.

Rick cleared his throat. 'You're a wonderful girl, Siobhan, really you are. I've never met anyone like you before. Karl's a very lucky man.'

'I don't think he sees it like that,' she said with a nervous laugh.

'Oh, no,' said Rick, 'he thinks you're marvellous. He

talks about you a lot – he made you sound amazing and he wasn't exaggerating.'

'Oh,' said Siobhan, 'well . . .' She was embarrassed.

'No, really, I think you're gorgeous . . .' he stopped, 'Do you mind me talking like this?'

'Oh, no, please carry on. I'm not going to look a gift compliment in the mouth.' She couldn't look at Rick, he'd see her vulnerability.

'I just think you're . . . you're . . . stunning. You're so funny and, and warm and clever and beautiful. God, I shouldn't say this, Siobhan, but if I was single and you were single . . .'

She turned to face him.

'Go on,' she said.

'Well, you know, if I was single and you . . . you were single, I'd just love to kiss you now.'

Siobhan's whole body was tingling with excitement and nerves. A flush was rising from her lap to her face.

'Do you think that would be wrong?' he asked, his body turned completely towards hers, his eyes searching her face for approval.

'Well, we could always try it and see if it *felt* wrong and then we could stop it if it did.'

'But what about Karl?' Rick pushed some stray hairs behind her ear.

'What about Tamsin?' she replied, every hair on her body to attention as a result of his touch.

'Well, to tell you the truth, we haven't been getting along so well lately. Tamsin . . . Tamsin's not a very stable girl, she's not a very happy girl. I sometimes think I may have bitten off a little more than I can chew with her. She's hard work . . .' He was stroking her cheek now, with the backs of his fingers. 'God, you've got wonderful skin,' he whispered, 'it feels like satin.'

Siobhan's groin felt like it had been plugged into the mains. She groaned softly.

Rick brought his face towards hers. 'Just like a child's skin.' He rubbed his nose gently along her forehead, teasing her with his lips. He held her neck with his hand and massaged her jawbone with his thumb. Finally his lips met hers and Siobhan succumbed, turning around to meet his body and his lips, goosebumps and tingles and deep hot flashes of sexual excitement and lust suffusing her body. She hadn't felt like this for years. She opened her mouth to allow Rick's tongue to caress hers. His lips were soft and warm, and his breath tasted of red wine and fresh air. Oh, God, French kissing was good. Why did people stop doing it after they got to know each other? Why was such an intimate and erotic act reserved mainly for strangers? She wound her tongue around his and up around his teeth, pressing her body against him as he leant her back against the steps and started to move his hands inside her coat and over the silky fabric of her tunic. She pulled his shirt out of his jeans and caressed the skin on his back, appreciating the solid feel of the muscle underneath and the tension, knowing it was his desire for her that was making him feel so good.

She was lost in their kiss, entirely oblivious to the wind-chimes and the owls, and to Karl, a few hundred feet away from her, inside the chapel. Rick moved his hands under her top and towards her bra. He let out a stifled moan as his hands found her breasts. Siobhan could feel his frustration at the fabric that encased them and sloped her shoulders slightly to enable him to slip the straps off and pull it down. Rick moaned again as his hands felt the bare flesh flow from her bra, she felt his excitement and she could understand it, two huge breasts in his hands: if she were a man she would be excited. He kneaded them gently, still kissing her, his tongue growing wilder and wilder in her mouth, her lips feeling wonderfully raw and sore. She wanted him to kiss her until they bled.

Suddenly he tore his lips away from hers and buried his head inside her coat, under her tunic, between her breasts. He was sighing and groaning and licking her breasts and sucking her nipples. 'Oh, God, Siobhan,' he kept saying. 'Oh, God, Siobhan.'

Siobhan bent slightly to watch him – she'd been staring at the stars, lost in desire and lust – and as her gaze fell upon the top of his head, his sandy blond hair glowing peach in the lamplight, the spell broke. What the hell was she doing? Why was she letting this man suck her nipples, this man with blond hair? For fifteen years she'd looked down on Karl's black mop, my God – Karl! – what was she doing?

Suddenly she was sober and she was cold, physically cold. Rick's hands were sliding down her body, towards the elasticated waist of her trousers, his fingers pulling at it, feeling their way down to the top of her knickers, but she was fully conscious now, wide awake, aware of her surroundings and her circumstances. She was with another man, on the banks of a loch on a sharp December night, her hair was unravelling, her back was aching, she was cold. She felt the last glimmer of passion desert her and anxiety begin to set in. Her body tensed and she pulled back slightly, wanting Rick to calm down too, wanting him to stop but not wanting to tell him to. She looked down at him again; he was completely consumed, carried away, he wasn't aware of Siobhan's change of mood. This was all wrong, all wrong, it was just supposed to be a kiss – she could've covered up a kiss, walked back into the chapel still feeling confident and in control. This was getting out of control, how could she hide this from Karl? This was all wrong! Oh, shit! What had she done?!

She sat up, and Rick moved his head from between her breasts and tried to find her mouth again. 'Oh, Siobhan, I want you,' he picked up her hand and put it to his groin. 'Feel how much I want you.'

That was it.

'Rick!' she said firmly, 'we've got to stop.'

'Oh, no, Siobhan, we've got to carry on. I want to be inside you, you feel so good, you smell so good,' he rubbed her hand up and down the solid shaft inside his jeans.

She pulled her hand away, pulled up her bra and her tunic, closed her coat. 'No, Rick, we've got to stop. Karl and Tamsin are in there. What if they come out and find us?'

'We can hide somewhere – let's go into the woods.' His hand still rested on her knickers.

She pulled his hand away gently. 'No, that's enough. I want to, I really do want to, but I can't, we can't. It's not right.' She tried to smooth down her hair.

Rick's face wore the expression of a thwarted school-boy who'd kicked his football into a forbidden garden. Siobhan took his hands in hers. 'I'm sorry,' she said gently, 'if circumstances had been different, if we weren't here, if

I didn't have Karl and you didn't have Tamsin . . . but, thank you.'

'What for?' asked Rick incredulously.

'Thank you for wanting me, for making me feel sexy and beautiful.'

'Why would you need me to make you feel sexy and beautiful? You *are* sexy and beautiful!' he said, kissing her hands.

'I don't feel it, Rick, but you made me feel it. I didn't used to be this fat, you know, I used to be slim. I'm not used to it.'

'You're not fat!'

'Oh, Rick, don't be such a typical man. Of course I'm fat.'

'OK, so you're not Kate Moss, but you've got a lovely body, really you have. It's . . . it's soft and warm and it smells good and it feels good and, OK, it might not look great in a mini skirt, but it looks great to me, like a real woman's. The first girl I had sex with was round and sexy. She was called Drew, and she was so pretty and full of life and love, and I've never really stopped loving her, you know. People are just prejudiced, Siobhan, because maybe they've never had a chance to really appreciate someone who doesn't conform to the ideal. Well, as far as I'm concerned, they don't know what they're missing. I mean, look at Tamsin, she's tiny and she looks great in Lycra and all that, but sex is just, you know – it's just not all that exciting, she's very unconfident, restrained. I'd rather have a big woman who loved it than a skinny woman who wasn't too bothered. And besides, you're firm, you're not all flabby. I think that's perfect.' He kissed her cheek. 'I think you're perfect.'

Siobhan smiled a small smile and squeezed Rick's hands.

'Thank you,' she said again, fighting back a little tear, 'thank you, you're a very, very nice person.'

'So, is that it then?' He smiled. 'I have a feeling I've just been therapy for you.'

Siobhan felt bad. 'Oh, no, I mean . . . well . . . I'd love to get to know you better . . . but, well . . . you know . . .'

'Yes, I think I do. You really love Karl, don't you?'

She nodded.

'So why all this? What was this all about?' he asked tenderly.

'Oh, God. I'm not sure any more. I thought he was interested in someone else. Well, I still do actually. I think. I don't know. I just thought he was changing, going off me, didn't fancy me any more. I've been feeling so insecure, incredibly insecure . . .'

'Have you spoken to Karl about it?' Rick pulled her jacket closer around her as a gust of wind hit them from the surface of the water.

'No, I just can't. I've got some kind of block, I don't know where to start. I've always been so confident and I don't know if Karl could cope with me being like this, knowing the truth about how I feel.'

'Look, Siobhan. I don't know Karl very well, but from what I've seen and the way he looks at you and talks about you, he could cope. What he *won't* be able to cope with is you not telling him. I wish things could be different, I really do. I wish I could have taken you into the woods and made love to you all night and then taken you home with me and made love to you some more, but things aren't like that, so I think you should use what's just happened here as a chance for a new start with Karl. Talk to him, tell him how you feel before it's too late.' He looked into her eyes seriously. 'Really, I mean it. Don't put it off – do it now, tonight, while you're feeling like this, now! Come on, let's go inside.'

They stood up and tidied themselves and slowly walked back towards the chapel.

'Thanks,' said Tamsin awkwardly to Karl's back as he poked at the fire. He turned around. 'Thanks for not saying anything earlier on, you know, about last summer. I was . . . it was . . . a strange time . . .' She brought a bitten fingernail to her mouth and began to chew.

'Hey. Forget about it. It's none of my business.'

They sat in silence for a second.

'I wonder where they've gone,' said Tamsin, as pleasantly as she could.

'Oh, they're probably looking at the view or something,' said Karl, sitting back on the sofa.

'Aren't you worried?' she asked impatiently.

'No – why should I be? Rick's with her, he'll look after her.'

'That's not what I meant. For Christ's sake, haven't you noticed what's been going on tonight?'

Karl looked blank.

'Your girlfriend. Flirting with my boyfriend. Blatantly. Don't tell me you haven't noticed anything.'

'Oh, that's nothing to worry about. Siobhan always used to be a terrible flirt, it doesn't mean anything. I'm just glad to see her enjoying herself for once.'

All the resentment Tamsin had been swallowing that night was starting to erupt. 'God, you really are stupid, aren't you! That wasn't just flirting, that was a fucking mating ritual going on in front of your very eyes. They're probably out there fucking each other's brains out right now!'

Karl laughed. 'I think you're being a bit paranoid, if you don't mind me saying so. I think you've probably had a bit too much coke and booze.'

'Look, why don't we go out and see for ourselves!' she shouted, jumping to her feet.

'Sit down, for Christ's sake. You're being ridiculous. Just because you don't trust your boyfriend . . .'

'This has got nothing to do with not trusting my boyfriend! It's your fucking girlfriend I don't trust. She's like a bloody black widow, all over him all night, spinning a web around him, like a great fat predator!'

'God, you're mad!' said Karl calmly. 'Siobhan is the sweetest, nicest, warmest person I've ever known and you're just jealous. And you should learn to trust your boyfriend.'

Karl's easygoing attitude and condescending manner were pushing Tamsin over the edge. 'That's it! I'm telling her! When she gets back, I'm telling her. About you. I know about you.' There was a wild glint in her eyes as she stabbed the air above her with a finger to accentuate her point. 'You tell me I should trust my boyfriend! You fucking hypocrite! Why should I trust anyone when there are men like you around? Adulterous, slimy, two-faced, dickled creeps who'll fuck anything with a decent pair of legs!'

Karl should have known this was coming.

'Oh, yes – you think no one knew about you and Cheri

in the office at the dance club? Did you think we were all stupid?! Cheri told me all about it. All the sordid details. She told me about the abortion, too – your baby that she had to get rid of. What makes you think Siobhan's any different to Cheri? What makes you think I should believe that Rick's any different to you?! It's what makes the world go round, you smug arsehole – sex, sex, sex! Siobhan wants it, you want it, Rick wants it, we all want it, and you can't trust anyone. So don't sit there telling me I'm paranoid, thinking that you're any different to anyone else, 'cos you're not. Wake up and smell the coffee, dick-for-brains: your girlfriend wants to have sex with my boyfriend and they're probably doing it right now!' Tamsin was crying, angry tears. 'And if they're not doing it they're sure as hell thinking about doing it!'

Karl adjusted himself in his seat and eyed Tamsin thoughtfully. He was still utterly collected.

'I have to say that I am not at all comfortable with the concept of blackmail,' he began, 'so let's just call this a deal, OK? But, if you even so much as think about mentioning my affair with Cheri to Siobhan, there are some things I could tell Rick over lunch one day that I feel sure you'd rather he didn't know about.'

'Huh!' said Tamsin, wiping at her tears, 'you don't really know anything. You can't prove anything.'

'OK, OK. Look, I'm not stupid either, y'know. Everyone knew what you were up to. Those two French guys couldn't keep their mouths shut about your little rosbif-sandwich interlude. There's no point going into this any more than necessary. As I say, this is a deal. I think we should just drop the subject now. If you're really that worried, then why don't you go and have a look outside, but I can assure you, it'll only make you feel worse about yourself. Trusting people has nothing to do with other people, it's in here' – he pointed at his head – 'and you can call it complacency, or smugness, but I call it dignity and happiness. I call it the only way to get through life and stay sane.'

Tamsin couldn't think of anything to say to that.

'Well, it doesn't look like we're going to be able to make any more small talk tonight, so I may as well go to bed,' said Karl. 'I'm very sorry things got a bit unpleasant there – I guess it's been a long day and a long night. Do you think we could make a fresh start in the morning?'

Tamsin shrugged and stared at the floor.

Karl put out his hand to shake hers. She gave him hers, limply.

'Whatever will be will be, Tamsin. Sleep tight.'

He tapped up the stairs, followed by Rosanne, who'd been sleeping in front of the fire, and Tamsin curled up on the sofa with the intention of crying and worrying and revelling in anxiety. Instead the huge amounts of alcohol in her system sent her into a deep and instantaneous sleep.

She didn't hear Rick and Siobhan tip-toe back in, and she didn't even wake up when Rick picked her up like a baby and carried her up the stairs to their room.

The lights went off around the house, toilet chains flushed, floorboards creaked, and suddenly it was silent.

Silent except for the windchimes, the owls and the gentle hum of the tape recorder still going round and round on the mantelpiece, where they had left it recording . . .

16

Ralph woke up with a start. He'd been dreaming, deep disturbing dreams he wasn't used to having. He tried to remember them, but the details had fled his memory already. Something was strange, something was different. The alarm? Yes, the radio, music blaring out from the other side of the room where he'd left it . . . Why? . . . What? He'd set the alarm, last night. What time was it? 7.30 a.m. – fucking hell. He pulled the thin pillow from under his head and put it over his face, trying to block out the music and the light strobing through the minuscule gap between the curtains. As consciousness returned to him, slowly and painfully, he became aware of the lyrics to the song playing on the radio: 'I feel so dirty when they start talking cute . . . I wanna tell her that I love her but the point's probably moot . . . I wish that I had Jessie's girl . . .'

Jesus Christ! Ralph took the pillow from his head and sat up slowly. It was seven-thirty in the morning and he could relate to Rick Springfield – this was a very strange start to the day.

Ralph pulled himself from under the warmth of his duvet towards the radio, trying to find the Off button on this alien piece of equipment. Eventually he unplugged it in desperation and sat back on his heels as silence returned to the bedroom.

Someone out there was trying to get at him; it was the first time in months that Ralph had set his alarm and it woke him up with fucking 'Jessie's Girl'. Unbelievable!

He was utterly disoriented. What the hell was going on? The studio – of course! He was going to go to the studio today. Why? Because he was an artist? Sort of. Because he wanted to? Not really. Because . . . because Jem had told him to . . . that's right. Because Jem had told him to. Well, not told him to exactly, but encouraged him to, advised him to, *wanted* him to.

He'd promised her he would, just to make her happy. You're right, he'd said. Tomorrow – I'll go tomorrow, bright and early. Don't do this for me, she'd said, do it for yourself, promise me. I promise you, he'd said.

So here he was, seven-thirty on a Friday morning, shell-shocked, exhausted, cold and confused. He certainly did not feel like he was doing this for himself – this was for Jem, plain and simple, to make her proud of him, milk her interest in him. He would be her little project if that's what she wanted: he didn't mind playing the tortured artist for her if it meant that he occupied her thoughts for a while and displaced Smith. Smith was a banker, more or less, a boring old bloody banker, nothing there to capture Jem's imagination.

He walked over to the windows and threw open the curtains, ready to face the day now he remembered why he was doing this. What a beautiful day! That helped. He'd borrow Smith's bike and cycle there, get some oxygen into his lungs, as his mother used to say.

He pulled on some boxer shorts from a pile on the floor and made his way into the hall, quite perky now, humming to himself, '"I wish that I had Jessie's gi-i-irl, I want Jessie's gi-i-irl . . ."'

'Didn't know you were a Rick Springfield fan.'

'What?' Ralph jumped. It was Jem, coming out of Smith's bedroom wearing one of his T-shirts that barely concealed her . . . her knickers? Her hair was unruly, her face sweetly sleepy and swollen; she looked like a baby mouse. She yawned.

'So,' she said, 'what do you think of seven-thirty in the morning, then? Horrible, isn't it?!'

Not so horrible after all – not when you got to see Jem, braless and fantastically dishevelled, in a T-shirt with the tantalizing promise of maybe, if she was to bend over just the weeniest bit, glimpsing the last centimetre or two of her bottom, or maybe . . . maybe . . . if she was just to stretch a little bit and the front of her T-shirt was to . . . augh, God. He pulled his gaze away from her legs.

'Grim!' he agreed.

'I got up especially early to give you some moral support. I hope you appreciate it!'

'Oh, God, you didn't have to. That's very sweet of you.' She'd got up early, just for him! Left Smith alone in bed, for him! Yes! 'D'you want to use the bathroom first?'

'No, you go first. I'm going to make you some breakfast, set you up for the day! I wouldn't mind a quick wee, though.'

'Oh, sure, of course.'

He moved out of the way to let her get to the bathroom, her body just barely brushing up against his as she passed, just enough to induce an unexpected erection inside his baggy shorts, which forced its way jauntily through the gap

148

at the front and emerged squinting into the brand-new day, like an overzealous mole. Shit. He pushed it back inside, buttoned the fly quickly with fumbling fingers and crossed his hands in front of his crotch. Jem had left the door slightly ajar and he could hear her peeing, that strange gushing, jerky sound of girl's pee hitting water, and then the sound of toilet paper being unravelled from the wooden holder and folded and wiped across her. And then she was out again, grinning widely at him.

'I didn't flush it – hope you don't mind. See you in the kitchen!'

She skipped off down the hall. Ralph watched her as she went, her T-shirt rising just not quite high enough with every bouncy step she took. He exhaled deeply the breath he'd been holding since their bodies had touched and walked into the bathroom. He stared down into the toilet bowl at Jem's pee and the raft of pink paper floating on top of it, sinking slightly as it became waterlogged, and aimed his semi-hard penis at the yellow water, feeling strangely gratified by the sight of their fluids mingling before his eyes. Yes, he liked the idea of their bodily effluents becoming as one . . . and he absolutely adored the idea of Jem now, in the kitchen, tinily T-shirted and cooking his breakfast . . . mmmmm! He smiled smugly to himself. Things were looking up.

It had been two weeks now since their first night together, their chilli night, and Ralph had been working incredibly hard to sustain the bond they'd formed. He realized now that this was more than a crush, more than jealousy or lust. He was most definitely in love and he had no intention whatsoever of ignoring it, of putting his feelings to one side. He'd never been in love before and he was not going to let this opportunity slip through his fingers. He was going to take it slowly and cautiously.

He had suddenly started taking an interest in Smith's social and professional affairs, subtly discovering when he was going to be out and making sure he, Ralph, was in, that he had some time alone with Jem. He'd bought a couple of new tops and had finally washed his jeans, a job he'd been putting off for six months. He also bought flowers regularly now, from Northcote Road – peonies, of course – and made sure that he timed it so that he was artistically and sensitively arranging them in a vase when Jem got in from work. He'd even cooked for her a couple of times. And they'd developed a banter about hot food. 'Oh, you must go to such and such a restaurant in Earlsfield/Bayswater/Brick Lane. Best vindaloo I've ever had – really, really hot'; or 'Guess what? They've started selling Thai Bird chillies in Asda.' Ralph had even found some chilli seeds for sale in Northcote Road, and Jem and he had planted them, taking it in turns to water them and discussing their progress together, anxiously, like fretful parents.

This was a particularly successful development as it not only brought Jem closer to him, but also alienated Smith, who suffered from a tendency to order lamb pasanda and things with almonds and cream in. It was a tiny but effective little spanner in the works of Smith and Jem's cloying complicity. Ralph shared something with Jem that was somehow outside the realm of a non-romantic relationship – their own complicity. And now there was the tortured artist thing.

They'd been watering the chilli seeds in the airing cupboard the night before, and Jem had brought the subject up.

'Had any more thoughts about painting, Ralph?'

'Painting what?' he'd replied absent-mindedly, thinking maybe she was suggesting a new lick of paint in the living room.

'You know. Painting. You – studio – artist,' she'd said, with her palms outstretched, emphasizing his obtuseness.

'No. Was I supposed to?'

'No. You weren't *supposed* to, I just thought you might have, that's all.'

'Why's that?'

'I don't know. You just seem different lately, somehow. More . . . more . . . purposeful. More alive. I had actually been wondering if you might have met someone!' she added playfully, nudging him in the ribs.

'No, I haven't "met" someone,' he retorted, nudging her back and laughing. 'I've got a girlfriend, remember.'

'Oh, yes – the lovely Claudia.'

'And what have you got against Claudia all of a sudden?' Ralph was surprised and faintly pleased by the mild sarcasm in her voice.

'Nothing' – Jem took a deep breath – 'except she doesn't make you happy and I think you could do better for yourself.' She patted ineffectually at the moist soil in the small plastic pots, for something to do to cover her embarrassment.

'Oh, bless you, Jemima. I didn't think you cared.' Ralph was coming across as light-hearted, but inside his chest his heart was racing like a Formula One car. Finally, finally, she was cracking – she cared, she cared!! 'So, who do you think would be better for me then?' he asked cocking one eyebrow slightly in an attempt to look coy.

'Oh, I don't know. Someone who makes you feel good about yourself, someone who appreciates what a lovely bloke you are and doesn't just complain the whole time, someone who would inspire you to do what you're best at and not just treat you like a . . . like a . . . like an airhead gigolo!' She was practically kneading the already smooth soil now, her face reddening slightly.

Ralph laughed, hard and loud.

'"An airhead gigolo!!" God that's funny. I've never thought about it like that before, but I think you're right! I think that's exactly how she sees me. A gigolo!'

'No, really, Ralph, I'm being serious. There's a desperate shortage of nice blokes around in this world and you're wasting yourself on Claudia. Believe me, there's thousands of girls out there, nice girls, who would just love to go out with a guy like you. And if you had a nice girlfriend you'd spend less time bloody worrying about what you were going to do wrong next, and being inadequate and not good enough for some souped-up Sloane, and more time doing what you're good at. Painting. Really. I mean it,' she finished, closing the door of the airing cupboard and heading for the kitchen. Ralph followed closely behind, not wanting to miss a syllable. 'Girls like that make me so angry – they give other girls a bad reputation. Dump her and start painting, Ralph. Please.'

Oh, blimey. This was getting a bit heavy now. 'Can I just try the painting bit first and then see if I still need to dump Claudia afterwards?'

She punched him playfully. 'God – can't live without the sex, can you!'

'I'm not going to deny it, I'm a voracious animal,' he smiled, leaning backwards against the work surface.

'Well, I wouldn't want you to do all this just because I say so,' Jem said, replacing the water-spray under the sink, 'but if you thought you were up to it you should definitely give it a bash, just one day at a time – see how you feel. That's always the way in life: the longer you leave things, the harder they are to do . . .' She trailed off. 'Do it, Ralph, go tomorrow. Get up early, get to your studio and see what happens. Maybe you won't paint anything, maybe you'll just come straight back again, but at least you'll have got out of this cycle of just staying at home all day doing nothing – eh?' She was standing in front of him, looking up at him through her eyelashes, a stern but amiable expression on her face which stopped Ralph from feeling that he was being pressurized and more like he was being cared for, warm and nice inside. It had been a long time since he'd felt that way.

'OK,' he said, feigning defeat under duress, 'OK. Just one thing, though – what exactly do you mean by "early"?'

'Oooh, no point being half-hearted about this. Seven o'clock?'

'No way! Eight,' he countered.

'All right. Seven-thirty and no arguing!'

'OK, but that stinks, it really does. Even you don't have to wake up that early.'

Jem smiled. 'You'll feel good about it, I promise. You'll feel happier with yourself.'

And then that all too familiar moment arrived – the

depressing sound of Smith's key in the lock, the twinge of pain in Ralph's heart as Jem's face lit up like the woman's in the Terry's All Gold advert, and she was gone, gone from him, and into Smith's arms.

But she was his again now, for a few delicious moments, before Smith got up; she was in the kitchen cooking him breakfast – she'd never cooked Smith breakfast – and she was wearing that teeny-weeny, itsy-bitsy T-shirt. He rushed his shower, not wanting to miss a moment, dressed quickly but thoughtfully in his cleanest clothes, splashed on a bit of designer aftershave (a present from an ex), fluffed up his hair and made his entrance.

Jem was coaxing the last few baked beans from the bottom of the can. 'I always feel mean if I leave a few stray ones,' she said, 'like they'll feel rejected or something.' She flicked on the gas ring and gave the beans a quick stir. 'Could you handle laying the table?' she asked. 'I'm just getting to the brain-to-hand co-ordination bit.'

She had put an apron on over the T-shirt, tied in a bow at the back, forcing the precarious garment a little higher up her legs but still . . . still just not quite high enough. Maybe if she had to reach for something from one of the cupboards higher up, like . . . the ketchup!

'Jem, would you mind passing me the ketchup? It's in that cupboard just over your head.'

He watched with bated breath; Smith's T-shirt had been clinging stubbornly to the back of Jem's thighs all morning like a prudish nanny, but now it was time. There was no way its resolute spirit could survive the impact of reaching for the ketchup.

Jem raised herself on to tiptoes, her back started to stretch, her arm left its side to begin the journey to the cupboard, the T-shirt moved a millimetre, two millimetres, three millimetres, and there it was! Almost. Oh, God, just another millimetre . . . Ralph was frozen to the spot with painful anticipation . . . Just another millimetre . . . Shit! Shit!! Jem's free hand suddenly grabbed the hem of the hateful T-shirt and pulled it down staunchly over her thighs as she completed the stretch and grabbed the bottle. Ralph couldn't believe it.

'There you go.' She handed him the bottle, seemingly unaware of his intense disappointment and frustration.

Let's face it, he thought, I was not meant to see her bottom, it's not going to happen, forget about it. But, dear God, he wanted to see her bottom. If it was anything like her silken thighs he absolutely had to see it.

'Sorry, Jem. Mustard?' He gestured at the same cupboard with his eyes.

She tutted good-naturedly and reached for the cupboard again. The mustard was further back in the cupboard and she had to stretch that little bit more, using her spare hand to steady herself on the work surface. Ralph stopped and stared again: one millimetre . . . two millimetres . . . three, four, five – Jesus! There it was! Six, seven . . . his mouth was dry, his eyes bulging . . . oh, sweet Jesus . . . the most beautiful, edible, luscious little bundle of bottom, pale and smooth and . . . bottomy . . . and, oh God, want to bite it want to bite it . . .

'I hope you're not looking at my bottom, Ralph McLeary!' laughed Jem, turning around.

Ralph spluttered. 'What? Me?'

'Yes, you. Here's your mustard.'

Ralph reached out for it with trembling hands, trying to look unfazed and innocent, turning too soon and missing the jar entirely. It dropped to the floor and, quite contradictory to Ralph's expectation of what would happen if you dropped a jar of mustard on to a linoleum-covered floor, it smashed into several pieces, depositing a splat of dirty yellow paste all over Jem's bare feet.

'Oh, God, Jem, I'm so sorry.' He rushed for the kitchen roll and pulled far too much off, bundling up the mass of paper and soaking it under the tap. 'I'll wipe it off for you. I'm so sorry.'

He got down on his knees at Jem's feet and began to dab at the mustard. 'There,' he said, 'it's coming off.'

'Of course it's coming off,' said Jem. 'It's mustard, not creosote!'

Ralph held her ankle tenderly as he wiped her tiny white feet. 'There,' he said, letting his hand slide a little further up her calf, his whole body stiff with the excitement of being so close to the hem of her T-shirt, his face inches from her naked groin, his hands encasing her legs and her feet, the mustard suddenly an erotic lubricant; he would quite happily have licked it off her.

'There. Almost done.'

He tore a single sheet off the roll and dried her feet with it, delicately, moving the paper in between her toes with his finger, his other hand still moving slowly further up her leg, almost behind her knee now. He was disappointed to realize that the job was finished; all the mustard was gone. He patted her leg and got slowly off his haunches, leaning his body in a little bit as he rose, keeping his nose close to her body, breathing her in deeply. Suddenly his eye was caught by a couple of small yellow specks on her legs.

'Oh,' he said, breathlessly, 'there's a bit more.'

He put his finger back in the paper and brushed at the splashes, wobbling slightly on his tired knees and grabbing the top of her leg quickly to keep himself steady. Warm, soft, lovely, lovely legs. She didn't flinch at all, just stood still, looking down at him with a small smile on her face.

'You're very thorough,' she said.

'All gone,' he said nervously, slowly, very slowly getting to his feet, his nose almost brushing against the protrusion of her breasts through the T-shirt. He was standing perilously close to her, towering over her, his heart beating so hard he could hear it in his ears.

She didn't move. 'Thank you,' she said.

He didn't move. 'My pleasure,' he said.

'No mustard for your sausages, then,' she said.

'I guess not,' he said.

Neither of them made any attempt to return to their respective chores. They stood where they were, for what seemed like eternity but was probably only a few seconds.

'Ralph?'

'Jem.'

'Remember what I was saying yesterday – you know, about thinking that you deserved someone better, how I think you're quite special?'

Ralph hardly dared breathe. He felt like he was being kept upright only by the magnetic force that Jem was radiating, like if she was to walk away he would just collapse in a heap on the floor. 'Yes?' he replied expectantly. Oh, God. What was she going to say?!

'Well, I just wanted to say . . . oh, shit!' Her face became panicked and she turned around abruptly, 'Shit – the bacon!' She pulled the pan off the heat and opened the window over the sink.

The kitchen was thick with grey, caustic smoke, the bacon annihilated, shards of brittle black charcoal sitting shame-facedly in the pan.

'Oh, bollocks!' she exclaimed, laughing. 'No bacon either, I guess.'

'Never mind,' said Ralph, 'the beans are my favourite bit anyway. Don't worry about it. Carry on. What you were saying, you know, just now . . .'

'Oh, yes,' said Jem, 'That. I was just going to say . . .'

A deafening wail obliterated her sentence, a high-pitched shriek emanating from somewhere in the flat.

'What the hell is that?' shouted Ralph over the din.

Smith was standing in the doorway in a green towelling dressing-gown, looking dazed, his hair all over the place. 'What's going on?' he mumbled with annoyance. 'Why's the smoke alarm going off?'

'Oh, God. I burnt the bacon,' said Jem. 'Quick, Smith, blow on it – blow on the alarm!'

The three of them congregated in the hall. Smith stood on a stool and blew on the alarm, fanning away the small amount of smoke with his sleeve.

'What were you making bacon for anyway?' he asked, bristling with irritation.

'For Ralph. For his breakfast,' she added unnecessarily.

Smith continued blowing and fanning until, eventually, the unbearable siren died down.

'Jesus,' he said, getting off the stool and smoothing down his hair.

'Sorry, boyfriend!' said Jem, holding out her hand to him. 'At least we know it works, though.'

'Hmmmm,' replied Smith, gruffly. 'Well, I suppose it was time to wake up anyway. Is there any breakfast for me?' he asked.

She smiled at him radiantly. 'Of course there is. Coming right up!'

Smith went for a shower then, and Ralph and Jem returned to the kitchen, Jem cracking eggs into a clean pan and turning the heat down under the now almost solidified beans.

'Jem,' said Ralph, putting out knives and forks, 'what you were saying . . . ?'

'I'll tell you later,' she said, and carried on with the breakfast.

Later. Later? It was another one, two, three, four, five, six, seven, eight, nine, ten, TEN! hours until later. How could he possibly wait ten hours to hear what Jem had to say? That was impossible.

'Can you not just give me a little clue?' he said, wincing.

'Oh, God, Ralph! It's no big deal. I'll tell you later, OK?'

'OK,' he said, taking a seat at the table and watching her deftly co-ordinating the final stages of the greasily aromatic breakfast.

Smith came into the kitchen and breakfast was served.

'There you go – a proper working man's breakfast for proper working men,' said Jem, placing plates covered with eggs and sausages and beans and mushrooms and huge slabs of hand-sliced toast dripping with butter in front of them. 'Get stuck into that!'

'You are an angel, you're a saint, you're totally and utterly perfect! Thank you!' Under the circumstances Ralph felt able to blast Jem with superlatives and adoration without arousing discomfort or suspicion (the way to a man's heart and all that) and Jem took it as it sounded rather than as it was meant, smiling happily at her satisfied customer.

His overpowering need for satiation, stimulated by the morning's string of oddly sensuous encounters, was projected on to his food, and he ate like an animal, wolfing down the huge plate of food in moments. He wanted to go now anyway. Smith and Jem were playing footsie under the table and smiling at each other over their breakfast plates. He took his plate to the dishwasher, packed a small rucksack with a radio, some mini Mars Bars and a spare jumper, grabbed Smith's bike and helmet and set off down the road. Smith and Jem waved him off sweetly from the top of the basement steps, arms around each other, looking almost like proud parents. The notion made him feel queasy, quashing the whole air of ripe desire and eroticism that had inflamed his morning.

17

Ralph cycled quickly, taking the scenic route along the river, over Battersea Bridge, past the desirable residences of Cheyne Walk, down Grosvenor Road towards Millbank.

'"Where can I find a woman like that – like Jessie's girl ..."' He sang loudly to himself as he pedalled, not caring who heard. He was bursting at the seams with pent-up everything – lust, jealousy, love, hurt, excitement, disappointment. This was unbearable, totally unbearable. How could he go on like this, living under the same roof with the two of them, Jem not minding if he saw her bottom, telling him he was 'special' and then playing footsie with Smith as if he didn't exist? Was she doing it on purpose? Maybe she was a nymphomaniac after all. No. No. That wasn't right. There was more to it than that, much more. There was something between them, something ... spiritual. Oh, what rubbish. Spiritual! No, they got on, it was as simple as that. They got on very, very well together, they had a 'special' relationship. If he didn't fancy her so much he could very well have been friends with her – that would have been novel, a female friend. But that was impossible now, especially after this morning, especially after the pee in the toilet and the T-shirt and the mustard and everything.

What was it she wanted to say to him? He couldn't get it off his mind. Oh, well – he only had one whole enormous, never-ending day to wait to find out.

He turned right and left at Parliament Square and followed the river on to Victoria Embankment, still cycling suicidally fast, ignoring the burning in his leg muscles and the possibility of errant pedestrians walking into his path.

It was a glorious day, cold in the nicest possible way, the sky an unfeasible blue, the Houses of Parliament gleaming like freshly washed bedsheets.

Fucking Smith. Fucking bloody Smith. Smith had always had the better luck. From early on. Smith had the smart house in Shirley, the nice liberal parents, the coolest friends, the best-looking girls after him, the flash car on his eighteenth birthday, the holidays, the job, the money, the flat, the career. Ralph had just tagged along to start with, feeling out of his depth and insecure.

His parents were old, much older than anyone else's parents, and timid of nature. He couldn't have invited anyone back to their house in Sutton – his mother would have laid a table of Viscount biscuits and cardboardy jam tarts and wanted to chat with his 'young friends' about school and the weather. His father would have taken refuge in the garden, pottering around in his twill cap with his rake and his hoe or whatever, looking like an elderly groundskeeper in a stately home. The television would be switched off – it was rude to have it turned on in company – and the small beige living room would have resonated with the sound of the old wooden clock on the wall ticking away the interminable seconds.

He'd had to work hard to find his feet in Smith's world. The first time he'd been round to see Shirelle, he'd been almost morally shocked by the attitude of Smith's parents, who swore frequently and shouted loudly over the din of every television in the house, and let Smith's friends come and go without the slightest interest in who they were or how their schoolwork was going or whether they were about to have sex with a foreign-exchange student in the spare room.

He hadn't lingered at first, servicing Shirelle as speedily as possible with one eye on the door, not quite able to comprehend the fact that Smith's parents didn't actually care, and leaving rapidly, dressing on the way out, not looking to the left or the right for fear of making eye contact with one of the many people who appeared to be constantly milling around the large, comfortable house.

And then of course he'd gone for that walk with Smith and found that he was not a bad bloke and was obviously disproportionately impressed by Ralph's supposed sexual prowess, and Smith had welcomed him into his life.

He'd been uncomfortable for a while, worried that he was the subject of some enormous joke, but he soon learned to relax and enjoy the advantages of having wealthy, happy friends. The jealousy he'd always felt towards Smith began to wane, and as the years went by and their friendship developed into one of brothers, the initial discrepancies between them faded and they became equals. Ralph was cool now, too, he could hold his own – he was the star of the Royal College, he had press coverage, beautiful blondes, a wide circle of friends and invitations to smart parties.

But now all those old feelings were rising to the surface again, the feelings of inadequacy, of being the country mouse, the poor relation, the social misfit, the butt of someone's joke. Because Smith had the one thing in the world that Ralph hadn't even realized until now he'd wanted – a real relationship with a real woman who really loved him.

Fucking Smith. Fucking bloody Smith. Not. Fucking. Fair.

He hurtled up Thames Street towards a bank of impatient cars queued four-wide at the traffic lights. He rode on, faster and faster, up Lower Thames Street and towards Tower Hill. The burn in his legs had stopped ages ago, he was an automaton, the bike was cycling itself. He heard a car horn for the millionth time that morning. 'Ah, fuck you!' he shouted out, sticking his finger in the air.

He took his hands from the handlebar, got to his feet and closed his eyes against the wind that whipped across his face like a leather glove. He took in a huge deep breath, bigger almost than his lungs, and opened his mouth wide enough to feel the rush of air against his tonsils.

He was about to yell but the sound was lost in the blaring screech of yet another car horn, of rubber against Tarmac, of metal grinding metal as Ralph's bike hit the bonnet of a shiny red Mercedes 350SL convertible, his dream car, and his body flew up into the London skyline, across a parked car, over a parking meter, finally landing with a menacing thud of flesh and bone against the wall of an office building on Minories.

His body was soon surrounded by a concerned group of strangers oohing and aahing and asking if anyone was a doctor, and shouldn't they call an ambulance, and putting their ears to his mouth to see if he was breathing.

'Shhhhh!' said a small fat man who, for some unofficial and peculiar reason had taken control of the situation, 'shhhhhh, everyone, he's trying to speak.'

He put his gelatinous face an inch from Ralph's mouth, his cheeks turning red with the effort of leaning over. He sat back, exhaled and scanned the faces of the attentive crowd gathered around him.

'He's saying that he wishes he had Jessie's girl,' he announced with confusion, 'over and over – "Jessie's girl."'

'"I want Jessie's girl . . ."'

'Why the hell does he keep singing that?' whispered Smith.

Jem shrugged and squeezed Ralph's hand again. 'Oh, God, look at him!' she wailed. 'It's all my fault! He would still have been in bed at that time of the morning if it hadn't been for me.' She put her head down on the side of Ralph's bed and began to sob.

'Oh, Jem, don't cry. Don't blame yourself.' Smith stroked her small, quivering head. 'It's *not* your fault. Remember what the driver of the car said. He was cycling unbelievably fast, with his eyes closed – it wasn't just bad luck . . .' He trailed off as the image of his poor mangled bike flashed through his head again. He'd only had it for two months and now it was a write-off, dead, deceased. Thanks a lot, Ralph.

The doctor had informed them that Ralph had a fractured wrist, severe bruising to the left side of his body, a broken rib and mild concussion. He would come round soon, he told them, any time now. He was very lucky apparently; the wall had, perversely, broken his fall. If he'd hit the pavement first he could have injured his back or broken a leg.

They were sitting with Ralph, in the quiet of the ward, either side of his bed, Jem holding his hands, Smith holding his own crossed in his lap, waiting for Ralph to do something, anything at all rather than lie there looking so pale and still and bruised, singing that bloody song over and over again.

'Let me get you a cup of tea,' sighed Smith, getting to his feet and stretching, looking quickly at his watch. He had so much work to do.

Jem turned back to observe Ralph. He looked so sweet, his face scuffed and tinged with purple, his big round eyes so distressingly closed, his left arm in plaster, a bandage around his chest holding his broken bones together. He looked like a child, a vulnerable, lovable, sweet, broken child, and it was all her fault. It didn't matter what Smith said, what anyone said, it was she who'd steered Ralph down that particular path of fate, whether he'd also been to blame or not. If it hadn't been for her he'd still have been in bed at that hideous moment when his bike hit the bonnet of that car; she'd determined his destiny that Friday morning, she and no one else.

'"Jessie's girl – I want Jessie's girl,"' Ralph was humming again in that strange, rasping voice.

'This is Jem, Ralph – can you hear me?'

'Where can I find a woman like that . . . ?'

'Oh, Ralph, this is Jem. Please, Ralph, open your eyes, look at me.'

Ralph just lay there.

'Ralph – Ralph – it's me!'

Ralph awoke. 'Jem . . .' Ralph's voice sounded weak, tired.

'Shhhhh . . . shhhhh,' said Jem, putting her hand to his cheek, 'don't try to speak.'

'Jem.' He smiled at her and closed his eyes again, nuzzling his cheek against her hand. 'Jem.'

Smith returned at that moment, grasping two polystyrene cups of tea.

'Smith, Smith, he's awake! He talked to me!'

Smith put the cups down on the bedside table and re-instated himself quickly on his chair. 'Ralph – Ralphie – can you hear me?'

Ralph nodded and opened his eyes slowly. He smiled at Smith. 'What the fuck's going on?' he croaked.

'You tell me,' laughed Smith, grinning widely at Ralph and taking his hand, 'you lunatic bloody kamikaze cyclist! What the hell were you playing at?'

'I – I don't remember,' he replied, speaking very slowly. 'Oh, yes, I do! I was singing. Singing. I was singing. I was on your bike. Yeah – that's right.'

'I'll get the nurse,' whispered Smith to Jem, 'they probably need to know.'

'Jem,' said Ralph, after Smith had gone, 'so nice to see you – you look . . . lovely.'

'Oh, Ralph, thank you, but I think your judgement's probably a little impaired at the moment.'

'Has Smith gone home?'

'No, he's gone to get a nurse. You've been unconscious for hours.'

She watched as he drifted into a happy slumber. She felt overwhelmed with tenderness and affection. All of a sudden she wanted to hold Ralph, to protect him, to look after him, to love him? . . . It had been such a strange morning. The whole episode with the mustard had unsettled her. There was something nice about it; she'd enjoyed the feeling of his hands on her legs, his finger between her toes . . . and there'd been that moment, before the bacon burnt, when the world had stopped for a second, literally stopped, and he'd stood over her, close to her and her heart had beaten so hard it had felt like her eardrums were going to explode and now . . . now . . . for some reason she was feeling very confused.

She looked at Ralph, his cheek still resting against her hand, his body still and shattered, his mind elsewhere. He looked so gentle, so in need of love and care.

Her heart tied itself up in a knot.

18

It had been a very happy fortnight for Siobhan and Karl, the happiest for months and months. Siobhan had taken Rick's advice that night at the chapel and talked to Karl about everything, absolutely everything. And Karl, in his usual strong and compassionate way, had listened and understood – even the bit about Rick.

'You kissed him,' he'd stated matter-of-factly, sitting bare-chested under the counterpane on the huge four-poster bed, Rosanne curled up at his side with her head on his lap.

'Uh-hum,' Siobhan had nodded, looking glumly at the floor, long strands of scruffy golden hair falling from the pins that had held it in place all night, her eyes streaked with black mascara and smudged eyeliner, her dainty heels clogged with mud from the banks of the loch.

Karl had felt a small jolt of surprise. That mad Tamsin girl had been right – sort of. They'd kissed. Rick had kissed Siobhan. Siobhan had kissed Rick. He found himself feeling a little sick.

'Jeez. What . . . what . . . er, how . . . how long . . . how long did you kiss for, exactly?' he said slowly, rubbing his chin, feeling awkward about this unexpected scenario but also that he needed to handle it like a grown-up.

'Ten minutes, twenty minutes, I don't know. I thought of you,' she added, wanting to turn the conversation back to what was important – them. 'I thought of you and I stopped . . .'

'Why? Was it . . . was it . . . because you were drunk, high – what?' Karl was talking calmly, rationally, genuinely trying to understand what had happened that night but still shaken by the image in his mind of Siobhan, his Siobhan, in the arms of another man, kissing him, her tongue in his mouth . . .

'Partly – well, no, not really at all. I was . . . I was thinking about it even before we started drinking, the minute I saw him, in fact,' she gulped, feeling maybe she'd admitted too much but then realizing that this was just the beginning of what needed to be said.

'Well, yes. He's a great-looking guy, I suppose . . .'

'Oh, Karl, stop it! Stop being so bloody reasonable. Do you think that's all there was to it? You think I just liked the look of him and suddenly, after fifteen years with you I just thought, Oh, what the fuck, I'll have him? Yes, he's good looking, of course he's good looking, but . . . but that's not it.'

'Well, then, tell me, Siobhan. Please tell me. Why?'

'To show you that I'm still attractive, that other men, good-looking men, would find me attractive. I wanted to make you jealous, Karl. I know how immature that must sound, how . . . how stupid. I wanted you to stop me, before, when we were flirting, I wanted you to get angry, to be possessive, to think, That's my girlfriend and if I'm not careful she's going to have sex with someone else – but you didn't. You were so typically Karl – so unfazed, cool, oblivious – so fucking smug! It didn't occur to you did it, Karl, it didn't cross your mind that someone else might want me? You just think I'm some great ugly ink-blot, some fat bird that no other man would look twice at . . .' She broke down in angry tears.

'Oh, God, Siobhan, this is what we were talking about before, before we went downstairs tonight. Shit. I wanted to talk to you then but you were so angry, so defensive, you wouldn't talk about it.' Karl could feel tears welling up behind his eyes now. 'Come over here, Shuv.' He patted the empty bed beside him. 'Please. I want to be close to you.'

She got up from the dressing table and walked slowly to the bed, sitting gingerly on the edge, wanting to be close also, but still full of so much uncommunicated anger and resentment that she was unable to yield herself to him entirely.

'Shuv,' he began, 'I'm not going to lie to you. You have put on quite a lot of weight. I've not mentioned it because it just didn't seem important. Really,' he added, registering the raised eyebrows and scepticism on Siobhan's face. He took her hand. 'You are the most beautiful woman in the world. And I'm not going to say "to me" because that's not true. You're beautiful to me, but I can also see that you're beautiful to other people as well. I've seen the looks men give you when we walk down the street. You're over-weight, yes, but that doesn't matter. I mean look at you – you're magnificent, Siobhan – your hair, those blue eyes, the way you carry yourself, the way you are with people, your laugh. And when you're naked you look voluptuous, feminine, round . . .'

Siobhan was smiling now through her tears, a soft spot in the pit of her belly aching with pleasure.

'I don't want you any less, Siobhan, if anything I want you more. That night, that night when all this started, after the drinks at the Sol y Sombra, I wanted you more then than I can ever remember, more than when we first met.'

Oh, yes – that night. Siobhan had to tackle this now, while she was feeling able to talk honestly. She took a breath.

'Karl – about that night. I want to explain.'

He held her hand encouragingly.

She continued. 'It was that girl, that Cheri girl – you know, the one who lives upstairs. Well. When I saw her there at your drinks party and she looked so young and slim and beautiful and you were obviously so . . . so in awe of her, I just felt really inadequate and ugly, and later, when you were, you know, trying to make love to me, I just kept thinking that you wanted me to be her, that you were imagining I was her, that I was young and slender and smooth and . . . and . . . and that's why I pushed you off me – I just couldn't bear it. I felt so hideous – like a freak, like a whore or something, like a great fat whore. I thought that that was why you were being so passionate, because you were turned on thinking about her, not me, and – oh, God – does this all sound really pathetic?'

Karl felt sick. What had he done? He was to blame. Why had he ever gone within a mile of that horrible, horrible bitch? He had the most wonderful girlfriend imaginable, a girlfriend who loved him and trusted him and cared for him. And his selfish, pathetic actions had forced her into the arms of another man. In a way he deserved this. He'd been plagued with guilt for months now, for what he'd done to Siobhan. It was time he paid the price for his treachery, his deceit.

'No . . . no,' he sighed, pulling her to him. 'It doesn't sound pathetic, not at all pathetic. I'm the pathetic one, Siobhan, not you.'

'What do you mean?' asked Siobhan.

'Nothing. Nothing. Just that you've always been the strongest one. Always. I've leant on you through the years, relied on you. It was you who made all the best decisions in our relationship. If it wasn't for you we'd still be living in that grotty bedsit in Brighton, I'd still be trying to be a rock star, playing to a bunch of pissed eighteen-year-old students in a stinking union bar knee-deep in snakebite and vomit, convincing myself I was enjoying it, that I was living some sort of worthwhile life. You made me grow up. I'm a better person because of you, Siobhan. And I promise you, really, really promise you, Siobhan, that when we got home that night, when we were in bed, it was you I wanted, it was you I saw when I closed my eyes, that I felt under my fingertips, with my mouth, with my tongue. Only you. That girl, that Cheri girl, she's very pretty, y'know, obviously but – oh God, Siobhan, it's you I want, you I've always wanted, eight stone or eighteen stone . . . Well – maybe not eighteen stone!' He laughed and Siobhan hit him playfully and let him hold her in his arms and love her and comfort her.

Well, that wasn't so much of a lie, about Cheri, Karl thought guiltily. Just selective truth, protective lying, protecting them, their love, their future. But, God, he felt awful, he felt so, so awful. He stroked her hair.

'Jeez, Shuv, your hair's full of stuff – bits of twig and

grass and God knows what. Are you sure you were just kissing out there?'

'Well, it was lying-down kissing, wasn't it?' she giggled nervously. 'Karl, do you forgive me? You know, don't you, it was nothing? It was me being childish and I used poor Rick to get at you . . .'

'Oh, I shouldn't imagine he minded too much. What man would, you devilishly beautiful woman, you!'

They'd hugged tightly and properly then and talked into the night, talked about the last twelve months, about Siobhan's unhappiness, and they'd made plans to make sure that Siobhan would be happy in the future, to make sure that never again would they allow their relationship to become stifled, silent and thick with unspoken thoughts. And then they'd made love, for the first time in nearly two months, and as Karl slid down between her breasts, Siobhan looked down at his mop of black curls and lay back and smiled.

They'd heard the rumble of Rick's Peugeot early the following morning – he and Tamsin had obviously thought better of hanging around to see what happened next – and spent a blissful day and night on their own in the enchanted chapel, talking, walking, eating and making love.

The first thing she'd done when they got back to London on Monday was to phone her gynaecologist to arrange an appointment to talk to someone about their options for infertility treatments. During their late-night conversation in the chapel, it had transpired that Siobhan had been in denial about her inability to conceive for years; it had been a long-held dream, an assumption about the path her life was going to take, and when she'd been told it was denied her, she'd brushed the dream under the carpet like a shrivelled-up dead spider, bought Rosanne and decided to get on with her life, refusing to consider the option of fighting for what she'd always believed would be her natural right. Not, she understood now, the action of a decisive, pragmatic woman, but the action of a woman in shock, a woman who didn't know what else to do. They would make the most wonderful parents, they realized that night. So many awful parents in this world, so many who didn't deserve children, who didn't want them, who hurt, stifled, spoiled and damaged their off-spring. As they talked and basked in the warmth of their revived closeness they knew that they deserved children, they were ready for them, and they wanted them more than anything.

The next thing Siobhan did, anticipating the advice she was bound to be given prior to any treatment being offered to her, was to enrol with her local Weight Watchers group. Funny, now she knew that Karl loved her any way she came it was so much easier to make the decision to do something about her weight. For herself, not just for Karl; for their future, for their baby. And, more practically, in the short term, so that she could resurrect some of her lovely old clothes from early retirement and throw away her horrible leggings. It was boredom that had led her to overeat, the hours and hours spent at home on her own, with a fridge full of unhealthy food, eating meals alone, huge plates the size of a funeral pyre, without the con-straints of the embarrassment of someone watching her.

She and Karl had decided that she needed more to do,

she needed to be busy, too busy to eat, so she'd put an ad in a bridal magazine advertising her dressmaking services. The ad had only been in for a week and she already had three commissions. The phone rang every day with enquiries from prospective brides, and she was turning the spare bedroom into a proper bridal room.

They'd discovered the hard way that the ease that had always been the bedrock of their relationship had also been its undoing. They'd never discussed things in any great depth because they hadn't needed to. Siobhan had always decided when to move on, and Karl, compliant and utterly full of faith in her foresight and wisdom, had followed blindly. He'd been too blind to see when the time had come for him to take the lead and take Siobhan firmly by the hand and into the future, their future.

It had been hard for Karl to come to terms with what had happened between and Rick and Siobhan that night on the banks of the loch. He'd had to control a lot of rather unpleasant feelings of jealousy and he really didn't like the emotion at all – it was alien to him, against his nature. But he'd managed, somehow, and now he was feeling strangely touched by the revelations that night at the chapel, touched that, for once, Siobhan had needed him. He was being called on to be a man, called up for service almost, except his country didn't need him, his lover did, and he felt proud and strong and ready to do whatever was necessary.

He felt very grown-up, and it was a great feeling. He wanted to spend some money on the flat, get rid of all the studenty artefacts and shabby bits of old furniture they'd brought with them from Brighton, take the posters off the walls, buy some light shades for the bare bulbs, buy a really nice duvet cover, maybe take out the horrible orange plastic bathroom suite and put in something expensive and Italian.

He couldn't be a rockabilly for the rest of his life; he was thirty-five years old: if he had children, their school-friends would tease them for having a father who looked like Bill Haley. It would be painful, but he was going to do it – go to the barber's and ask them to remove his beloved quiff and sideburns. On the bright side, it wouldn't take him so long to get ready for work in the mornings, and he could stop using that Black and White gel that Siobhan hated. Maybe build some cabinets for his oversized record collection too; the yards and yards of neatly stacked rows of records currently dominated their living room, like some dubious modern-art exhibit at the Tate Gallery. They were a trophy, a testament to his life to date. It was time to hide them, maybe even sell some. Time to move on.

They'd been so happy for so long that Karl and Siob-han had forgotten to press Play after depressing the Pause button of their lives – they'd been stuck in the freeze-frame for years, transfixed by its perfection, by the smiles on the faces of the people in it. It had taken that night in Scotland to remind them that there were new scenes to come, new developments to be worked through and that the important thing, the most important thing in the world, was to keep the film moving, whether the film had a happy ending or not.

Karl's work was going better, too. He'd been called to Jeff's office on his return to work on the Monday afternoon, and he was smiling. He'd just received the latest ratings and figures were up for Karl's show – only a fraction, but enough to suggest to Jeff that it would be best to leave things be for a few weeks, give things a chance to settle down, see how the figures went. 'Keep hold of the tape from Glencoe, though,' he'd said, 'Rick tells me you came up with some blinding stuff – keep it, just in case.'

But Karl felt confident that they wouldn't need the tape. The following week's figures had shown a further increase and he felt sure that the trend would continue. He didn't mind playing the odd bit of Top Ten bilge to keep the younger listeners on board if it meant that he could educate them by playing pop classics in between.

Karl had decided from the outset to be honest with Rick about the events at Glencoe. He liked him, he respected him and he wanted their relationship to work.

'Rick,' he'd said in the station canteen after his show on Monday, 'I know what happened. I know what happened with you and Siobhan on Saturday night.'

Rick had visibly receded in his seat then and stared down at his suddenly unappetizing plate of broccoli and cheddar bake. 'Oh,' he'd managed to reply in a voice a few octaves higher than his normal bass.

'Look, I'm not the jealous type, Rick. I was a bit shocked, it has to be said. But I hear that you were very kind to Siobhan, offered her some very wise advice and, well, we needed it, to be frank with you. I just want you to know that I don't feel bad about what happened, you know, that night . . .' This wasn't true. It wasn't true at all. Karl still felt sick about what had happened, but he knew that if he allowed his jealousy to get a foothold the whole situation would turn in on itself and become negative. He had to keep things positive, it was the only way.

Rick finally exhaled and began to regain his bulk. 'You know, she's a great girl, Karl, really, really . . .' he said nervously.

'Yeah, I know. I know.' Karl didn't want to hear this; he had no interest in Rick's opinion of his girlfriend. He took a breath to control himself. 'Look, all I'm saying is, basically, no hard feelings, eh? I respect you and I don't want this to come between us, especially when it's turned out to be such a . . . such a positive thing ultimately – for both of us, for me and Siobhan. We needed a kick up the arse – you know, we'd got stale, stuck, complacent, so anyway,' he smiled then, and stuck his hand out to Rick, who took it uncertainly but gratefully and shook it hard, 'forget about it – eh?'

'Yeah,' said Rick, still feeling a little embarrassed by Karl's candidness and his part in the situation.

'So, how are things with you and Tamsin? She was a bit upset that night?' said Karl, thickly buttering an insipid bread roll, wondering how much he could say to Rick about his patently unstable girlfriend.

'Um.' Rick gulped. 'Gone . . . she's gone.' He spoke quickly, in that strange, high-pitched voice.

'Oh, Jeez, mate, I'm sorry. What happened?'

'Well, I told her – what happened.'

'You told her! Why?'

'Well, she guessed really. I woke up the next morning and she was just sitting at the foot of the bed, staring at me.' He shuddered. 'It was scary actually. And she was holding my clothes, from the night before, and they were sort of . . . dirty. You know, grass stains and stuff.' He averted his gaze from Karl's at that moment. He breathed in deeply and let it go slowly and audibly through puckered lips. 'She just went fucking ape, completely mad, you know? Telling me I was a cock-sucking bastard motherfucker son of a syphilitic bitch – that sort of thing. I'm surprised you two didn't hear, she was screaming so loud.'

'Jeez,' said Karl.

'You know, I've been with Tamsin for six months, but I don't think I know even half of what makes her tick. There's a lot of stuff going on under the surface with her, d'you know what I mean? She's got a lot of secrets, that girl, a hell of a lot of secrets.'

'Hmmmm,' said Karl. That was undoubtedly true.

'I guess it's just as well I found out sooner rather than later, eh?' he added with a small, nervous laugh.

'How are you feeling about it?' asked Karl.

'Worried, more than anything. I don't know how she's going to cope.'

'Look, if she needs help, she'll contact you. She'll probably change her mind and try and come back. She's a grown woman, she can look after herself. It's the people who seem weak who are always surprisingly strong, and the ones who seem strong who are unexpectedly weak. She'll be just fine.'

'Yeah, I hope so, I do hope so. Oh, by the way' – Rick dipped into his leather briefcase – 'I . . . er . . . I brought this.' He handed Karl the small silver tape recorder from the night in Glencoe. 'I haven't listened to it yet, and it doesn't seem like you're going to need it now, but you may as well have it.' And then he'd passed the little machine to Karl who nodded his thanks and put it in his back pocket.

Karl got up to leave and they shook hands. The cleaning-up operation was over for the time being; everything that had to be said had been said. Karl was glad he'd done it, glad he'd been so controlled, so mature. But he still couldn't rid himself of the feeling that he'd like to take Rick outside and break his jaw.

It had been a most, most excellent two weeks for Karl and Siobhan and now it was almost Christmas and Karl had left the ALR building in Olympia and was driving up Kensington High Street. It was dark, the streets glowing phosphorously orange, and the pavements on both sides were thick with shoppers and slush from the snow that had fallen briefly that lunchtime and melted quickly in the brilliant white sunshine that had followed. A Salvation Army band played carols outside Barkers and the pleasant noise of shiny brass and scrubbed voices added to Karl's already great sense of well-being. He miraculously found a parking space in Derry Street and quickly pushed his way as charmingly as possible through the dense hordes of shoppers towards the warm welcoming doors of the department store, fully appreciating the gorgeous gust of artificially warm air that hit him as he entered. He walked briskly through the perfumery department, avoiding the plastic-faced assistants wielding large bottles of headache-inducing fragrances and headed through to the quiet inner sanctum of the jewellery department. This was no good, he thought, eyeing up the display cases of oversized pieces of gold and amber and cubic zirconium, they were all costume pieces, gaudy and garish.

'Excuse me, please,' he said to a friendly looking young

man behind a counter, 'excuse me. Can you tell me where I'll find the real jewellery?'

He pointed Karl in the right direction. Oh, yes, he thought, this is more like it, this is the stuff.

'Can I help you, sir?'

'Yes, please,' replied Karl eagerly. 'Yes. Can you show me a selection of rings, please, in the region of . . . ' – he quickly calculated how much he could afford – 'in the region of £1,000 to £1,500. No, sorry, actually can you make that £2,000?' He smiled widely. It was going to be worth it.

'Certainly, sir. And what sort of ring were you looking for?'

Karl would have thought that was obvious – there was only one kind of ring, wasn't there?

'Oh, engagement rings, please.'

Yes! He was going to marry her. He was going to marry his beautiful, beautiful Siobhan. He was so excited he could barely breathe. Why had he never thought of this before! He stared down at the glistening tray in front of him, rows and rows of shiny, perfect troths, tiny sparkling symbols of love. Oh, which one? Which one would end up on Siobhan's delightful finger for the rest of her life? Because it would be for the rest of her life; for the first time ever, the concept of being with Siobhan for the rest of his life seemed unbearably romantic, not just some inevitable destiny, some unspoken certainty, but the most wonderfully, fantastically romantic notion imaginable. Just think, the two of them for ever, children, grandchildren, a nice house in . . . in . . . Chelsea maybe, glittering careers, and the two of them, always the two of them – Karl and Siobhan Kasparov, that fabulously grown-up, happy couple, still so in love after fifty, a hundred, three hundred years together . . . aaaaaaahhh. Makes your heart melt, dunnit . . . ?

He had to think about what Siobhan would like, not what he liked. He'd have chosen some great hunk of rock; Siobhan would prefer something more subtle, daintier, maybe something with a coloured gem in it, blue maybe to match her eyes, or yellow to match her hair. The salesman patiently showed him every tray in the department, calculating his commission with each ring Karl looked at, encouraging him and sharing his enthusiasm. Finally Karl saw it – the right ring, the one that had 'Siobhan' written all over it: an intricate cluster of tiny pearls, diamonds and sapphires mounted on a white-gold band, feminine and unusual, with a vaguely Celtic feel to it, and entirely unpretentious – just like Siobhan.

The excited salesman placed the ring in a beautiful red-leather box and Karl left the store £2,200 poorer and in a rush to get home. They'd invited their friends Tom and Debbie over for dinner that night, nothing fancy, just some pasta, maybe watch a video after. Now he was hoping they wouldn't want to stay for the 'maybe-watch-a-video-after' bit and would leave as early as possible, giving him time to propose before they were both too tired to celebrate.

He could barely contain himself as he flitted around Siobhan in the kitchen that night, watching, or rather hindering her while she prepared the evening meal, chopping up huge flat mushrooms and strips of streaky bacon for a carbonara sauce (made with virtually fat free crème fraîche, she hastened to inform him).

'Tom and Debbie are running a bit late,' she told him. 'They called just before you got back.'

'Oh, God. How late?' he asked impatiently.

'I don't know, only about half an hour or so, I suppose.'

'Oh, God.'

'What's the matter with you? Since when were you a stickler for time-keeping in other people?' asked Siobhan, laughing at Karl's curious vexation.

'Oh, nothing – I just want this evening to be over, that's all. I want to be alone with you and I can't wait because I'm an impatient fecking bastard, that's all,' he said, grabbing her from behind and planting a vampire kiss on the back of her neck.

'Control yourself, Karl Kasparov!' giggled Siobhan. 'Another half-hour won't kill you!'

'It might well do, it might well do . . .'

Karl was bursting at the seams. It had been Jeff, Jeff of all people, who'd put the idea into his head. He hadn't done or said anything in particular, it was just the way he referred to his wife all the time – Jackie this and Jackie that. And his kids, he talked about them constantly, called them 'the kids' even though they were probably in their twenties by now. 'Jackie and the kids.' 'Siobhan and the kids.' It seemed that Jeff and Jackie had a great marriage; it had lasted more than thirty years already and they were still very much part of each other's lives, firmly interwoven like threads in a piece of fine silk, not a rag-bag fraying old patch of canvas like a lot of marriages seemed to be. There was a wonderful, dignified finality to their marriage, an immutable permanence. They hadn't reached a dead end and stopped, they'd gone on and on, growing and changing, up the same path, towards the same horizon, hand in hand. It was corny but it was also exactly what Karl wanted. He wanted a great marriage.

Tom and Debbie finally arrived and the four of them enjoyed a relaxed evening together. Before too long it was eleven o'clock, too late to watch a video and, as far as Karl was concerned, time for them to go, time for the big moment. He'd contained his excitement long enough, imagined the look on Siobhan's face, the plans they would make about venues and guests and which church and what vows and talking into the night and going to bed to make love and celebrate their future together. The past was important, of course it was, but nothing was more important than the future now.

Eventually Tom began to yawn and look like he was going to leave.

'Do you want me to call you a cab?' asked Karl.

They saw them to the door as the cab waited outside, its engine breaking the silence of the still December night. Siobhan yawned, too, as the front door closed behind their guests. 'I'm going to brush my teeth,' she said.

'No! Wait!' said Karl, his smile so lively that it pulled his face in a hundred different directions at once. 'Just wait there. Don't move.' He motioned to her with his hands.

'What are you up to?' asked Siobhan, Karl's ludicrous smile infecting her.

He returned from the hall with his hands behind his back. 'Siobhan,' he began, 'this is the most important thing I've ever done. It's also the best thing I've ever done and I only pray that you agree with me!' He laughed nervously and Siobhan stared back at him with curiosity, amusement and apprehension.

'Siobhan McNamara, the most beautiful woman in the world' – he pulled the red box from behind his back and clumsily forced it open – 'Siobhan McNamara, will you marry me?'

He stood, for what felt like an eternity, holding the little box aloft, searching Siobhan's face for a reaction.

'Oh, my God, Karl, you daft bugger! You madman! What the hell have you done?' She picked the box cautiously from the palm of his hand.

His face dropped and a look of panic spread across it.

'Yes, please!' She threw her arms around his neck. 'Yes, please!'

19

Smith had gone away for an entire weekend. Some idea of James's apparently, an office 'team-building' exercise, completely bizarre given that the members of the small office were so vividly disparate it was obvious no amount of 'building' would ever make a team of them. But James had been sweet-talked by a charming, long-legged rep from a management consultancy and persuaded that after a weekend of 'motivational, incentivizational, inspirational deconstruction and reconstruction' not only would his odd little company somehow be transformed into a model of modern working practices but that he would also live longer, attract women and suddenly experience a regrowth of his long-absent hair.

So Smith had grumpily packed a small bag on Friday morning, and he, Diana, James, three ageing account executives, two dumpy secretaries and a bad-tempered receptionist had squeezed themselves into a rented Renault Espace and trundled up the Al to a hotel in Hertfordshire. Jem had been heartily amused though, of course, very sympathetic and embraced him tightly as he left the flat, looking stony-faced and muttering, 'Only get one fucking weekend a week and I've got to spend it with a bunch of psychos.'

Jem had arranged to meet up with some friends at the Falcon on St John's Hill that night for someone's birthday and had gone home after work to change.

Ralph was in. He hadn't been out since he'd got back from hospital two weeks ago. He was still a bit sore, especially around the ribs, and it hurt like buggery when he laughed, but his doctor was pleased with his progress – he was young and strong and healing well.

Jem joined him on the sofa with a can of lager. Ralph had looked at her, a strange smile hovering about his lips. 'What is it?' asked Jem.

Ralph kept smiling. 'Guess what?'

'What?'

'I've done it!'

'Done what?'

'I've been a good boy,' he beamed. 'I'm sorting my life out.'

'Oh, yeah? Meaning what?'

'Meaning I've finished with Claudia,' he said smugly.

'What!' she shrieked. 'What do you mean, you've "finished with Claudia"?'

'Well, what do you think I mean? I've finished with Claudia, simple as that.'

'Good God. I don't believe it! Let's get this straight. You saw Claudia – Claudia with the legs, Claudia with the face of an angel, Claudia who lets you have sex with her – you saw her, and you said, "I'm sorry, it's over, I don't think we should see each other any more," just like that?!'

'That's right,' he replied, his arms folded across his chest, grinning indulgently.

'Not "It's over but can we still have the odd shag for old time's sake?"'

He shook his head.

'Not "It's over but do you mind if I sleep with your best friend?"'

He shook his head again.

She'd thrown her arms around him then and hugged him quickly.

'Bloody hell, Ralph. I'm so proud of you! How did she take it?'

'Oh, typically Claudia. "You would do this just before my sister's wedding, wouldn't you, you're so selfish, who am I going to go with now, all my sisters will have their boyfriends and husbands there and I'll be the sad old spinster – God I hate you!"' He finished his impersonation with a camp flounce. 'And then she cried. Wasn't expecting that, I have to say, old Clauds, crying. She tried to play it down, y'know, but I think she was really upset.'

'So what next?' Jem asked. 'How are you going to control your sexual urges? What are you going to do on Friday nights? Who's going to be your next girlfriend?'

'What makes you think there has to be a next girlfriend? No, I think I'm going to steer clear for a while, "find some time for myself."' He said this in a cheesy American-therapist voice. 'I haven't been single since I was, since I was . . . ever. I've never, ever been single – I think it'll do me some good. And I reckon I can live without sex for a while, a little while anyway. I've got my sources if I get desperate, I've got my Little Black Psion Organizer!'

'Well,' said Jem, moving to get up, 'it's a start, it's a very good start. Well done. Now we've just got to find you someone to fall in love with . . .'

A strange mood fell across them both briefly at that moment, and for a second they sat, suspended. Ralph noted the fleeting tension with some satisfaction. He had realized that Jem thought he was a little sad, going out with a girl he didn't care about purely for the sex, and so he was putting a new plan into operation: Operation Mature and Available. His decision to chuck Claudia hadn't been entirely rational and prescient. It had been hard for him lately, spending time with Claudia, wishing she were more like Jem, everything she did and said irritating him with its cloying girlishness and irrational female 'logic'.

But mainly he'd finished the relationship because Jem wanted him to, because Jem would think more of him if he did and because, more than anything right now, he wanted Jem's respect. He'd done a lot of thinking since the accident and understood that there was no point in mooning around after Jem, trying to impress her with his choice of flowers or the latest vindaloo. Jem was twenty-seven years old, the age when a woman, consciously or not, starts to look for different qualities in a man, an age when charisma alone is not quite enough to clinch the deal, when a healthy bank balance, a solid future and a practical nature become just as attractive as a trendy hair-cut, a wacky sense of humour and the romantic allure of a failed artist.

That was another reason she'd chosen Smith, and he didn't blame her really, he'd always been quite taken with the thought of being supported by a rich woman and could see no reason why Jem should be beyond the allure of a man in a position to keep up the mortgage payments and pay for Baby Gap clothes in the event of a maternity break, a man you could seriously envisage making a good impression at a Parent–Teacher meeting, a man who would have no qualms about assembling a set of bookshelves, a man with AA membership. So, there was no point in getting all bitter and resentful about Smith and his seemingly obscene good luck. He just needed to rise to the level of the competition. Surely a girl would rather a fabulously successful artist type than a fabulously successful banker type.

He'd been in touch with his 'mentor', Philippe, who had unexpectedly been pleasantly surprised to hear from him after so many months. They'd discussed the future, the market, the prevailing stars, his past work, his state of mind, and Ralph had left feeling nicely needed and worth while and itching to get the cast off his wrist so he could start painting again. He'd made another, less eventful trip to his studio and pottered around for a while, clearing out the cobwebs and rat droppings, throwing out dead-bristled brushes and dried-up tubes of paint, familiarizing himself with the draughty old shit-hole.

Less is more, he'd decided, and he'd backed off from Jem in the two weeks since his accident, spending more time with his friends, even when he knew that Jem was going to be on her own in the flat, deliberately forgetting about the chilli plants in the airing cupboard, dispensing with the constant flower-buying and compliments. And the more he backed off, he'd been gratified to note, the more she came to him. Part of that was to do with guilt, he realized that. She still blamed herself for the bike accident and fussed around him like a delightful little hen, making sure he was comfortable, fetching him things from the kitchen, cooking for him. But she was missing the rapport they'd developed, it was obvious – she'd talk to him about the chilli plants, give him progress reports, like a sad mother to an absent father who needed reminding about the welfare of his children. She took up his flower-buying role and brought home unusual chillies she'd discovered in food halls and Asian supermarkets.

Once Ralph had established that Jem cared, truly cared, it was time to put step two of Operation Mature and Available into practice: finish with Claudia. And now this remarkable opportunity had arisen, Smith, away, for a whole weekend, two whole days. He didn't know what was going to happen but he knew something would. Definitely. He could feel it in his water.

Jem could feel something in her water, too. Ever since the day of the accident she hadn't experienced a moment's peace. She had spent the last fortnight battling with feelings she'd never encountered before. Jem had always been so solidly sensible in love, a serial monogamist, as they called them these days, two years here, a year there, all nice blokes and clean breaks.

Despite the fact that for one reason or another Jem usually ended up breaking men's hearts, it wasn't because she was cruel or unkind or had anything against men. She didn't *want* to hurt them, she just had to sometimes. She'd never been unfaithful and, as far as she knew, no one had ever been unfaithful to her. She'd never had a 'bad' relationship, just relationships that didn't work out because men wanted more than she could give. She wasn't one of those girls who was constantly attracted to the wrong sort of man, who suffered from unrequited love, who couldn't commit or who 'loved too much'. She'd never had a passionate love affair with someone, been consumed with desire. She'd never experienced irresistible lust. She'd loved, or at least been fond of everyone she'd ever been out with, and they'd loved her back. All her relationships had been strong learning experiences, passing the time until the right man came along. And now, when finally she thought the right man *had* come along, and she was happy and could see a long-term future ahead of her with Smith, she was suddenly feeling horribly attracted to someone else. To Ralph. It was utterly ridiculous. This wasn't how she operated.

Jem wasn't stupid, she could read people like books, had always been able to, and it was quite obvious that Ralph was attracted to her, too. It was touching, the way he'd been so pleased when she'd congratulated him on his choice of flowers that he'd gone out and bought them every week, and the way he was always making nice comments about her clothes, and that he was happy just to hang around the flat with her when Smith was out and chat about things which were 'their' things now, like chillies and music and recipes. She'd ignored the signs at first, put it down to vanity on her behalf. Why would Ralph, with his penchant for willowy, upper-class blondes, be interested in her? She was imagining it, paying herself compliments. But then there'd been that peculiar morning, the morning of the accident, and she'd found herself behaving quite outrageously by her standards. She knew he'd been titillated by the shortness of her T-shirt and she'd been conscious of the fact that she wasn't wearing any knickers; she had known, deep down, that he'd deliberately asked her to reach for items from the top cupboard so that he could look at her bottom. She'd been wickedly happy to oblige, titillated by his titillation.

She hadn't been fully aware of any of this at the time, of course. People never really are. Jem believed that very few people were as calculating as other people assumed them to be when they did something wrong. Things *did* just happen, and it was only afterwards that you could look back and see the points at which you allowed yourself to lose control, to make the wrong decision, to behave badly. Ralph's interest in her made her feel good, and she couldn't ignore it. She'd been ashamed of herself when she'd experienced a flutter of excitement at the prospect of spending a weekend alone with him. But nothing, absolutely nothing, of any description, shape, size or form was going to happen this weekend, or ever for that matter. *Nothing. No way. Never.*

His announcement tonight about Claudia had unleashed a whole new set of unwelcome emotions. He was free, he was available. Jem had no idea why this was important, but the moment he'd told her her stomach had done a backward flip and triple pike. She was pleased because over the two and a half months she'd been living at Almanac Road she'd become very fond of Ralph and wanted him to be happy, not henpecked by a dissatisfied, uptight, walking nightmare; she was pleased that he at last appeared to be taking his life in hand. But there was also a part of her that was pleased just because he was single, because he was no longer with someone else. And then she'd made that remark about finding him someone to fall in love with, and a strange feeling had overcome her, for a second she'd felt awkward and uncomfortable. Stupid, really. After all, she wasn't in love with him, she was just day-dreaming; she was in love with Smith and that was that. She was flattered by Ralph, fond of him, cared about him. But she was *not* in love with him. And he was not in love with her.

'What are you doing tonight?' she asked him abruptly, to diffuse the peculiar mood that had descended on her. 'Your first night of freedom,' she added, finally getting to her feet.

'Not a lot,' he replied. 'I was going to stay in and do a bit of sketching, now that my wrist's stopped hurting so much.'

Jem looked down at his bandaged wrist and started laughing.

'What's so funny?!' asked Ralph, laughing too.

'I just thought of something.'

'What?' said Ralph, smiling widely.

'I just thought, you sure chose a bad time to finish with Claudia! No sex and now no wanking! You're going to get pretty frustrated!'

Ralph looked down at his impotent right hand as well, and a look of dismay came over his face. 'Shit,' he muttered, 'I hadn't thought of that. Supposed to be good for you, though, isn't it?' he added, brightening. 'A bit of abstinence, holding on to your seed. Good for the mind and soul. Still . . . shit . . .'

Jem continued to laugh at the look on Ralph's face. 'Looks like it's the old hoover attachment for you, then,' she cackled, slapping her thighs with her hands.

Ralph winced.

'Come out with us tonight, Ralph, we're only going down

the Falcon. Come on, it'll take your mind off your predicament!'

'Who's "we"?'

'Oh, just some friends. It's Becky's birthday, it'll probably be quite a big group.'

Ralph quickly weighed up the pros and cons: night in alone *v.* night out with Jem. 'OK. When do we have to be there?'

Ralph rolled a spliff for the walk, using some grass he'd just acquired from a friend of a friend.

'I don't know what this is like,' he said, pinching it out of the bag between his fingertips, 'but it was fucking expensive and it smells amazing.'

'Looks like skunk,' said Jem. 'Go easy on it.'

'Nah,' said Ralph, smiling wickedly and piling it on to the Rizlas with the abandon of a man who has a brand-new bag of weed.

They took the spliff and a can of lager, wrapped themselves up in as many clothes as possible and began the freezing walk down St John's Road, smoking as they walked. Halfway down they both suddenly realized that they were completely stoned.

'Shit,' said Jem, 'I'm wasted.'

'Me, too,' agreed Ralph. 'That's completely taken me out.'

'I told you to go easy on it!'

St John's Road was empty and gaudy, brash chain stores twinkling with fairy lights and sale banners, the occasional group of revellers passing them drunkenly in swaying bands. It was the last weekend before Christmas.

They walked up to the traffic lights giggling at their

predicament, quickly finishing the lager, finding a bin for the empty can. St John's Hill was busier, chilly commuters still pouring out of Clapham Junction station clutching Blockbuster Video cases and hoping they weren't too late to make it to Marks and Spencers. They crossed the road and pushed open the door to the Falcon and were greeted by a blast of warmth and Oasis and loud male talk, accented by the occasional shard of female laughter. The huge U-shaped pub, replete with traditional Victorian fixtures and fittings, was packed, and they had to push their way to the bar.

'I'll get these,' said Jem. 'What do you want?'

She stood on the foot rail to gain a few inches and leant into the bar, years of experience teaching her that this was her only chance of being served at a busy bar lined with tall men, smiling at the barmaid, who was serving someone else – barmaids always served girls first.

'Two pints of Löwenbräu, please,' she shouted, when it was her turn.

They took their drinks and Ralph followed Jem while she manoeuvred her small frame through clusters of office workers in suits and skirts, circles of friends in jumpers and jeans, scanning the room for a familiar face.

Eventually, the glimmer of recognition, the raised hand, the introductions, the sea of strange faces and barrage of instantly forgotten names, the echoing question, 'Where's Smith?', the quizzical looks, the friendly handshakes, the gradual separation of the group back into the individual conversations which had been momentarily halted by their arrival.

'Jem tells me you're an artist.'

Oh, God. Ralph turned to face the architect of this

dreadful opener, a lanky young man with an agreeably lop-sided face wearing a *Reservoir Dogs* T-shirt and drinking a pint of cloudy bitter that looked like it contained frog spawn.

'Um, well, sort of . . . lapsed, you could say, but trying.' He managed a snigger and looked down into his glass before taking a large gulp.

'Actually, I'm a sort of artist, too – sort of,' replied Reservoir Dogs, unfazed by Ralph's lack of interest. 'I'm a graphic designer; Jem tells me you do a bit of that, on the old Mac.' He was grinning and wriggling with excitement as he spoke, and Ralph knew what was coming: 'You know, I think Macs are finally coming into their own . . .'

And he was off. Ralph died inside. He loved computers but he hated talking about them. And he was stoned. So stoned. It was all he could do to keep up with what Reservoir Dogs was saying, let alone think of one single response that wouldn't make him sound like he'd just landed in a time machine from the year 3000 BC. It was loud; the music was so loud, he kept asking Reservoir Dogs to repeat himself and then wondering why he'd bothered. He'd lost the ability to make eye contact. He glanced across at Jem every now and then, and she would glance back from the conversation she was conducting with an unattractive girl with a squandered bosom, and he could tell that she was having a hard time too. He smiled, he chuckled, if the intonation of Reservoir Dogs's voice suggested that that was appropriate, he nodded agreement, he shook his head with disapproval, he said 'Yeah, I know' a lot. But he didn't have the first idea what the man was talking about and he didn't care. He had to get away, this was a nightmare. He finished his pint; he'd only had it for ten minutes.

'Can I get you a drink?' he asked, affecting an angled glass with his empty hand in case his voice got lost in the atmosphere.

'Yeah – thanks. I'll have a pint of Parson's Codpiece please.'

Ralph made his way gratefully to the bar. This was such a bad idea. Why had he loaded that spliff? He was a paranoid, twitching, nervous wreck. The vibrant pub was electric with colours and movement and noise. He felt like he was walking on a moving carousel and everyone, but everyone was looking at him. He wanted to go home.

'How you doing?'

He turned around. Oh, thank God. It was Jem. 'I'm completely fucked, I can't cope. Who *is* that bloke? He's so weird.'

'What – Gordy?! He's not weird, he's lovely – that's just you being stoned.'

'How are you doing?'

'Oh, I'm fucked too. I've been trying to talk to Becky but I've got no idea what she's talking about, and I can't take my eyes off her tits.'

'I don't blame you – better than looking at her face!'

Jem hit him with mock indignation and then laughed.

'Listen, Jem, d'you mind if I go after these drinks? This really is not a good night for me to meet a bunch of new people.'

'This is not even a good night to be with a group of really close friends. I'll come with you.'

They took their drinks back to the crowd. Gordy

slapped Ralph on the back: 'Thanks mate, nice one.' They had strange disjointed conversations with people with overexpressive faces and booming voices, concentrating hard to keep up, losing the thread, worried that they had HOPELESSLY STONED written all over their blank, uncomprehending faces. They finished their beers, made their excuses, pushed their way back through the crowd, '*Mega Mega White Thing,*' clouds of smoke, faces, backs, voices, shouting 'Excuse me, please, excuse me,' '*Lager Lager Lager,*' until they reached the doors, opened them and, as the last few bars of Underworld died away, emerged into the cool, beautiful, empty silence.

'Aaaaaaaaah!' they both exhaled in unison.

'Nightmare,' said Ralph.

'Shit,' said Jem, adjusting her furry wrap and putting on her gloves. 'OK, I need to be somewhere very quiet and very mellow where I don't have to talk to anyone I don't know . . .'

'Shall we go home?' asked Ralph, blowing coils of steamy breath into his hands.

'No, come on, let's turn this to our advantage. Let's go into town and have a really weird time. Let's pretend to be German tourists and go to all those places we don't normally touch with a bargepole. Come on. Look! There's a number 19: it's an omen, quick!' She grabbed his hand and they ran towards the bus stop on Falcon Road. They leapt on to the platform just as it began to pull away.

20

They started in Piccadilly Circus, and for the first time in their lives they sat with the tourists under Eros. A duo of African drummers provided a suitably irregular soundtrack as they sat and watched the lights of Piccadilly from, they both agreed, a far superior vantage point to the more well-trodden areas. They wandered in zombie-like awe around the Trocadero, blinking at the harsh illumination, gawping at the peculiar array of shops. They took a ride on the Emaginator and screamed themselves hoarse as they careered down bottomless pits and around blind corners at a million miles an hour. They walked up Gerrard Street, a street that Jem walked down every day of her life, which in her current state of mind took on the air of a film set filled with a cast of weird and wonderful extras. London was alive; it smelt of Christmas. Everywhere they went they were filled with wonder. What a fascinating city, what an interesting shop, look at that person, look at that restaurant, those noodles look good. The world was full of colour and activity and sound and music and the most remarkable people.

They went into the Chinese supermarket and wandered up and down the aisles for ages, oohing and aahing over packets of all sorts of God Knows What. Jem's friendly Mancunian butcher was there.

'Hello, Jem,' he said.

'Oh, hello, Pete!' she replied. 'Don't you ever get a day off?'

'Nah, I love it, don't I? Can't get enough of touching raw meat and playing with offal.'

He was just finishing up, they were about to close, and he only lived just up the road. He invited them back to his flat for a beer and a smoke. This evening was becoming more and more bizarre.

He lived in a flat over the Hong Kong bank. It belonged to his boss, the manager of the supermarket and, by the sound of it, most of Chinatown. Pete would not be drawn on the subject of Triads, but Jem and Ralph had reached their own conclusions. It wasn't the smartest of flats, the stairway overwhelmed by camel high-gloss paint and tan shaggy carpets with shiny track-marks, the furniture in the high-ceilinged living room obviously expensive but sparse and tasteless.

They followed Pete down a cavernous hallway, papered with beige bamboo-design paper and lit by grimy faux-candle wall-lights. He pushed open a white plywood door at the end.

'This is my boudoir,' he announced proudly.

Ralph and Jem laughed out loud. The room was huge, three large sash windows framing the bright lights of Gerrard Street outside, the changing colours bouncing off the mirrored walls and ceiling. But it was the bed that had really made them laugh. It was at least eight foot square and topped by an enormous arched bedhead which looked like the console on the *Starship Enterprise,* with flashing white lights and an abundance of knobs and switches.

'Shit,' said Ralph, 'have you got a licence for that thing?'

'Wild, isn't it?' laughed Pete. 'D'you fancy a ride?'

Ralph and Jem looked at each other. It had suddenly occurred to them that they were in a strange butcher's flat late on a Friday night and he was getting undressed and inviting them on to his potentially perverted bed.

Pete sensed their unease. 'It's not mine, you know,' he smiled, 'it's my boss's. This is his Shag Palace, like – it's where he brings his birds. Come on. I'm totally sound. I promise ya. It's just a laugh.'

He leapt on to the bed and it wobbled like a fat girl's stomach.

'It's a water-bed!' Jem shrieked with delight. 'I've always wanted to go on a water-bed!'

'Well, now's your chance – get your shoes off.'

She threw her shoes aside, joined him on the bed and began to bounce around a little. 'Come on, Ralph,' she called, 'this is fun! Get on.'

Ralph still wasn't sure. He was feeling less stoned than earlier but he was still nervous, a bit edgy. Maybe there was a gang of twisted psychotic fetishists hiding in the mirrored wardrobes that lined the walls. Maybe this Pete guy regularly brought gullible strangers back to his sick flat so that he and his mates could have a bit of fun. Maybe they were Triads. Maybe it was part of the deal for living in his boss's flat. He scanned the room for video cameras, shackles, handcuffs, lengths of rope, torture implements. All he could see was a thousand reflections of the strange tableau of him and Jem and the butcher and a kaleidoscope of coloured lights. He was totally weirded out.

'Um, nah. I'm all right, thanks,' he muttered, shoving his hands into his coat pockets and stepping nervously from one foot to the other.

'Suit yourself,' said the butcher.

'What do all these buttons do?' asked Jem.

He smiled and hit a knob. The bed started to vibrate. He hit another one. The bed undulated like a belly dancer. He flicked a switch and the lights started to flash and the bed began to play music. A tray popped out of the flush console bearing a gold pot of cigarettes, an inbuilt lighter and an ashtray. Another panel opened to reveal a shelf of miniature gin bottles and two tumblers.

'This is the best one, though,' said Pete, fiddling with a joystick.

With a gentle hydraulic hum, the bed lifted itself a few inches off the ground and slowly turned on its axis through 180 degrees until it faced the other way.

'Wow!' laughed Jem.

'Isn't it great!' agreed Pete 'And this is *my* secret compartment.' Another panel lifted to reveal a small wooden box. He brought it out, opened it and gave it to Jem. It was a stash box full of Rizlas and cardboard and a large lump of black. 'Help yourself. I'm going to have a quick wash and a shave – I'm going out later. Make yourselves at home on the bed and I'll be back in a mo.'

He closed the door behind him and Jem peered around the bedhead at Ralph, who was still standing on the same spot.

'You all right?' she asked.

'No, actually I'm totally freaked. What are we doing here? This is really dangerous, you know – he could be anyone. There could be anyone here.' He moved across the room and began to open and close the mirrored doors.

'What on earth are you doing, Ralph?' asked Jem, getting off the bed and walking towards him.

'I'm just checking, that's all,' he replied, a little embarrassed by his own paranoid behaviour.

Jem crossed her arms and looked at him, smiling fondly.

'What?' he demanded gruffly. 'What are you smiling at?'

'You.'

'Why?'

'Because you're sweet.'

'Oh, stop it.' But a small smile had started twitching at the edge of his lips.

'Come here,' she held out her arms, still smiling.

Ralph's stomach flipped. She wanted to give him a hug! He moved shyly towards her, his smile now almost fully formed. She was tiny in her bare feet. Her hair was falling down. Radiohead played 'Creep' quietly in the background. The lights on the bedhead flickered in rhythm. The room was dark but alive with light and colour. It seemed to spin around them. He would never forget this moment.

He wrapped his arms around Jem's neck. He wanted to say something but he didn't want to talk. She wrapped her arms around his waist. They squeezed each other tightly. She stood on her tiptoes and buried her head in his chest. It was the best hug of Ralph's life. The moment was magical, enchanted. She smelt like happiness. She felt like happiness. If only, if only she was free, free to lift her head up and offer him her ripe, red sweet mouth . . .

'Ralph . . .'

'Um?'

'D'you remember that morning, the morning of the accident?'

'Uh-hum.'

'When we were in the kitchen and I was going to tell you something?'

They separated and held each other's hands.

'Yes.' Finally. He had known it would only be a matter of time before she remembered that unfinished business.

'Well, I just wanted to say . . .'

'Yes.'

'I just wanted to say that I think you're very special . . .'

So fucking special.

'. . . and that I'm very, very glad to know you and that . . . that . . . well, whoever you finally fall in love with is going to be a very lucky girl. I really enjoy being with you and I feel very close to you – very close. I hope you feel the same way.'

Ralph smiled and squeezed Jem's hands. 'Oh, God, oh, yes, I really do. Really, really. I . . . I . . . I . . .' Was it the moment? Was this the time to come clean, to tell Jem that he was hopelessly in love with her? 'I . . . I . . .'

'What?' urged Jem. 'Spit it out!'

He exhaled. 'Nothing – nothing. I'm very glad to know you, too, that's all. I think you're extremely special, too. Smith's a very lucky bloke.' He laughed nervously. No, it wasn't the right moment. Not yet.

Jem kissed him on the cheek and leapt on to the bed again. 'Come on!' she grinned, 'chill out. This is one of life's great surreal experiences – don't miss out on it!'

He smiled, finally relenting to the spirit of the night, unlaced his shoes and joined her on the bed.

'It's your fault if we get gang-raped and hacked to pieces by twenty-two Triads with machetes and stainless-steel dildos, though.'

Jem made them a spliff and they sat on the gently bob-bing bed watching Chinatown from the window, feeling like they were on the deck of a huge white yacht moored in the middle of Soho. Pete came back into the room with a handful of lagers and they passed him the spliff.

'What a place to live,' said Jem, cracking open her can. 'Something to tell your grandchildren about.'

'Too right,' he said, inhaling. 'But it's got its draw-backs. I have to be out of here in seconds if the man wants to bring a whore back. And then I have to change the sheets afterwards. And if I want to chuck in the job – bang goes the flat. But you're right, it's a real experience.' He wandered towards one of the wardrobes, rustled around for a few moments and came back clutching hangers.

They watched him slip into a pair of flat-fronted purple jacquard trousers, a silk lilac-patterned shirt with a mon-strous collar and enormous flapping double cuffs, a fat orange satin tie and a black frock-coat with preposterous lapels.

'So,' he said, giving them a twirl, 'whaddaya think? Cool or what?'

'Incredible,' said Jem, stunned by the transformation. He looked amazing. He looked like a pop star. 'You look amazing,' she said, 'you look like a pop star.'

'Thank you,' he said, smiling happily. Jem had obviously

said the right thing. 'This is all vintage stuff, you know – collectors' items. I get it all from a stall at Greenwich market,' he said, clipping on enormous diamond-studded cuff-links. 'Here, do you two fancy coming out for a boogie? I'm going to Nemesis, it's just around the corner,' he added, noting the blank expressions on their faces. 'It's a really nice place, not pretentious or anything.'

Ralph and Jem looked at each other. They both knew that the other didn't really fancy it and shook their heads.

'Nah, thanks, Pete. Not really dressed for it, are we?' Jem said, looking at Ralph.

'Thanks anyway, mate,' said Ralph, who had finally satisfied himself that Pete wasn't about to make them the grizzly victims of a butchering that would have hardened Soho detectives turning green and throwing up into their hands. Psychopathic murderers just *didn't* wear silk lilac shirts and diamond cuff-links.

Pete stood at the mirror, adjusted his sideburns, tweaked his hair and straightened his cuffs. He offered them his flat for the night as he wouldn't be back till mid-morning. When they declined, he insisted they take a spliff for the road and a couple more beers.

'Any time,' he said, 'any time you're round here, just come and see me at the supermarket or this place, and we can go out for a drink next time.'

'Do you always let strangers into your flat?' asked Ralph.

Pete snorted. 'Of course, mate. There's no adventure in life if you don't trust people, is there? No experiences. I work hard, I play hard, and if I die tomorrow, at least it would be better than ending up like me dad. Hates change, complains if they alter the layout in Tesco's or if *Countdown* starts five minutes late. Doesn't trust anyone, thinks everyone's out to get him. He's never been to London, let alone out the country. How I see it is like this: Some people have like, a travel-bug thing, don't they? Want to go to Thailand and Africa and have adventures and wear shit clothes and carry all their stuff around in a fucking great bag on their back.' He shook his head and grimaced. 'Not me. I can have all the adventures I want right here. You've just got to have the right attitude. Look where we are – the greatest city in the world . . . all the people in the world are right here. Poor people living in dog-shit and second-hand clothes, rich people driving cars that cost as much as houses, artists, bankers, models, drug dealers, the ugliest people in the world, the most beautiful people in the world, Cambodians, Swedes, Nicaraguans, Israelis, Ghanaians, Portuguese. Go to Stamford Hill and look at the Hassidic Jews there, that's an adventure. Rich Americans in St John's Wood, or South Kensington. Japanese in Finchley Central. Arabs on the Edgware Road. Irish in Kilburn. Greek Cypriots in Finsbury Park. Turks in Turnpike Lane. Portuguese in Westbourne Park. But I love it. I'm open to anything that comes along in this city.

'Ninety-nine per cent of the people in this city wander around in a little bubble. Like you, Jem. I see you at least twice a week and we have a little chat, and I can tell you're a really nice girl and that you've got a bit of spirit, like, a bit of adventure, but you were still too scared to take it any further, weren't you? We'd reached our little London point of contact, you were comfortable with that and if it hadn't been for tonight we would have gone on like that for eternity.

'Nah – life's too short to live in Beckenham and lock your door every night when you get off the six-fifteen, not to let strangers into your flat. See you two, tonight, I bet you never thought you'd end up on an eight-foot water-bed watching some butcher getting tarted up for the night. I bet you're glad you did though, arntcha?' He laughed.

'Ever seen that film *After Hours* about that straight guy who follows Rosanna Arquette into downtown New York and ends up stranded in the middle of the night with no money and meets all these weirdos and freaks? Now, some people might have watched that film and thought, Oh, God, what a nightmare, I hope nothing like that ever happens to me. Not me. That's what I want my life to be like, every day – *After Hours*. I always think of it like this: You're walking down the street and you pass a phone booth. The phone's ringing. Now, there are two kinds of people, people who think, Don't want to get involved, and walk on by, and people who are curious, nosy, and want to answer it. Chances are it's a wrong number. But there's always a chance you could be getting involved in some mysterious rendezvous, a lover's tryst, anything. A phone ringing on the street – it could be anything. It could be the start of a film, like, or a book' – he paused for effect – 'I love it!' He looked at his watch and slapped his thighs. 'Anyway, enough of me philosophizing, I've got some partying to do.'

They followed him down the dreary stairwell and back into the bright, multicoloured mayhem of Chinatown.

'If I don't see you before, Happy Christmas and all that – have a good one,' said Pete, shivering a little in the icy midnight air.

He gave Jem a kiss on the cheek. He leant into Ralph's ear as they shook hands.

'Lucky man, Ralph,' he whispered, 'very lucky man.'

Ralph almost corrected him, almost said, 'Oh no, she's not my girlfriend,' but stopped himself. He wanted Pete to think he was a lucky man; he wanted Pete to think he had something special.

And then he went. Jem and Ralph stood where they were, not quite sure what to do next that wouldn't feel like an anticlimax after their rather peculiar experience and Pete's closing inspirational philosophy.

'Gosh,' said Jem.

'Indeed,' said Ralph.

'Food, then?' said Jem.

'Guess so,' said Ralph.

Jem's face suddenly lit up with a wicked smile. 'Come on,' she grabbed his hand, 'can we just do something before we eat – there's something I've always wanted to do.'

Ralph shrugged, smiled and followed her.

21

A fat Mexican in a sombrero played panpipes by the pagoda phone boxes, watched and appreciated by no one. Restaurants closed down for the night, scrawny men in grubby overalls wheeled large bins of leftovers into the street. Two drunk drag queens in feather boas and Baby Jane make-up passed them noisily and disappeared into a bar above the Chinese barbers' with red velvet curtains at the window and fairy lights around the door. A couple stood outside the Dive Bar lost in a neverending kiss.

They crossed Shaftesbury Avenue, weaving through the perpetual traffic jam and crowds of coated, scarved and hatted people.

'Where're we going?' asked Ralph.

'Just you wait!' smirked Jem.

They turned left from Greek Street into Old Compton Street, Ralph peering as inconspicuously as possible into the steamed windows of chrome-and-glass gay bars, into a world he had no place in, an exclusive world. Funny, he thought, how the word 'exclusive' had come to mean chic, fashionable, private, select, when what it really meant was that you weren't allowed in, you were excluded. It was quite a horrible word really.

Right and left into Brewer Street.

'Here,' said Jem, stopping outside a darkened shop with beaded curtains at the doorway and an amateur window display filled with sun-bleached packaging and nasty nylon underwear. A sign in the window proclaimed WE SELL POPPERS. A grotesque mannequin with chipped skin like a horrific burns victim sported a leather basque and brandished a whip in arthritic fingers. Unfeasible dildos stood side by side on a shelf, like suspects in a police line-up.

'Here?' asked Ralph, his voice betraying a little middle-class disapproval. 'What for?'

'Just for the hell of it, of course, I've never been in a sex shop before.' She was excited, a bit nervous. 'Come on,' she urged.

They entered the shop together, trying to look blasé, as if they often browsed around Soho sex shops on a Friday night. A statuesque woman with backcombed black nylon hair down to her thighs, wearing more black eyeliner than the average woman would apply in a lifetime and a tight leather dress that must have required the removal of at least a couple of ribs glanced up at them with a look of practised disinterest and then continued to read the vintage comic she had spread open on the counter in front of her. Her skin was a dead, matt white which appeared to have been sprayed on with an aerosol can. She looked like she might have fangs.

A large Black guy in a T-shirt and jeans stood silently by the door, his hands clasped in front of him, his legs a couple of feet apart. Security. At the far end of the shop an unlikely couple browsed through a rail of French-maid outfits and Miss Whiplash leather ensembles. She was tall, young, perfectly blonde, expensively dressed; she would have looked fantastic on a large black horse in a pair of jodhpurs and a hairnet. He was small, old, powerfully bald, expensively dressed; he would have looked intimidating at the head of a huge corporate boardroom table. Maybe not such an unlikely couple. They'd done this before. There was no humour between them as they quietly discussed the preposterous pieces of shoddy nylon and PVC which hung like oversized dolls' clothes from cheap plastic hangers – this was a business transaction. What were they? Boss and secretary, client and high-class whore, husband and second wife? Maybe she was his daughter's best friend at boarding school? Another couple stood and examined the video racks. He was fat and unkempt. So was she. Again no humour. They might have been browsing through the reference section of the local library.

The shop was silent, there was no music, no television, just the reverent, businesslike hum of muted embarrassment. This was not what Jem had expected.

She wandered towards the video display and the fat couple moved a little to the left to give her some space. She picked up a box. A shocked-looking peroxide blonde with a mouth like a vagina squeezed her dome-like breasts together while a faceless, torsoless, armless man pinned beneath her penetrated her anally and another man who appeared to have only a two-foot penis and a fabulous head of hair impaled her from the front. No wonder she looked shocked. Jem put the box down. She surveyed the display of extraordinary leather and chrome bondage accessories that hung from the ceiling like carcasses in a butcher's window. Masks, hoods, cuffs, straps, whips and chains, implements for hanging someone from the ceiling, tying them to the bed, gagging them, constraining them, contorting them, whipping them. An all-in-one, head-to-toe PVC bodysuit with a barely sufficient mouth-slit straddled the wall. It looked uncomfortable, sweaty.

Jem walked towards Ralph, who was flicking through a magazine filled with badly photographed images of men and women looking uncomfortable and sweaty in similar erotic garb.

'I'm going to buy a vibrator,' she whispered to him, cupping his ear with her hand.

'What?!' he exclaimed, almost silently.

The vibrators were located in the glass-fronted cabinet which served as a counter to the vampire woman with the comic. Jem felt a little uncomfortable as she eyed the selection, trying to look expert, trying not to look self-conscious under the stagnant aura of the bizarre shop assistant. She wasn't sure what she was looking for. Did she want a sixteen-inch shiny black one or a discreet, cream, handbag-sized model? She beckoned to Ralph, who put back his copy of *House of Correction* monthly and crouched down next to her in front of the cabinet.

'What d'you think?' she whispered.

Ralph shrugged. He felt like the unwilling boyfriend in a clothes shop on a Saturday afternoon. This was girl's stuff – how was he supposed to know? He was feeling awkward. He'd been inside a sex shop before, of course he had. With his mates, when he was younger, for a laugh, to buy poppers, leer over dirty magazines. But this was different, very different. Now his head was full of images – Jem on her unmade bed, lying on her Chinese-dragon dressing-gown, her knickers around her ankles, her skirt hitched up, knees apart, applying her new vibrator to herself. Oh, God, it was fantastic. But he didn't want to think those things about her; as erotic and exciting as the image was, he didn't want it in his head. He wanted the hug in Pete's bedroom in his head. He wanted the subtly erotic image of Jem's bare toes smeared with mustard in his head, the barely there glimpse of her soft white bottom. He wanted her face, open, smiling, bright and joyful. He wanted to imagine them together, in the future, in love, laughing, making love, taking their dog for a walk.

He looked down at her smiling face, the tip of her nose pink and pinched, her eyes looking brightly and fondly at him, and the unwanted image disappeared. This was Jem, gorgeous, lovely, wonderful, angelic Jem. He didn't want to be like Smith. He didn't want to be a fusty old stick-in-the-mud. She was asking him to be open-minded, to go with the flow. He smiled and turned to eye the display.

'I mean, I don't suppose it really matters how big it is, as long as it vibrates – unless you want to stick it inside you, of course,' he offered helpfully.

'That's true,' whispered Jem thoughtfully. 'I don't think I want a black one, or one with veins. They're a bit vulgar, aren't they?'

'Yeah,' agreed Ralph. 'I think you should just go for a cheapo one. There's no point in spending a lot of money.'

'Hmm. What about attachments?' she asked, gesturing to the pop-up tongues, cactus-like probosces, alien plastic fingers and fierce nodulated rubber balls.

'Nah,' said Ralph, warming to the subject now that he was no longer embarrassed, 'just gimmicks, waste of money. That's a good one,' he said, pointing to an innocuous slim cream model with no veins, helmet, tongue, balls or inadequate pulsing movement, 'and it's only £7.99. I'd go for that one.'

'OK,' said Jem, getting to her feet, wishing suddenly that they were available in boxes on shelves, like in a supermarket, so she wouldn't have to ask the frightening androidal creature above her to get her one. She took a deep breath and forced herself to be brave. This was like having a smear test. Unpleasant for the recipient but all in a day's work for the administerer. Old Morticia must have seen all sorts – a nice middle-class girl buying an inoffensive vibrator on a Friday night would be nothing to her. The girl looked like she'd had a frontal lobotomy anyway.

'Can I have one of those, please?' she asked, as confidently as she could in such a low voice.

Morticia leant down to see where Jem was pointing, unlocked a cabinet behind her, took out a box, opened it, showed the contents to Jem, waited for her to nod approval, put it back in the box, put the box in a white plastic bag, took the ten-pound note from Jem's hand, handed her two pounds and a penny and a receipt and carried on reading her comic. The whole transaction took place in deathly silence.

'Thank you very much,' said Jem, reeling as she heard her nice home counties voice and good manners resonate inappropriately around the hushed shop.

The black security guard remained waxwork-still as they passed him at the door. Ralph held back the clacking beads for Jem and they stepped out into the street, relieved that it hadn't suddenly turned into a strange, uninhabited ghost town, that there were still normal-looking people milling around the streets, queuing for night-clubs, waiting on corners for non-existent cabs to take them home.

They walked back towards Lisle Street and enjoyed an MSG-rich meal of crispy beef and chilli, chicken in chilli-and-black-bean sauce and Kung Po chilli pork in a near-empty restaurant, under the watchful gaze of a bored young waitress who had appeared thoroughly confused by their request for their food to be 'extra spicy' and was now observing them curiously for signs of spontaneous combustion or insanity while they chatted about Pete and the sex shop and their strange evening.

'What Pete said just now, before we left – it really made me think you know,' Jem said, pouring the remains of a Tsingtao lager into her glass, 'about adventure, and trusting people and everything. He's right, you know. I like to think of myself as a bit of a "free spirit" ' – she fashioned the quote marks out of the air with her fingers – 'I like to think I'm up for anything, open to adventure. But Pete was right. Everyone in this city is scared, aren't they? There are lots of weirdos out there, but I don't suppose many of them are likely to kill you or kidnap you, are they?

'It's like, d'you ever walk past people in a train station, say, or walking down the street, a group of friends meeting up, talking about their other friends – "Oh, how's so and so?" – talking about their lives, and you can tell they're quite close, known each other for a while, shared experiences? D'you ever get a twinge like maybe you're missing out on something? Like, how come their paths crossed and ours didn't, maybe they're great people but I'll never get to know them? I'm just a stranger on the street to them, I've got my own friends, my own shared experiences with

218

other people who *they'll* never know. And it just seems sort of sad. D'you know what I mean? So many people in this world and the law of averages says that you can only ever get to know such a tiny percentage of them. And fear means that you'll get to know even less. Why are we so scared of each other? Someone at work invites you over for dinner and you're filled with horror, you bump into an old friend on the train, they suggest going out for a drink, you swap numbers and then pray they won't call you, you've got your nice safe circle of friends, your Tuesday friend, your Thursday friend, your weekend friends, you've got your night in on a Monday, your gym night on a Wednesday, and all of a sudden you haven't got any room left for anyone new. Is that what God intended? Is that right? Surely we're all living point nought nought nought nought one per cent of our potential lives. I'm only twenty-seven – what am I going to be like when I'm fifty? Don't you think it's sad?'

'I think you're being a little rose-tinted about the whole issue, to be honest, Jem. Friends are an investment, they're not always easy. It's not always fun and laughter and super shared experiences. Friends have needs, problems, demands, insecurities, expectations, and in order to be a good friend you have to at least try to satisfy all of those things as well as enjoying the good times. I just don't think it's possible to offer that sort of relationship to everyone you pass on the street. I think we're forced to be selective, to take just a couple of chocolates out of the box and leave a few strawberry creams and hazelnut whirls for someone else.'

'Ah,' said Jem, enjoying Ralph's analogy, 'but who gets the montelimar?'

Ralph smiled. 'I think the montelimars end up working in Soho sex shops and going home to an empty flat covered in bat droppings.' He picked up the bill that the eagle-eyed waitress had prematurely planted on their table.

'Yeah, I suppose I'm being a little idealistic. Friends can be a pain. They can be demanding and hard work. But maybe that's because they're the wrong friends. I read a quote once, can't remember who by, but they said that your friends aren't necessarily the people you like the best, they're just the people who got there first. You spend your whole life searching for the right partner but maybe you settle for your friends too soon and then just make do for the rest of your life, never knowing what you're missing out on. Oh, I don't know,' she sighed, resting her head on her hands and smiling at Ralph across the table, 'maybe I'm talking complete crap. I just feel . . . Pete's just made me feel like I'm missing out, like I'm not living properly. I'm grieving for all the strangers I've never known!' She turned the bill around on its saucer to have a look at the total.

'Pete's one in a million,' said Ralph, 'it just isn't possible for everyone to be like that. We really would be in trouble if they were – human nature couldn't support that level of openness, there's too many of us, we're not equipped for it. We've evolved like this for a reason: survival, the most basic of all human instincts, adapted to living in a city with eight million other people. It makes sense.' Ralph peeled a ten-pound note from his wallet.

'I guess I've just always been the sort of person that can't bear to feel they're missing out on anything. If I've got a choice of two parties to go to I'm always convinced

I've chosen the naff one and the one I missed is going to be the party that people will be talking about for years to come. Grass is always greener sort of thing . . .'

She stopped abruptly and they looked at each other. There was a moment's silence. Jem stopped fiddling with her napkin.

'Does that apply to your relationships, too?' asked Ralph, semi-flirtatiously, semi-seriously.

'Not usually,' Jem said, looking down at her hands and examining them nervously.

'Not usually?' Ralph stared at the top of her head. 'So, sometimes?'

The atmosphere was suddenly deliciously awkward.

'Yes, sometimes,' Jem lifted her head slightly and smiled behind her hand.

Ralph could feel that they were clinging on to the precipice by their fingernails – one more millimetre and they'd be there, falling. He couldn't blow it now, couldn't say the wrong thing. He took a deep breath and waited to see if she'd say anything more. She didn't. They stared at each other, breathlessly, across the table. She opened her mouth, lowered her eyes. Ralph's heart stopped beating. Still she didn't say anything. His turn.

'When?' he asked gently. Jump, Jem, he thought, I'll catch you. It'll be fine. Just jump, please, let go . . .

Jem pleated her napkin into a fan. 'Oh, just sometimes – not usually.'

'So, you have felt that the grass was greener while you were in a relationship? Was it? Greener?'

The waitress removed their bill and two ten-pound notes without either one of them noticing.

Jem shrugged and carried on pleating. 'I don't know.'

'You never found out?' Ralph was fishing.

Jem stopped pleating and looked up at him.

'No,' she said, 'I haven't found out. Shall we go?' She got up abruptly from her seat, which lost its footing and fell backwards. She flustered and tried to pick it up but got her bag tangled on the table leg. Ralph helped her untangle herself and straighten the chair. They stood inches from each other. Jem awkwardly adjusted the strap of her bag on her shoulder. She looked up at Ralph. He was gazing at her with an intensity that made her glance away immediately.

'Excuse me,' she said, making a pointless effort to get past him.

Ralph took her shoulders and looked into her eyes. 'You haven't yet – that's what you said. Do you think you might find out? Ever? In the future? Maybe?'

Please say yes, Jem, please, for the love of God, say yes.

'No,' she lowered her eyes, 'I don't think so. It doesn't work like that does it?'

'You mean Smith?' said Ralph.

'No, I don't mean Smith. We're not talking about Smith, are we? We're talking hypothetically here.'

'Oh, right – I see,' Ralph felt himself shrinking. 'Cross wires!' He attempted a small laugh. Fucking Smith. 'Guess we'd better go. Let's see if we can find a cab.'

Neither of them had allowed the atmosphere to linger. The conversation, as blatant, as explicit as it had seemed at the time, seemed more and more ambiguous as it receded into memory.

They took a deft U-turn in the conversation as they sat

in the back of the heated cab and watched early-hours London flash by in a multicoloured series of twinkling vignettes. By the time they got home they were friends again. But it was a rather poor patch-up job, a temporary fix, because they both knew deep inside that they hadn't imagined the conversation – there were no cross wires.

Ralph lay in bed that night, flat on his back, his duvet up to his chin, his hands clasped together underneath on his chest, staring at the ceiling. He was tired but he didn't want to close his eyes. If he did his head would fill with images, images that hurt too much now. Images of a parallel universe in which he had brought home the peonies, had made more of an effort, hadn't gone to bed first on that fateful evening, had taken more care over his career, his destiny, a parallel universe in which Jem had made the right decision, had chosen him. Tonight had been one of the best nights of his life. He'd never had such fun with a girl before, never had such adventures. The whole night had been like a film – magical, surreal, wonderful. And he was more in love with Jem than ever before.

A tear formed, he blinked and it ran down the side of his nose. She'd said no, it wasn't going to happen. He'd never felt so sad in his life.

'Morning, Jem,' chirruped Stella.

'Morning, Stella,' Jem replied.

'New jacket?'

'No – very old jacket, actually.' Maybe Stella was finally beginning to exhaust her repertoire of compliments.

'It's lovely – it suits you. How was your weekend? How's your poor flatmate?'

'Oh, he's much better now. The bruising's gone down, his wrist's starting to heal – the doctors reckon there won't be any lasting damage.'

'Oh, good, good. That's marvellous news. My auntie Kate broke her wrist – it never healed, gave her pain for the rest of her life, she was never able to use it again, but then, she was eighty-two, I suppose, and old bones are so weak. Like my mother's hip – she broke one hip and had to have it replaced, waited three years for that operation, dreadful NHS, and then her knee went and she had to wait another two years to have that replaced, she walked like a duck after that, waddle, waddle, waddle, and . . .'

Jem's thoughts began to wander, as they did on the rare occasions that Stella talked about her own life. They wandered back to her weekend, such a strange, but wonderful weekend. It had been magic, their night in Soho. And then there'd been that big, plump moment of awkwardness in the Chinese restaurant, when they'd nearly . . . oh, God.

They'd been so close to going to a place that Jem didn't want to visit. Ever.

Jem's feelings were all over the place and she suddenly found herself subconsciously making mental pro and con lists:

Smith: sweet, generous, handsome, peonies, her friends liked him, she liked his friends, good job, lots of money, nice flat, reliable, affectionate, easy to be with, man in her dream?

Ralph: sweet, generous, handsome, sexy, stacks in common, great sense of humour, easy to talk to, always in a good mood, creative, passionate, vulnerable, potential for *After Hours* living, man in her dream?

Smith: a bit restrained, tendency to moodiness, not very adventurous in bed, predictable, likes kormas, thinks girls should drink dry white wine, not creative, introverted, settled, no potential for *After Hours* living.

Ralph: unstable career (but he *was* trying), bad taste in women (but he *had* finished with Claudia), oversexed (no, she crossed that one off her mental list) . . . she racked her mind for more cons . . . longjohns (no, he didn't wear those any more) . . .

Jem shuddered slightly, trying to shake the thoughts out of her head. Stella had finished her catalogue of OAP joint-replacement stories and Jarvis, her boss, had arrived in a flurry of paper and camp complaining. 'Oh, Jemmy, darling, please, please can I relieve myself on your desk – I'm desperate,' he whined, dropping a thick folder in front of her. 'It's that repugnant Scots witch, she's in full broomstick mode – wants me to negotiate another 5 per cent for her from Carlton for that dreadful quiz show. I ask you!

She's lucky anyone will hire her at all – face like a rhino's arsehole with piles. Could you, would you, Jemmy darling? I've got the hangover from Gomorrah and my back feels like Roy Castle's been tap-dancing on it all night in stilettos – thank you, thank you.' He blew her a kiss, disappeared into his office and fell asleep face down on his sofa.

Jem and Stella looked at each other and exchanged a small smile. Jem sighed and pulled open the folder. What a start to the week. She hated having to negotiate rates, especially with the people at Sin 'n' Win, who were notoriously tight with their budget. The phone saved her from having to contemplate this unpleasant job.

'Good morning, Smallhead Management,' she trilled in her silly phone-answering voice.

'Morning, Smallhead Management,' said a strange nasal voice, 'I've got quite a small head and it's a bit out of control at the moment and I was wondering if you could manage it for me. And, do you do big ears and fat ankles by any chance?'

Jem smiled and turned away from the office towards her desk.

'Ha ha ha, McLeary – funny boy, very, very funny.'

'Too quick for me, Ms Catterick, and how are you today?' He sounded terribly bouncy but just a little nervous, a slight breathlessness catching in the back of his throat.

'Not bad, not at all bad. How are you, and to what do I owe this delightful honour?' Her heart was pounding. This was Ralph, for God's sake, dear old Ralph. Why on earth was she feeling so . . . so . . . giddy?

'Oh, knackered, bored, miserable without you.' He produced a peculiar strangulated laugh that said he shouldn't have said that – that was the sort of thing you said to your girlfriend, not your flatmate, not your best mate's girlfriend.

'Not going to the studio today?' Jem replied, deliberately ignoring his last comment.

'Yeah, yeah,' he said, 'I'm here already. I've been here since nine o'clock. My fingers feel really supple today, I think I might be able to use them – give it a bash anyway.'

'That's the spirit.'

They were silent for a second, awkward, almost.

'And I just wanted to say, thank you – for the weekend – I really enjoyed myself.' Ralph cracked the silence.

'Yeah – it was good, wasn't it? I enjoyed myself too.'

'And I wondered if maybe . . .'

'Uh-huh . . .'

'. . . Well, there's this restaurant in Bayswater . . . and I know Smith's working late tonight . . . does the best jal frezi in town . . . and maybe . . . well, you're probably going out or maybe you fancy a night in, but if you fancied it we could meet up later . . . er . . .'

'Uh-huh . . .'

'It was just a thought. Nothing fancy, you know, just a curry . . . and . . . um . . .'

'OK.'

'Yeah?'

'Yeah, OK. What time?'

'Straight from work? Six-thirty maybe. I could meet you outside the Tube. Bayswater, not Queensway.'

'OK.'

'OK, then. Excellent. Well . . . have a good day and I'll, er, see you later, then.'

'Yeah, see you later. Work hard.'

'I will. You too. Bye, then.'

'Bye, then.'

'Bye.'

'Bye.'

Jem put the phone down. She needed to take a few deep breaths to bring her heartbeat back to normal human resting levels. Bloody hell. If she wasn't quite mistaken, Ralph had just asked her out on a date – and she'd accepted. This was it. The beginning of the end.

She ignored Stella's curious gaze and began fumbling through the folder on her desk.

Shit. What had she done? And why was she so bloody excited?

23

The tape recorder made a hissing noise, then a whirr, then a click. The room fell silent. Siobhan jumped slightly. She lifted her hand heavily to tuck her hair behind her ear. She put her head in her hands. She stood up. She paced the room. She sat down again. The clock said eight-thirty. She stood up. She squeezed at her temples and stared at the floor. A car pulled up outside. She went to the window and threw open the curtains. It wasn't him. She looked in the mirror, adjusted her hair and wiped away the deathly streaks of mascara that had formed under her eyes from the tears she'd cried. When she was hurt. Just before she got angry. A long time before she'd started hating him.

She searched through the debris on the floor for her hairbrush, pushing pieces of broken vinyl out of the way, lifting cushions off the floor and putting them back, peering under the up-ended Christmas tree and shattered picture frames. She found it in the hallway, where she'd thrown the contents of their 'bits and pieces' tray — the carpet glittered with multicoloured foreign coins and hairpins, plectrums and keys. She untangled her hair from its velvet elasticated band and began to comb it vigorously, till it gleamed and every strand was in place. She tied it back again, making sure there were no ridges or tangles in it, and smoothed it down with her hands. She felt calmer now.

Another car pulled up outside. It wasn't him. She paced the room again. Fucking bastard. Fucking smug Irish piece of shit. Cunt. Cunt cunt cunt cunt cunt. She was ready for him now. She stood at the window, waiting. She saw the dark-haired man and the girl from downstairs leave the basement flat clutching cans of lager and laughing. Out for a normal Friday night – lucky them.

Come home, you bastard, come home, you bastard.

She tapped her fingernails on the windowsill. Come home.

Finally, the familiar rumble of the old Embassy. She watched him slowing down, looking for a parking space, not finding one – good – reversing back down the road with his chin on his shoulder and his arm over the passenger seat, into the space in one smooth movement – he'd always been a very good parker – reaching into the back seat to pull out his briefcase and a carrier bag from the off-licence, locking the door, striding up Almanac Road. Look at him, she thought, just look at him. Who the fuck does he think he is? Prick. Oh, yes, skipping up the stairs now with a bounce in his step. Cunt. She remained where she stood by the window and waited for the sound of his key in the door.

'Hi.' Bastard.

Silence for a second and then his voice from the hallway.

'Shit. What's happened here? Shuv, where are you? Are you all right? What's this stuff doing all over the floor? Shuv? Shuv? Shit!' He walked into the living room and a tiny pink-glass bauble crunched under his foot. He took a step sideways and looked around the room in horror. 'Jesus

Christ, Shuv, what's happened?' He walked precariously towards her. 'Are you all right?' He reached out a hand to touch her arm. She jerked it away from her.

'Get your filthy hands off me. Don't you dare touch me!'

He backed off. 'Oh, Jesus, what's happened? Who did this? Has someone hurt you?'

Siobhan laughed bitterly. 'You could say that.'

'Who? Tell me.' He attempted to touch her again.

'It's you, you revolting piece of shit. Get off me!'

'Me?' asked Karl incredulously. 'How?'

'Yes – you! You'd love it if it was someone else, wouldn't you? Then you could get all angry and phone the police and roam the streets seeking revenge. But there's no one else to blame. I trashed the house and it's your fault, you fucking bastard.' She pushed him out of the way and stormed into the bedroom.

'What are you talking about? Shuv – please – talk to me.' He followed her through the hall and into the bedroom. 'What've I done wrong?'

Siobhan turned to face him. Her face was red with anger. She slowly lifted her head up to the ceiling and pointed above her with a finger. She put her other hand on her hip and stared at him.

'What!?' asked Karl in exasperation. What the hell was going on? This was insanity. All day long he'd been looking forward to coming home. It had been a hectic, problem-ridden day of hassle upon hassle, but at the end of the tunnel were Siobhan and Rosanne and the flat and a blissful weekend of relaxation and warmth and television and the pub. Not this. What was this?

'That!' she hissed, still pointing upwards, 'that's what

you've done wrong. That trashy little tart up there. In the office at the dance club, apparently . . .'

Karl's jaw dropped and his heart began to hammer against his ribcage. This could not be happening. Not now. His mind hurtled through a million possible responses in a couple of seconds. Denial? Admittance? Tears? How the hell did she know? Had he left something lying around the flat? No. It must have been that venomous little bitch. She must have told her. Why? Why now after so long?

'Are you going to say something or are you just going to stand there looking like a moron? You know what I'm talking about, don't you? You're not going to deny it, are you? I'd hate you even more than I already do if you did.' She folded her arms and regarded him with icy disdain.

Karl felt his stomach constrict and the contents swill around nauseatingly. He sat down heavily on the bed and exhaled a deep, painful breath. He had to find out how she knew.

'Shuv, oh, God, I . . . er . . . who told you?' He looked at her desperately.

'You did. You told me, you stupid fucking careless bastard. Here,' she said, turning to walk out of the room, 'wait here.'

Karl heard the sound of glass and vinyl crunching underfoot as Siobhan walked through the living room. He felt, like people he'd heard on talk shows and films say a thousand times before, as if his world was falling apart. He knew, without a shadow of a doubt, that this was the worst thing that had ever happened to him.

Siobhan returned a second later holding something small and silver in her hand: Rick's state-of-the-art tape recorder. Karl mentally rewound and fast-forwarded through his memories until he found what he was looking for. That night at the chapel, when Siobhan and Rick had gone outside, he and Tamsin. He heard Rick's voice in his head, word for word: 'This thing's brilliant, it tapes for six hours.' Siobhan rewound the tape a little and pressed Play – it was Tamsin's voice, shrill with bitterness and alcohol: *'you think no one knew about you and Cheri in the office at the dance club? Did you think we were all stupid?! Cheri told me all about it. All the sordid details. She told me about the abortion, too – your baby that she had to get rid of . . .'* He screwed his eyes closed. How stupid. Oh, God, how painfully stupid.

'OK, so now you know,' said Siobhan, waving the gadget at him. 'You fucking bastard.' She threw it on to the bed beside him. 'I want you to go, Karl. I want you to pack a bag, right now, this instant, and leave. I'm going to my mother's tomorrow. You can come and move back in then. I can't live under this roof any more, I can't share a roof with that whore. I don't want to talk about this and I don't ever, ever want to set eyes on you again.' She choked on her tears as she left the room, slamming the door behind her.

Karl sat numbly on the edge of the bed for a minute. This could not possibly be happening. His stomach churned and his head ached with tears that he was too shocked to set loose. This could not be happening. But it *was* happening. This was real. This was horribly, horribly real. He had to stop it!

He leapt to his feet and strode into the living room. Siobhan was sitting on the sofa, their new sofa, staring into space, Rosanne lying uncertainly across her lap, her eyes darting awkwardly around the room. Karl got down on to his knees and began to collect small shards of coloured glass and black vinyl.

'Leave it, Karl!'

'It's dangerous,' he whispered. 'Rosanne might hurt her paws.'

'I'll do it,' Siobhan snapped, 'after you've gone. Talking of which – can you please leave.' She wouldn't look at him.

'Siobhan – please – can't we talk about this . . . ?'

'Why on earth would I want to talk about this?! Listen to your excuses. Hear all the sordid details. It's pathetic. You're pathetic! Nothing means anything any more. Just go!'

'Oh, God, Siobhan! No! Please! Please don't do this! I love you. I need you. I . . .'

'Oh, stop it, for God's sake, stop it – you sound pathetic! Look, Karl, I mean it. I want you to go. I don't want to talk about it!'

Karl's face crumpled and he began to cry.

'Shuv – no!' He dragged himself on his knees to her feet and wrapped his arms around her legs, his whole body quaking with silent sobs. 'No . . . no! I won't go . . . it was nothing, it was a mistake, it was crap, rubbish, I was stupid, I was weak. It was . . . all a huge mistake. I'm so sorry, so sorry . . .'

The sight of Karl prostrate at her feet, crying, opened Siobhan up. It broke through the cold hard shell she'd been determined to wear, and she started to cry too. 'I trusted you. I always trusted you. I asked you about her, remember, in Scotland? And you made me feel like a silly little girl. How could you?! I was honest with you, about Rick. Why couldn't you be honest with me too? That's what really hurts. The lies. The dirty, ugly, stinking lies. You made a mistake. I made a mistake. Why couldn't you admit it? And why, Karl – why did you do it? Because I was fat, that's why! "Oh, no, Shuv, you're beautiful, I love you whatever size you are." Bollocks! You lied to me! You must have thought I was so fucking stupid. I hate you, Karl, I hate you so much!' Tears flowed down her face and her shoulders heaved up and down. Karl gripped her legs even tighter and cried even harder.

'I'm so sorry. I'm so sorry! Oh, God – what have I done?'

'Ruined everything, that's what you've done, you stupid cunt.' The unfamiliar word felt like poison spilling from her lips. 'Ruined absolutely everything.'

For a few moments they sat stock-still, Karl still wrapped around Siobhan's legs, crying so deeply and painfully that neither of them could talk. Rosanne looked from one of them to the other, her dark eyes full of concern and confusion. She whimpered quietly and snuffled at the top of Karl's head. Karl raised his head and looked up at her. He kissed the top of her head. He caught Siobhan's eye, the first eye contact they'd had since he'd got home. He knew what to do. His face brightened slightly. He took Siobhan's hand.

'It doesn't have to be ruined, Shuv. We can work on it. We're strong enough. We can get through this. Other couples couldn't. We're not like other couples. We're special, we can get through this. I'll do anything it takes – anything. I'll move out for a while if that's what you want. But please, let's fight for it. We can't give up on this because of something so ... so ... stupid. If we gave up it would be the most tragic thing imaginable, we'd regret it for ever – please.' He squeezed her hand tightly and looked up at her pleadingly. 'Imagine it, Shuv. Us, not being together. Me, on my own here. You, somewhere else. Not together. Imagine what it would really be like. Imagine it. We can't do it, we can't let that happen to us – can we?'

Siobhan looked down at him in her lap. She couldn't imagine it. It filled her with dread and pain. But she couldn't imagine making it work again either. She didn't trust him any more. He'd had sex with their neighbour, impregnated her, he'd lied to her, he wasn't the man she'd thought he was, the honest George Washington, incapable of telling a lie. How many other lies had there been? She would become an insecure wreck, worrying constantly when he was out of her sight, like one of those women she'd always pitied. She'd go through his jacket pockets, interrogate him about his activities, sniff the air for perfume when he came in from work, steam open suspicious-looking mail, eavesdrop on his telephone conversations, look for his love, his attention, all the time. She didn't want to become like that. She couldn't live with someone she didn't trust. She'd rather be alone for the rest of her life. She looked away from Karl's intense gaze and withdrew her hand from his. Every muscle in his body was taut with anticipation. She shook her head sadly.

'No,' she said quietly, 'it's too late. It's over.'

Karl wailed. 'No! Please, God, no! Don't say that. It's not over, it'll never be over. We're soul mates. We have to be together, Siobhan, we just have to!'

She pushed him gently off her lap and stood up heavily.

'I don't trust you any more, Karl. I can't live with someone I don't trust. Now, please, I beg of you, pack a bag and go. If you really care about me you'll go. Please!'

Very slowly, Karl got to his feet. 'Tomorrow,' he sighed, 'I'll go tomorrow.' Siobhan shook her head again. He walked numbly to the bedroom while Siobhan waited in the living room, listening to the desolate sounds of cupboard doors opening and shutting, drawers being slid back and forth, the zipper being pulled open around the circumference of Karl's suitcase, and then pulled shut again. The saddest sounds she'd ever heard in her life. Her tears ran silently.

Karl stood slackly in the doorway, weighed down by his suitcase and his misery. Siobhan wanted to ask him where he was going but didn't let herself. That would be too caring, too personal, too . . . ordinary. She saw him for a second, as he'd looked skipping up the front steps just half an hour before, light-footed, ready for the weekend. In another world they'd be eating now, watching a video, drinking a bottle of wine, curled up together on the sofa, bathed in garish, twinkling reflections from the fairy lights on the Christmas tree they'd put up the weekend before. They'd discuss his show like they did every evening and Siobhan would tell him how the wedding plans were progressing. One of them would take Rosanne out for a walk and then they'd go to bed together, cuddle up in each other's arms for a while to get warm and fall asleep.

But this was a different world, a world in which she'd been bored in the afternoon and had found that little tape recorder of Rick's. She'd switched it on and enjoyed listening to it, laughing out loud to herself. Because she was cooking she hadn't switched it off at the end, she left it playing. And then everything had gone psychedelic. She'd thought it was a joke at first, Tamsin and Karl messing around together, so she'd rewound it and played it again. And then she was sick, physically sick, shivering and gasping and heaving over the toilet bowl. She'd splashed her face with cold water and the shock woke up the anger in her and she'd gone insane for quarter of an hour, destroying their home. This was the world she was in now. This was reality, Karl standing in the doorway with a suitcase about to leave home. The tears kept coming.

'I'll phone you later,' he said quietly.

'No,' she said. 'No. Don't phone me.'

'I'll phone you later,' he repeated. Rosanne jumped off the sofa and walked up to Karl. He crouched to hug her, muttering tear-stained farewells into her soft ears, and then he stood up, looked at Siobhan and walked out of the front door. The slam echoed around the barren flat.

Siobhan walked slowly to the window and watched him unlock the boot of the little black car, swing the suitcase in and then manoeuvre himself into the front seat before starting the engine and driving away.

As his car passed the window he slowed down and looked up at the flat. Their eyes met for less than a second and a look of unbearable intense pain passed between them. The Embassy made a small, bloodcurdling screech before disappearing from view and out of Almanac Road.

24

Ralph checked the clock on the bare white walls of his studio for the hundredth time that hour. It was 5.18. Time to go, nearly. Well, if he took his time, dawdled a bit, he could probably leave now. It wouldn't matter if he got to Bayswater a bit early; it was a nice evening, he could wait outside the station. And that way, if Jem got there early, too, they'd have longer together.

He switched off the little radio, put it in his rucksack, picked up his jumper and coat from the chair by the blow-heater where he'd been warming them up, threw them on hastily, turned off the light and locked the doors behind him.

The concrete corridor was cold and filled with the clackety-clack of interlock machines from the dressmaker's studio next to his and muted drum 'n' bass coming from her CD player. He took the steps two at a time out into the dark courtyard, past Murray, the permanently stoned security guard, and into the bleak, traffic-infested thoroughfare of Cable Street.

Another wasted day. Another totally wasted day. He hadn't even picked up a brush. He'd spent the first hour pacing the studio, getting up the nerve to go to the payphone down the corridor and phone Jem. And then, when he'd finally done it, he'd spent the rest of the day pacing the studio in anticipation, watching the minutes die slowly on the studio clock, his stomach clenched tight in a knot of excitement, fear and dread. Shit. He didn't know what the hell to do, how to handle it. His loyalties were split asunder.

Smith, you arsehole, you stupid, stupid fucker. Why did you have to tell me? And that was the irony of the whole situation. Smith had told Ralph because Ralph was Smith's best friend – who else was he going to tell? And since Jem had moved in, that was something that Ralph had almost forgotten. For the last three months he hadn't seen Smith as his mate any more, his best buddy. He was his rival, his opponent. He was the person who was getting in the way of his dreams and his destiny, the person who stood between him and happiness. Ralph had forgotten, forgotten that, first and foremost, before Jem, before nearly everything else, Smith was his best friend. He'd felt bad about it – but not as bad as he'd felt about Smith's pathetic little outburst of childish excitement when he had got back from his team-building weekend the night before.

Smith had been edgy from the moment he'd got back to the flat on Sunday night, overanimated, overblown, loud and irritating, going on and on about his weekend. Jem had gone to have a bath. Smith had waited until he heard the bathroom door bang shut and then leant towards Ralph conspiratorially.

'It's happened!' he'd said, his face almost splitting at the seams with delight and excitement.

'What's happened?'

'Finally, finally!' continued Smith, oblivious to Ralph's lack of comprehension, 'I knew it. Didn't I tell you? Didn't

I tell you!' He punched Ralph playfully on the thigh and grinned at him like the Cheshire Cat.

'Spit it out, Smith, for Christ's sake. What the hell are you going on about?'

'Cheri, of course! Cheri!' He was rocking back and forth. '*Ma Cheri amour*! Ha!'

'What? What are you talking about?'

'Well, Ralph, my friend. My patience has paid off. It is, as they say, in the bag. Tonight I bumped into the glorious Ms Dixon outside Sloane Square Tube station. Uh-huh! We shared the bus stop for a while and we just chatted . . . like you do.' He raised his eyebrows mock-nonchalantly and then broke back into a ludicrous smile. 'Can you believe it? Me and Cheri. Just chatting! I didn't stutter, stammer, grimace, drop anything, break anything, sweat or trip over. We . . . just . . . chatted. Ha! And she is *only* about three hundred and eighty-five times more beautiful when you're talking to her than when you just glimpse her in passing. God! It was amazing. Anyway, we waited ages for a bus, just chatting, as I said, and then I suggested we go for a quick drink at Oriel to warm up and then maybe get a cab a bit later. Cool, or what?! So we did. I asked her what she wanted and she ordered a bottle of wine. A whole bottle! So I knew she wasn't just being polite – she'd have ordered a tomato juice or something then, wouldn't she? And she is just unbelievably nice, you know – really, she is. I know you think she's a snooty cow but she isn't at all. Oh, Jesus, Ralph. She is beautiful. She is *so* beautiful. I have never seen skin like that in my life. And her hands are perfection and her hair is like . . . like . . .'

Ralph had been momentarily speechless. He'd breathed

in deeply as he felt his heart fill with a mixture of joy and horror. Smith still loved Cheri! In spite of Jem, in spite of everything. This was wonderful news. But it was terrible news, too. Poor Jem. She didn't deserve this. As much as he wanted Smith and Jem to split up, as much he wanted her for himself, he couldn't bear the thought of her being treated so badly by anyone.

'Oh, my God, Smith. I thought this was all over. I thought you were over this. What the fuck are you playing at?' He'd eyed Smith with horror and disgust.

'I thought I was, too. I thought it was over. But then I saw her tonight and . . . and, well, God. She's just so beautiful. And I can talk to her, Ralph. I can really talk to her . . .'

'But what about Jem? You can talk to Jem, too. I've never met a woman as easy to talk to as Jem . . .'

'Oh, yeah. I know that. But Jem's Jem and Cheri is something completely different . . .'

'What, Smith? What *is* Cheri? What the fuck is going on here?'

'OK. OK. Keep your undies on. Look. I don't know. I don't know, all right!' Smith had put his head in his hands. 'Christ – talk about pissing on a bloke's fireworks. Jeez . . .'

'Look, Smith. I am not here to piss on your fireworks. I'm here to point out to you that you have a girlfriend. Remember? Jem? Sweet, trusting, loyal, faithful, loving Jem? Christ . . .' He looked away, revolted. 'So,' he sighed resignedly, 'what happened next?'

Smith brightened a little and sat up straighter. 'Well, so, we were in Oriel, chatting, drinking wine, just getting on, really. And she was telling me all about herself, about how she used to have loads of lovers, but now she's got rid of them all because – and get this – she's looking for Mr Right! Is that amazing, or what! She's basically cleared the decks for the right man. It's got to be, hasn't it? It's got to be me! I've waited five years, I've wanted that woman for *five years*, I've dreamed about her, I've thought about her, I've even . . . Shit, I've even imagined her when I've been in bed with Jem . . .'

Ralph wrinkled his face in distaste. 'You really are a cunt, aren't you?'

'Jem was just all a big part of the way things panned out. Jem took my mind off Cheri for long enough for my obsession to shrink to a manageable size, so that when Cheri was ready for me, I wouldn't blow it. D'you see? It's all timing. It's destiny.'

'I thought you didn't believe in all that.'

'I don't . . . I didn't. I do now. I didn't believe in Jem's destiny, but I believe in my own. This is it, Ralph. This is it!'

'This is *what*?! Will you please tell me what the fuck is going on? You have a drink with the girl from upstairs, she tells you she's not going out with anyone at the moment and you're already making plans for the future. I mean – *what*?' He shrugged and held up his hands in frustration. 'You're just going to dump Jem, are you? Just throw her away like a used tissue?'

'Fuck, Ralph – I can't believe you're reacting like this! I thought you'd be pleased, excited for me. You know how long I've been in love with that woman, you know the hell I've been through. Christ, before Jem came along I hadn't had sex for five years. Five years! Do you have any idea what that feels like? Jem's been great for me, really great. She's brought me out of myself, reminded me about shared physicality, about sharing everything. And, no, I'm not going to dump her. Not yet, anyway. It's still early days for me and Cheri. I've got to earn her trust. Just because *I* know we're meant for each other, it doesn't mean that she'll know. No, I've got to take it slowly . . .'

'. . . and meanwhile, you'll just tag good ol' Jem along for the ride, will you? Smith, I'm horrified. I am horrified and I am disgusted by you. In fact, I am so disgusted by you that I can no longer talk to you.' Ralph stood up and looked down at his friend. 'Jem is just about the best person I have ever known – no, actually, she *is* the best person I have ever known, and I refuse to sit here and allow you to treat her like this. I'm going to tell her, and I'm going to tell her now!'

Smith leapt to his feet. 'Don't you fucking dare! Don't you fucking *dare*! One word, just one word leaves your lips and you're homeless, mate' – his face was millimetres from Ralph's – 'and I mean that. *One word,* and you're out of here. You're my mate, Ralph,' he said, running his fingers through his hair, 'and I hope you'll always be my mate. But mates stick together, don't they? They don't take sides with girls. You've known me for fifteen years. You've known Jem for fifteen minutes. It's your choice. OK? But don't think I wouldn't do it. Because I would.'

He'd picked up the remote control, then, stretched his legs out on to the coffee table and switched on the telly.

Ralph had looked at him there on the sofa in his rumpled suit and tie, his blandly handsome face bare of feeling, and wondered for one stupefied moment how a girl as perceptive, wise and reasonable as Jem had ever thought that an emotional cabbage like Smith could be the right man for her, the man she'd been dreaming about since she was sixteen.

Ralph quietly and sadly left the room, and headed straight for his bedroom.

He hadn't got a wink of sleep that night. His emotions were all over the place. Excitement, because he knew something that would put a speedy end to Jem's silly infatuation with Smith. Frustration, because to tell her would be apocalyptic. Feelings of hypocrisy, because he was no angel himself. He felt sorry for Smith because he was an arsehole, and he felt sorry for Jem because Smith was making a fool of her. In a way, this was all his dreams come true, confirmation of everything he'd always thought – that Smith was not worthy of Jem and her unconditional love. Confirmation that Smith didn't deserve a girl like Jem.

He tossed and turned and turned and tossed, his emotions going around in his head like marbles in a tumble-drier, and then he'd got up early, before Jem and Smith, and made his heavy-hearted way to the studio. He still hadn't decided what he wanted to say when he'd phoned Jem, he just knew that he had to talk to her. They'd had such a wonderful weekend together and, despite the scene the night before with Smith, he didn't want to break the spell.

And now he was standing on the dreary platform of Limehouse DLR station, waiting impatiently for a rare sighting of a train, his mind still in total and utter pandemonium, wondering what the hell to do. Should he? Shouldn't he? The complete devastation if he did. Smith would know it was him who'd told Jem and would throw him out of the flat. But then, he'd had a free ride for long enough now. Smith was going to settle down with someone at some point, whether it was Cheri, Jem or anyone else, and he'd be out on his ear then anyway.

Maybe it was about time he learned to stand on his own two feet, stopped using Smith as a security blanket. But he'd have lost a friend, his best friend. Did that matter any more? He was vaguely surprised to feel a twinge of pain in his heart when he contemplated it. But it was nothing like the enormous spear of agony that pierced right through the fibre of his being when he imagined losing Jem; that really would be the greatest loss imaginable. Maybe Jem would hate him for telling her, for dismantling her happiness and taking apart her dreams. Maybe she'd take out her anger at Smith on him, direct her hurt and her disappointment at him. That would be the worst-case scenario – then he'd have lost everything.

He realized that the safest possible alternative was to say nothing. Smith was a slimebag, he'd proved it now, and the best decision all round would be to say nothing, bide his time, capitalize on his wonderful relationship with Jem and then be there for her, help her to pick up the pieces when it all came tumbling down, as it was bound to, at some point in the future.

But that was the problem – the vagueness of that concept: 'some point in the future'. What sort of way was that to live a life, waiting for your best friend to break your true love's heart before you could claim your destiny, before you could be happy? And, in any case, maybe all this bullshit about Cheri would come to nothing and Smith would keep Jem hanging on in second place for the rest of their lives. Maybe he'd fuck up in ten years' time when he and Jem had four children and a house in the country and invited Ralph over for dinner once or twice a year because they felt sorry for him. No. He couldn't let that happen. He didn't want to be staring wistfully and meaningfully at Jem over the dinner table when he was forty, still resenting Smith.

A train finally slunk apologetically into view, and Ralph boarded it, too grateful for the warmth to feel angry about the wait.

And then there was the matter of personal morals. In some people's books, and maybe in Jem's, reading someone else's diaries would be perceived as being on a heinous par with infidelity. Did he really have any right to moralize about Smith's actions? Did he have any right to unload Smith's secret on to Jem without coming clean about his own sneaky, dishonest behaviour? Not really. But how could he do that? How could he tell Jem in one short sitting that (a) her boyfriend had been fantasizing about an unattainable woman he'd been in love with for five years while he was in bed with her, (b) her flatmate had been reading her diaries and snooping in her room for the best part of three months and (c) aforementioned flatmate was hopelessly, passionately and devotedly in love with her and wanted to spend the rest of his living days with her. And how're you finding your jal frezi, by the way? Shit.

As he made his way towards the Circle line, he was no closer to deciding what to do. Every option seemed to offer nothing but down-sides – not an up-side or a fringe benefit in sight. Where was the option that resulted in Jem realizing she was madly in love with Ralph, leaving Smith without telling him why and everyone living happily ever after? Non-existent, that was where.

He'd have to play it by ear. See how he felt when he was

sitting there in the restaurant, with Jem. Maybe she had her suspicions, you never know. Then he would only be confirming what she already knew, not maliciously sabotaging Smith's life. Yes, that's what he'd do. Plan nothing, decide nothing, Play It By Ear . . .

The Tube finally arrived at Bayswater station and he tumbled off and up the stairs towards the bright lights and open-all-hours bazaar atmosphere of Queensway above. Jem wasn't there yet. He glanced around him for a clock – it was six twenty-three. He stood at the lip of the station, his hands deep in his pockets, his nose starting to run slightly in the cold night air, brusquely dismissing thoughts from his head as they entered, chanting mantra-like to himself, *Play It By Ear, Play It By Ear.*

An old woman in the opposite corner to him was muttering obscenities to herself and slowly hitching up yards and yards of filthy grey skirt. He looked away, embarrassed, but then couldn't resist a quick look back. She was showing him her prune-like, hairless fanny and smiling at him through blackened, wizened teeth. 'That's what you want, innit darlin'?' she was chuntering. Ralph looked away again. How disgusting . . .

Queensway never slept, but that was because no one English lived there – it was all company lets and pay-by-the-week hotels, Australians and Arabs and Africans, big-screen sports pubs, all-night coffee shops, noisy restaurants, and the sound of loud foreign chatter everywhere you went. It always felt vaguely like being on holiday when you were in Queensway. Not the place for cocoa and slippers and *Coronation Street* with your shepherd's pie.

Ralph glanced at the clock again, careful not to attract

248

the attention of the repugnant female flasher still standing across from him and now, he suspected, urinating down the wall. It was six twenty-nine.

Play It By Ear. Play It By Ear.

'Who's your mate?'

Ralph spun around as he heard a soft female voice centimetres from his ear. It was Jem.

'Oh, shit. Thank God. It's you. I thought it was my knickerless friend over there.'

'Lovely, isn't she! Has she shown you her fanny yet?'

They began to walk.

'So, how was your day?' Jem asked.

'Oh, crap. Didn't get a thing done . . .'

'Oh, that's a shame. Why not?'

'Just had a lot on my mind, I guess.'

'Like what?'

'Oh, nothing much. You know, just stuff . . .'

'Anything you want to talk about?'

'Nah – not really – maybe. I may bend your ear yet.' Yes. That was good, Ralph thought. Lay the foundations for possibly discussing it later. 'How was your day?' He looked down and smiled at her. He loved that he had to look down to smile at her. It was so . . . so . . . beguiling . . .

'Dreadful, absolutely dreadful. The Monday from Hell. But far too boring to talk about. So, tell me about this jal frezi.'

They chatted as they walked, about curry, about this and that, about nothing. Ralph began to feel himself simmering to the surface like boiling milk, but he couldn't turn the heat down. He didn't want to make small talk. He didn't want to pretend that they were just friends. He didn't want to just go and have a curry with Jem and come home and watch Jem disappear into Smith's slimy, second-rate arms. He wanted . . . he wanted . . . *Play It By Ear,* he reminded himself, *Play It By Ear.* But it was no good. He was playing it by ear and his ear was telling him to do it, to take a risk with everything in his life, gamble the lot. Yes, please, Mr Croupier, I'll put it all on red, the limousines, the yacht and the house in Colorado . . .

He took a deep breath and then exhaled. They'd reached the restaurant. The abrupt change in atmosphere brought his temperature back down to a simmer for a few moments.

'Wow!' exclaimed Jem, 'what a place!'

Dozens of unsmiling waiters in skinny black trousers ran nimbly through a vast sea of tables, holding aloft huge silver platters filled with red, green, brown and creamy pink curries, and cushiony white naan breads like miniature moonscapes. Hundreds of loudly conversing diners sat framed by colonial murals in mint green and ice blue, between towering wrought-iron palm trees and under six-foot ceiling fans spinning desperately to keep the intense heat down.

A frenetic waiter showed them to their table, threw a pair of menus at them and disappeared without a smile.

'It's not the friendliest place in the world,' whispered Ralph, 'but just take a look at the prices.'

They discussed the menu, decided on their order, and within less than a second of them closing their menus the same wiry waiter was back, gruffly taking their order and disappearing quickly again. Their Cobra beers arrived in thirty seconds.

'Fast turnover,' Ralph laughed, suddenly realizing that he'd chosen a bad venue for a heart-to-heart – if you took longer than fifteen minutes in this place they sent waiting customers to hover over your table.

'Well,' said Jem, smiling up at Ralph over the top of her beer glass, 'this is very nice, isn't it?'

Ralph was slightly taken aback. He'd forgotten that this was very nice. He'd just been thinking of it as purgatory.

'Yes,' he said happily, 'I suppose it is – very nice indeed.'

'Um' – Jem looked away from Ralph and then back towards him – 'what's it . . . what's it in honour of?'

'What d'you mean?'

'It's just that – I hope you won't take this the wrong way – I kind of had the feeling, when you phoned this morning, to ask me about tonight, that you were . . . asking me out?'

'Really! What made you think that?' Ralph choked on his Cobra.

'Oh, I don't know. You just sounded sort of nervous and the conversation was a bit stilted. It just . . . reminded me of being asked out on a date. That's all,' she finished, waiting for a response.

The small talk was over.

'So' – Ralph rubbed his chin – 'let's get this straight. I phoned you, entirely innocently – bored, nothing better to do than phone boring old Jemima Catterick – invited you out for a curry, purely, of course, so I wouldn't have to sit here on my own, and you thought I was asking you out on a date. The cheek of it!'

'Oh, stop it!' laughed Jem.

'And then,' Ralph was getting into his stride now, 'and

then, having quite unbelievably mistakenly thought that I'd asked you out on a date, which is, of course, ridiculous, instead of saying "But, oh, Master Ralph Sir, I couldn't possibly, my heart belongs to another, you are a scoundrel and a cad," proceeded to accept what you had so brazenly misinterpreted as an invitation of an *amorous* nature and are here now, sitting at this table with me, *unescorted*!! What am I to make of this?'

'Oh, Ralph, you old git!' Jem was blushing furiously.

'I'm sorry,' Ralph laughed. 'Your face. It's a picture. You look so sweet.' He looked down at his large, long-fingered hands, now covering Jem's tiny white ones, and felt a glow in his stomach. They looked so right together, those hands. He wanted to see them together for the rest of his life. He caressed the side of Jem's hand with his thumb. She made no attempt to move it. 'Such tiny hands,' he murmured. He squeezed them and looked at Jem, giving her a slightly cheesy smile because it was all he could manage, and then looked down at their hands again. 'You were right.' He glanced at her shyly through his eyelashes. 'I *was* asking you out on a date earlier. It's true.' He smiled again and gave her a 'Caught me' look with raised eyebrows. 'I . . . we had such a great time at the weekend – it was . . . it was one of the best weekends of my life – honestly. And I wanted to see you again – away from the flat and from Smith and everything. I just . . . I just love being with you, Jem, I really do, and . . .' He gulped and looked quickly up at Jem, who was watching him with an expression of anticipation and warmth. He sat up straight and looked her in the eye. 'I hope you don't mind,' he finished, looking away again.

'Of course I don't mind,' replied Jem. 'I've told you

before, I love being with you, too. I know I've only known you for three months, but I already think of you as one of my best friends.'

'Oh, God, Jem, that's sweet. But it's not what I'm talking about. I'm talking about love. Real love. Not palsy-palsy love, not matey love. I *really, really* love being with you. I . . .' He faltered for a moment and felt a tingly sweat begin to break out on his brow as the floodgates opened. 'Oh, God, Jem. I love you. I've never said that to anyone before. But I mean it. I'm mad about you. I think you're the most wonderful person I've ever met. I think about you all the time and I can't pretend I don't feel this way any more. I'm jealous as hell of Smith for having you. I never really thought about love before, about the right woman, about settling down with one person. And then you moved in and at first . . . at first I didn't realize how special you were – you were just a flatmate I didn't really want. And then I got to know you, got used to having you around, and gradually started liking you more and more. And then one night I knew – the night we had the chilli challenge. I suddenly knew, without a doubt, that I was in love with you. Jem, we were destined to be together. We're right for each other. We fit. We would be the most special couple in the world, you know – magic, it's magic when we're together, haven't you noticed? I can't just be friends with you any more, Jem, d'you understand? I don't want you to like me as a friend. I want you to feel the same way about me as I do about you, and there are times . . . sometimes, when I think you already do.' He breathed out, a long, cool wonderful breath, full of relief and elation. He felt about ten stone lighter, the weight of the feelings and emotions he'd been hauling around with him for the last two months finally lifted from his soul.

'I also know that you've heard all this before. I know about Nick, and Jason, and the other ones. I know you've had enough declarations of love to last you a lifetime . . .'

'What!' Jem's eyes were saucers.

'. . . but I promise you, I'm not like that. I wouldn't want to change you, to control you. I want you exactly as you are now. So, if I don't hassle you and I don't bombard you with flowers and poems and love letters, it's not because I don't love you, it's because I do. D'you see?'

'What!? Rewind! How the hell do you know about Nick and . . . and Jason, and everyone?'

Ralph looked across at Jem's furious face and exhaled heavily. Oh what the hell, he thought. Nothing to lose now. May as well go for broke. He took a deep breath.

'Oh, God. Jem. Please don't overreact to this, please try to understand. This is going to sound dreadful, but . . . but . . . I read your diaries. I'm so sorry. I've been reading your diaries since the day you moved in. I mean, not just reading your diaries, it was more than that. I've spent hours sitting in your room, just breathing you in, just being among your things. I know everything about you. I know how ugly you felt when you were growing up, I know about all those lovesick boys, all those clingy, demanding men who tried to change you, tried to control you. I know everything about you and I think it's only fair that you know everything about me. I know it was wrong – I've never done it before, I promise you. I was just sort of . . . drawn to them . . . drawn to you. I know that sounds like bullshit, but it's true. And it made me feel so close to you. I wanted so much to feel close to you. I'm not good with intimacy, Jem. It was the only way I knew. I'm very, very, very sorry. Really I am. I'm so sorry, Jem.' He smiled nervously, his gorgeous, lop-sided, lazy smile, from left to right. 'Please, Jem – say something.' He held his breath and awaited her response.

Jem's face was puce. 'I can't believe it! I can't believe you read my diaries! That's . . . horrible! Christ, Ralph. I thought you were my friend! Well, look. You can forget about that, you can forget *all* about that. Friends don't destroy their friend's sense of privacy, friends don't snoop around their friend's personal things. It makes me feel sick just thinking about it . . .'

'Please . . . Jem . . . please try to understand . . .'

'No, Ralph. I don't understand. And from this day on, from this *moment* on, you and I are flatmates – nothing more, nothing less – no more curries, no more chat, no more anything. Just keep away from me and everything will be just fine. Let's just forget any of this ever happened – OK?!'

'No! Jem! Please! I don't want to forget this ever happened. I'm glad this happened. I *wanted* this to happen. Please – let's talk about this.'

'Ralph, didn't you hear what I said? No more. It's over. I want to go home. Let's get the bill.'

She leant down to pick up her handbag then, rustling around in it for her purse, her chest rising and falling violently with the effort of not crying. Her world was spinning around her head like a broken helicopter. She had never felt so confused in her entire life. She was angry, so angry, about Ralph reading her diary, snooping in her room. But she was feeling more than that. She could live with the idea of Ralph reading her diaries. She wasn't a secretive person, she had nothing to hide. It was a terrible thing for him to have done, but she could handle it. What she couldn't handle was the avalanche of feelings triggered by Ralph's declaration of love, his declaration of what, if she was honest with herself, she'd known all along. Ralph was in love with her! He'd laid his hand on the table, he'd let the cat out of the bag, and there were beans all over the bloody place. This was no longer a game. The situation was no longer under control. And she wished she could have laughed lightly, patted Ralph's hands and told him sweetly that she loved him too, but not in that way, that her heart and her destiny belonged to Smith, that she wanted nothing more from him than friendship. But she couldn't. Because it wasn't true.

Damn and blast and fuck it. She loved him. She loved Ralph. She loved the way he held his pint and his fag in the same hand. She loved that he watched *The Waltons* in bed every Sunday morning. She loved the way he always stopped to pet dogs he passed on the street. She loved the way he shouted at people on the telly he disagreed with. She loved his hands and his long bony feet. She loved his lazy smile and the way he started wheezing when he was hysterical with laughter. She loved the fact that she could say absolutely anything to him and he'd make a conversation out of it, no matter how silly or banal. She loved his fascination with the detail of life, how he always noticed a good sunset or an unusual cloud formation, a hidden gargoyle on the side of a building or a ladder in someone's tights. She loved the gap at the back of his mouth where he'd lost a tooth in a football match and she loved the little scar that ran into his hairline where he'd head-butted an amp by mistake at a Clash gig in 1979.

She loved him and now he loved her. They could be together, they could just hold hands, disappear into the sunset together and live happily ever after. They could love each other.

She looked up at him quickly. He was facing away from her, forlornly trying to attract the attention of a waiter She looked at the sweet V-shape of hair at the nape of his neck that she'd always wanted to touch, the defeated slump of his shoulders. He was adorable. Even as the adrenaline of anger flooded her body, even as she put a dam over her feelings towards him, she yearned to turn around and take him in her arms and kiss the living day-lights out of him. She loved him. She wanted him. She'd never even kissed him . . .

But she couldn't love him. She just couldn't. *What about Smith?* The floodgates snapped closed.

Ralph turned around and met her gaze.

'Jem . . .' he beseeched.

'No!' she snapped.

'Please . . .'

'No!'

They left the restaurant in a heavy cloud of silence, hailed a cab and went home, the atmosphere between them setting like cement as they drove.

25

Karl drove straight round to Tom and Debbie's that night, after Siobhan had kicked him out, and phoned her, repeatedly, every ten minutes, listening with disbelief to the sound of his own voice on the answerphone, informing him that he wasn't there, but that he could leave a message. Of course he wasn't fucking there!

The following day he tried her at her mother's, every half-hour, until Mrs McNamara had finally snapped and told him she'd call the police if he tried again; Siobhan did not want to talk to him. He couldn't really remember much about it all now, it was a big, black, drunken blur. He'd got himself to work somehow on Monday afternoon.

And that was when it happened – when everything changed.

He hadn't planned it at all. The last thing he'd been thinking about in the previous seventy-two or so hours was work, his show. But he was a DJ. He couldn't phone in sick. So he'd driven in, in a daze, his automatic pilot changing gears for him and looking out for traffic lights.

'You all right, mate?' his producer John had asked, as he stumbled blindly into the studio.

'Yeah, yeah.' Everything was different. His studio felt different. John seemed like a stranger. They went through the playlist. Funny, he thought, he was the DJ, he was the man who played the records, the man who played the songs with the lyrics that cut right through the heart-strings of the broken-hearted throughout London. How many times, he wondered, had he put on 'The Sun Ain't Gonna Shine Any More', and how many times had some poor, devastated, lonely fucker in an empty flat switched on his radio and heard it and felt the pain of loss even more greatly than before. He'd done that to people, without even realizing it. And now it was his turn. But he could control it, he could change the playlist. He could play the Spice Girls and 'I Will Survive' and 'Aga-fucking-doo' and keep it all at bay, all the pain. He could play God.

But he didn't want to. He would stick with the playlist and deal with the consequences. Who wanted to be God anyway?

He'd glanced through the list, viewing it for landmines, but he knew the emotions wouldn't hit him until he was listening to the song, till the lyrics were real in his ears.

'Are you sure you're OK?' asked John, again.

'Yeah, yeah.'

Why wasn't he feeling anything? He *wasn't* feeling anything. Just numbness and weirdness and emptiness. He didn't want to cry. He didn't want to run. He didn't want to be here. Things were just happening to him, words were coming from his mouth, his hands were moving, holding his cup of coffee, his legs crossed and uncrossed themselves, his eyes read and translated words for him, but he had nothing to do with any of it, it was all just happening. He wondered if his face might actually smile, if his throat might just laugh out loud. Probably.

'Mr Pitiful', Otis Redding: that was first up. He remembered that song. It was on a tape he'd made for Siobhan when they'd only just met. You know, how you used to, when you were too young to know who you really were so you'd make tapes for each other, a way of saying, 'This is me, this is who I am, this is what I like, and because I like you so much, I want you to like it, too,' before you had a job or a car or a flat or a history or a proper personality that could say all that for you. So he'd made her endless tapes, spent hours painstakingly picking through his record collection for just the right track, hours recording them on to C90 tapes he bulk-bought from Woolies. And then he'd handed them to her proudly, wanting her so much to love them, to love his music as much as he loved it. And she had. And that had made him love her even more than he already did . . .

The news was read, the weather forecast and the traffic reported. Karl's mind went blank. What was he supposed to say? What did he usually say? He had no recollection. He couldn't even remember what day it was, what month. The clock ticked down the seconds. Five . . . four . . . three . . . two . . . one. Karl's mouth was bone dry. His voice had vanished. His whole spiritual being had disappeared from sight. Karl had ceased to exist . . . His jingle ran, and then there was a minuscule moment of silence, magnified ten-thousand-fold by the number of people who heard it. John stared at him, bulgy-eyed, the studio assistant reached for the mike, ready to step in, and then, finally Karl opened his mouth.

'Good evening, London, you're tuned in to ALR, London's finest, and I'm Karl Kasparov. It's 3.30 p.m. and it's *Drivetime* here in the country's capital. Just three shopping days left till Christmas, so I've been told, and here's one of my favourite songs, for all you useless guys, just like me, who haven't bought a single gift. It's called . . . "Mr Pitiful".'

He slipped the cans from his ears and stared in wonderment around him. He hadn't given a single thought to what he was going to say when he went on the air, and then he'd managed that – it was second nature. John gave him the thumbs up, relieved. Karl was a pro. It was going to be all right.

And it was all right. For the next fifteen minutes or so, at least, he was quite amazingly good. He breezed through the link-ups; sailed through REM and the Manic Street Preachers; 'Oliver's Army' was a piece of piss; 'Respect' by Aretha, no problem; 'Wonderwall' didn't even come close to cracking his professional veneer. He had some on-air banter with John, drank his coffee, smiled and even laughed a little. He was just doing his show. He began to feel almost normal again.

And then . . . he wasn't expecting it, it wasn't one of his favourite songs, it didn't really remind him of Siobhan, or even of his youth: 'The Bitterest Pill', the Jam.

Something about the song tore right through his emotions. He loved the Jam. Siobhan had loved the Jam, too. And it was so true – this was the bitterest pill he'd ever had to swallow, the end of everything, the beginning of nothing. And it was all his fault. His mind filled involuntarily with images of Siobhan, smiling, laughing. His senses filled up with the smell of her and the sound of her.

And then he started crying. Slowly at first, tears just trickling down the side of his nose. He turned away from John and the rest of the team, wiped them away, took deep breaths. There were forty-five seconds left of the song. His breath came faster and faster, the tears thicker and thicker; thirteen seconds to go.

His body started to heave, and he suddenly realized that there was no way he was going to be able to stop the flow. John was talking to someone on the phone, the assistant had gone to the toilet, no one had noticed. Three seconds . . . two . . . one. He should have lined up another song, segued straight into something else, given himself a chance to recover. But he didn't, it hadn't occurred to him. The airwaves were silent, except for the sound of his laboured breathing as he tried to regain control of himself. It was like an awkward silence at a dinner party except a thousand times worse. John put down the phone and stared at him in horror. The silence continued. Karl kept crying.

And then, at last, he spoke. He knew he shouldn't. He knew that eventually John would have played a jingle, a trailer, something. This wasn't what radio was about. Radio was about professionalism, seamlessness, technology, music. It wasn't about his heartache or his misery. It wasn't about him.

'I . . . I'm sorry,' he began, his voice quavering dangerously, his vowels thick and doughy with mucus, 'I'm . . . I'm . . .'

Everything in the studio stopped; John was rooted to the spot, his jaw hanging open, his hand glued to his cheek. There was no bustle, none of the usual activity, just an unhappy man talking quietly into a microphone like it was his best mate down the pub, while tears poured down his cheeks.

'I've had a bad weekend . . . my girlfriend left me.'

John winced and covered his face with his hands. 'Oh, my God,' he muttered, 'he's doing a Blackburn, he's doing a fucking Tony Blackburn.'

'Siobhan, my girlfriend. Fifteen years. And . . . it's all over . . . and . . . oh, God, I'm sorry. I thought I'd be able to do this but . . . but, it's so hard. God, it's *so hard*. It's only just hit me, y'know. She's gone. Siobhan's gone!' He let loose a gigantic sob. 'Oh, God! If you knew what Siobhan was like. She was . . . she was like an angel. Just like an angel. I wanted her so badly, I've never wanted anything in my life like I wanted Siobhan and then I got her – I don't know how, I didn't deserve her, y'know. She was too good for me, *way* too good for me – a different class. She was so beautiful. And, God, you should've seen her hair, it was like pure gold, y'know? She could've had anyone and she chose me. And I don't know what I'd've done without her all these years, without her smile and her laugh and her goodness and her wisdom. God, she was wise. And her love. She loved me so much – d'you under-stand? D'you know what it's like to be loved that much by someone so beautiful and so . . . so good. And I . . . I . . .' His voice began to crack up again. 'I never took it for granted. Really. I never did. I always thanked God for that woman, always appreciated her.

'But . . . but, but . . . listen! Now just you listen to me, all you men out there. And women. This is important! This is just so bloody important, you must pay attention. If you've got a man, or a woman, and you love them and they love you, don't mess around, don't cheat on them. Please. Just don't do it. I did it. I took the trust of the most incredible, beautiful woman in the world and I made a mockery of it. And for what? For nothing! For disposable sex with a disposable woman who meant less than nothing to me. Can you believe it! Can you believe anyone would do something that stupid?! It was a pathetic little ego-boost. I can see that now. I always thought Siobhan was too good for me, too beautiful, too special. I tried to pretend it didn't bother me, but I always felt smaller than her, and then this other girl came along and made me feel like the Man, y'know? I was cleverer than her, nicer than her, better than her, or so I thought. And she wanted me. And my sad little male ego just took what was on offer, just grabbed it without a thought, for anything or anyone, not even myself probably. Oh, God! I didn't even enjoy it that much, y'know! But at least I felt special – *I* was the special one. It made me appreciate Siobhan even more, when the affair ended. It made me realize things about love and relationships that I hadn't thought about before. About continuity, about growing old with someone. How that can be as romantic as falling in love. I wanted to marry Siobhan, then, be with her for ever and ever and ever. But it was too late. She found out about the affair, she found out exactly what I was like. That I was pathetic and selfish and weak. And she deserved someone better than me. So she left. And now I'm alone. And it's over. I'm going to go back to our flat tonight, where we used to live together, and she won't be there. It'll be empty. And . . . and . . . and I didn't know it was possible to feel this unhappy and this sad and this bad. I loved her so much, and I broke her trust, and now I'm swallowing my bitter, bitter pill, and I deserve it. So – so just don't do it,

OK? Just don't. Because if you're with someone you love, who loves you back, then you're the luckiest person in the world. *Ignore* that sexy bloke in the marketing department or that horny girl who lives upstairs, or whatever. Because it is not worth it. D'you hear? It . . . is . . . not . . . worth . . . it.' Karl took a deep breath and sat up straight. The tears had stopped. 'Well,' he began, looking cautiously around him at the open-mouthed assistants and secretaries and producers who were now standing five-deep in the booth, gathered together from all corners of the ALR building, staring at him, some glossy-eyed, some embarrassed, some horrified. One young girl wiped a tear away from her eye and looked away from him. There was absolute silence. 'I . . . erm . . . I'm sorry. I – er – sorry. Sorry.' He laughed a tight little laugh and looked around again at his waxwork audience. Jeff stood at the front now, his arms crossed, eyeing Karl with a look that was impossible to define. 'I've got a feeling this might be my last show on ALR – I'll put another song on. And, I'm sorry . . .'

He slid up the volume, pushed the cans away from his ears and rubbed his face hard with the palms of his hands. Shit. What the fuck had he done? He'd just lost control. All he'd been aware of was the mesmeric, sooth-ing sound of his own voice in his earphones, nothing else – not the listeners at home, not the procession of shell-shocked people gathering in his studio, certainly not the fact that he was waving goodbye to his career. He'd been talking to himself, sorting out his own head, over the airwaves, to thousands upon thousands of stran-gers. He felt better for it. It was better than the dreadful, numb nothingness he had been hauling around with him all weekend. At least things felt real again now . . . painfully, horribly real.

'Karl.' He felt a warm hand on his shoulder and turned around. It was John. 'Shit, Karl. That was something else. You OK?'

'Oh, Jeez. John. Shit . . .'

'Jules is out there. She'll take over for you. Come on, let me get you out of here.'

'Shit. Am I going to get the sack? Is that it? Is this over too?' He got heavily to his feet and pulled at the hem of his denim jacket, awkwardly.

'Nah, nah, nah. Come on, Karl. Let's go. Jules is here.' He put his arm gently around his shoulders and guided him through the swing doors and out into the corridor.

It was like a film: people just stopped and stared at him, shamelessly, craning their necks over partition walls and around doors; a hush fell wherever he went. He felt he should have a blanket thrown over his head and be bundled into a waiting van. They passed the reception desk.

'Karl – Karl!' June had one hand over the mouthpiece and was calling his name across the foyer and beckoning him with her eyes.

Oh, God. What did she want? Karl just wanted to keep walking, until he was out of the building and on the pavement and in his car.

'Karl, stop!' June was wobbling across the marble floor on her stiletto-heeled ankle-boots. 'Stop, it's Jeff – on the phone.'

Karl looked helplessly at John. This was it. He was going to get the sack. He took the phone from June.

'*Karl – mate – get back here this instant.*'

Karl's heart sunk deep into his stomach.

'*The fucking phones are going fucking ape, Karl – hmm, hmm – they want you back on the air. Get up here right now.*'

And then Jeff dropped the phone halfway through his last sentence like he always did, like only powerful people ever do.

'It's true,' cooed June, aflutter with unexpected Monday-afternoon excitement, 'the phones haven't stopped ringing for the last ten minutes – and they all want you. What *have* you been up to, Karl?' she asked with a middle-aged, happily married, flirtatious smile.

Karl turned to John again. John shrugged and smiled and led him back up the corridors, into the lift and back to the studio. It was mayhem. Three extra secretaries had been brought in to help man the phones. The atmosphere was electric. A small ripple of applause broke out as Karl walked slowly back into the room.

'Karl – mate.' Jeff strode towards him, smiling widely, and slung his arm across his shoulders, giving them a bone-crunching squeeze. 'They fucking loved it! You're a star, mate! We've taken two hundred calls in ten minutes! Get back on the air – give 'em what they want – tell 'em what you're feeling.' He guided him back towards his seat.

Jules smiled, slipped off her headphones, stood up and kissed Karl on the cheek, handing him the cans.

Karl sat down and looked around him at the sea of warm, sympathetic faces.

'I don't know if I can,' he muttered.

'What?' said Jeff. 'Of course you can, 'course you can. Just carry on – just as you were.'

'But . . . I've said it now, said everything I wanted to say.'

'Well, just say it again! They want it, mate. You can say anything you like. Just keep talking. We'll put some calls through to you, there're some fucked-up people out there who can really relate to you – they want to talk to you. You can do it, Karl – hmm, hmm. Jules will stay here if you need back-up. Go on, just be yourself, no rules at all . . .' He squeezed his shoulders again and began to back out of the room, 'No rules . . .'

Karl was terrified. He wanted to go home. All this . . . expectation. All these people, staring at him. Fucked-up weirdies waiting to talk to him on the phone. Jeff winked at him. Jules patted his arm. John brought him another cup of coffee. The clock said he had forty-nine seconds. Shit. He felt so alone . . .

The clock ticked away the last three seconds. Karl took a deep breath, and held it. He cleared his throat. 'Well,' he began, 'I've er . . . I've been asked to come back. Ha!' He laughed nervously. 'It seems that you all like me better miserable than happy! Um, I'm going to try, to keep things going and we can all, maybe, just be miserable together. I'm not quite sure how this is going to work . . . but . . . I think I'll play another song now. This one's for Siobhan. For us. It makes me think of university, before I knew her, when I just used to watch her, y'know, and dream about her. When she was just a fantasy, something out of my reach. It's one of the most perfect pop songs of the last ten years. It's the La's. "There She Goes" . . .'

Thumbs up all around the room. Karl breathed a sigh of relief. He grabbed the playlist and began to scribble all over it, striking through it with his pen and rewriting it.

This show was going to be for Siobhan. There were no rules, that was what Jeff had said. No rules. So he'd do the whole show for Siobhan, for them, play all their songs, all their favourite songs. Wallow in it. And if people wanted to listen to him wallowing, then they were most welcome to. He didn't mind in the slightest.

So for two hours, he talked about Siobhan, he played hauntingly sad and heartbreakingly happy music. He took phonecalls from listeners who'd made the same mistake as him, some of them in tears, from listeners who just wanted to wish him all the best. He played requests for them, *their* songs.

It was two solid hours of pure emotion, of honesty and humanity. The phone rang constantly, there were tears and torment and anger, sadness, misery and regret. All the sad, lonely people in London came out from under their emotional duvets and felt part of the world again. It was unbelievably naff. It was horribly corny. It was Oprah on a bad day. But, it seemed, it was what people wanted. And it was what Karl needed.

There were people queuing on the pavement, clutching bunches of flowers and autograph books when Karl left the building that night. They'd been waiting for him. It was bizarre, it was madness. 'Thank you,' they kept saying. 'Chin up.' Pretty girls in clumpy boots gave him their phone numbers, pale men with dark eyes shook him by the hand. The atmosphere was peculiar. Karl shuffled through, said 'thank you' a lot, took the phone numbers, accepted the flowers, signed the autograph books and finally made it to his car, slamming the door behind him.

'Jeez,' he muttered to himself, 'what the fuck's going on?'

Little did he know that this was just the start of the madness. For the next few days, he was London's best-loved celebrity. They did a piece about him on *Newsroom South East,* his picture was on page three of the *Evening Standard,* accompanying an article about infidelity in the capital, every day there were increasingly more people standing around outside the ALR building, waiting to speak to him, to thank him.

But as far as Karl was concerned it was all completely ridiculous. It didn't make any difference to him; Siobhan didn't call.

He stayed with Tom and Debbie that night, and the next, and the next. He couldn't face going back to the flat. Siobhan knew where he was staying; he'd left a message with her mother, dictating the number twice, to make sure she wrote it down properly. She never called. She must have read the newspapers, listened to the radio, seen the news, but it didn't seem to have touched her at all. Not that that was why he'd taken on this role as the capital's favourite agony uncle, but you'd think, wouldn't you, that if the rest of the metropolis was awash with sympathy for him, that she would have felt it too? She really didn't want to know.

So, for three days he went to work, went home, got drunk, talked to Tom and Debbie about Siobhan, talked about life, talked about finding himself single, childless and alone in his mid-thirties when he'd always assumed he'd be just like everyone else, and wondering what the hell had gone wrong.

After the third day, he began to get angry. For fuck's sake – she'd gone off with Rick, hadn't she? She'd betrayed his trust too. After all, what's the difference between lying down and letting someone kiss you for half an hour, and lying down and letting someone shag you for five minutes? Which is the more intimate really? And supposing he *had* told her about Cheri, before she found out, would she have forgiven him? Would she have said, 'Karl, you've done a dreadful thing but, because you've told me all about it, and I didn't have to find out for myself, I forgive you and I know I can learn to trust you again'? Of course not. She'd have felt just the same, just as awful, just as unforgiving. She'd still've moved out.

Finally, after the show on Thursday night, Christmas Eve, he plucked up the courage to go home, back to Almanac Road.

He sat in the back of the cab, staring out of the window at the miserable, wet, dark night, his head pounding with frustration, anger, misery, loss and rage, and a blinding, all-consuming, heart-palpitating terror.

His key sounded strange in the lock. Like a distant echo of something from his past, a shadow of a memory from a forgotten dream. He'd never noticed the sound of his key in the lock before, never been aware of the sharp metallic click and the smooth hydraulic movement. It was so familiar yet so new.

It was cold in the flat. The central heating had been off for five days. Siobhan had always had it on full blast, claiming she felt the cold more than most, something to do with her circulation. He'd always wished it was cooler, complained, tried to open windows when she wasn't looking or slip the thermostat down a bit. It was cold now and he wished it was so hot that the paint on the walls would melt . . .

She'd cleared away all the mess. There were three huge black bin-bags in the kitchen, full of his broken records, and the Christmas tree stood naked and pitiful on the fire escape by the kitchen door, what was left of its decorations piled into a carrier bag and left by the fireplace. She'd taken all the nice bits and pieces that had made it their home, the vases, the clocks, the dhurrie rug. It was spotlessly clean. Everything was in its place. It smelled of furniture polish and Windolene. It was horrible.

He'd wanted to turn around and leave the moment he'd walked in. Rosanne's scruffy wickerwork basket, outside the bedroom door, was gone and her lead no longer hung from the hook in the hallway. It was silent, cold, dead and empty.

Karl sat heavily on the sofa, their sofa. Where she had sat six nights ago and told him it was over, where he had clung on to her legs and begged her to let him stay. He put his head in his hands and let the silence and the chilling emptiness of the flat engulf him. It occurred to him, for the first time since she'd gone, that she wasn't coming back. They hadn't had a tiff; they weren't having a breather from each other; it was over. She wasn't coming home.

For the very first time in his whole life, Karl was alone.

26

Cheri had seen him come home on Christmas Eve, two months ago now. It was the first time he'd been back since that radio show. She'd stood in her pure-white fluffy bathrobe and watched him from the window; he looked grey and dull and monotone, not like the Techni-colored Karl she remembered. She'd watched him put his key in the lock and had almost been able to see the pain flicker across his face as he slowly pushed open the door . . .

She could imagine what he was feeling. Of course she could, the whole country knew what he was feeling, for God's sake. He was a celebrity – which was just so bloody typical. When she'd met him he'd been nothing but a lowly dance-teacher. Then she'd dumped him, and now, because of their affair, because of *her*, he was famous, splashed all over the papers, his face popping up with grating regularity on the pages of gossip magazines and on TV chat shows. He'd even – and it made Cheri's blood boil just thinking about it – been interviewed by Richard and Judy. Richard and Judy! First London and now the whole bloody country was enraptured, smitten, head-over-heels in love with Karl bloody Kasparov. Poor Karl Kasparov.

Poor Karl, my arse, Cheri had thought. Poor Karl, who'd taken her with such ferocity and regularity on that chair at the Sol y Sombra. Poor Karl who'd caressed and licked every inch, every corner, every soft, supple, delightful nook and cranny of her firm, ripe body, groaning and grunting like an animal with undisguised desire. Poor Karl, who lied to, cheated, deceived and betrayed the woman he'd publicly professed to loving so much. Cheri really didn't feel much sympathy.

OK, so she'd made the running. He'd been harder than most. In fact, he'd been her greatest conquest. She'd wanted him because she thought he was unattainable, because every Saturday morning she'd look out of her window and see Karl, Siobhan and their sweet little dog walk back from the shops, laden with bags, and they'd be laughing and chatting about wonderfully domestic issues and mutual friends and their plans for the day, and he would casually place a hand on Siobhan's shoulder and look at her as if she was the only woman in the world, as if she wasn't fat, as if it didn't matter. Karl patently had no idea what he was missing. He was a handsome man. The hair and the sideburns were a bit silly and some of his shirts were a little loud but she could see that he was fit; he had a good solid neck, wide shoulders, a great bum, accentuated by his tighter than currently fashionable trousers and wonderful thick black hair, shiny with gel. And she just loved Irish accents, had never been able to resist them. He could do better than that, she'd decided. He just needed something, or someone, to make him realize. She was doing him a favour.

It had been hard at first, getting his attention. 'Come on,' she'd wanted to shout at him, 'come over here, take a look at a real woman, look at what you're missing – you can have me, I'm yours. I promise you, you'll never look back, never be happy with a fat woman again.' But to no avail. He looked at her, he smiled, he said 'Morning' when they passed in the entrance or on the street, but he didn't 'notice' her. And the more he didn't notice, the more she wanted him. It became almost an obsession, deciding what to wear in the mornings, listening out for the slam of his front door, ensuring that their paths crossed at least once a day. She'd followed him once, wondering where he went every evening at six o'clock in his Hawaiian shirts and peg trousers, and had discovered that he taught a dance class. At last, a connection, a way in. She could jive, her father had taught her when she was a little girl. She'd waited until the class finished and then followed him home again, colliding with him at the front door and engineering a conversation towards an invitation to join his next class.

Even then it had been hard. She'd turned up every Tuesday and summoned every ounce of her passion to inject into the childish steps of the dance, ensuring that she always partnered Karl, that every move she made shouted 'sex', lassoing him with her eyes, hooking him with a grind of her hips, and smiling, always smiling. But still, nothing. He would compliment her on her dancing, express his gratitude that at last he had a partner who had a true appreciation of Ceroc, buy her a beer, walk her home afterwards. But nothing. Siobhan this, Siobhan that, he talked about her all the time and eventually she understood that if she wanted Karl she would have to take him. So she did. But she'd soon tired of him.

And now he was famous – rich and famous. And where was her credit, her glory? Where would Karl be now if it hadn't been for Cheri? Just another low-profile, anonymous DJ on local radio, that's where.

It wasn't fair. All her life Cheri had dreamt of fame, had dreamt of being a prima ballerina, until she'd suddenly shot up to five foot ten and realized that she wasn't going to be the next Margot Fonteyn, she wasn't going to be showered with roses and pursued by millionaires. And as far as she was concerned, her unwanted growth-spurt was the only reason why Darcey 'bitch-face' Bussell had ever made it; it should have been her.

It wasn't right that Karl was famous and she wasn't, that she received no recognition, stuck in the chorus line of undistinguished musicals in London's less dazzling theatres while Karl was partying it up with celebrities all over town. She was twenty-six, talented and beautiful, but she wouldn't be for ever – it would be too late one day; she'd be old and ugly and her chance would have gone.

The more Cheri thought about Karl and his sudden fall into the lap of celebrity, the more she wanted to take up her role. She was, after all, the woman referred to constantly in interviews with Karl, in newspaper articles, she *was* that 'disposable woman'. In a way, she was famous already – famous for being a marriage-wrecking bitch from hell.

And, then, one day the previous week, she'd had a sudden revelation. She'd been watching something on the telly, about a woman who regretted her part in breaking up some relationship or other, so had plotted and planned and brought them back together, and then everyone thought she was wonderful. She could do that! Of course she could. And then *she* would be famous. And famous for being good, not for being a bitch, famous for bringing

Karl and Siobhan back together. She'd be a heroine, everyone would love her. She could already imagine the stories in the newspapers: '*34–24–34beauty Cheri said she could bear the guilt no longer. "I never meant to hurt anyone," she said today from her Battersea penthouse, "I was just lonely. All I want now is for Karl and Siobhan to be happy."*' Cheri knew how the media worked – a griefstricken DJ publicly emptying his soul over the airwaves was great, great press; the unnamed ex-lover suddenly emerging from the woodwork to mend his heart was pure media nectar.

Cheri felt a small shiver of excitement fizz down her spine – this might just work! All she had to do was work out the logistics. Where was Siobhan? How could she contact her? How would she convince her that she had her best interests at heart? It would mean playing the 'nice girl', she realized that, but she reckoned she could pull it off.

Cheri let the curtain drop and curled herself up on the sofa with a mug of fragrant peppermint tea and a bottle of pale-oyster nail polish. She had some thinking to do.

Siobhan had been a wreck when she and Karl had first split up, as the full realization of what had happened began to sink in. It was over, she and Karl were over, and for the first week she'd done nothing but pull Rosanne to her and cry into her fur. Karl had kept phoning and kept phoning and she'd resolutely refused to take his calls even though a soft, aching part of her heart was desperate to talk to him, to hear his gentle voice and make him feel better. She'd heard his radio show and listened to every single song he'd played for her, sat and hugged her knees in her old bedroom while Karl shared their most intimate memories with half of London. She'd talked to his voice on the radio, hoping that he'd answer back, and when he hadn't she'd cried and cried.

Her mother had tried to reason with her, tried to persuade her to take Karl's calls. It was a mistake, darling, she'd said to her, that boy really loves you, you know that, why can't you give him a second chance? Siobhan knew that part of her mother's wish for a reconciliation was an instinctive maternal fear that her daughter would be left on the shelf, that she was thirty-six years old and Karl might be her last chance, but she also knew that her mother was talking sense. After the horror of discovering Karl's secret had faded away and she was left, alone, in her draughty old bedroom in her mother's house in Potters Bar, it did occur to Siobhan that Karl should be forgiven, that she could, probably, learn to trust him again, that he did love her as much as she deserved to be loved and that the two of them could repair the damage and still make a beautiful life for themselves in the flat in Battersea. But something stopped her thought processes from advancing beyond these vague notions, something stopped her from taking his phonecalls or picking up the phone or packing her bags and driving back to the flat and saying 'Darling, I'm home.'

She was haunted, haunted by images of Karl, naked and sweating, pumping up and down and in and out of Cheri. Every time she closed her eyes, she imagined it, Karl's rump clenching and unclenching, quivering and wobbling, ramming and pounding, driving himself in and out of Cheri, deeper and harder and faster. It made her feel sick. It disgusted her. And try as she might, she couldn't exorcise the image. It was with her every moment of the day, inexorably linked with her thoughts of Karl, tainting every attempt she made to be reasonable about the whole sorry situation. It was like someone had spilt a bottle of ink over all the wonderful memories she had of Karl and their life together.

So she didn't call and she didn't go back and she stayed in her room in Potters Bar growing more and more unhappy, waiting, she supposed when she thought about it later, like a princess at the top of the tower, for Karl to come and rescue her. But he didn't. He talked about her to half the entire population of London, about them and their relationship, he tried to talk to her on the telephone. But he didn't come for her.

Then, one Sunday evening, at the end of January, she picked up the phone in her mother's hallway and she called Rick. It was a most unexpected thing to have done. She hadn't really thought about it, hadn't given herself a chance to feel nervous about what she was doing, she'd just picked up the phone and dialled. She supposed, in retrospect, that she'd needed a lift, an ego boost. Her confidence levels had never been so low, and the only thing that lifted her spirits was the memory of that night in Scotland and the way Rick had looked at her, touched her, made her feel.

She and Rick chatted for half an hour, about how cold it was, about how dreary Potters Bar was, about Christmas and New Year, family and friends, Fulham and food. It was an ordinary conversation, it was full of small talk and inconsequentialities, but it was warm and bound together with unspoken words of friendship and caring, and after

Siobhan had put the phone down she'd felt better than she'd felt for weeks.

They'd chatted a few more times after that and then, one day in mid-February, Rick had suggested she get out of Potters Bar for a night, come for a night out in Fulham; he'd take her to the Blue Elephant because she'd mentioned that it was her favourite restaurant, and she could stay at his, in the spare room, of course.

It hadn't sounded like a date when he'd suggested it, just an invitation from a friend, worried that another friend was about to die of boredom. He'd come in for a cup of tea and utterly charmed Siobhan's mother. 'What a delightful, delightful young man,' she'd said, with a slightly girlish tone to her voice, 'and so handsome. And fancy driving all the way from Fulham to Potters Bar to pick you up. Not many men would do that, you know.'

Rick had raved about how much weight Siobhan had lost – which she had; she couldn't eat when she was unhappy and had gone down to a healthy size fourteen. 'Not that you weren't gorgeous before, of course!' he'd smiled. They hadn't talked much in the car on the way into London, just listened to music and grinned at each other a lot. 'It's so good to see you,' Rick kept saying, 'so good.'

And Siobhan had smiled and told him how good it was to see him, too. Which it was. Absolutely wonderful, in fact. He'd put his hand over hers and squeezed it, beaming at her and then beaming to himself.

In retrospect, Siobhan could see that it was really quite strange. After all, they didn't really know each other, had only actually met once before, but there had just been so much *warmth* between them, they were like old friends. It had felt so comfortable sitting there in the passenger seat of Rick's new BMW, not talking, just listening to music and smiling at each other. It was as if they'd known then that they had all the time in the world, that this was just the beginning.

Rick had parked outside his house and then they'd walked, arms around each other and terribly slowly, like new lovers do, down Fulham Broadway, towards the Blue Elephant. It's easy to gauge the newness of a relationship by how slowly a couple walk together. Siobhan and Karl had reached the medium canter of the established couple years earlier, their motivation for walking becoming a desire to get from A to B rather than a chance to spend time together.

But even though any passing stranger might have assumed that they were brand-new lovers in the first blissful throes of romance, as far as Siobhan was concerned, they *weren't* on a date. They just weren't. She was still raw and in pain, and the idea of a date, of getting involved in another relationship was quite out of the question. She was enjoying Rick's company more than she could possibly have imagined, but she was still in love with Karl.

Which is why, after the tiny little Thai waitress had taken their order and removed their menus, the first question Siobhan had asked Rick was, 'So, how's Karl?'

Rick had shrugged, wryly. 'You tell me.'

'What – haven't you spoken to him?'

Rick shook his head.

'Really?'

'Of course not. He blames me, doesn't he?'

'What for?' Siobhan was confused.

'For you finding out about his affair. Because it was me who gave him *that* tape recorder.'

'What?! God, that's so pathetic! So unfair. You didn't make him take it home with him, you didn't make me press the Play button and you *certainly* didn't shove his dick into that slag!' Siobhan looked around her as she realized that she'd started shouting. 'Sorry,' she said. And then she'd started crying. 'I'm sorry. It's just . . . it just hurts so much.'

Rick had passed her a tissue, made a joke, made her smile through her tears. He'd ordered champagne and they'd talked all night, about Karl, about Tamsin, about love, about life, about everything. It was the first chance she'd had to really talk about her feelings, to put into words the disgust that she felt about what Karl had done with Cheri. None of her female friends were single and they were all Karl's friends, too. She hadn't wanted to put them in an awkward position. But it was different with Rick. *He* was different.

'OK,' Rick had said as they left the restaurant three hours and two bottles of champagne later, 'enough talktherapy – you need some fun. You need to drink a lot more champagne and get horribly drunk.'

'Oh, Rick, I don't know,' Siobhan had laughed. 'Look what happened last time you and I drank too much champagne together.'

They'd both giggled, but then Rick had turned and held Siobhan's hands in his and looked into her eyes. 'Siobhan,' he'd said, 'you know how I feel about you. And I have to say that nothing's changed. I still think you're the most amazing woman. You're . . . you're . . . well, you know. But right now you don't need that of me. You need a friend. And I really, really want to be your friend. Hey!' he smiled, 'I'll be your girlfriend, if you like! I can do that!'

'What?' Siobhan had laughed.

'Yeah! Come on. Let's go back to mine, have a couple of Sea Breezes and get tarted up, and then we'll go to a club and see who can pull the ugliest person, and then we can come home, put on our dressing-gowns and moan about men over a cup of decaff! It'll be excellent!'

So they had. Rick had put on a Boyzone CD, they'd drunk more than a couple of lurid-pink Sea Breezes and danced around his flat together while they got ready, Rick camping it up ridiculously: 'What do you think – does this make my bum look fat? Beige chinos or the khaki chinos – or do they clash with my hair?'

They'd caught a cab to a dive of a club off the New King's Road, full of foreign-language students, Australians and South Africans, and Rick had ordered them white-wine spritzers at the bar. 'Mmmmmm,' he'd said, 'I've never had one of these before, they're quite nice, aren't they!'

They'd danced for ages, to Oasis and Counting Crows and REM, chatting and laughing and eyeing up everyone on the dance floor. 'See that guy over there,' Rick had said, 'he's looking at you.'

'Which one?'

'That tall one, with the white T-shirt on – brown hair – over there.' He'd indicated with his eyebrows.

'No, he's not – don't be stupid.'

'Yes he is! Look – he can't take his eyes off you. D'you want me to go and say something to him?'

'No!' Siobhan had grabbed his arm. 'No! Don't you dare! Please – don't!'

But it was too late. Rick was already winding his way across the dance floor. Siobhan had turned away in horror and stood rooted to the spot, hoping that the flashing plastic tiles would open up and swallow her until, a few minutes later, she'd felt Rick's hand on her shoulder.

'His name's Mike, he's American, he's an engineering student, he's nineteen and he thinks you're gorgeous.'

'Oh, don't be ridiculous.'

'I'm not! Look! He's waving at you.'

And sure as could be – he was. Siobhan had waved back, a feeble little gesture and turned away again.

'Aren't you going to talk to him?'

'No way!'

'Oh, go on!'

'No. Really. I couldn't. I just couldn't. I don't even fancy him.'

'What! How can you not fancy him? Look at him. He's handsome, he's clever and he's only nineteen!'

'Exactly! What the hell am I going to have in common with someone who's probably never seen a black-and-white television, who's never owned a vinyl record and who thinks that all-night TV is a God-given right?'

They'd both dissolved into hysterical laughter then, and Rick hadn't pushed it. 'Fair enough,' he'd said, 'fair enough!'

By the time she and Rick got back to his flat, at three o'clock in the morning, they'd drunk another five spritzers, chatted to dozens of people, all young enough to conceivably be their children, had two phone numbers a piece,

Rick had been thrown out of the ladies' toilets twice and Siobhan was laughing so hard she could barely breathe.

'Oh, Rick,' she'd giggled, 'you really are the best friend a girl could possibly ask for!' Siobhan hadn't had so much fun since Brighton, before she'd met Karl. She'd never been a single girl around town. She and Karl had moved to London together and made all their friends together, and because she'd never worked in an office she'd never really had 'girlfriends' as such, just couple friends. And even though tonight had just been a joke, a piss take, it had given her an idea of what she might have been missing out on for the last fifteen years. Fun. Spontaneity. Childishness. Silliness. It had been brilliant.

'Feeling a bit happier now?' he'd asked, handing her her coffee and joining her, dressing-gowned, on the sofa.

'Well, let's see. I've been taken out to dinner to my favourite restaurant, I've drunk champagne, vodka and white wine spritzers, I've been lusted over by a nineteen-year-old American, a twenty-year-old South African and a twenty-two-year-old Estonian, I've danced myself silly for three hours, I've walked home in the rain singing motown and now I'm wrapped up in an airing-cupboard-warm dressing-gown on a squidgy sofa in a beautiful flat, drinking real Colombian coffee. Yes, I'd say I'm feeling a bit happier now.'

'Glad to be of service,' he'd said.

They'd fallen silent for a moment then and stared awkwardly into their coffee cups feeling that something more should be said, that this was a special moment. Siobhan had been the first to look up and had been suddenly startled by the blue of Rick's eyes, by the softness of his skin, the sincerity of his expression, the kindness of his mouth and the warmth of his smile.

'Oh, Rick,' she'd said, 'who are you? You always seem to be in the right place at the right time, saying the right things. You always make me feel so much better, so much like I want to feel.' She'd looked deep into his eyes. 'Are you an angel?'

He'd smiled and put down his cup, taking Siobhan's hands in his. 'No,' he'd said, 'no, I'm not an angel.' And then they'd instinctively moved towards each other, across the ivory damask skin of the sofa, and grabbed hold of each other in a deep, warm embrace.

She'd clasped him to her and rested her head against his, breathing him in, breathing through the layers, the slightly herbal aroma of his hair gel, the fruity tang of his shampoo, the oily pungency of his warm scalp and, underneath it all, the base notes that words couldn't describe – the smell of him. It seeped through her nostrils, down the back of her throat and rushed into her heart. She caught her breath and held him tighter.

Siobhan really hadn't expected to fall in love with Rick. She'd thought she was still getting over Karl. And maybe she was. But she was unable to control the feelings that swept through her like a magical hurricane whenever she was with him. He made her feel as special as Karl had always told her she was, he made her feel beautiful and secure and brand-spanking-new, like she'd just been taken out of the box.

She truly felt that Rick was an angel. They were two angels together and she had never felt so serenely, perfectly happy in her whole life as she had in the last month, since she'd been going out with Rick. This was as good as it got, as it could ever possibly get.

And one day soon, she didn't know when, she was going to have to tell Karl all about it . . .

27

The Evening Standard 27 February 1997

A STAR IS REBORN

In today's faddish, fickle world, in which fashion, fame, opinion and favour are fleeting and so dependent on the vagaries of the media and its self-appointed pundits (and I include myself in this possibly quite disagreeable fraternity), it is gratifying to discover that from time to time a talent can emerge that is so unquestionable, so prodigious, so undeniably brilliant, that it can survive a backlash from even the most vicious hack's keyboard. I stand humbled.

The name on the invitation sounded familiar. Ralph McLeary. Those of you with elephantine memories may well recall the artist – I certainly didn't. The accompanying press release filled in the gaps for me. Ralph McLeary was a Royal College luminary back in 1986, whom I, in this very column, once described in a glowing, almost embarrassingly gushing manner as 'a young man with an incestuous relationship with his medium, a young man who has created, at the tender age of twenty-one years, works in oil on canvas of such magnitude and importance, of such precocious maturity that I am obliged to employ the word "genius" to describe him.' I was not alone at the time. The press was united in a froth-mouthed frenzy. It all came flooding back to me.

However, I have no recollection of his works, not one brush-stroke or colour or shape; the detail has been cleared from my ageing and ragged memory to make room for the proliferation of fresh young painters paraded before my jaded eyes in the intervening years, whose works I am contractually bound to find words, daily, to describe.

I am, I fear, a fickle old man, my head so easily turned by a pretty canvas and the indulgent pleasure of my own words on paper. But, like the abandoned wife who makes a dramatic re-entrance – years after she has been traded in for a younger model, whose charms soon fade – thinner, happier, more confi-dent, and glowing with inner beauty, Ralph McLeary has re-emerged to put us all to shame. His show, currently on dis-play at the Notting Hill gallery of his one-time mentor Philippe Dauvignon, is a reminder that art is not, and nor should it ever be, prey to the same fads and foibles as the eminently more dis-posable, high-turnover worlds of fashion, film or popular music, and that a true genius can quite happily survive and, in McLeary's case, positively flourish without the ego-driven attentions of some fossilized Fleet Street flunkey.

These are McLeary's first works in over five years and I find my fingertips nervously twitching above my keyboard with the effort of not gushing forth, once again, in the manner of a lascivious old man. I will restrain myself.

McLeary's work has matured in a most satisfactory manner, his earlier anarchic stabs, jabs and thrusts at the canvas being replaced by a soft, almost romantic realism in a series of por-traits of heart-breaking beauty and haunting eloquence. Maybe the previous McLeary incarnation was suffering from a delayed and troubled adolescence, but the McLeary of today is all grown up with a freshly pressed shirt, a decent haircut and is, no doubt, nice to his parents. And all the better for it. In these days of toilet bowls, chocolate bars and maimed animals masquerading as art, it makes an old man very happy to view a collection of paintings that speak so traditionally and with such beauty of the simple concepts of love and happiness and light and dark. I will not say another word . . .

Ralph's back was a mess, his shoulders ached, his hands felt arthritic. His nose was streaming, his throat was raw, his sinuses felt like they had fishing hooks stuffed into them. His clothes hung off his rake-like, emaciated body like enormous flaps of skin, dark circles surrounded the grey pits of his eyes, he hadn't had a haircut in nearly two months and his hair was matted into small grimy peaks of grease and paint and dust.

He looked appalling, he felt appalling, but he didn't care. He was a man possessed. He hadn't had a decent night's sleep since Christmas, he hadn't been out for a meal, touched a drink, seen his friends, watched telly, been to the shops, had sex, had a bath, read a paper, sat on a sofa. Nothing. All he'd done, for nine weeks, was paint and smoke. Paint and smoke. Paint and smoke.

He'd survived on Ginster's pasties, plasticy sandwiches and microwaved burgers from the Esso station around the corner on Cable Street. His social life consisted of sharing the occasional spliff in the wheelie-bin area with Murray the security guard.

Bed was a large, smelly piece of foam, covered over with an old dust-sheet, and his pillow a couple of T-shirts folded into each other. Entertainment was his paint-splattered old tranny and sex was the odd half-hearted wank.

Everything else was painting and cigarettes.

It had been a small life, an uncomfortable life. It was cold and dark and lonely and unhealthy. He lay on his mattress at night, listening to the wind whistling through the cracks in the window-panes, the scurrying of rats outside his door, the never-ending drone of four lanes of traffic speeding by on Cable Street. He awoke each morning at five, he washed in the toilets down the corridor, he painted, he popped out to the Esso station, he ate something, he painted, he painted and he painted, he went to bed at midnight, one in the morning, two in the morning, and then he woke up and did the same thing all over again.

He was prolific. Pro-lif-ic. After so many barren, stagnant years, he was unstoppable. He'd phoned Philippe, who'd been to visit him after the first two weeks, seen what he'd already produced and immediately written him out a Coutts account cheque for five hundred pounds, which Ralph had banked and spent on canvases and paints.

Day by day the walls of his studio were lined with more and more paintings – twenty-one paintings to be precise, small and large, portraits and still lifes. Twenty-one paintings in sixty-four days. Quite an achievement. Philippe said he'd never known anything like it.

What Ralph didn't explain to Philippe, because it sounded so naff, was that his inspiration through it all had, strangely enough, been a DJ, a DJ called Karl Kasparov.

Ralph had tuned into ALR one afternoon, by mistake. He didn't usually enjoy commercial radio, all those adverts and brain-dead DJs. But something about the desolate tone of the Irish DJ's voice had appealed to him and then he'd understood what he was talking about – lost love – and he'd been almost moved to tears by the empathy he felt with him. He sounded like such a nice bloke and his honesty was breathtaking. And then he'd seen a picture of him on the front of some trashy magazine in the petrol station and had put two and two together and realized who he was. He was the guy from the upstairs flat at Almanac Road, the one with the quiff and the spaniel and the fat girlfriend, the guy he'd said hello to in passing dozens of times, but had never really spoken to . . .

He'd started listening to his show every day, like the rest of London, just to make sure Karl was all right, to find out how he was feeling, poor bastard. And he'd found that Karl's misery had fuelled his own, motivated him, inspired him. Cut off from humanity, from reality, and from the source of his own unhappiness, Ralph had needed Karl to remind him why he was there in the first place. Three-thirty p.m. had been the high spot of his day, his chance to feel something again, to feel human. He had a lot to thank Karl Kasparov for. He'd never really met him, but he felt like an old mate now, a really good mate. Once this is over, he'd promised himself, I'm going to buy that bloke a drink; actually, I'm going to buy that bloke a lot of drinks.

Ralph sat back now, a cigarette burning between his fingers, his stiff, sore back against the wall, his knees brought into his chest. He sucked hard on his Marlboro and blew out a thick cloud of soft, white smoke. He had finished. He couldn't paint another stroke even if he wanted to. His collection was complete and he was satisfied. He looked around his studio and breathed a sigh of relief. And then he felt a small stab of sadness.

God, he missed Jem. He missed Jem so much. He couldn't wait to go home.

He'd managed two days of attempting normality at Almanac Road after their disastrous curry in Bayswater, two days of hiding out in his bedroom, trying to avoid Jem, trying to avoid Smith, controlling his urge just to leap on her, shake her by the shoulders and tell her all about Cheri, to tell her that Smith was a tosser, before he realized that he had to go. Jem barely acknowledged him, the atmosphere was foul. He couldn't live like that. So he'd packed a small bag and gone to the studio, started painting and not stopped since. He spent Christmas Day painting, New Year's Eve painting. He'd phoned Smith to say he didn't know when he'd be back, he'd phoned his parents to wish them a Merry Christmas and a Happy New Year and, apart from Philippe, he hadn't contacted anyone else for more than two months.

But now it was over and time to start living again. Besides, he had a party to organize. Thursday night was the press launch but Friday was his night. Invite whoever you want, Philippe had said, your mum and dad, your friends, your flatmates, your Uncle Fred. Get some caterers in, a sound system, have a party, you deserve it – and for God's sake, get a haircut, you look appalling.

He had a plan. He'd go back to Almanac Road now. He'd have a bath, he'd get one of those £3.99 spit-roast chickens from Cullens and have it with mashed potato and gravy and eat it with *cutlery*! The thought excited him. He'd dig out his address book, he'd whack out some sort of groovy party invite on his Mac, print off a few dozen, go down to the Post Office, buy some stamps and send them out to all his friends. He'd put one in Jem's room and one in Smith's room.

And then he'd go upstairs. On the way to the first-floor flat he'd stop and put an invitation through Karl Kasparov's letter-box. It was the least he could do for him after everything he'd, albeit unwittingly, done for him.

Then he would wander up the stairs to the first floor and he'd knock on the door and ask that Cheri girl if he could come in for a moment. He'd accept her offer of a cup of tea and then he'd ask her a favour. She'd be confused at first but then he'd explain, in graphic detail, why he wanted her to do this for him and, hopefully, she'd smile and say 'Sure', and she'd be glad to help. He'd finish his tea, thank her from the bottom of his heart, shake her hand, maybe even kiss her cheek and go back downstairs.

And then he'd walk into his bedroom, take off his shoes, strip to his boxers, peel back his soft, heavy duvet and slip into bed. Aaaah! And then he'd sleep, all night and most of the next day, and he wouldn't wake up until the sun had already started to sink in the sky, until the sky was the colour of blueberries and plums and the football scores were tap-tapping their way through to *Grandstand*. And then . . . and then what?

And then he'd smile from ear to ear because he'd be halfway to happiness, halfway to where he wanted to be, halfway to Jem.

28

His coat was hanging in the hallway, his clumpy boots stood side by side by the doormat, laces loose and undone, toes slightly turned in, just like his feet. Jem's heart missed a micro-beat. She hung her coat over his and wandered into the living room, looking for more signs of his return.

The ashtray on the coffee table overflowed with Marlboro butts and the remote control sat where he had always left it, on the arm of the sofa. In the kitchen a plate smeared with congealed gravy and shreds of crispy chicken skin sat at an angle in the sink, half-heartedly rinsed. A packet of Smash sat on the counter, by the kettle, surrounded by hard, floury nuggets. The door of the dishwasher was open, again like he had always left it, and a tea-bag sat in a pool of its own tan emissions on top of the bin.

So, thought Jem, the Phantom Diary-Reader is back.

The bathroom was humid and slick with condensation – large wet footprints steamed on the bathmat still on the floor, his old green toothbrush with the long-flattened bristles lay on the side of the sink. Small globs of toothpaste clung to the white enamel.

Jem allowed herself a smile and walked quickly across the hall to Ralph's bedroom, her heart racing with anticipation. She knocked tentatively at the door and pushed it slowly open when there was no reply. Her spirits dropped as she encountered an empty room. He was out. He was out, but he was definitely back! Ralph was back!

She'd really, really, *really* missed Ralph. She'd missed everything about him, his sleeping presence behind the closed door of his bedroom while she got ready for work in the mornings, his half-drunk mugs of old, cold, milky tea lying around the flat in the most unexpected places – she'd found one in the bathroom cabinet once – his bare-footed padding around the flat, the packets of Marlboro stored all over the place like a squirrel's nuts, but most of all she just missed him being there.

She'd tried her hardest to put all that love stuff to the back of her mind. It was just silly. She didn't love Ralph – how could she love him? She didn't really know him, she'd never kissed him, never slept with him – she was just fond of him. And he was just being silly, too, as silly as all those other boys, all those other 'I Love You's. She was sure he'd realized how silly he'd been over the past couple of months, probably had a new posh, skinny girlfriend by now. And she'd got over her anger about the diary-reading business. It was good that Ralph had gone away, away from Almanac Road. It had given her time to put her mind into order and make sense of that night in Bayswater. If he'd stayed around she'd have been confused and bewildered, constantly comparing Ralph and Smith, wondering what to do. She'd have worried about the falling-off of her feelings towards Smith, the growing intensity of her love for Ralph. She might even have started to believe that Ralph was right, that they were supposed to be together and Smith wasn't her destiny.

Which, given the way things had been going between

them for the last two months, was not quite such an outlandish theory.

Things weren't going well. Things were, in fact, quite hideous. Smith had changed so much lately, since his weekend away in St Albans. At first she thought maybe he was sulking, maybe he was jealous about her and Ralph having such a great weekend together, going out for *that* curry together, maybe he *was* just like all the other boys after all. But after a while she'd realized that he wasn't jealous, he wasn't sulking, but that he quite simply wasn't interested in her any more. And she didn't have the first idea what to do about it. He was no longer affectionate, no longer funny, he didn't make an effort, hadn't been out with her and her friends for two months, hadn't held her hand, taken her out for dinner, phoned her at work, nothing. Jem was well aware that she didn't have very high expectations as far as men were concerned, she didn't demand much in the way of attention or romance, but this was ridiculous! She'd tried to talk to him about it, tried to voice her concerns without coming across as insecure or paranoid, which she most definitely *wasn't*, but each time he'd reassure her that really, he was fine, of course he was, he was just a bit tired, a bit stressed, a bit overworked, a bit preoccupied. And he'd apologize and stroke her hair absent-mindedly and that was that. She didn't like to go on about it because she knew from her own experience how trying that was, the incessant questioning: 'Are you all right? . . . Are you *sure* you're all right? . . . Why are you so quiet? . . . What's the matter? . . . Is it me? . . .' etc etc. She'd hated it and she refused to inflict it on somebody else. Even if they quite patently *weren't* all right,

At first she'd been worried by Smith's change in attitude, alarmed, had spent hours agonizing over what might be the problem. Boredom? Depression? Someone else? And then a couple of days ago she'd stopped thinking and stopped worrying and all of a sudden she'd stopped caring. And that was more worrying than anything. If she truly loved Smith, surely she'd still care? No matter how awful he was, how cold, how distant? But she didn't.

Somewhere along the line, she realized with horror, they'd turned into one of those hideous middle-aged couples you see staring into space together in restaurants and pubs, seething with uncommunicated resentment and loathing, staying together for years on end, compromised to the nth degree, because neither one of them ever had the guts just to get up and walk out, one of those couples who just *don't care about each other any more.*

Jem had tried to be positive about it; she knew that the early pheromone-induced passionate phase of a relationship was not a long-lived state of affairs and the fact that she and Smith had been living together from day one had probably hastened the whole process towards its inevitable conclusion a little, but still, it had only been five months. Surely they were allowed a little more love-hued bliss than that? But it appeared not.

And now, Ralph was back. Ralph who *did* care about her. Lovely, lovely, lovely Ralph. Dearest, darling, gorgeous Ralph. It was the happiest she'd felt in weeks.

She wandered into her bedroom and kicked off her shoes.

There was a small red envelope sitting on her bed, addressed to Miss Jemima Caterick, in Ralph's untidy handwriting. She leapt upon it and ripped it open. Inside was a brightly coloured invitation on shiny colour-printer paper.

Ralph is about to be stinking rich.
So come and celebrate at

RALPH'S PARTY

Get drunk, dance, flirt, do whatever you want – I'm paying. You can even have a look at my paintings if you like.
Galerie Dauvignon, 132 Ledbury Road, London W11,
Friday 6 March 8.30 onwards.

RSVP

Jem's spirits lifted substantially. A party! How thrilling! She could wear that lovely rose-printed dress with the skinny straps and all those little buttons down the back that she'd never had a chance to wear before. She'd be able to see Ralph's paintings, as well, these amazing paintings that the press were raving about. There'd be dancing, she hadn't danced for ages – Smith didn't like dancing, of course, boring old git. But she'd dance anyway. With Ralph. She'd dance with Ralph. Sod Smith. Sod him.

She penned a reply and propped it up against Ralph's door.

'Ten pound forty, mate.'

The cab driver held out his hand and peered up at Karl through the open window. Karl slowly ransacked the pockets of his jacket, his coat, his jeans, swaying ever so slightly in the cold, damp night air. He eventually located his wallet, licked the tips of his fingers with a delicate pink tongue, and awkwardly pulled out a twenty-pound note.

'Keep the change,' he slurred, turning heavily on his heel and weaving towards the front steps of number thirty-one. The cab driver eyed the twenty, eyed Karl, shook his head and drove away.

Karl lumbered precariously up the stone steps, left foot, right foot, left foot, right foot, leaning in towards the door to maintain balance, scraping his front-door key around the lock in clockwise and anti-clockwise circles before it finally, more through luck than judgement, slid into the hole. The door opened heavily under his weight and took him somewhat by surprise. He closed the door gently behind him and surprised himself again when a loud slam echoed around the hall. He winced and put his fingers to his lips. Shhhhhhh! He giggled and fell back against the door.

A small pile of letters sat on the shelf in the hall. He picked them up between unwieldy fingers and his face puckered into an absurd mask of concentration as he screwed his eyes open and closed in an attempt to focus his two perfect fields of vision into one perfect field of vision and read the envelopes.

'Miss Shee Dickshon – ha! – shlag.' He tossed the top one away from him, towards the stairway leading to the first-floor flat. 'Miss Esh McNamara – huh! She's no' here, nah – she's fucking *gone*!' he shouted at the envelope. He fished in his inside pocket for a pen, removed the lid with his teeth and began to scrawl all over the front of the envelope: *'She's not fucking here – she's at her fucking mother's – 78 Towbridge Road, Potters Bar, Herts – send her my fucking love.'*

'Siobhan-fucking-McNamara, Mish McNamara, Mish Dickshon, Mish Dickshon, Siobhan.' Cheri's letters flew from his hands all over the carpet and up the stairs. He turned towards his front door in disgust and negotiated the lock, falling on to the floor of the hall, front first. Picking himself up, he noticed a red envelope on his doormat, handwritten, with no stamp.

He tore the envelope open, wobbling gently from side to side and stifling a dainty hiccup. He moved the letter within away from him and towards him until it made itself readable, squinting like an old man reading the *Times*. There was some handwriting scrawled on the back.

'. . . *listened to your shows . . . made me cry . . . live downstairs . . . know lots of beautiful single women . . . thought you could do with a good party . . . next Friday . . . just a thought . . . bring a guest . . . champagne all night . . . just turn up . . .*'

Karl smiled crookedly.

Free champagne, huh? He'd be there. What a nishe bloke, he thought to himself. What a nishe, nishe, nishe, nishe bloke. He smiled again, left his overcoat where it fell on the floor, stumbled into his bedroom and collapsed on top of his unmade bed and into a deep and instantaneous sleep.

Cheri watched Karl from her window, sliding into the front seat of his funny old black car and driving away down Almanac Road. She waited until he was out of view and then strode quickly and lightly to her front door and down the communal stairs, her cashmere-socked feet barely making a sound as she tiptoed across the floorboards.

She stopped outside Karl's door and quickly peered

through the hall window, checking that he hadn't unexpectedly returned, before reaching into the back pocket of her jeans and taking out a screwdriver, a nail file and her expired American Express card.

Cheri's plan was starting to gather momentum. She'd had a most unexpected visitor the day before, one of the guys from the basement flat – not the good-looking one she'd had that drink with at Oriel just before Christmas, but the scruffy one – Ralph. He'd asked her for a favour. It was all a bit weird really, and her first instinct had been to say no, but then Ralph had told her who else was going to be there and she'd thought about the journalist at the *Daily Mail* she'd phoned the day before, the one who said they'd be interested in her story, and she'd decided that it might be to her advantage to help out. And besides, he'd been really quite sweet, that Ralph bloke, and such a nice smile.

So she'd said yes and now all she had to do was get into Karl's flat somehow to find what she needed. She knew it was possible. One of her old boyfriends had managed to get her door open a couple of years ago when she'd locked herself out. All the doors in the house were the same, the original ones that had been put in during conversion, so the locks were probably the same, too.

After a good fifteen minutes of manipulation and stress and desperate attempts not to damage the paintwork and gouge large chunks of wood out of the doorjamb, the door suddenly and happily creaked open. Cheri smiled with satisfaction, put her tools back in her jeans pocket and wandered into the flat. She wrinkled her nose a little with distaste. It was a mess: the curtains were drawn, there were piles of old Sunday papers all over the floor, mugs and plates everywhere, takeaway containers balanced precariously on top of the television, and the whole flat was imbued with an overwhelming odour of musty bedsheets and old shoes.

She surveyed the room and wondered where to begin. She didn't even really know what she was looking for. An address book would be a start, she thought, so she headed towards a table that looked like it might, at one point, have been a desk. Her heart was racing under her sweatshirt, reverberating against her ribcage. Her hands were shaking and her breath was short and sharp. She was enjoying this! She began leafing through piles of paper on the table and then trying the drawers. Nothing.

She wandered into the kitchen and then backed out again when she saw the state of it. Why didn't the stupid bastard get a cleaning lady for Christ's sake? He could afford it. To think that she could have . . . yuck . . . with someone so unclean, with such low standards. She shuddered a bit and put the thought to the back of her mind.

Gingerly, she pushed open the bedroom door and took a deep breath against the assault of the smell of his unwashed bedclothes and un-hung-up clothes strewn about the room. She switched on the light and balked at the sight of a pair of unappetizing-looking boxer shorts resting at her feet. She sneered and stepped daintily over them, towards the dressing-table at the far side of the room. Bingo! There it was – exactly what she was looking for. A letter, addressed to Siobhan but covered now in a barely legible scrawl. *78 Towbridge Road, Potters Bar, Herts.* She memorized the address, repeating it to herself several times before placing the letter back on the dressing-table, switching off the bedroom light and softly retracing her steps back to her flat upstairs.

It was all systems go!

Ralph? Ralph? Ralph?

Who the fuck was Ralph?

Siobhan had gone to school with a boy called Ralph – Ralph Millard, a pretty, fey boy with a reputation for being 'posh', but he wasn't even in her year. Her doctor was called Ralph, or was it Rupert? Rodney? No – she didn't know any Ralphs.

So who the hell had sent her this invitation?

She picked it up again and looked at it, turning it over to see if any give-away clues had suddenly appeared on the back. No. Nothing.

It had arrived a week ago, in a parcel of forwarded mail from her mother, in a red, handwritten envelope. It was addressed correctly, to Siobhan McNamara, but without a postcode. The postmark said it had been posted in W1 – could have been anyone. She certainly did not recognize the handwriting and, although it had been marked RSVP, there was no address or telephone number enclosed to which to do so. It was a total mystery. And Siobhan did love a mystery.

She'd deliberately passed by Ledbury Road earlier on that week and satisfied herself that Galerie Dauvignon did actually exist and was actually showing a collection of paintings, but she'd suddenly been too shy to go in and, besides, she was quite enjoying the suspense and didn't want to spoil whatever surprise it was that was awaiting her on Friday night. Maybe it *was* Ralph Millard. He might well have been the type to end up an artist. Maybe he'd always had a secret crush on her and had kept her mother's address all these years, waiting till he'd made a success of his life before getting in touch again, to show off. Or maybe he'd been bearing some sort of grudge for twenty years and now it was pay-back time? No, Siobhan had never said more than two words to the boy.

It was all a wonderful, great, gooey mystery and, as the days had gone by since she'd first opened the invitation, she'd become really quite excited at the prospect, planning her outfit and booking an appointment at the hairdresser's. Whatever it was, *whoever* it was, she was ready for it. The worst thing that could happen would be that it was all a mistake – so what? At least she'd have a chance to get dressed up and show off her new figure and her trendy new haircut. If it was an awful party, all she had to do was leave, hail a cab and go back to Rick's. Back home. She'd only been living at Rick's for a couple of weeks and hadn't quite got into the habit of calling it home yet.

Rick hadn't decided yet whether or not he was coming, although he was every bit as intrigued and excited as Siobhan by the mystery of it. Siobhan knew he was just trying to be cool, trying to play the easygoing boyfriend, giving his new girlfriend some 'space', showing that he was happy to let her go out on her own to a strange party on a Friday night, just like Karl had been in the early days of their romance. 'Oh, no,' Rick had said, so sweetly, 'you don't want me hanging around, cramping your style, you go on your own.' Bless him. Such a sweetheart. Siobhan secretly hoped he wouldn't come. She was still enjoying the euphoria of new-found freedom, the reincarnation of her old independent spirit, which had been buried away for years inside layers of routine, boredom and fat. She wanted to enjoy her adventure tonight alone.

She wandered into the bathroom, the expensive designer bathroom in Rick's flat with the stainless-steel shower compartment and the curved mirrors, the expensive designer bathroom that was polished every two days by the Hungarian cleaning lady who came in every day to clean all the rooms in Rick's expensive designer flat.

She'd lost even more weight after she moved into Rick's flat; it just wasn't the sort of flat that a fat girl could feel comfortable in, it was a thin girl's flat. Something about the sparse fixtures and fittings, the long, flowing swags of curtains, the elegant vases of slender flowers, the glass and chrome objects on skinny, barely-there shelves, the tall, thin Georgian windows, high ceilings and shutters, the soft, elegant minimalism of the place, had just sort of *sucked* the fat off her. She hadn't had to try. And of course, it was a well-known fact that falling in love was one of the most effective diets known to woman.

Once the excess weight had gone she'd been filled with confidence to try different things. So she'd gone to the hairdresser's and winced while they snipped painfully through her pony-tail, screwing her eyes shut as she heard the severed hair fall quietly to the floor, like a whisper. They'd cut her hair to just below her shoulders, into big chunky layers, a 'Rachel' she supposed it was called, although she hated to admit it. They'd put some blonder streaks at the front and blow-dried it upside-down. She'd shaken her shorn hair and thrown back her head, and there in the mirror in front of her was a young woman! A young, modern woman of the nineties. Karl would have been horrified. He'd loved her hair almost as much as he loved her, Siobhan had sometimes thought, and he hated change.

From the hairdresser's, Siobhan had gone straight to Covent Garden, to Oasis and Warehouse and French Connection, and bought herself a rather extravagant amount of clothes – fashionable clothes to go with her fashionable hair! And not a pair of leggings among them.

Rick had loved her new look, commenting in a very unboyfriendlike way on how her old hair had dragged her down, as beautiful as it was, and how much better the new cut framed her face and accentuated her fine, Irish features, the blonde streaks bringing out the dazzling blue of her eyes.

She was shampooing her new hair now, marvelling still at how much less hassle it was and wondering why she'd saddled herself with such a ridiculous amount of hair for so many bloody years. She was free – free of her hair and free of her fat and free of the past.

She rinsed it through, stepped out of the shower and into a soft, cream towel, shaking her head to loosen the droplets of water from her ears, while she dried her neck and shoulders. She picked up the glass of wine she'd left sitting by the sink, now sparkling with beads of jewel-like condensation, and took a large gulp. She rolled the glass between the palms of her hands, turned to look at her reflection in the mirror behind her and smiled a little smile of excitement.

29

'Oh, ma' God – look at you! You are elegance personified – no?!' Philippe slapped Ralph on the shoulder and looked around the room for a reaction from the caterers who were wheeling in trolleys of food and champagne from a van parked outside. Philippe always did everything for effect.

Ralph pulled at his tie and shifted nervously from foot to foot. He'd felt self-conscious all the way to the gallery. It was the first time he'd worn a suit and tie since his aunt's funeral the previous year. It was a nice suit, though. Dolce & Gabbana. Ha! If Claudia could see him now! It was grey (this season's black, apparently) with nice neat little pockets. They'd talked him into a rather radical stripy shirt with a cutaway collar. 'Natural clothes-horse,' the small, painfully fashionable Spanish assistant had told him admiringly as he held ties up to his chest. 'Yes – 'ave you ever thought about modelling?' the tall, painfully fashionable French assistant had agreed. 'You 'ave the 'eight, the post-yure, you know? Ees so nice, for me, when you wear these clothes, ees so nice!' They'd stood and beamed at him.

Ralph had been flattered but embarrassed. But he'd liked the suit and the groovy shirt and he particularly liked the natty thin black tie they'd chosen for him – more Madness than Kid Creole, and not too trendy. He'd walked out into Bond Street, six hundred pounds poorer, but feeling ten inches taller. He'd faced the trauma of designer-clothes shopping and he'd triumphed. Male model indeed!

It was important that the suit was right. Very important. He wanted everything to be right tonight. This was more important than the opening night, more important than any of those overblown old farts and pretentious tossers who'd come to criticize his work for the papers. He'd been up to James Street to have his hair cut that morning and had finally relented to one of those proper old-fashioned wet shaves with steaming towels that his barber had been offering him for years. New shoes. New whistle. Soft chin. Best socks. It was party night.

'So, Ralph, for what honour do we owe these new clothes, this 'andsomeness, this' – Philippe sniffed the air to either side of Ralph's collar – 'this sexy perfume.' He raised his eyebrows and patted Ralph's cheeks gently with both hands.

'You'll see, Phil, you'll understand,' he replied, a little stiffly. He wasn't in the mood for piss-take. He was far too nervous.

'Is a woman, no?' Philippe's brown eyes sparkled with mischief.

'No – is not a woman – it's just a suit, that's all.' He bristled slightly. His heart was racing. He slipped a finger under the collar of his shirt. 'God, it's fucking sweltering in here, Phil – is the aircon switched on?'

Philippe nodded. 'Full power. Here, come see the beautiful flowers – they just arrived. Peonies, just like you asked. Come – see.' He guided Ralph across the gallery, over flawless bleached-blond maplewood flooring, to the office at the back.

Ralph's head moved to the left and right as he walked, looking at his paintings, trying to see them through Jem's eyes. What would she think? Would she freak? Would she laugh? Would she love them? Oh, God, he hoped she'd love them. They were all for her, after all. He'd hung them with Jem in mind, placed them on the walls in the exact order he wanted her to see them in, imagined her in her black coat, furry stole and gloves, imagined her swivelling her head this way and that, stepping closer to look at the captions, turning and smiling at him every now and then.

The small office at the back was awash with peonies – Ralph had ordered two hundred and fifty pounds' worth – and the fresh floral aroma permeated his nerves and dissolved his tension a little. He ran his fingers absent-mindedly over the soft, silken tips of the multicoloured petals and slowed his breathing.

'Any chance of a glass of wine, Phil?' he asked, adjusting his tie.

Philippe raised his eyebrows. 'Wine? Ralph. What is going on? Yesterday, and the day before, and the day before this, it was jeans and lager – now, today, is suits and wine. Is me – yes? I am rubbing off on you – you are becoming a Frenchman – no?!' He giggled and pulled a bottle of wine from the fridge behind him and took two glasses from the cabinet.

Ralph picked up his wine, lit one of Philippe's cigarettes and walked back into the gallery. He reached beneath the reception desk and changed the CD on the music system located there. Radiohead. There. That's better.

And then he paced for a while, enjoying the muted thud

of his leather soles against the springy floorboards, following the lines between the boards, balancing on one foot, seeing if he could splay his feet, heel to heel, into a one-hundred-and-eighty-degrees angle, without falling over. He could.

He put his hands in his pockets and pulled them out, admiring the expensive sweep of his trousers and the perfection of the creases that ran from hip to ankle. He buttoned his jacket, felt even hotter and unbuttoned it. He flapped the sides of the jacket back and forth to ventilate his armpits. Shit, it was hot.

He stood at the front door, his cigarette and wine in one hand, his other in his pocket, leaning against the doorframe. He probably looked like a pretentious twat, hanging out in a trendy Notting Hill gallery in his Dolce & Gabbana suit, drinking wine and smoking French cigarettes. He didn't care. He was nervous.

He watched people walking past. Most of them didn't look in. Art. Not Really My Cup Of Tea. Don't Care For It Much. He didn't blame them really. It was a funny old thing, art, when you thought about it. His paintings. They were for him. Bits of him. His fantasies and dreams. No wonder most people wouldn't want it in their homes. The sort of people who did want it, the sort of people who were prepared to pay £2,500 for one of his paintings, didn't really have proper homes, they had houses, or offices, or 'spaces'. He tried to imagine one of his paintings on the living-room wall at his mother's, next to the clock with the swinging pendulum. He smiled.

A glance at the clock on the wall behind him told him it was only 7.30 p.m. Another hour to go. Again he paced the room. He drank more wine. He smoked a dozen cigarettes. 'You want we call this exhibition "Study in Nicotine"?' Philippe had complained.

The caterers worked around him, placing artfully designed platters of canapés on to white-clothed tables. Miniature Thai crabcakes festooned with sprigs of fresh coriander, dwarf sticks of satay with tiny little bowls of gloopy peanut sauce, diminutive pink bundles of prawn wrapped around baby butts of sugarcane, the smallest samosas Ralph had ever seen in his life, saucers of sweet chilli sauce, hot chilli sauce, chopped green chillis, minced red chillis and chilli pickle. Ralph had taken a lot of care over the food order.

Two large black bins behind another table were full to brimming with ice and champagne and a young girl in a black skirt and smart white blouse was busy putting shiny glass flutes in rows on the table in front of her.

Philippe was fussing with the peonies, arranging them around the room in huge extravagant bouquets, humming quietly to himself as he went.

Ralph felt his stomach contract and his bowels move. He tried to ignore it, but as his excitement mounted it got more and more unbearable. He rubbed his stomach through the cotton of his stripy shirt and clenched his buttocks tightly. The hair on his arms stood on end. He paced the room some more. He squeezed his buttocks some more. He smoked another cigarette. He stood at the door again and watched the traffic and the w11 trendies and the foreign couples walking into expensive restaurants. He took off the Everything but the Girl CD Philippe had chosen and put Radiohead back on. He put 'Creep' on repeat play. 'You want your guests to die of depression?' muttered Philippe. His stomach kept churning. His bowels kept moving. He could feel sweat patches under his arms. It was 8.28 p.m. Where the bloody hell was she? Christ – if she didn't come – no, she'd come, she would . . .

His bowels were going crazy now, every cigarette he smoked loosening them even more. She wasn't here yet – she should have been here by now – he wanted to wait for her, be at the door when she arrived, but he *had* to go to the toilet. He dashed through the office and into the cubicle by the back door. He sighed with relief as his nerve-racked insides fell into the toilet bowl. He pulled up his lovely new trousers, tucked in his shirt, straightened his tie and mopped under his arms with some balled-up toilet-paper. He looked at his reflection in the mirror. He looked frightening – pale and clammy with an expression of pure terror in his eyes. And he was so thin. Shit. He'd wanted to look so together, so successful. He looked like a drug addict in an expensive suit. He dried his hands and walked into the office, taking deep breaths and pinching at his cheeks to restore some colour.

There was so much to think about, so much to worry about. What had started off as a nice idea, a little party with all his friends to celebrate his success and the end of his self-imposed exile, had turned into a potential soap opera peopled with strange, complex characters and woven through with convoluted story-lines. It could all go horribly wrong. He hoped it wouldn't end in farce.

Oh, where was she?

She said she'd be here before everyone else – she said

she'd be here at quarter past, and it was now 8.45 p.m. He walked back across the gallery towards the door just as she arrived, gliding into the room in an electric puff of perfume and glamour. Her silken hair was piled tousily on top of her head and her burnished skin gleamed like copper under the merest hint of make-up.

'Oh, God, Ralph, I'm so sorry I'm late, I couldn't get a cab and . . .'

'Don't worry, it's fine, they're not here yet anyway. Here, let me take your coat.' He slipped it awkwardly from her shoulders, revealing long, bare brown arms and an ankle-length sliver of sheer, black, body-clinging lace.

Ralph's mouth sprang open like a cash register. 'Jesus Christ – you look absolutely – Christ – you look fantastic!'

Cheri smiled, trying not to look as if she was too used to such compliments.

'And I can't thank you enough for this, really I can't. Thank you so much for coming and thank you for looking so . . . fucking gorgeous. You're absolutely perfect . . . umwah, umwah.' He grinned and kissed her theatrically on each cheek. Suddenly his muscles relaxed, his heart rate slowed down and a smile returned to his face.

'This is going to be great,' he said, clasping Cheri's arms and smiling widely into her eyes. 'It's going to be great!'

30

Smith hadn't so much as given Jem a second glance, let alone commented on her appearance when she'd emerged from her bedroom, looking, quite frankly, stunning, in her rose-printed dress, with her hair pinned up all over her head with tiny little satin rosebuds, and wearing a pair of extremely sexy strappy sandals that fastened all the way up her finely-turned ankles with suede laces.

'Have you finished in the bathroom yet?' he'd asked with a hint of impatience in his voice that was wholly misplaced as it was *his* fault that they were running late in the first place, and Jem had only been in there for fifteen minutes, not really a terribly long time for a girl to make herself look so utterly ravishing.

He'd refused to wear the white shirt that Jem had suggested he put on, and was now grumpily undoing the shirt he'd chosen because he'd discovered a stain on the sleeve that was, to judge by the tone of his voice, also Jem's fault (although she'd never laid a finger on the shirt in her life) and moaning under his breath about what a bloody hassle the whole evening was turning out to be and he hadn't even left the house yet.

The cab finally arrived twenty minutes after the third time the increasingly unconvincing man at the cab office had informed them that it was 'just around the corner'.

By the time the cab had fought its way through an

unexplained, slow and extremely long traffic jam on Holland Road and pulled up outside the gallery, it was 9.30 p.m. and Smith and Jem had lost all interest in talking to each other.

They paid the driver, who may well have been in a good mood when he'd arrived at Almanac Road to pick them up but had obviously been infected by the general atmosphere of hostility and resentment that had suffused his cab for the last thirty minutes and was now as grumpy as both of them, if not more so.

Jem adjusted her furry wrap and waited on the pavement for Smith to get his change.

'I'm not staying late,' he muttered, tucking his wallet into his back pocket and joining Jem on the pavement. 'Ralph's friends are a bunch of nobs.'

Jem raised her eyebrows behind Smith's back in a very married way and they walked towards the door, at precisely the same moment that Karl sauntered towards the gallery.

'Oh, all right, mate! Didn't recognize you for a moment there, out of context sort of thing!' Karl grasped Smith's hand.

'Yeah, nice to see you.' Smith shook hard, a look of confusion spreading over his face at the sight of his upstairs neighbour. 'What are you doing here, then?'

'Your mate, Ralph, he sent me an invite. Said he'd been listening to me on the radio and felt sorry for me. Hah! Half of London feels sorry for me y'know – it's a strange predicament. But then again, I do get invited to an awful lot of parties these days.' He winked and nudged Smith in the ribs and Smith and Jem both saw that he was drunk.

Realizing that Smith's general mood was unlikely to bring forth an unprompted introduction to the large Irishman, Jem stuck out one small hand and pointed it towards Karl. 'Hi, I'm Jem. I live downstairs with Smith and Ralph. Nice to meet you.'

'Ah, yes – you're the flatmate. Is that right?'

Jem smirked. 'Yeah, sort of.'

'Nice to meet you, too. I'm Karl.' Karl smiled a warm drunken smile and squeezed Jem's little hand, a bit too hard. 'You're a lovely looking girl, if you don't mind me saying.'

Jem didn't mind him saying, in the least. It was the only compliment she was likely to get tonight and she embraced it warmly.

'Not at all,' she smiled, looking towards Smith to make sure he'd registered the comment and was feeling suitably inadequate for not having matched it earlier. He was already halfway through the door.

The party appeared to be in full swing. Smith, Jem and Karl wove their way through the room, looking, respectively, for the toilet, Ralph and the champagne. Bloody hell, thought Jem, as they squeezed past bare backs, designer labels, skinny blondes, male models and fashion victims, Ralph really has got some glamorous friends. She felt very short. The air was thick with Issey Miyake, pretentious talk, dense clouds of cigarette smoke blown from bored round mouths and the high-pitched whine of plummy girls moaning about other plummy girls. They were greeted with disinterest as they moved through the room, or the occasional slow and deliberate eyeing up and down, followed by a look of vague disappointment when no labels of note or drop-dead good looks were spotted among their number.

Jem started to feel her spirits droop. Smith was right. Ralph's friends really *were* a bunch of nobs. She could actually feel Smith's bad mood increase as he followed behind her.

She scoured the room desperately for Ralph now. She was scared that he'd have suddenly turned into a pretentious artist-type and that he'd ignore her when he saw her and pretend not to recognize her in front of all his super-cool friends: 'Excuse me, do I know you?' She shuddered. She had to see him, to reassure herself that he was still lovable, gorgeous Ralph, despite the throngs of two-dimensional magazine-cut-out people he'd surrounded himself with. She kept walking.

Karl was glad he'd had a few drinks before he came out. He looked around him at the plastic people and suddenly felt very alone and very old. He was glad he'd bumped into these two at the door, at least he hadn't had to walk in on his own. Karl hated this 'being single' business. He absolutely hated it. All his friends kept telling him he'd get used to it, come to enjoy it, in fact. He'd soon realize the benefits, they insisted. Instead, Karl came to hate it, more and more, every day. Not a day went by that he didn't miss Siobhan and their cosy lifestyle and their nights on the sofa. Life was so simple, then, he hadn't had to make an effort, hadn't had to go to parties full of strangers and make conversation with people he didn't like. Life with Siobhan had been pure, domestic bliss.

He was still sure she'd come back. She couldn't stay in her dreary little bedroom in Potters Bar for the rest of her life. She'd forgive him soon enough, she just needed time and space. It was his birthday next week. He was sure she'd phone him then – it was the perfect opportunity to start afresh, to forgive and forget.

In the mean time he had a party to get through. He reckoned he'd put away a few glasses of champagne, down some of those delicious-looking morsels of food he'd spotted over the other side of the room, make a wee bit of polite conversation with his lovely neighbours and then slip off and back to the rather good bottle of single malt he had waiting for him back at the flat. He started fulfilling his evening's resolutions by grabbing a glass of champagne off a passing tray and knocking it back in one, wiping at his mouth with the back of his hand and stifling a little burp.

Smith had spotted Ralph's head at the far side of the room. 'There he is,' he muttered with relief. His little band of followers shadowed him as he headed Ralphwards.

Ralph was wearing an incredibly smart grey suit and had finally had his hair cut. He was, thought Jem, looking absolutely delicious. He had his body turned away from them and was chatting to yet another tall, skinny blonde in a black lace dress whose face they couldn't see. The conversation seemed quite animated and their heads were pressed close together, their body language insinuating that they were making more than polite chit-chat. Jem felt a little nausea rise in her gut and swallowed it quickly. Ralph could talk to whoever he liked; it had nothing to do with her.

Ralph spotted them approaching and broke away from his intimate chat. When he saw Jem his face broke open into an enormous smile and he opened up his arms to embrace her. Jem breathed an enormous sigh of relief – he was being Ralphy – and let him absorb her in a bear-hug.

'Jemima Catterick, you look breathtakingly beautiful,' he whispered in her ear and brushed her cheek with a tiny kiss that sent shivers down her spine. She blushed and felt her heart pump under her breast.

'So do you,' she giggled.

The tall, golden woman had turned around now and Ralph broke away from their embrace to put an arm around her bare shoulders. Jem felt jealous again.

'Um, I think you all know Cheri, don't you?'

Cheri beamed at the trio.

'Cheri, this is Karl . . . you know each other, don't you? . . . Smith, my flatmate – I believe you've met . . . And this is Jem – Smith's girlfriend – I think you've met her, too, haven't you? Well, isn't this a nice, neighbourly little gathering! Sorry about all these pretentious bloody Notting Hill trendies . . . didn't invite them . . . someone else's friends. My real friends are probably still in the pub . . .'

Ralph continued talking, but no one was listening.

Smith was swaying on the spot, his hand still where he'd left it, in Cheri's, when they'd been introduced. He'd gone a rather bilious shade of puce and looked like he was about to faint. He was grimacing and was obviously trying to form a word in the back of his throat, his dry mouth forming and unforming circles, like a tongue-tied trout. He wished he'd worn that white shirt.

'Didn't know you knew Ralph?' he finally managed, in a rather unattractive squawk.

'Well,' said Cheri, trying delicately to extricate her hand from Smith's, 'he's a new friend' – she imbued the word 'new' with half a ton of innuendo and put her arm around Ralph's waist, proprietorily – 'and he's just such a little sweetie.' She puckered up her voluptuous lips and kissed him softly on the cheek.

Jem stood rooted to the ground, feeling even smaller, and foolish and over-flowery. She felt unexpected and entirely uncalled-for tears well up from her chest and breathed deeply, clinging on to Smith for dear life, while he stuttered manically about how much he liked Cheri's dress and how stunning she looked and what a pretty hair-do that was.

In the general atmosphere of hatred, jealousy, lust, embarrassment and shock, no one had noticed Karl, whose face was slowly turning from a pale lobster-pink to a bright, lurid crimson and whose large frame was filled with so much anger and rage he looked like he might explode like a microwaved sausage at any moment.

'What the FUCK is going on?' he began, slowly and deliberately, looking directly at Cheri. 'Is this some sort of FUCKING joke?' This was said almost silently except for the final 'fucking' which was bellowed so loudly that they all jumped from their skins and clutched their throats.

The group turned towards Karl. Cheri put out one nervous hand towards his arm. 'Calm down, Karl. It's not what you think. I promise you, you'll understand . . .'

Karl jerked his arm away from her touch. 'You FUCK-ING SLAG. Don't you fucking touch me. JESUS! I feel sick. Isn't it enough that you destroyed my life?' He leaned in towards Cheri, who cowered into Ralph's shoulder, and began spitting into her face. 'Now you're going to destroy this fella's life too . . .' He pointed viciously towards Ralph.

'Now, mate, come on . . .' Ralph tried to intervene with an outstretched arm. Karl swiped it away like it was an annoying fly. He was approaching boiling-point.

'No, mate, *you* come on. I don't know what the fuck's going on here, but I don't like it. Not one bit. Is this all a joke, huh? Is that it? Why did you really invite me here tonight? Did this BITCH put you up to it?' he snarled.

'Karl, please! I promise you, it's not a joke. You'll see,' Cheri beseeched, theatrically, 'it's just not like that at all, it's because I care . . .'

'WHAT!' Karl began to laugh, a deep, ominous, unpleasant laugh that made all three of them flinch. 'You! Care! You're incapable of caring about anyone or anything but yourself. You are the most selfish, self-centred, manipulative and evil woman it has ever been my misfortune to meet. You've already ruined my life once and I'm not going to stick around here while you and your "friends" entertain yourselves at my expense.' He slammed his empty glass down on a shelf. 'Thanks for the invite – *mate*,' he spat at Ralph.

'Please, Karl, don't leave – you can't leave now!' Cheri was desperately holding on to him. If he left now, then all her work would have been for nothing and she'd be stuck at a party she didn't really want to be at, with a bunch of people she didn't even know, and she'd never be famous.

But Karl extricated himself from her grip, turned on his heel and began to stride through the room, knocking dahlings and It girls out of the way with his large elbows as he moved. The twittering and chattering had died down during the confrontation and everyone now fell silent, apart from one hooter-nosed idiot on the far side, who was so taken with the sound of his own voice that nothing, it appeared, could stop him talking.

Karl had almost reached the door when someone grabbed him from behind and spun him around. It was Smith, who had watched the whole sorry scene unfold in utter horror and had chased Karl uncertainly across the floor of the gallery, through the gap in the crowd that Karl had left behind him, and to the door.

'Now listen here . . .' he began.

Jem watched from the other side of the room and winced, thinking for the first time how silly Smith really was. 'Now listen here' – it was the sort of thing that only a really silly man would ever say. It would be entirely his fault if Karl were to wallop him one.

'. . . now listen here. I don't know exactly what your problem is, but you are *way* out of order and I suggest you go back immediately and apologize to Cheri. That is no way to talk to a lady.'

Karl stared at Smith. He suddenly looked a lot taller than six foot and certainly a lot taller than Smith. His lip curled up in a Rottweiler-like sneer.

'That BITCH over there is no lady. And what – the fuck – has it got to do – with you?' he asked, poking Smith in the shoulder in what looked like an extremely irritating manner. 'Oh – don't tell me – she's got you in her nasty little grip as well, has she?' Karl laughed and pushed Smith gently away from him. 'Well, good luck to you, mate, you'll need it.' Karl turned away and towards the door.

Smith bridled a bit, looking as if he was seriously

contemplating grabbing Karl's arm again and taking this argument outside, but was saved by the timely entrance of another guest, a pretty blonde woman in a black coat and heels.

'Oh, my God! Siobhan!'

'Karl!'

'Christ! What . . . what the . . . what're you doing here?'

'What are *you* doing here?'

'I don't know. Who invited you?'

'I don't know. Wasn't it you?'

'No.'

'I've got no idea.'

'Christ, Shuv, you look amazing. What happened to your hair?'

'I had it cut. Look, what the hell's going on? Whose party is this?'

Karl pointed at Ralph, who was watching with an open jaw at the far end of the room. Cheri had repositioned herself discreetly behind a pillar.

'His?' said Siobhan, her face contorted with confusion. 'But . . . why? Who is he?'

'He's Ralph.'

'Oh, yes. Ralph. Of course. The invite. But who is Ralph?'

'*That's* Ralph. He lives downstairs, Almanac Road. Remember?'

Siobhan struggled to recall. 'Oh, yes, but – why? I don't understand, Karl. What the fuck *is* this?'

Karl shrugged. 'I have no idea.' His frame relaxed, his face softened and he smiled. 'Jeez – who cares? Shuv, it's so good to see you. It is *so* good to see you . . .'

He petted her hands and grinned manically down at her.

Smith was still standing behind him, his fists clenched, his hackles still at attention. He turned to face the rest of the room, which had already grown bored of the drama and resumed halted conversations as if nothing had ever happened. What did you have to do to entertain these people? He looked down at his fists and unfurled them slowly, rubbing at the indents his fingernails had left in the palms of his hands. He straightened his tie, ran his fingers through his hair and began walking slowly back across the room, embarrassed that his attempt at a fight, his only ever attempt at a fight, had been stalled like that in front of a room full of Ralph's twattish friends.

He headed straight towards Cheri, who had now emerged from behind the pillar, and put an arm protectively around her shoulder, rubbing gently at the bare skin under his hand. His heart raced. She felt exactly as he'd expected her to feel – like silk spun from the thread of the silkiest silkworm that ever lived.

'Are you all right?' he asked in his best sensitive and caring voice.

Cheri nodded glumly. 'Yes,' she said, 'but I suppose after everything I've done, I deserved it.' She looked away poignantly.

'What! Don't be ridiculous. He was drunk. He had no idea what he was talking about.' Smith was quite beside himself with indignation.

'No, Smith – really. He was absolutely right about me. It's all true.'

'No!' Smith made them all jump with the ferocity of his dissension. 'He's mad. Really, Cheri. Don't you pay any attention to him.'

Cheri sighed and Smith continued to rub the small patch of lustrous skin that lay just beneath his thumb. It was the best piece of skin he'd ever touched; he could quite happily rub it all night.

'Look, Smith,' Cheri continued, 'I told you all this – don't you remember? – at Oriel? All about my past, my problems with men.'

Jem stiffened and gripped her glass in her fist as if she was armwrestling it. Smith finally stopped rubbing Cheri's shoulder and let his hand drop to his side, aware of Jem's existence seemingly for the first time that day. Ralph flinched and looked away. It was starting. He hooked his hand through Jem's arm and deftly began to wheel her away from Cheri and Smith.

'Jem, let me give you a personalized tour of my exhibition – a true honour for you.' He smiled cheesily and dragged her away, just as she was beginning to open her mouth to say something. Jem didn't resist. Oriel? What? Smith didn't know Cheri. What the hell was happening? Why was he being so protective of her? What did he know about her? All that thumb-rubbing and concern and all those compliments about her dress and her hair. And, anyway, wasn't Ralph supposed to be with Cheri?

'Ralph,' she asked in a small, confused voice, 'what the fuck is going on here?'

Ralph was beginning to feel a little guilty now, but not in a bad way – a bit like a vet giving an injured animal a painful injection. This was for Jem's good; she might not like it at the moment, but she'd appreciate it in the long run. He put his hands on her shoulders and steered her towards the front of the gallery.

'I dunno,' he laughed, 'it's just one of those nights, I guess.'

Jem's head was in too much turmoil to demand a more articulate response and she let him move her around like a mannequin. What was all that business with the couple from upstairs – that Irish DJ guy and his ex-girlfriend? They were standing together now at the door, Siobhan giving Karl a little twirl to show off her new figure, Karl grinning from ear to ear, looking like he'd never been happier in his life. And what did he have to do with that Cheri girl? And how did Ralph know Cheri? And Smith? And . . . and . . . and . . . oh, God. Jem felt quite giddy. Up until this evening Jem had thought that Cheri was just the girl who lived on the first floor, the one she'd had that chat with ages ago, the one who used to be a dancer, the one who was getting married. Yes, that's right, she was getting married wasn't she? And now she was Ralph's date, Karl's enemy and Smith's . . . Smith's what? And she certainly didn't seem to be getting married any more. She glanced across the room and saw that Smith had placed his hand back on Cheri's shoulder and was whispering into her ear, his groin twisted pointedly towards her thigh, his eyes glued to her face. Cheri was smiling and laughing and looking very coy.

'Jem? Jem, are you all right?' Ralph was leaning into her face and staring into her eyes, looking concerned.

'Yeah . . . sure . . . I'm fine.' She tore her gaze from the unpleasant and unsettling little scenario; she couldn't deal with all this right now. Besides, she had Ralph to herself for a few moments and he was about to show her his paintings, which, in all the drama, she hadn't even glanced at yet. She took a deep breath.

Ralph was still staring into her eyes. He opened his mouth as if he was about to say something, closed it and opened it again. 'I know I've already said this, Jem – but I'm going to say it again anyway. You look drop-dead gorgeous. You really do. That dress is . . . stunning. And I love, absolutely *love,* all these little roses in your hair.' He touched one gently with a fingertip. 'You are, without a doubt, the most beautiful woman in this room. I'm so glad we're friends again – so glad.' He picked up her hand and gently kissed the back of it.

'Oh, Ralph, so am I. I really missed you, you know.' Jem blushed and giggled and kissed the back of his hand too, feeling immediately that this was an embarrassing thing to have done, clearing her throat and turning away to hide her blush. 'So, er, are you going to show me these famous paintings of yours, then?'

Damn Ralph, she thought, always sending me into these paroxysms of confusion.

Ralph flushed slightly, pleased as punch with the little damp patch on the back of his hand that Jem had left there with her lovely soft lips.

'OK.' He placed one hand gently on her waist and pointed her towards the first painting. 'This one's called "Pink Lipstick and Peonies".'

Jem gasped and put her hand over her mouth. 'Ralph – that's – is that? It's me, isn't it?' She spun around towards him with wide eyes.

It was a small portrait, rich in colour and detail, a close-up of Jem's face wearing a huge, open smile that showed all her teeth, her head surrounded by a bed of pink, purple and mauve flowers in full bloom.

Ralph nodded and steered her towards the next painting.

It was Jem again, head and shoulders this time, in a field of shiny red and green chillies. The next one was of Jem, and the next, and the next. There were still lifes, too, of flowers and spices and chillies. Jem suddenly felt embarrassed and self-conscious.

'Ralph . . .' she began.

'Shhhhh' – Ralph put a finger to her lips – 'just look – just enjoy.' And there she was, just as he'd envisaged, twisting her head this way and that, peering at the captions, turning towards him every now and then with a quizzical look on her face that said 'You're mad,' but that was also full of affection, wonder, excitement and, he was absolutely sure of it, love.

31

'So, is there any particular reason why you didn't tell Jem about our little drink at Oriel at Christmas?'

Smith looked momentarily nonplussed and scratched his chin. 'Oh, but I did. I guess she just forgot,' he sniggered, and pushed his hands deeper into his pockets.

'Hmmm.' Cheri let it pass. 'She's a lovely girl, isn't she? I bumped into her once, outside the house and we had a little chat. I thought she was gorgeous.'

'Yeah. Yeah. I suppose so.'

'It's funny, because we spent all that time talking at Oriel and you didn't mention her once . . .'

'Well . . .'

'Quite gave me the impression you were single, actually.'

'Yeah, well . . .'

'Which is a shame, because I sort of hoped that you would be.' She circled the rim of her glass with one long, brown finger. 'We got on very well that night, didn't we?'

Smith's eyebrows shot up to his forehead and he stood up straight. 'Oh, God – I mean, Jem and me – it's nothing serious, really.'

'That's not what she told me.'

'Huh?'

'That time I chatted to her outside the house. That's not what she told me. She told me all about her dreams and

330

how you and she were – how did she put it? – destined, that's right, *destined* to be together.'

'Well, Jem's very sweet but she can be a bit –' He pulled an extraordinary face involving crossed eyes, a protruding tongue and an index finger circling around his temple, then snorted and shoved his hands back into his trouser pockets.

'Really! Hmmm, I have to say she seemed very sane to me. But she's absolutely mad about you, she really is.'

Smith smiled smugly and shrugged. 'I know,' he said.

'But I thought you said it wasn't very serious . . .'

'Well' – he scratched the back of his neck – 'it's not – for me. D'you know what I mean? I think' – he looked around him and lowered his voice an octave – 'I think it's a bit of a case of unrequited love, to be honest. I mean, I'm very fond of Jem – don't get me wrong – really very, very fond of her. She's a lovely girl, as you so rightly said, but . . . she's not "the One". You know what I mean, don't you, about "the One"?' He raised his eyebrows conspiratorially and moved his body an inch or two closer to hers.

'Oh yes,' she replied, 'Mr Right. That sort of thing.' She flashed him a dazzling smile. What a slimy bastard, she thought to herself, gritting her teeth. Ralph had been so right about him. She'd had her misgivings about this whole scenario – she was only here for Karl and Siobhan, after all. And now they were happily ensconced together at the other side of the room, looking terribly pleased with themselves – it looked like her plan had been a resounding success – and she could just call it a night, go home. But she was in full flow and after just five minutes with this scumbag she was keen to do whatever it took to get him out of Jem's life. She watched Jem and Ralph move across the room, his large hands on her small shoulders, guiding her gently around the pictures he'd spent nine weeks locked in a damp, cold studio painting for her, pictures of *her*. She'd noticed the little *frisson* of discomfort that had flickered across Jem's face when she'd walked in and seen her and Ralph together, looking like a couple. Cheri knew that look better than most. She'd been jealous. She felt more than friendship towards Ralph, it was obvious. They looked right together. Ralph had been right, she could see that now. This awful Smith character was just an obstacle.

She looked across the room again at Siobhan and Karl, deep in conversation and laughing together, and smiled to herself. She was having so much fun being a good person! Now, if she could just get Smith out of the way tonight and clear the path for Jem and Ralph, then she really *would* be a fairy godmother! Cheri smiled again as a lovely feeling swam through her stomach, a big, fat, happy fish of goodness. She turned back to Smith and stunned him with another of her prize smiles.

By eleven-thirty, most of the fake guests had left – they had to get up early the following morning to catch flights to New York and Tokyo and Sydney, for shows and shoots and castings – and Ralph's real friends had arrived, fresh from the pub around the corner, loud and drunk and ready to party. The evening, it seemed, was only just beginning.

Someone put Abba on the CD system and within the first three bars of 'Waterloo' pretty much everyone was dancing, clutching champagne bottles in their hands and swigging from them as they moved to the music, singing along to the lyrics at the tops of their voices. Smith had Cheri by the waist and was spinning her around the room, rather heavy-handedly.

Siobhan and Karl were sitting quietly in a corner absorbed in conversation.

And Jem was in the toilet, crying her eyes out.

She hadn't spoken to Smith all night. Not one word since they'd got there. First of all he'd been so deeply involved in conversation with that Cheri girl that she hadn't liked to interrupt, and then he'd whisked Cheri off on to the dance floor and they hadn't stopped dancing since. And Smith didn't even *like* dancing. She brought her tissue to her face as fresh tears began to cascade down her pink cheeks. She was embarrassed and she was humiliated. She wasn't used to being treated like this. Ralph had tried to console her, tried to put her mind at rest, convince her that there was nothing to worry about, but for God's sake, Smith was all over that girl.

And then there was Ralph. It looked like all that love stuff was going to come to the surface again any minute. Jesus – a whole room full of peonies and paintings of her and all their favourite food and compliments and hand-kissing and tingles up and down her spine and the way . . . the way he'd put out his finger to touch one of her little satin roses . . . it was all so intimate, so exciting, so gorgeous and so fucking wrong. It was all so fucking wrong. Smith was her boyfriend – although you wouldn't think it judging by his behaviour tonight – and Ralph was her friend, and now her feelings were every bit as confused as they'd been before Ralph had gone away. No, they were more confused, much more confused . . .

Jem marched out of the cubicle, splashed her face with water from the sink, mopped it off with a paper towel, adjusted her dress, poked at her hair and squared her shoulders. She needed reassurance. She needed to know that Smith loved her. For the first time ever, she needed to hear him say it. She was going to walk out there and grab him away from that horrible girl and make him tell her then and there, so she could hear it, so she could get her mind straight and stop all this Ralph nonsense once and for all.

She gave herself one last stern look in the mirror, turned on her heel and strode out into the gallery.

Siobhan had been trying to tell Karl, all night, about her and Rick. She'd taken a dozen deep breaths at appropriate moments, steeled her nerves, and then lost it. How could she? He looked so happy, his face was aglow with joy. He was so thrilled to see her and was trying so hard to make a good impression, to say all the right things. He'd asked her how things were going at her mother's; that would have been the perfect opportunity to have said something, but she just couldn't. He'd be so hurt, so angry. She'd said something inconsequential in reply and changed the subject. She'd suggested that they get up and dance, to avoid conversation, but he'd said no – I just want to sit here and talk; I've missed you so much; I want to talk all night. So they sat and talked and now they were talking about Karl's radio show, the infamous one, and Siobhan knew that any moment now the conversation was going to get serious – very serious indeed.

*

Smith was absolutely plastered. Completely, totally and utterly hammered. It was only because Cheri was such a good dancer and was so strong that he hadn't fallen over yet. His thick hair was matted to his forehead with sweat, his shirt was damp and crumpled, and he had a ridiculous expression on his face which he probably thought was a suave smile but which looked more like the village idiot's on a bad day. He was hopelessly out of rhythm and kept singing the wrong lyrics to the songs, without noticing.

Cheri had had enough of dancing with this cretin – he was making her look bad – and she encouraged him off the dance floor with the suggestion of getting a drink. He followed her like a pissed puppy.

'Cheri,' he slurred, leaning awkwardly against the wall, clasping a glass of champagne, quite obviously trying to look cool and failing miserably, yet again, 'you and me. We should get together, y'know – some time.' He raised his eyebrows lazily, in a 'How about it?' sort of way.

'Oh, yeah?' Cheri replied wearily. She was tired of this now.

'Yeah,' leered Smith. 'You and me – we're good together, aren't we – we've got something – special. Can't you feel it?'

'Yeah, I suppose so.'

'That night at Oriel, that was great, wasn't it?'

'Uh-huh.'

'And tonight. Shit – it's been brilliant. We've talked all night and danced and everything . . .'

Cheri was looking frantically around the room, for Ralph or Jem or anyone to come and rescue her. She was bored stiff.

'. . . and I really think that you and I – well, I think it's destiny . . . d'you agree?'

Cheri wasn't even listening any more. 'Yeah,' she murmured. 'Yeah, sure.'

Smith had failed to notice that Cheri was stifling a yawn and looking at her watch. He'd decided that enough was enough. He'd waited long enough and now, this instant, this very moment, was the right moment. This was it!

He slammed his drink down on the bar, threw himself to his knees and grasped Cheri's hands in his. 'Oh, God, Cheri! I love you. I've always loved you!' His voice rang out around the room; he didn't care who heard! Ralph looked away from the conversation he was having with his mate John's girlfriend and watched with horror. He closed his eyes and covered his face with his hands. Smith was up to his old tricks. 'I've loved you for five years and . . . I want us to be together for ever.' Smith slavered wet kisses on to the backs of Cheri's hands. Ralph's eye was caught by someone emerging from the toilet at the back of the room. It was Jem, looking red-eyed and walking forcefully towards Smith and Cheri with a determined look on her face. He saw her jaw drop when she noticed Smith's lips on Cheri's hands and he watched her stop in her tracks when she heard Smith, at the top of his voice, with all the abandon of a man in love who has had too much to drink and is no longer in control of his senses, shout out for the world to hear, 'Cheri, I love you. Will you marry me?'

For the second time that night, the room fell silent. Cheri looked horrified, Ralph gasped, and Jem screamed. Smith turned around, almost falling from his knees in the process, saw Jem and began one of his trout impersonations, turned back to Cheri, saw the look of disgust on her face and dropped his head into his chest. Jem picked up her coat from a chair, threw on her furry wrap, grabbed her handbag and ran from the gallery, out on to the dark, wet street, her sobs swallowed up by the sound of passing traffic as the door opened and closed. Ralph threw Smith a look of pure contempt, picked up his coat and ran out after her.

Cheri looked down at Smith's slumped figure at her feet. She tugged at his hands and pulled him into a standing position. 'Pathetic,' she sneered at him. 'Absolutely pathetic.'

Siobhan and Karl had missed all this drama. They were already in the street, having some of their own. Karl was pacing up and down the pavement, gesticulating wildly with his hands. Siobhan stood with her head downcast and murmured gently under her breath. They stopped their conversation momentarily as first Jem and then Ralph emerged from the gallery and began running down Ledbury Road, Ralph shouting 'Wait, Jem, please,' after her receding figure. They looked at each other, shrugged and continued. What they were talking about was too important to allow even the most dramatic of goings-on to disturb them.

'So – if you're not living at your mother's – where exactly are you living?' Karl turned away from Siobhan, not wanting to watch the discomfort on her face. 'With your *new boyfriend*?' He spat this out. He felt sick, violently sick.

Siobhan nodded glumly.

'Oh! And where exactly does this *new boyfriend* live? Somewhere nice?'

This was horrible, truly horrible. They'd been getting on

so well, and then Siobhan had dropped the mother of all bombshells. She was seeing someone. 'Is it someone special?' Karl had asked. 'Yes,' she'd nodded. 'Is it – serious?' She'd nodded again. 'Jesus – how long?' Karl was becoming increasingly distressed. Siobhan had shrugged. 'A few weeks.' Karl's face crumpled and his lip began to quiver. 'But . . . but . . . we've only been split up a few weeks.' Siobhan had started crying then and had buried her head in Karl's chest. They'd hugged and Karl had moved their trauma out on to the pavement to avoid becoming a topic of conversation amongst the party-goers.

'Well?' he demanded, a sob catching at the back of his throat. 'Do you and your *new boyfriend* live somewhere nice – Siobhan – tell me, tell me all about it . . .'

'Oh, please, Karl, don't . . .'

'No. Siobhan, I want to know everything. Tell me everything. What's his name? What does he look like? What does he do for a living? Is he handsome? Huh? Is he? Is he good in bed?'

'Oh, Karl . . .'

'Well – is he? Jesus. Siobhan. What's going on here?' Karl ran his fingers through his hair and drooped backwards into a shop doorway, draping his coat over his knees and rubbing his face with his hands. 'I thought we were having some time apart. Why couldn't you wait, Siobhan? Shit – how did you manage to get over me so quickly? Over *us*?'

'I don't know, Karl, I don't know. It didn't feel quick, it felt like an eternity, sitting in that bedroom, alone, missing you, missing the flat, missing everything. It felt like for ever, just waiting, hoping that you'd come and get me.'

'I called you! I called you every day, every hour of every day. You wouldn't take my calls.'

'Oh, God, Karl, it's easy to call. I wanted you to take action. *Do* something. I wanted to hear the sound of your car engine turning over in the driveway, wanted to hear the car door slam and your footsteps in the gravel. I wanted to hear the doorbell and I wanted my mother to call up the stairs to tell me that you were there, that you'd come for me. Every night I waited – and you never came . . .'

'But your mother said she'd call the police if I even *phoned* again. How could I, Shuv? How could I just turn up? I didn't know what to expect.'

'Oh, please! Don't tell me you were so scared of my mother, my tiny little sixty-nine-year-old mother, that you couldn't fight for what you really wanted. I always had to do *everything,* Karl – everything. Don't you see? That was the whole problem. You just always wanted everything to stay exactly as it was – me, the flat, life, everything. If I hadn't dragged you up to London all those years ago, we'd still be living in that shithole in Brighton. If I hadn't phoned Jeff after that wedding you'd never have gone for that interview. If I hadn't sat up half the night with you, persuading you, you'd have turned down the job. I even had to be unfaithful to you to get you to notice that I was unhappy, that there was something seriously wrong with our relationship. I had to kick you out when I found out about you and Cheri and I was *damned* if I was going to be the one to make the running again, Karl, to reconcile our relationship – it was your turn! It was your *fucking turn*! I waited for you, Karl, and you didn't come. You didn't write. You didn't give me one decent reason why we should try to save our relationship. You just sat around, drinking whiskey and feeling sorry for yourself, crying down the airwaves to a million total fucking strangers, making everyone feel sorry for *you*! Well, what about me! Who felt sorry for *me*! No one. No, Karl, you had your chance. You had a thousand chances and you blew all of them. I have to take control of my life again, Karl. Be me again. And there's no room for you any more. I love you. I will always love you. You've been my best friend for half my life. But you're a dead weight, Karl, and I've cut myself free. Just like I cut my hair, see' – she pulled the shorn locks to her chin and waved them at Karl – 'and don't you think it suits me better?' She turned away then and began to cry.

Karl felt like someone had slapped him in the face with a side of salmon. Tears stung his face. What could he say? What could he do? She was right. Shit! He wanted to kick himself. He wished that he could be split in two so that he could chase himself down the street, into an alley and kick twenty-six different types of shit out of himself.

'Shuv . . .' He reached out to touch one quivering shoulder with his hand. She spun around.

'Oh, Karl – I'm so sorry. I'm so sorry that you thought there was still hope. I heard you on the radio and you sounded so defeated, so much like you knew what I already knew – that it was over, finished. If only I'd known. We could have talked before. We *should* have talked before.'

'It's too late now, huh? Too late for all those could'ves and should'ves.' He exhaled noisily and began to cry again.

'Oh, Shuv, what the fuck am I going to do without you? What am I going to do, Shuv? Eh?'

He turned towards her and the two of them held each other in a sad, wet, desperate embrace, sobbing loudly into each other's ears.

So loudly in fact that, at first, they failed to hear the engine of the car that pulled up on the road next to them and the gentle whine of an electric window being lowered, and then the soft, shocked tone of Rick's confused voice calling out, 'Siobhan?'

32

Ralph finally caught up with Jem at the junction with Lonsdale Road. She was striding purposefully but awkwardly in her skinny heels. 'Jem – please – stop!' He followed quickly behind her, accelerating a little to overtake her. 'Please – stop!' He grabbed her wrists and pulled her to a halt. 'Stop!'

'What?' Jem barked, struggling to free herself from his grip. 'Leave me alone!'

She began to thrash out violently at Ralph, futilely flailing her arms around. 'Jem, I'm sorry,' Ralph said, bringing her arms into his chest and putting his around her, restraining her in a tight embrace. 'I'm so sorry.' She relented to his mollification and collapsed silently into his arms. 'I'm so sorry. Oh, Jem.' He rested his cheek on the top of her head, feeling the little indentations in his skin made by the satin roses and smelling the floral freshness of her shiny hair. 'My poor, poor Jem.' Her small body heaved under his arms for a moment and he hugged her tighter.

Jem sniffed and wiped her fingers across her nose. 'Ralph,' she said, 'I didn't just imagine that, did I? That was my boyfriend in there, proposing to that girl? Was it a joke, Ralph? Tell me it was a joke. What the fuck is going on? Huh? What is that girl doing here? How do you know her? How does Smith know her? Don't give me any bullshit, just tell me the truth. Is this all some sort of sick joke? Huh? Huh!'

Ralph exhaled. He knew he had to explain. He had to explain everything and not leave out one single detail, including his own sneaky part in the whole hideous scenario. He led Jem to a bench and they sat down.

'Well,' he began, 'this all started five years ago, when Cheri first moved in upstairs . . .'

And he told her, all about Smith's pathetic obsession, about his self-imposed celibacy while he waited for Cheri to notice him, about the night he'd bumped into Cheri on his way back from St Alban's and they'd gone for that drink in Oriel, about how Ralph had wanted to tell Jem *then* but Smith had threatened him with homelessness. He told her how Smith had laughed at her dreams and destinies and how he thought she was a bit mad but that having a girlfriend would make him more attractive to Cheri. He even told her how Smith had fantasized about Cheri when he was making love to Jem . . .

'Oh, my God! Oh, God, I feel sick! I can't believe you didn't tell me all this, Ralph,' Jem sobbed, 'that night, in Bayswater. You just let me . . . oh, God, I feel so humiliated – I've never been so humiliated in all my life!'

'Think how it would have sounded, Jem! You wouldn't have believed me! I'd just told you I was in love with you, it would have sounded so convenient, so . . . untrue! I had to prove it to you, that Smith was a slimebag. You had to see it with your own eyes. That's . . . that's,' Ralph lowered his eyes, 'that's why I invited Cheri tonight. I've never been friendly with the girl, never even really liked her very much. But I just had to let you know what was going on – I couldn't let him treat you like that any more. And I knew that was the only way you'd really believe what was going on.'

'So, you deliberately ruined my evening, did you? You deliberately humiliated, hurt and destroyed me in front of dozens of people! You deliberately made a complete and total arsehole of me, and . . .'

'No! No! Not of you – of Smith. I made an arsehole of Smith. And I have to say, he surpassed himself. Even I had no idea that he was that ridiculous, Jem, I promise you. I thought he'd flirt with her, at worst, but *that* – that was quite remarkable. And I'm sorry that I ruined your evening, but I thought it was a small price to pay for the potential ruination of the rest of your life, which, as you well know, I happen to care a great deal about, so, please, Jem, don't take this anger out on me – take it out on Smith. He's the one who deserves it, not me. I know I've managed to develop something of a reputation with you for being devious and underhand but please, please, please believe me – I *had* to do this. I couldn't watch him making a fool of you for one second longer. Smith's an arsehole. He's my best friend, but he's an arsehole. I know it and now you know it. Please don't be angry with me, Jem – please!'

Jem caved in visibly and began to wail. 'Oh, Ralph, I hate him! I never ever want to see him again.'

'No, Jem. Don't let him get away with it. Give him hell. If I were you I'd want to go in there and kick him right in the bollocks, kick them so hard that he could cough them up and use them for tonsils. He's made a fool of you, Jem – he's treated you with a complete lack of respect. And you, more than anyone I know, more than anyone I've ever known, deserve to be treated with respect.' He stroked a crooked finger against the wetness of her hot, red cheeks. 'You're so special, Jem. You are so fucking special.'

Jem looked up at Ralph through her tears and into his eyes and suddenly she saw it. Destiny. The man in her dreams. She had never seen love like that in anyone's eyes, ever before. Ralph really, really loved her. And it *wasn't* like all the other I Love Yous. He didn't want anything from her, he wasn't besotted, he wasn't obsessed, he wasn't looking for her to fill any holes in his life, he didn't want to change her, control her or adore her – he just loved her. Plain and simple. He loved her. She reached out one small, cold hand and placed it on his cheek.

'Thank you, Ralph. Thank you for caring so much. Thank you for the paintings and the food and the peonies. Thank you for being there for me and for what you did tonight. I'm sorry I got angry with you, I'm sorry I'm so stubborn. It's just . . . it's just . . .'

'Yes – I know – you like to be in control. I know that. I know *you*. That's why I knew I had to do what I did tonight.'

'You really care, don't you?'

Ralph nodded and took Jem's hand from his cheek and put it to his lips. 'You know I do, Jem. And you know I love you . . .'

'Oh, Ralph!'

'. . . and you know that that was part of why I did what I did tonight – because it would give me a chance, a chance to be with you, because as long as you were in love with Smith, that wasn't going to happen . . .'

'Oh, Ralph!'

'. . . and I have so much respect for you for not wanting to hurt Smith. You're a better person than I am – he's my best mate and I don't have that level of loyalty to him. But now, now you know, now you know what he's really like, and you're free, Jem! Free! I'm not expecting you to tell me you love me, I'm not expecting anything from you at all. I know that reading your diaries was a bad thing to do and I don't expect you to forgive me, but now we can be friends, and then, if nothing else ever happens, at least I'll know it's because you don't love me and not because of some misguided sense of love and loyalty you have for a pathetic little man who doesn't deserve to even breathe the same air as you. D'you understand?'

Jem smiled, enigmatically. Ralph continued. 'So, if we both live to be a hundred and you never fall in love with me, then that's cool, because at least *you could if you wanted* and . . .'

Jem put a hand on each of Ralph's cheeks and kept smiling at him.

'. . . I mean, especially so soon after all this stuff with Smith, you're probably feeling a bit *vulnerable* right now and so I wouldn't expect, you know, *anything,* you know, like that . . .'

Jem watched while Ralph talked, a look of tenderness and love spreading, like the rising sun, over her face. She leaned her body in a little nearer to his.

'. . . so, as long as we can still be friends, you know, go out for meals, go to the pub sometimes, I don't need you to fall in love with me, well, you know, not yet anyway, not immediately . . .'

Jem brought Ralph's face close in to hers and put one finger over his lips.

'It's all right, Ralph,' she whispered, grinning from ear to ear. 'It's all right. I love you.'

'What?' Ralph stopped his blabbering and screwed up his face.

'I love you!'

'But . . . but . . . but . . . really? Really and truly! You love me?'

Jem nodded.

Ralph's insides stood up and performed a standing ovation, his heart let off a volley of fireworks, his stomach fluttered with the wings of a million doves and a shower of ticker-tape spiralled joyfully through his mind. Jem loved him! She loved him! He leapt up from the bench and ran around it in circles, punching the air and whooping with joy. 'She loves me! She loves me!'

'Oh Jem,' he beamed, sitting down next to her and gripping her hands in his, 'you have just made me so happy. You'll never know how happy I feel right now. I love you! And you love me! We love each other, Jem, we love each other.' He pulled her to him and almost crushed her in the best hug in the history of the world and then, suddenly, just when Jem thought he was going to kiss her, he stood up, grabbed her by the hand and began to run with her towards the party.

'Come on,' he laughed, 'we've got some unfinished business to attend to, haven't we? We've got to go back to the party and retrieve your dignity! Let's go!' he said, 'let's go and crucify Smith!'

But their mission was unexpectedly delayed by the sight, as they approached the gallery, of Karl, red in the face, showing all his teeth and smashing his fist into the terrified face of a pretty blond man who lay stretched precariously across the bonnet of a showroom-new silver BMW while Siobhan stood and screamed, tugging ineffectually at the back of Karl's shirt.

'You FUCKING BASTARD!' Jem and Ralph winced at the sound of cartilage cracking under knuckle and the sight of a small plume of blood erupting like red ink from the flattened nose. 'You FUCKING BASTARD!!'

'Karl, get *off*! Get off him! Please! Leave him alone!' Siobhan tugged again at the hem of his shirt, but it was useless to try to pull him off Rick: Karl was strong at the best of times; in his current rage he was superhuman.

'You FUCKING BASTARD!' Jem and Ralph flinched as another blow cracked off the unfortunate Rick's cheekbone and yet another burrowed deep between his ribs with a sickeningly brittle popping sound.

'*Help me! Help me!*' Rick's voice sounded tiny beneath Karl's armpit. '*Will someone please help me!*'

'Ralph?' Jem nudged Ralph.

'What?'

'Can't you do something?'

'Oh, right – yeah.' He wandered uncertainly towards Siobhan.

'What's going on?' he asked.

'Oh, please,' sobbed Siobhan, 'please do something. He's going to kill him!'

Oh, God. This really wasn't Ralph's scene at all. But he took a deep breath and launched himself at Karl's waist, linked his hands around him and tried to peel him off Rick like a mussel from a shipwreck. Without turning, Karl swung a seemingly double-jointed arm at him and clouted him around the ear, but Ralph clung on, using his foot against the side of the car for leverage. Karl turned to see what exactly this annoying little parasite was playing at, realized it was Ralph and immediately let Rick drop, like an out-of-favour toy, on to the bonnet of the car, with a resounding thud.

'It's you!' he boomed, 'it's you, you fucking bastard. This is all YOUR FAULT!'

Ralph's expression changed from one of a hapless have-a-go hero to one of terrified incomprehension within a millisecond.

'What?'

'You FUCKING BASTARD!'

Oh, God – hadn't Ralph heard that somewhere before?

'Why are you doing this to me, eh? What have I ever done to YOU? Why are you trying to RUIN MY LIFE?'

Ralph shrugged and began to back away from Karl, surreptitiously. And then, unfortunately, he smiled.

'What THE FUCK are you laughing at, you FUCKING BASTARD!! You think this is FUNNY! You invite me to your party, to humiliate me and break my heart and you think that's FUNNY!'

'Look, mate, I'm sorry, I really am, but I promise you, I'm not laughing at you and I'm not trying to ruin your life and I have no idea what the hell is going on here . . .'

'Oh! You don't know,' Karl laughed, ominously. 'So, you *didn't* invite that slag Cheri, in there then, eh?'

Ralph nodded tautly. 'Yeah – I did.'

'Right. So I suppose you *didn't* invite me then, huh?'

Ralph gulped and nodded again. 'Yeah, sure, I invited you.'

'And of course, you *couldn't possibly* have invited my girlfriend Siobhan then, could you?'

Ralph shook his head violently. 'No – no! I didn't. I didn't invite her. I don't even *know* her – I promise!'

Karl grabbed Ralph by the neck of his lovely new Dolce & Gabbana shirt and brought his face inches from his own. Jem gasped and gripped hold of Ralph's arm.

'So, who did? EH? Who invited her? It's your party, isn't it, you're the FUCKING HOST! So! Who else could it have been? I want to KILL YOU, you bastard, this has been the worst night of my life and I want to kill you!'

Siobhan gently touched Karl's elbow.

'Karl, please, it's not his fault. It's not anyone's fault. Please leave him alone.'

'No, Shuv – you keep out of this! This BASTARD's playing games with me and he's not going to get away with it.'

'I really don't think he invited me, Karl. Please, leave him alone. Please don't fight any more.'

'But, Shuv, I thought this was what you wanted! I thought you wanted me to be like this, to take action, defend your honour, fight for what I want . . .'

Siobhan looked him deep in the eyes and held his now limp hands. 'Karl – it's too late. It's me you should be shouting at. I should have told you about Rick. I should have been more honest with you. I should have told you everything. It's too late for fighting, Karl. It's too late.'

'But . . . but . . .' he looked helplessly from a breathless Ralph to a beseeching Siobhan. He didn't know what to do any more. He didn't know what to think. He didn't know who he was or why he was or where he was. He lifted his hands to his eyes and began to cry.

'Oh, God,' he mumbled through spitty breath, rubbing his eyes hard with the heels of his hands. 'Oh, God.'

Siobhan put an arm around him and led him away from the small group of onlookers. She turned to give Rick a reassuring wink as she went, which he returned with a small, pained grimace through the encrusting blood surrounding his nose and mouth. He knew what Siobhan had to do. He understood. He straightened himself painfully, dabbing gently at his nose and mouth.

'Any chance I could come in and use some ice, mate?' he asked Ralph quietly, after they'd gone.

'Oh – sure – yes – of course.' Ralph came to his senses – he'd been in some sort of fear-paralysis ever since Karl had first called him a FUCKING BASTARD – and gave Rick a shoulder to lean on as they walked slowly back into the party.

'Oh, thank God, you're back.' Cheri approached Jem and Ralph anxiously as they returned. 'You've got to get rid of Smith – he's doing my brain in.' She indicated Smith, at the far end of the room, stumbling towards the toilet, unaware of Jem's return. 'He won't leave me alone,' she whispered.

He'd spent the hour since Jem had fled desperately trying to convince Cheri that he wasn't drunk, that he wasn't pathetic, that he wasn't a sad, ridiculous bastard, and that his proposal of marriage was not only sincerely and passionately intended but was also a fabulously good idea and that Cheri would regret it for the rest of her life if she turned him down.

Cheri looked at Jem with pity and compassion and put a hand on her arm. 'Are you all right?' she mouthed. Jem nodded and smiled at Ralph, and then back at Cheri. 'I'm fine now, thank you. Angry, embarrassed and humiliated, but fine! Unlike this poor bugger.' She moved out of the way to reveal poor Rick, slouched against Ralph's shoulder, his face quickly swelling up into tight shiny bumps of purple and grey.

Cheri eyed Rick's bloody, broken face with concern, and then a flicker of recognition passed across her face. 'Rick?' she questioned, taking his hand and helping Jem and Ralph to lead him to the large black bin full of semi-melted ice behind the bar.

Rick's face crumpled with the strain of remembering.

'Cheri,' she said, placing her hand on her chest, 'remember? I'm – I was – a friend of Tamsin's. We all went out one night, last summer, to that restaurant on Fulham Broadway and your car got clamped, remember?'

'Oh, yeah. Of course. Cheri. I remember you, yeah. What are you doing here?' He winced as Jem and Ralph gently lowered him into a chair.

'Oh, God,' Cheri laughed, 'don't ask!'

Ralph and Jem looked at each other. This evening was in danger of collapsing under the weight of too much drama and coincidence.

Cheri wrapped some ice in a linen napkin and rested it

against Rick's face. 'Are you OK?' she asked. 'Are you sure you don't need to go to a hospital, or something?'

Rick shook his head and smiled bravely. 'Nah, it's just superficial. Really. I'll be fine.'

Cheri smiled kindly and continued her administering. She was enjoying playing the role of a benevolent Florence Nightingale-type. There was a time when she'd have been ill at the thought of touching someone else's wounds, someone else's blood, when it would have been a huge inconvenience. Now it was a pleasure. Maybe she should have been a nurse? She smiled again.

The party had started to thin out a little now. Ralph's friends had begun asking for minicab numbers and people milled drunkenly about on the pavement outside the gallery, waiting for black cabs.

Abba were still playing on the CD a little forlornly now, as only one drunken, maudlin-looking fellow with lipstick kisses all over his face was dancing to it, holding an empty bottle of champagne to his chest and humming along sadly to 'Dancing Queen'.

Philippe was wandering disconsolately around the room with a bin liner, collecting cigarette butts and licking the tip of his finger occasionally to moisten the small, barely visible burns left all over his lovely maplewood flooring, and tutting softly to himself.

A few couples lined the room, still absorbed in conversation and unaware that the party was closing down around them, and a group of Ralph's friends surrounded him, thanking him noisily for a great night, congratulating him on his exhibition and his good fortune and making the scrag ends of conversation that only get used at the close of a party – invites to other parties, promises to phone, last-minute exchanges of news and gossip – trying to cram into two minutes all the chat and talk that hadn't been shared earlier in the evening because you were talking to someone else. Or, in the case of this particular night, because you were showing your muse your paintings, watching your best friend propose to a woman he shouldn't have, convincing your true love to fall in love with you and breaking up a fight between an extremely angry jilted lover and his girlfriend's new boyfriend.

Siobhan and Karl had still not returned from their cooling-down walk, Cheri continued to tend poor Rick's wounds, Jem stood with Ralph while he saw off his friends, and Smith ... where was Smith? Smith was nowhere to be seen.

No one had seen him, in fact, since about half an hour ago, when Jem and Ralph had first returned from their drama on the street.

'I think I saw him heading towards the toilet,' Cheri offered helpfully, patting daintily at Rick's wounds with a napkin-wrapped fingertip.

Ralph and Jem looked at each other mischievously. It usually meant only one thing when someone disappeared into a toilet for that long at a party. They walked softly across the wooden floor towards the toilet door, and Ralph tried the handle. It was unlocked, and he pushed the door open slowly, while Jem held on to his arm and peered over his shoulder.

Jem and Ralph had seen all sorts of sorry sights in their

life before, all manner of pathetic, drunken individuals in undignified positions and situations, but nothing they'd ever seen before could have prepared them sufficiently for the sight that confronted them when they opened the door to the toilet in Philippe's gallery.

A huge cloud of steam fled the room as the door opened, revealing Smith, completely unconscious, slouched on the toilet seat, his trousers unfurled around his ankles, his penis flopping sadly and shrunkenly to one side amid his shirt tails, while his head rested in the sink, surrounded by a halo of putrid-smelling yellow and green vomit, matched by the Pollockesque lumps splattered all over his face and embedded in his wet hair. The hot tap ran violently down the side of the sink, missing the vomit entirely and kicking up billowing fugs of steam into the room. Nestling in the bottom of the toilet bowl, plainly visible thanks to the perky angle of Smith's naked bottom, sat an enormous and rank-smelling turd. It was quite the most undignified vision that either Jem or Ralph had ever encountered.

'Oh, dear,' said Jem, putting her hand over her mouth and turning away.

'Oh, dear,' repeated Ralph, stifling a laugh. 'Stupid bastard.'

'What shall we do? Poor Smith.'

'Huh!' exclaimed Ralph. 'Poor Smith, my arse!'

'What's going on?' Cheri had heard the commotion from the other side of the room and was standing behind them, unaware that she was about to witness a scene that would put her off her food for at least a week. She peered curiously over Ralph's shoulder and squeaked a little when she saw what was in the toilet, turning away in horror.

'Smith!' shouted Ralph, kicking at his shins. 'Oi, wake up – wake up! Your fiancée's here! Ha! Wake up!'

Smith slowly opened one eye and made a strange groaning noise under his breath, which sounded like 'Leave me alone', but no one could be sure.

'Cheri's here, mate – your fiancée! Wake up.'

'Ugh,' said Smith, opening his other eye and lifting his head an inch or two from the gory sink. 'Cheri?'

'Yes. Cheri.' Ralph smirked to himself.

'Oh, Ralph,' cried Jem, 'leave him alone. That's enough!'

Ralph knew Jem was right. He was enjoying himself, but it was cruel and mean and wholly unchristian. 'OK,' he said, 'you're right.' He leaned in towards Smith and shouted in his ear: 'I'll just leave you to make sweet talk with Cheri here, shall I then?' and he and Jem left him there, gradually gaining consciousness and, with it, the dreadful realization that there was vomit in his hair, shit in the toilet, his penis and naked arse were on full view and that his beloved Cheri was standing over him, eyeing him with an almost tangible expression of pity, disgust and horror.

'Ugh, God,' he mumbled, as he let his head fall back into the sink and kicked the door shut with one outstretched, half-naked leg, 'ugh, God.'

Siobhan and Karl had returned from their walk and found the gallery almost empty, except for poor Rick still sitting where Cheri had left him on the chair by the bar, his face now so swollen and purple that it was almost unrecognizable. Karl shuffled uncomfortably in the background, while Siobhan gently lifted Rick to his feet.

'It's all right, mate,' Rick said, as he and Siobhan shambled past Karl, towards the front door. 'I deserved that.'

Karl followed them out on to the street and watched Siobhan place Rick tenderly into the passenger seat, buckling him in and lightly brushing away a tendril of hair from the blood that was coagulating around his eye.

She walked over to the driver's seat, opened the door, sat down, adjusted the chair, put the key in the ignition and stared up at Karl as the electronic window wound itself down. She put a hand on top of Karl's hand, resting inside the window.

"Bye, Karl,' she said. 'I'm glad I saw you tonight. I'm glad this happened. Well,' she indicated Rick, 'maybe not *everything*. But, whoever it was who invited me, and I'm pretty sure I know who it was' – she indicated Cheri standing in the window of the gallery, watching them sadly – 'I'm glad they did it.'

Karl couldn't deny it. It had been the most painful, awful night of his life. It had been worse than the night Siobhan kicked him out. But it was good that it had happened. It had to happen. They'd had a much needed talk while they wandered together around the twinkling old lamp-shops and cosy, over-priced antique shops of Ledbury Road. They'd talked about everything, but mainly the future, and Karl realized now, without a doubt, that he had no place in hers . . .

'We're better off apart,' she'd said, smiling brightly at him. 'You've got to let go, Karl. The sooner the better. Start looking at the world with different eyes – you'll be surprised what you see – it's quite amazing! Think of the last fifteen years as a myopic haze and the last few months apart as brand-new glasses. I've been wearing mine. And you haven't. Now you've got to put yours on. Really, Karl! Put them on and see how bright life can be, how new and fresh and colourful.'

Karl wasn't too sure about this strange analogy. It sounded unlikely. And, whatever Siobhan might think, he was glad he'd had the opportunity to kick the shit out of Rick. He'd enjoyed it – right or wrong, he'd enjoyed it. He gripped Siobhan's hand hard and smiled at her through gritted teeth as the window began to close. 'Maybe we could go for a drink, one night.' He squeezed the invitation through the final inch of open window and drew his hand away from the car.

Siobhan nodded, put the car into drive, smiled one last smile at Karl and pulled away.

Karl stood on the pavement, swaying slightly in the wake of the car and the brisk winter wind that was picking up around Ledbury Road. He put his hands into his coat pockets, watching until the car had disappeared from view, and then he turned around and began to walk back into the gallery. He wiped a small tear away from the side of his nose, took a deep breath and put a spring in his step.

It was time to go home. Time to start afresh. Time to see things differently.

It was time . . .

It was a strange quintet who shared a black cab back to Almanac Road that night. Karl sat quietly on one side, staring intently from the window, nursing his scuffed knuckles absent-mindedly with the thumb of his other hand, wishing that the cab would hurry up and get him home and trying not to look at Cheri, who was sitting primly on one of the fold-out seats, desperately trying to keep her distance from the foul-smelling Smith, who'd attempted to wash every trace of sick and bile from his person but still carried with him a strong and heavy aroma of vomit. He had his head out of the window, like a dog, the bitter wind gusting through his hair and making his eyes water, but at least it meant he didn't have to watch Cheri eyeing him with contempt and reminding him that never, in the whole history of mankind, had one man managed to blow it so spectacularly and so completely. It also meant that he didn't have to look at Jem, snuggled up under Ralph's arm and watching him with a small sad look of pity and regret, designed to make him feel even worse than he already did about the awful unfolding of events that had occurred tonight, at Ralph's party.

Nobody spoke as the cab trundled dejectedly across Battersea Bridge. The sky was jet black overhead and illuminated brightly by a fat, white full moon. A party boat lit with fairy lights and loud with chatter and music passed beneath the bridge as they crossed. A skinny girl in a tight Lycra dress waved a bottle of champagne at them from the deck. Smith waved back half-heartedly.

The cab pulled up quietly outside number thirty-one and its passengers spilt heavily and gratefully on to the pavement, all glad that the cab ride from hell was finally over.

Cheri made her way briskly to the front door, keen as ever to avoid Karl, especially given the disastrous outcome of her attempt to bring him and Siobhan back together by sending her that invite. He caught up with her on the front step and waited awkwardly behind her while she unlocked the door.

'Well,' he began, unexpectedly, 'that was some night, wasn't it?'

Cheri spun around at the sound of his voice. 'Yeah,' she laughed nervously, 'unbelievable.'

'Um,' he scratched at the back of his neck, 'I don't know who, er, invited Siobhan tonight. I suspect it was you' – he put a quieting hand out as Cheri began to explain – 'it's fine, Cheri. It really is. I'm glad, you . . . someone . . . invited her, and I'm glad I saw her tonight and I'm glad I hit Rick. So . . . just don't worry. OK? It's all all right and I'm sorry, as well, about earlier, shouting at you like that. It was unfair. I was drunk. Sorry.' He smiled at her, a warm, sincere smile full of hope for the future and death to the past. Then he slipped his key into his lock and disappeared quietly into his flat, leaving Cheri standing at the bottom of the stairs, her coat clutched in her hands, a look of surprise, gratitude and pleasure slowly pinkening her face.

She turned and walked up the stairs, towards the top floor, smiling to herself, and wondered, yet again, at the joys of goodness . . .

Smith vanished quickly into the basement flat. He wanted to go to bed, more than anything in the whole world. His head ached, his throat was sore and his heart felt like it was slowly bleeding to death. He let the door slam behind him, not caring that Jem and Ralph were on their way, not wanting to look at them for one more single, solitary second. Everything was a mess now. Ralph was a bastard, Jem hated him, Cheri despised him. He had no friend, no girlfriend and no fantasies left. It was all over. Everything. But he was too tired to start trying to wonder about the future now, about his living arrangements, about Cheri, about everything. He'd deal with all that tomorrow. He'd buy flowers for Cheri tomorrow, to apologize, and he'd give Ralph and Jem their marching orders, kick them out. Tomorrow.

Right now, he was going to bed . . .

Jem and Ralph stood at the top of the basement steps and watched the full moon for a while.

'It was a full moon the night I first came to see the flat, you know?' said Jem, her arm tucked firmly around Ralph's waist.

'Oh, yeah?' he murmured happily, dropping a kiss on to the top of Jem's bedraggled head. 'Weird stuff always happens on full-moon nights, doesn't it? People behave strangely, act differently.'

'They certainly do!'

They fell quiet for a moment, contemplating the unbelievable sequence of events that had occurred that night.

'D'you remember,' asked Jem, suddenly, 'd'you remember when I first came to see the flat? You were on the phone, to Claudia, you didn't even look at me!'

'Ah, but what I bet you don't know is that seconds before you arrived, I'd been sitting on the sofa – there' – he indicated the sofa through the window – 'sitting there, waiting for this mysterious girl called Jem to arrive and . . .

smoking a cigarette. So, you see, it was me all along. The man on the sofa, the man of your dreams! Maybe you'd have realized sooner if fucking Claudia hadn't phoned at that precise moment . . .'

'And if you'd bought peonies! And hadn't worn those disgusting longjohns! And . . .'

'OK!' laughed Ralph, squeezing Jem to him, 'you're right! Destiny moves in mysterious ways, doesn't it?'

'You know Smith will probably make us move out, don't you?'

'Yeah. Well. We'll deal with that when it happens. I know a lovely little place on Cable Street!'

They started to walk down the steps and then Ralph stopped abruptly and turned to face Jem. 'Wait!' he exclaimed, beaming. 'Wait! I've had an idea. Just stand there and don't move until I tell you! OK?' He leapt down the steps two at a time and disappeared through the front door, letting it close behind him.

Jem stood on the steps, uncertainly, shivering a bit in the cold wind and wondering what the hell Ralph was playing at.

A moment later, she noticed a light shining from the living-room window and turned to look down.

A man was sitting on the sofa. A long plume of pink-tinged smoke hovered above his head. He had a slender neck and an oval skull covered in short black hair that ended in a sweet triangle of stubble at the nape of his neck. Jem shuddered. It was her dream. Exactly! And then she smiled, a huge, belly-achey, involuntary smile. The man on the sofa turned slightly in his seat. He looked at Jem and shared her smile.

And then Jem lifted the hem of her rose-printed dress with one small fist and ran down the steps, her heels echoing on the concrete, pushed open the front door, and the living-room door, grabbed hold of her destiny, threw him down on the sofa and kissed the living daylights out of him.

Acknowledgements

Thank you, Katy, Sarah and Nic, for reading as I wrote, chapter by chapter, month by month, and being unfailingly positive, constructive and enthusiastic. And thank you, Yasmin, for putting me up to this in the first place and continuing to encourage and inspire me throughout. I truly couldn't have done this without you. And lastly, thank you, Jascha, for not knowing anything about contemporary women's fiction but for being a great boyfriend and taking a risk anyway. Thanks for paying the bills, paying for dinner, buying me a computer and keeping a roof over my head. What a man!

Discover the romantic side of
Lisa Jewell . . .

Thirtynothing

Dig Ryan hasn't seen Delilah for twelve years, but when she bursts back into his life, he can't help falling for his first love all over again. Nadine has been in love with Dig for fifteen years, so she can't help feeling cheated when her best friend has his head turned again by her old nemesis Delilah. But how low will Nadine stoop to make Delilah go away, and how can she make Dig realize who he really loves?

One-hit Wonder

Bee Beahorn had it all – a successful music career, fabulous friends and a glamorous celebrity lifestyle. At least, that's what her estranged sister, Ana, had always believed. But when Bea is found dead in her flat, Ana realizes that everything she knew about her sister had been a lie. Ana is determined to find out the truth about her sister – and she might just find herself along the way . . .

Vince and Joy

Vince and Joy have their whole lives ahead of them on the day they meet as teenagers, and instantly fall in love. But two weeks later, a misunderstanding forces them apart, and when they cross paths seven years later they've been living very different lives. Yet neither of them has been able to let go of their first love. What happens when you meet the right person at the wrong time?

A Friend of the Family

The London family is in crisis. Newly divorced Tony is fantasizing about someone he shouldn't, prize-winning writer Sean has a hot new girlfriend, and a dose of writer's block, and their brother Ned has just come back from Australia, leaving his girlfriend behind. Now they have a new lodger – a mysterious stranger – but is he the friend this family needs, or a troublemaker they could do without?

31 Dream Street

For years, Toby has opened his door to the people who needed his help. For years, Leah has been fascinated by the mysterious house full of people across the street. They've never met – until Toby receives a letter that draws Leah inside and she gets to know the lives of the people she's wondered about for so long – a group of artists who have each lost their way. When Toby decides he needs to move on with his life, he knows he needs to help his tenants, too. Leah insists on helping him to bring them all happiness, but can she also make Toby's dreams come true?

Read on for an extract of Lisa Jewell's latest
number one bestseller **None of This is True** . . .

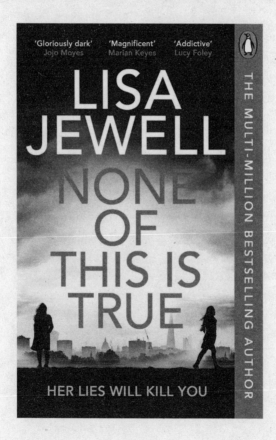

Prologue

Stumbling from the cool of the air-conditioned hotel foyer into the steamy white heat of the night does nothing to sober him up. It makes him feel panicky and claustrophobic. A sweat that feels like pure alcohol blooms quickly on his skin, dampening his spine and the small of his back. How can it be so hot at three in the morning? And where is she? Where is she? He turns to see if the girl is behind him, and sees her wishy-washy, wavy-wavy, in double-vision through the glass windows of the hotel. And then he sees a car indicate to pull over and his heart rate starts to slow. She's here. At last. Thank God. This terrible night is coming to an end. He squints to bring it into focus, to search the driver's seat for the reassuring gleam of her white-blonde hair, but it's not there. The window winds down and he recoils slightly.

'What?' he says to the dark-haired woman behind the wheel. 'What are you doing here? Where's my wife?'

'It's OK,' says the woman. 'She sent me. She'd had too much to drink. She asked me to bring you home. Come on. In you get.'

He looks behind him for the girl, sees her leaving the hotel and walking quickly away in the opposite direction, her hand-bag clutched tight against her side.

'I've got water. I've got coffee. Come on. You'll be home in no time.'

The dog on her lap growls at him softly as he slides into the passenger seat.

'I thought you'd left?' he says, fumbling behind himself to find the seatbelt. 'I thought you'd gone away?'

The woman smiles at him as she unscrews the lid from a plastic bottle of water and passes it to him.

'Yes,' she says. 'I had. But she needed me. So. Anyway. Drink that. Drink it all down.'

He puts the bottle to his dry, dry mouth, and gulps it back. Then he closes his eyes and waits to be home.

Coming to Netflix in May:
Hi! I'm Your Birthday Twin!

Now here's a strange one, coming your way from the people behind *The Monster Next Door* and *The Serial Date Swindler*. It's a podcast within a documentary, a kind of podumentary, if you will. In June 2019, popular podcaster Alix Summer, better known for her *All Woman* series of podcasts about successful women, branched out into a one-off project, which she called *Hi! I'm Your Birthday Twin!*, about a local woman who was born on the same day as her. As the project progressed, Summer started to learn much more about her unassuming neighbour than she could ever have imagined and, within weeks, Summer's life was in shreds and two people were dead. Absolutely spine-chilling stuff, with some shocking glimpses into the darkest corners of humanity: we guarantee you'll be bingeing the whole thing in a day.

Hi! I'm Your Birthday Twin!
A NETFLIX ORIGINAL SERIES

Screen is dark. Slowly the interior of a recording studio is revealed.

The text on the screen reads:

Recording from Alix Summer's podcast, 20 June 2019

A woman's voice fades in slowly. 'You comfortable there, Josie?'

'Yes. I'm fine.'

'Great. Well. While I'm setting up, why don't you just tell me what you had for breakfast this morning?'

'Oh. Erm . . .'

'Just so I can test the sound quality.'

'Right. OK. Well, I had toast. Two slices of toast. One with jam. One with peanut butter. And a mug of tea. The posh stuff from Marks. In the golden box.'

'With milk?'

'Yes. With milk.'

374

There is a short pause.

*The camera pans around the empty recording studio,
zooming in on details: the lines going up and down on the
monitor, an abandoned pair of headphones, an empty coffee
cup.*

'How is it? Is it OK?'

'Yes. It's perfect. We're all set. I'll count down from three,
and then I'll introduce you. OK?'

'Yes. OK.'

'Great. So . . . three . . . two . . . one . . . Hello, and welcome! My name is Alix Summer and here is something a
little different . . .'

The audio fades and the shot goes back to darkness.

The opening credits start to roll.

Saturday, 8 June 2019

Josie can feel her husband's discomfort as they enter the golden glow of the gastropub. She's walked past this place a hundred times. Thought: *Not for us.* Everyone too young. Food on the chalkboard outside she's never heard of. *What is bottarga?* But this year her birthday has fallen on a Saturday and this year she did not say, Oh, a takeaway and a bottle of wine will be fine, when Walter had asked what she wanted to do. This year she thought of the honeyed glow of the Lansdowne, the buzz of chatter, the champagne in ice buckets on outdoor tables on warm summer days, and she thought of the little bit of money her grandmother had left her last month in her will, and she'd looked at herself in the mirror and tried to see herself as the sort of person who celebrated her birthday in a gastropub in Queen's Park and she'd said, 'We should go out for dinner.'

'OK then,' Walter had said. 'Anywhere in mind?'

And she'd said, 'The Lansdowne. You know. On Salusbury Road.'

He'd simply raised an eyebrow at her and said, 'Your birthday. Your choice.'

He holds the door open for her now and she passes through. They stand marooned for a moment by a sign that says *Please wait here to be seated* and Josie gazes around at the early-evening diners and drinkers, her handbag pinioned against her stomach by her arms.

'Fair,' she says to the young man who appears holding a clipboard. 'Josie. Table booked for seven thirty.'

He smiles from her to Walter and back again and says, 'For two, yes?'

They are led to a nice table in a corner. Walter on a banquette, Josie on a velvet chair. Their menus are handed to them clipped to boards. She'd looked up the menu online earlier, so she'd be able to google stuff if she didn't know what it was, so she already knows what she's having. And they're ordering champagne. She doesn't care what Walter thinks.

Her attention is caught by a noisy entrance at the pub door. A woman walks in clutching a balloon with the words *Birthday Queen* printed on it. Her hair is winter blonde, cut into a shape that makes it move like liquid. She wears wide-legged trousers and a top made of two pieces of black cloth held together with laces at the sides. Her skin is burnished. Her smile is wide. A group soon follows behind her, other similarly aged people; someone is holding a bouquet of flowers; another carries a selection of posh gift bags.

'Alix Summer!' says the woman in a voice that carries. 'Table for fourteen.'

'Look,' says Walter, nudging her gently. 'Another birthday girl.'

Josie nods distractedly. 'Yes,' she says. 'Looks like it.'

The group follows the waiter to a table just across from Josie's. Josie sees three ice buckets already on the table, each holding two bottles of chilled champagne. They take their seats noisily, shouting about who should sit where and not wanting to sit next to their husbands for God's sake, and the woman called Alix Summer directs them all with that big smile while a tall man with red hair who is probably her husband takes the balloon from her hand and ties it to a chair back. Soon they are all seated, and the first bottles of champagne are popped and poured into fourteen glasses held out by fourteen people with tanned arms and gold bracelets and crisp white shirt sleeves and they all bring their glasses together, those at the furthest ends of the table getting to their feet to reach across the table, and they all say, 'To Alix! Happy birthday!'

Josie fixes the woman in her gaze. 'How old do you reckon she is?' she asks Walter.

'Christ. I dunno. It's hard to tell these days. Early forties, maybe?'

Josie nods. Today is her forty-fifth birthday. She finds it hard to believe. Once she'd been young and she'd thought forty-five would come slow and impossible. She'd thought forty-five would be another world. But it came fast and it's not what she thought it would be. She glances at Walter, at the fading glory of him, and she wonders how different things would be if she hadn't met him.

She'd been thirteen when they met. He was quite a bit older than her; well, a *lot* older than her, in fact. Everyone was shocked at the time, except her. Married at nineteen. A baby at twenty-two. Another one at twenty-four. A life lived in fast forward and now, apparently, she should peak and crest and then come slowly, contentedly down the other side, but it doesn't feel as if there ever was a peak, rather an abyss formed of trauma that she keeps circling and circling with a knot of dread in the pit of her stomach.

Walter is retired now, his hair has gone and so has a lot of his hearing and his eyesight, and his mid-life peak is somewhere so far back in time and so mired in the white-hot intensity of rearing small children that it's almost impossible to remember what he was like at her age.

She orders feta and sundried tomato flatbread, followed by tuna tagliata ('The word TAGLIATA derives from the verb TAGLIARE, to cut') with mashed cannellini beans, and a bottle of Veuve Clicquot ('Veuve Clicquot's Yellow Label is loved for its rich and toasty flavours') and she grabs Walter's hand and runs her thumb over the age-spotted skin and asks, 'Are you OK?'

'Yes, of course. I'm fine.'

'What do you think of this place, then?'

'It's . . . yeah. It's fine. I like it.'

Josie beams. 'Good,' she says. 'I'm glad.'

She lifts her champagne glass and holds it out towards Walter's. He touches his glass against hers and says, 'Happy birthday.'

379

The smile fixes on Josie's face as she watches Alix Summer and her big group of friends, her red-haired husband with his arm draped loosely across the back of her chair, large platters of meats and breads being brought to their table and placed in front of them as if conjured out of thin air, the sound of them, the noise of them, the way they fill every inch of the space with their voices and their arms and their hands and their words. The energy they give off is effervescent, a swirling, intoxicating aurora borealis of grating, glorious entitlement. And there in the middle of it all is Alix Summer with her big smile and her big teeth, her hair that catches the light, her simple gold chain with something hanging from it that skims her gleaming collarbones whenever she moves.

'I wonder if today is her actual birthday too?' she muses.

'Maybe,' says Walter. 'But it's a Saturday, so who knows.'

Josie's hand finds the chain she's worn around her neck since she was thirty; her birthday gift that year from Walter. She thinks maybe she should add a pendant. Something shiny.

At this moment, Walter passes a small gift across the table towards her. 'It's nothing much. I know you said you didn't want anything, but I didn't believe you.' He grins at her and she smiles back. She unpeels the small gift and takes out a bottle of Ted Baker perfume.

'That's lovely,' she says. 'Thank you so much.' She leans across and kisses Walter softly on the cheek.

At the table opposite, Alix Summer is opening gift bags and

birthday cards and calling out her thanks to her friends and family. She rests a card on the table and Josie sees that it has the number 45 printed on it. She nudges Walter. 'Look,' she says. 'Forty-five. We're birthday twins.'

As the words leave her mouth, Josie feels the gnawing sense of grief that she has experienced for most of her life rush through her. She's never found anything to pin the feeling to before; she never knew what it meant. But now she knows what it means.

It means she's wrong, that everything, literally everything, about her is wrong and that she's running out of time to make herself right.

She sees Alix getting to her feet and heading towards the toilet, jumps to her own feet and says, 'I'm going to the ladies.'

Walter looks up in surprise from his Parma ham and melon but doesn't say anything.

A moment later Josie's and Alix's reflections are side by side in the mirror above the sinks.

'Hi!' says Josie, her voice coming out higher than she'd imagined. 'I'm your birthday twin!'

'Oh!' says Alix, her expression immediately warm and open. 'Is it your birthday today too?'

'Yes. Forty-five today!'

'Oh, wow!' says Alix. 'Me too. Happy birthday!'

'And to you!'

'What time were you born?'

'God,' says Josie. 'No idea.'

'Me neither.'

'Were you born near here?'

'Yes. St Mary's. You?'

Josie's heart leaps. 'St Mary's too!'

'Wow!' Alix says again. 'This is spooky.'

Alix's fingertips go to the pendant around her neck and Josie sees that it is a golden bumblebee. She is about to say something else about the coincidence of their births when the toilet door opens and one of Alix's friends walks in.

'There you are!' says the friend. She's wearing seventies-style faded jeans with an off-the-shoulder top and huge hoop earrings.

'Zoe! This lady is my birthday twin! This is my big sister, Zoe.'

Josie smiles at Zoe and says, 'Born on the same day, in the same hospital.'

'Wow! That's amazing,' says Zoe.

Then Zoe and Alix turn the conversation away from the Huge Coincidence and immediately Josie sees that it has passed, this strange moment of connection, that it was fleeting and weightless for Alix, but that for some reason it carries import and meaning to Josie, and she wants to grab hold of it and breathe life back into it, but she can't. She has to go back to her husband and her flatbread and let Alix go back to her friends and her party. She issues a quiet 'Bye then' as she turns to leave and Alix beams at her and says, 'Happy birthday, birthday twin!'

'You too!' says Josie.

But Alix doesn't hear her.

1 a.m.

Alix's head spins. Tequila slammers at midnight. Too much. Nathan is pouring himself a Scotch and the smell of it makes Alix's head spin even faster. The house is quiet. Sometimes, when they have a high-energy babysitter, the children will still be up when they get home, restless and annoyingly awake. Sometimes the TV will be on full blast. But not tonight. The softly spoken, fifty-something babysitter left half an hour ago and the house is tidy, the dishwasher hums, the cat is pawing its way meaningfully across the long sofa towards Alix, already purring before Alix's hand has even found her fur.

'That woman,' she calls out to Nathan, pulling one of the cat's claws out of her trousers. 'The one who kept staring. She came into the toilet. Turns out it's her forty-fifth birthday today too. That's why she was staring.'

'Ha,' says Nathan. 'Birthday twin.'

'And she was born at St Mary's, too. Funny, you know I always thought I was meant to be one of two. I always wondered if my mum had left the other one at the hospital. Maybe it was her?'

Nathan sits heavily next to her and rolls his Scotch around a solitary ice cube, one of the huge cylindrical ones he makes from mineral water. 'Her?' he says, dismissively. 'That is highly unlikely.'

'Why not!'

'Because you're gorgeous and she's . . .'

'What?' Alix feels righteousness build in her chest. She

loves that Nathan thinks she's pretty, but she also wishes that Nathan could see the beauty in less conventionally attractive women, too. It makes him sound shallow and misogynistic when he denigrates women's appearances. And it makes her feel as if she doesn't really like him. 'I thought she was very pretty. You know, those eyes that are so brown they're almost black. And all that wavy hair. Anyway, it's weird, isn't it? The idea of two people being born in the same place, at the same time.'

'Not really. There were probably another ten babies born that day at St Mary's. Maybe even more.'

'But to meet one of them. On your birthday.'

The cat is curled neatly in her lap now. She runs her fingertips through the ruff of fur around her neck and closes her eyes. The room spins again. She opens her eyes, slides the cat off her lap and runs to the toilet off the hallway, where she is violently sick.

He just wanted a decent book to read ...

Not too much to ask, is it? It was in 1935 when Allen Lane, Managing Director of Bodley Head Publishers, stood on a platform at Exeter railway station looking for something good to read on his journey back to London. His choice was limited to popular magazines and poor-quality paperbacks – the same choice faced every day by the vast majority of readers, few of whom could afford hardbacks. Lane's disappointment and subsequent anger at the range of books generally available led him to found a company – and change the world.

'We believed in the existence in this country of a vast reading public for intelligent books at a low price, and staked everything on it'
Sir Allen Lane, 1902–1970, founder of Penguin Books

The quality paperback had arrived – and not just in bookshops. Lane was adamant that his Penguins should appear in chain stores and tobacconists, and should cost no more than a packet of cigarettes.

Reading habits (and cigarette prices) have changed since 1935, but Penguin still believes in publishing the best books for everybody to enjoy. We still believe that good design costs no more than bad design, and we still believe that quality books published passionately and responsibly make the world a better place.

So wherever you see the little bird – whether it's on a piece of prize-winning literary fiction or a celebrity autobiography, political tour de force or historical masterpiece, a serial-killer thriller, reference book, world classic or a piece of pure escapism – you can bet that it represents the very best that the genre has to offer.

Whatever you like to read – trust Penguin.